STORMBORN

Books by Eric R. Asher

Shop ebooks, audiobooks, and paperbacks at ericrasherstore.com

The Theme Park at the End of the World

The Steamborn Series

Steamborn

Steamforged

Steamsworn

Skyborn

Skyforged

Skysworn

Stormborn

Stormforged

Stormsworn

The Vesik Series
(Recommended for Ages 17+)

Days Gone Bad

Wolves and the River of Stone

Winter's Demon

This Broken World

Destroyer Rising

Rattle the Bones

Witch Queen's War

Forgotten Ghosts

The Book of the Ghost

The Book of the Claw

The Book of the Sea

The Book of the Staff

The Book of the Rune

The Book of the Sails

The Book of the Wing

The Book of the Blade

The Book of the Fang

The Book of the Reaper

Dreams of the Forgotten Dead

Garden Gnome Graves

The Vesik Series Box Sets

Box Set One (Books 1-3)

Box Set Two (Books 4-6)

Box Set Three (Books 7-8)

Box Set Four: The Books of the Dead Part 1

Box Set Five: The Books of the Dead Part 2

Mason Dixon: Monster Hunter

Episode One

Episode Two

Episode Three

Episode Four

Want to receive an email when one of Eric's books releases?

Visit ericrasher.com to get started.

STORMBORN

THE STEAMBORN SERIES, BOOK SEVEN

By

ERIC R. ASHER

History is not always written.

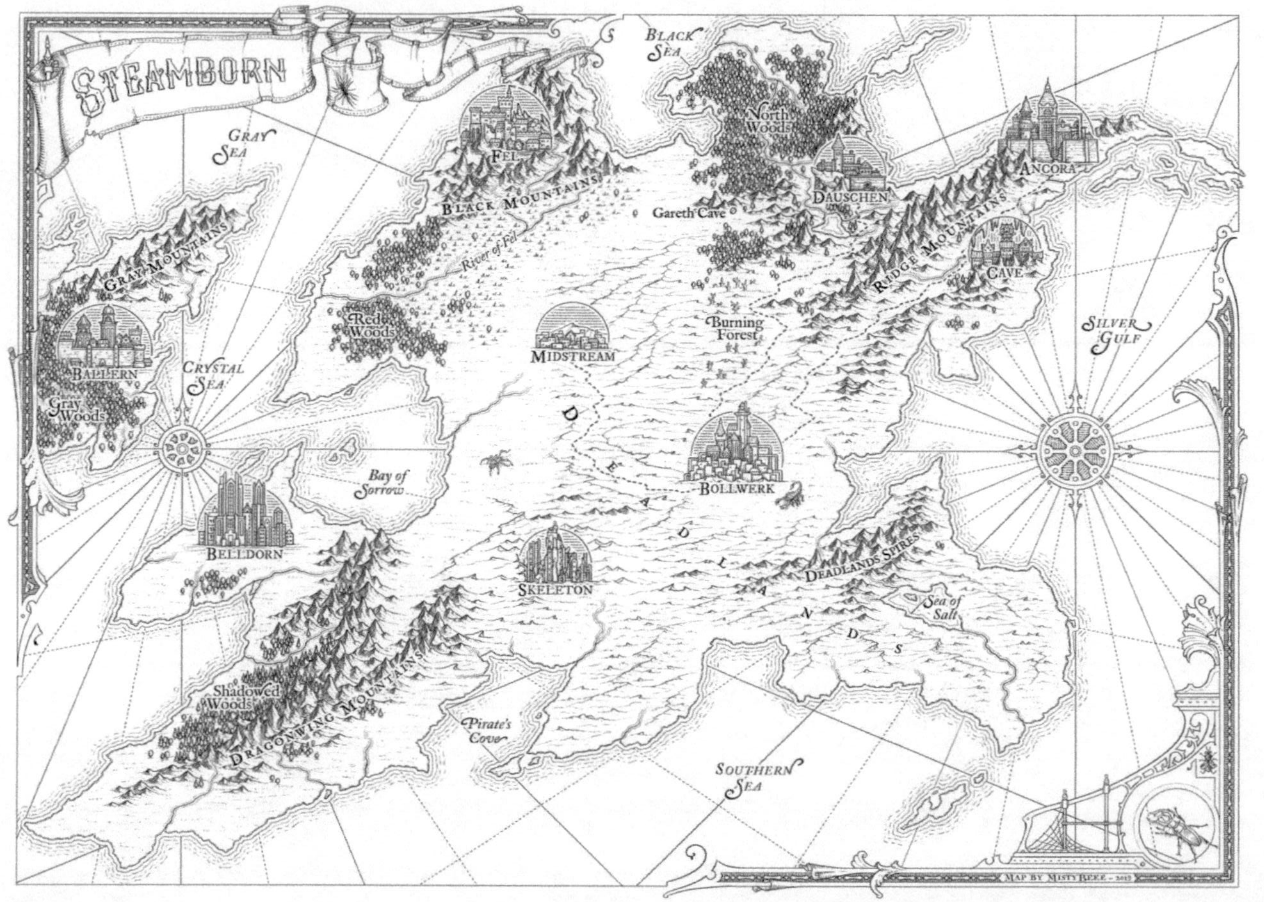
STEAMBORN
GRAY SEA
BLACK SEA
NORTH WOODS
ANCORA
FEL
BLACK MOUNTAINS
DAUSCHEN
Gareth Cave
RIDGE MOUNTAINS
CAVE
GRAY MOUNTAINS
River of Fel
Burning Forest
SILVER GULF
Red Woods
MIDSTREAM
BALLERN
CRYSTAL SEA
D E A D L A N D S
Gray Woods
BOLLWERK
Bay of Sorrow
BELLDORN
SKELETON
Deadlands Spires
Sea of Salt
Shadowed Woods
DRAGONWING MOUNTAINS
Pirate's Cove
SOUTHERN SEA
MAP BY MISTY REESE - 2017

CHAPTER ONE

OWEN WOULD NEVER escape the vision of his brother on the Red Hand's blades. It was a mercy he'd been dead by the time they strung him up on the wall, but Owen also knew enough of the outside world to know Fel was a cruel place. A cruel home. Part of him wished he had taken his family away from Fel long ago. He wished he'd taken them onto that strange airship with Jacob and Alice, but he couldn't leave Hefina behind, and he couldn't ask those outsiders to wait.

He reached out and rested his hand on his wife's shoulder. Hefina glanced up at him, her forehead creased as though she expected him to deliver more terrible news.

Owen spoke after a long silence. "It's good we're leaving, Hefina."

She squeezed his hand. "We'll be home one day. I know it."

He didn't answer that thought. In some ways, she was right. They'd find a home. Maybe in Dauschen, if their family had survived there. Or perhaps they'd take to Ancora, where the Ancorans apparently raised children as warriors to face down the likes of Mordair.

Wherever the tides took them, Owen was thankful his son hadn't seen what had happened to his uncle all those years before.

Even as the thought entered his mind, his gaze trailed to the bow of the speeder, where Vaughn watched the waters like his father had taught him. There was no windscreen at the speeder's bow, but his son didn't mind, clearly enjoying the wind on the sea even now.

The Black Sea wasn't a kind place for speeders, with tall waves and a chill that would cut through the best of the blacksmiths' diving suits. Owen knew if they sank, they were doomed. But he still guided them past the mouths of the rivers that led through the North Woods.

It wasn't until they passed the second that Vaughn questioned him. "Why not head inland here?"

"The North Woods haven't been fond of anyone from Fel in a long time, son. Best to avoid them. And best to keep distance between us and anyone who might have followed."

Vaughn frowned and looked back at the dark waters. "No one's going to follow us out here."

"I lost your uncle, and I'm not going to lose you from a lack of caution." It was a low blow. Owen didn't like prodding at old wounds, but he also didn't like the idea of Vaughn doing something ill-advised in a spur-of-the-moment decision. He remembered being that age, and he'd managed to make terrible decisions, even without his entire city being overthrown.

Maybe that's what it needed in the end. Maybe it was time for Mordair's terrible reign to be finished. But the cost was too high. And the thought that Vaughn could die alongside his uncle, and Owen might never see either of them again, was enough to drive him to Dauschen.

He wouldn't forget his last vision of Fel. The gamble he'd taken, docking their speeder once more after the wall had fallen and those Carrion Worms had crawled up from the depths of the earth. Leaving Vaughn onboard to wait and mind the boat was one of the hardest things he'd ever done, but he'd had to find Hefina.

She'd been smart to shelter between the walls. They'd built small cabinets in the spaces there, and after Mordair had started hanging citizens from the crenellations, Owen had built hiding places into their home. He'd hoped they'd never need them, but they'd become dreadfully useful.

Hefina stood and stepped toward the bow when they reached a calm patch on the waters. She took a seat at her son's side. Even in silence, Vaughn sat a little straighter, as if her mere presence gave him support. That was good. Support was something they would all need in the days to come.

✧　　✧　　✧

OWEN EYED THE shore of the small bay. Fingers of the sea stretched inland between the sandbars, empty but for a scattering of driftwood and the forest beyond. A few worn boulders stood sentinel in the surf, but Owen didn't see any immediate threats.

"What is it?" Vaughn asked.

"We need fuel."

"You're not going to find any solid fuel in the middle of nowhere."

Vaughn was right, of course, but they could burn wood if they were desperate to keep the boilers running. It wouldn't be as clean as solid fuel, but a little extra maintenance was a small price to pay for survival.

Nothing moved on the shore. No docks waited on the edge of the Black Sea, its cold waters avoided by all but the fisherfolk of the North Woods. And Owen knew they preferred the western bay when hunting Sea Claws.

"We need sleep," Hefina said. "It's been over a day, Owen."

"I know. Sleep and fuel." He looked toward the horizon, where the sun had started to vanish. "We'll camp here tonight. Without a lantern, we aren't going to do ourselves any favors, sailing at night."

Hefina frowned and studied the shore. "You mean to burn wood as fuel?"

"Yes. We're less than half a day from Dauschen. This old speeder can handle the soot and tar." He ran his fingers along the starboard railing, feeling the raised sawtooth pattern in the wood.

Vaughn sighed and turned his attention to the water. After a short time, he pointed slightly off to port. "Clearance to the shore here. Looks sandy, so I don't think we'll run aground."

Owen slowed the speeder and followed Vaughn's guidance exactly, running between two sandbars until the hull grazed the base of the nearest. It was there Owen hurled the anchor chain over the starboard side.

Vaughn followed it down with a long metal spike in his hand. He pulled the links tighter before driving the spike through an eyelet on the chain, deep into the sand. Owen dropped another anchor off the bow and sighed.

Hefina jumped to the sand and stretched. "We've been on the water too long. I still feel like everything is swaying."

Owen shut the vents to the boiler. It would die out soon enough and give them a little fuel left to start the wood burning. He gathered up a leather satchel and followed his family down to the sands.

"We can camp on the speeder or build a lean-to."

Hefina looked to the shadows of the woods, then down at her feet. "As much as I want to be on stable ground, let's stay on the boat. All we need is a tarp to keep the elements at bay. We don't have enough food to keep our energy up, Owen."

"We're out of food?" Vaughn might have tried to hide the panic in his voice, but Owen could pick it out easily enough.

Owen smiled at his son. There was no greater peril for a teenager than running out of food. "We'll be fine, Vaughn. Now help me gather some wood so we can settle in for the night."

Normally Owen would find a mindless task like gathering wood to be relaxing, but so close to the villages of the North Woods, that couldn't be further from what he felt.

"What's wrong?" Hefina asked.

Owen shook his head and raised his ax. "It's nothing. It's just … I'm listening for anything that could be a threat, but I can't shake the memory of what happened in Fel."

"We've not been gone even two days. It'll be a long time before any of us shake that memory, Owen."

Hefina was right. It had taken months before Owen could sleep without waking to nightmares of his brother's body on the wall. Even then, he hadn't escaped them entirely. He didn't think he ever really would.

Owen tightened his grip on the ax, hard wood digging into his palms as he squared up, raised his arms, and let his anger at Mordair and the Red Hand flow into that blade. The log split along the grain and left the ax embedded in the tree stump below.

Vaughn gathered up the wood and started toward the speeder. "Think that's enough, Dad?"

"Probably so. I'll split one more just to be safe."

Hefina waited for him to set the next log up before stealing his ax. It might have been therapeutic for him to take his frustration out on innocent wood, but Hefina was far better with an ax. A sharp exhale came with each crack of the blade, and she had the last log split in half the time.

They followed Vaughn back to the speeder. It would be a cold night, but one they could survive together.

Owen and Hefina took turns keeping watch. The curve of the stern was perfect for leaning back and eyeing the shore behind them. Nothing could cross the beach without being seen. And plenty of things came in the night.

It was the Mantises that made Owen the most worried and grateful they hadn't camped by the woods. Curious creatures, sifting through the sand and even approaching the boat. But the Mantises weren't fond of water, and their curiosity ended soon enough.

A small cadre of wild Pillies snuffled through the sands later on, their antennae flicking around like whips. And it was during that watch he saw the lights on the sea. Far to the east, so much he'd initially mistaken them for a star, but the lights bobbed ever so slightly.

Owen wondered who would be that far out in the Black Sea. It had to be at least half a day's journey north of Ancora. Or it was a trick of the light. Almost as fast as the curious sight had come, it was gone. Soon enough, the sky brightened, and the knot of dread in Owen's chest loosened just a fraction.

✧   ✧   ✧

THEY PASSED THROUGH the strait between the North Woods and a large, uninhabited island. Or at least uninhabited and unnamed, as far as Owen knew. It had been almost two days on the boat, but the voyage was nearly done. To the south, he could no longer see the North Woods. Instead, the rolling foothills of the Ridge Mountains obscured everything that waited beyond. Snowy peaks in the distance provided a backdrop to the walls and docks of the cliff-side city known as Dauschen.

"It doesn't look so different from here," Hefina said.

Vaughn leaned forward. "Other than that weird tower."

Owen laughed and patted his son's shoulder. "That's an airship dock. I'd wager a good sack of coin on it."

But his laughter faded as they passed a jetty that had obscured the eastern skyline. It wasn't that a new airship dock had been built in Dauschen, but many of the roofs and old stone he knew from his childhood were simply gone.

Everyone knew the stories of what had happened in Dauschen. The Butcher had tried to stop an uprising. But Owen had had family on the other side of that conflict. He knew better than most that Dauschen had been a slaughter.

He guided the speeder into the low stone docks behind the city. Farther south, between two peaks, he could just make out the railroad tracks that connected Dauschen to the city of Ancora in the east. But that glimpse came and went, concealed once more by the mountain range.

Vaughn hopped off the bow and grabbed a rope line, tying them off on a cleat.

"It's a ghost town," Hefina whispered.

"Not entirely." Owen gestured to the winding stairs that climbed the wall to the city proper. Two guards watched them, their expressions hidden in shadow.

"Is this the place that used to have markets like Ballern?" Vaughn asked.

Owen hesitated, brief visions of that vibrant history flashing through his mind. A violent contrast to the dead gray and rotted wooden stalls that peppered the docks of Dauschen.

"And where are all their boats?"

Owen looked closer at the docks, at the scarce lines haphazardly thrown down, charred wood, and darkened stone, before his stomach sank.

"They're still in the water." Hefina stood at the dock's edge, studying what waited in the deeper sea beside the mountains.

Owen stepped up next to her. One thing that hadn't changed was the clarity of the water behind Dauschen. It gave them a clear view of the carnage waiting below. Broken and burned vessels lay on the sea floor. Wood that did not move beneath the currents. Fishing nets that would never feed a family again. Empty armor and skeletal remains told of far more than a burned fleet.

"Come," Owen said, ushering his family away from the sight. "Leave the ax. No weapons. This place has seen enough violence to put the guards on edge."

They made their way to the stone stairs. Owen raised a hand in greeting, but the guards simply turned and stepped away, vanishing from sight.

"Let me talk to them when we reach the top," Hefina said. "You can be a bit brash sometimes, Owen."

He was about to protest before thinking better of it. "Probably for the best."

Hefina passed him on the stairs, leading the way up to a wide gate that Owen had never seen closed. Tight iron bars formed either door, with only a small gap near the center where they could see one guard.

"What brings you to Dauschen?"

Hefina leaned closer. "We're refugees from Fel. We're looking for my husband's cousin, Cage."

The guard stood up a little straighter, his brow furrowing.

"Did she say Cage?" the second guard asked, walking into view.

The first guard nodded. "I warn you, if you're lying, you're going off the cliff."

Owen almost snarled at the man. "I've seen enough of that in Fel. Did the Butcher destroy your compassion too?"

The first guard stepped back as if he'd been struck. "I … I'll take you to Cage." He unlocked the gate with a heavy thunk, revealing a scene of destruction and restoration that took Owen's breath away.

Vaughn passed through the gates, his gaze racing across the landscape from the scorched mountainside to the missing base to the missing homes. So many missing homes.

Owen placed a hand on Vaughn's shoulder and pulled him closer. "This is why Mordair must lose."

CHAPTER TWO

"THIS ISN'T OVER!" Mary shouted as she threw two levers, forcing the Skysworn into a violent dive before pulling up behind an ailing destroyer.

Jacob cursed and gripped his jump seat harness ever tighter. He glanced at Furi, who had her eyes shut against the airship's wild movements, but it was Alice's laughter that grabbed his attention.

"She's lost her mind," Furi said, her voice cracking with something between fear and concern.

"I know what I'm doing," Mary snapped. "Fire, Smith!"

The chainguns roared to life beneath the Skysworn.

"I meant Alice," Furi muttered. "We should have stayed in the library. Why didn't we stay in the library?"

Something crashed against the hull. Jacob glimpsed the smoke and fire of another distant airship. Their lines were fractured, but more than one of Belldorn's ships floated on the sea in pieces.

"You got it, Smith!" Mary shouted. "The rear destroyers are broken. Get back to the engine and get us ready to jump."

"I can do that," Jacob said.

"No. If I have to make any sudden moves, Smith knows how to keep himself from getting thrown into the bulkhead. We're jumping to the next destroyer, and then we're out of ammunition."

"Then take us into the clouds," Alice said. "We can drop bombs from above. You *know* we're good at it."

"Against a handful of ships, yes. In the middle of this chaos? No. And this was supposed to be recon to assess their retreat. I didn't expect them to fire on us, or I *would* have left you all in the library!"

The transmitter crackled to life, and Lady Katherine's voice brought the cabin to silence. "All ships, draw back to the docks. Your orders are to reinforce the city."

Mary flipped to the channel used by the captains. Several voices came and went, transmissions tumbling one over the other. But the sentiment was almost all the same. She turned to another frequency and clicked the transmitter.

"Eva, are you getting this?"

Static echoed through the cabin before Eva's voice answered. "Mary! Did you take down that destroyer?"

Jacob looked out the window as the entire afterdeck of the destroyer pulled at the remaining structure. It might be able to limp back across the sea, but he doubted it.

"Yes, but what does Kat have us doing? We have them on the run, and she's calling off the pursuit?"

"We don't know if they have more forces ready to attack, Mary. It's a good strategy. The city has taken enough damage, and we can't afford to be caught off guard."

Smith cursed over the horn. "Ready to jump, Mary."

The captain of the Skysworn took a deep breath and glanced at the trio behind her. "Alright, we're heading to the docks."

"I'll see you soon," Eva said, disconnecting with a click.

"We can't!" Jacob said, almost standing up in protest, only to be held down by his harness. "The more ships that escape, the more forces will be waiting in Ballern."

"We can't lose Belldorn," Mary said. "As much as I hate to admit it, Kat's right, Eva. We'll see you on the docks."

"I don't like it," Smith said. "Mordair's fleet is in Ballern now. It will be stronger with these remnants."

"We can't take them all on alone."

The transmitter crackled again. "Skysworn. Mary, this is Kat."

Alice and Furi both waited at attention for her to say more. Jacob's gaze wandered back to the carnage outside the windows, both near and far.

Mary eyed the transmitter. "Kat, what is it?"

"I need you to extend your reconnaissance. Follow them home. Can you do that? The Skysworn should blend in well enough at a distance."

Mary closed her eyes and popped open the horn. "Smith, what do you think?"

"We'll need to refuel in Ballern, but we could do it."

"Yes!" Furi said. "I can talk to the Skyborn. Bring more to our side. Kura has a lot of influence on the docks, and I could help."

"Understood," Mary said. "We'll continue west."

"Be careful. I don't want to have to explain to Eva why you flew into a mountain."

Mary let out a low laugh. "I imagine she'd make that a problem for you. Are you sure about the withdrawal, Kat?"

"I have to protect our people. Come home when you can." Lady Katherine disconnected with a click, and then static.

The Skysworn angled higher into the air, turning toward the northwest at Mary's command. A terrible vision lit the dark skies, fires casting light like a thousand dying suns drifting through the air and water.

"Hold on."

The thrusters engaged, slamming Jacob back against his jump seat and drawing a gasp from Furi.

✧　　✧　　✧

THEY WERE IN sight of Ballern's brightest lanterns and docks before the transmitter sounded again. Mary frowned at the rhythmic bursts of static before switching to another frequency.

"What is it?" Furi asked. "Is something wrong?"

Mary shook her head. "No, it's a signal from Baddawick." She clicked the transmitter. "This is the Skysworn."

"Mary? Good, good. It's, uh … well, I suspect you know who it is. Can we use our names?"

The ship rattled under the force of the thrusters, but Jacob didn't miss Mary's smile.

"Yes, Baddawick, we're secure."

"Good, that's good. You know, I didn't expect so many steps and annoyances to simply talk to you. The others, well, it's not so complicated with them."

"Our enemies don't know about all our locations. They know about me."

"Fair, that's fair. To the point! I have a message for Alice. From her mother, in fact."

"My mom?" Alice asked, almost jumping out of her seat despite the thrusters.

"Stay down. We're docking soon."

Alice huffed, but she kept her harness fastened.

"Alice is here," Mary said. "She can hear you."

"Good. Alice, I'm to tell you they're starting to move some residents back into the Lowlands."

"What?" Alice snapped. "Are they insane?"

Baddawick couldn't hear Alice's protests and continued without interruption. "She's volunteering to help, so you may not find her at the mansion should you return to Ancora. Look for her by the cliff near your old street." Baddawick's voice faded. Jacob couldn't make out what he was saying, but Baddawick's words cleared soon enough. "Mary, I have to go. Do tell Alice her mother is in good health. I've spoken with her several times. Lovely lass. Be safe. For the Steamsworn."

Mary pressed the transmitter's button. "For the Stormborn."

Baddawick's voice returned with a chuckle. "Word has already reached Ancora about your alliance with the Skyborn. May it end well."

"Thanks, Baddawick." Mary cut off the transmitter. "Brace yourselves. Cutting thrusters."

Jacob wasn't sure what was more intimidating, the sudden pull of inertia against his harness or the growl that emanated from Alice's chest.

"The Lowlands!" Alice didn't wait for the Skysworn to stop rocking or for Smith to stop shouting over the horn about Mary's overzealous braking. "Has Mom lost it? Going into the Lowlands? There's nothing there but death and ruins!"

"Maybe it's getting better," Jacob said. "Ambrose and his crew, you know?"

Alice rubbed at her forehead. "Ambrose is amazing, but no one is that good, Jacob. Not even with your Mech design. The Fall took everything from the Lowlands."

That was all it took for Jacob's memories to return. The roiling swarm of Red Death and invaders, a dark mass of shadows that swept across his home, churning everything he knew below their chitinous mass. To remember the people who vanished into them, and the city that would never be the same. *Could* never be the same.

"Jacob!"

He shook himself and looked up, finding Alice's stare boring into him.

"Are you ok?"

Jacob smiled and nodded. "I'm fine. Just ... just remembering the Lowlands."

"You're still a terrible liar."

Furi glanced between the pair, offering a crooked smile.

Mary turned in her seat. "You look as uncomfortable as I feel, Furi. Figured you'd be used to these two by now. Or is the battle still getting to you?"

"No," Furi said. "It's definitely these two."

At that, Jacob and Alice exchanged rather large grins.

✧   ✧   ✧

IT HAD BEEN some time since they'd last seen an enemy ship take any interest in them. Jacob hopped out of his jump seat once the thrusters had been cut and Mary's deadly dance was done with the destroyer. The Skysworn itself might pass for any number of small, antiquated vessels in the air, but the thrusters would be a dead giveaway to a great many people they'd be better off avoiding.

"Eva's going to worry, Smith."

A sigh came back across the horn. "Do what you have to do, Mary. She has a good crew. If we can't trust them, what are we even doing up here?"

Mary spun the dial for the transmitter before Smith finished speaking. It was a private frequency, and one she could almost always find Eva on. It wasn't a surprise when she didn't get a chance to speak, instead trying not to cringe when Eva's voice snapped over the line.

"Skysworn, where the hell are you? I've been looking all over the docks and found nothing. And no one's heard a thing about you."

"Kat needed some recon. We're heading to Ballern."

"Where?" Eva bit off the word. "I'm sorry, I thought you said Ballern. On your own? Right now?"

"I can see it through the windscreen, actually." Mary winced at Eva's muffled shout.

"What if they recognize you?"

"Those who know us know us as a trading vessel, Eva. It'll be fine."

"And if someone from Fel knows different? Where are you even going to dock?"

Furi leaned against the dashboard beside Mary. "On the Bones. Right below the warehouse district. It's hard to see, and generally ignored by everyone who's been paid to look the other way."

Jacob was somewhat impressed at how sharp and awake Furi sounded. After the battles earlier in the day, he was ready to fall asleep. And he *had* fallen asleep for a short time. Sleep before and after a battle was never easy for him, and he glanced over at Alice with quite a bit of jealousy. Watching her quietly snoring while Eva shouted over the transmitter was something to behold.

"Why didn't you tell me?" Eva almost hissed.

"We were halfway across the sea by the time we got the order. What was I going to say? It's not like a brig or any small vessel is going to make it that far."

"I don't know … something, at least. Just tell me next time."

"I really hope there isn't a next time."

Eva sighed. "Me too. Be careful and let me know when you've docked."

"Yes, Mother."

"Don't. You. Dare. Say. That."

Mary's cackle had more than a little evil in it. "We'll talk soon. Skysworn out." She looked up to meet Furi's gaze. "Tell me where. I could use the guidance."

"You know where Kura meets with everyone? The school?"

Mary nodded.

"Just below that. There are more than a few of the old bays still open. Fisherfolk and a few others use them."

"They fish from airships?" Jacob asked.

Furi turned and blinked at him. "After they land on the water, yes."

"Back in your jump seats," Mary said. "We'll be to the Bones soon enough."

Alice stirred when Jacob flopped into the seat beside her. "Five more minutes." It took Jacob a second to understand what she'd mumbled.

"Almost there," he said.

Alice cracked an eye open and yawned when Jacob and Furi clicked their harnesses back into place. Sometimes the maneuvers around the docks didn't make for the smoothest experience. "It's still dark out. What are we doing?"

"Same plan," Mary said. "Were you asleep for the whole plan? We're docking on the Bones."

"Then sleep?"

"Yes."

"Good. That's good."

"But it'll be an early morning," Furi said. "We have to find Kura first thing. There's a lot to talk about."

The lights of the docks brightened across the windscreen. Jacob couldn't see Mordair's warships on the sea below them, but he could easily pick out the shadows of the destroyers peppering the airship docks. Even if the Skyborn joined them in full, they would be surrounded by enemies. And yet all Jacob wanted to do in that moment was sleep.

Mary swung the Skysworn around a small line of ships waiting to be guided into the main docking areas. Lanterns on the docks flashed patterns to each captain in turn, giving them instructions on where to dock. Mary pulled wide. So wide, Jacob almost wondered if they were going back to sea, leaving the light shadows of Ballern's towers far behind them.

Before he could finish the thought, Mary turned back toward Ballern, raising the Skysworn's nose before angling down again. The ship tilted forward, and the full sprawl of Ballern opened below them. Ballern's white towers and sun-bleached stone rose far beneath them, peppered with warm yellow lights in the darkness.

Somewhere in that maze of streets and buildings and people, Mordair and the Children of the Dark Fire waited. Jacob's stomach soured at the thought before Smith's voice pulled him back into the moment.

"Chainguns are clear below."

"Understood." Mary leaned closer to the windscreen, focusing on something above them.

Furi groaned. "We are *really* close to that warehouse."

Jacob squinted and then almost jumped in his seat. The distant shadow wasn't distant at all. Any normal airship couldn't have squeezed into that space. Only the low-profile gas chambers of the Skysworn allowed them to do it, and they would have to tie the ship down tight to keep it from rising into the platform above them.

"Hold her steady," Smith said. "I'm headed out. I'll signal when we're anchored."

Jacob couldn't see Smith out on the deck, but he heard his bootsteps on the ladder and the thunk of the hatch. The familiar crack of the gangplank on metal told him the tinker was well on his way to tying off the Skysworn.

"As soon as we're shut down and tied off, head to your berths," Mary said. "We aren't doing anything else tonight but sleeping."

"Best idea I've heard all day," Alice mumbled.

Jacob grinned at her. It was only a couple of minutes before Smith appeared at the cabin door.

"All set. I'll get the engine cooled down. The rest of you get some sleep."

For all of Alice's nap and apparent grogginess, she was the first out the door and down the hatch. Everyone else followed with a bit less energy.

CHAPTER THREE

Jacob didn't startle awake. It was a slow shift from dreaming to realizing he was awake. He didn't hear anyone else moving on the Skysworn yet, but when he tried to move, Alice wrapped her arms around him tighter. He thought about trying to disentangle himself, but instead waited in the dark, thinking about what was to come in Ballern and wondering just what exactly was happening in Ancora.

Eventually, he turned to focus on the small sliver of light at the edge of the far door. In that moment he realized he needed a shower, and badly. The day had been long, and now that he'd had a chance to rest, a shower sounded like the next best thing.

Mary was next to wake. The sudden crash of her boots on the floor woke everyone else in short order. "Let's go, crew. We have mischief to get done."

"That's one way to put it," Furi mumbled from a bed nearby.

"How about a shower?" Jacob asked.

"Yes, please," Alice muttered. "I smell like I'm ready for the Carrion Worms. Or maybe that's Jacob?"

Jacob pursed his lips. "Pretty sure it's both of us."

"No time," Mary said. "We can get cleaned up later. After we find Kura."

Smith groaned and stepped toward the door as he pulled his shirt on, giving a brief glimpse of the biomechanics in his chest. "You're giving me flashbacks, Mary. All I need is to be knee-deep in a barrel of rotten Pilly eggs, and it'd be like the North Woods all over again."

"What happened in the North Woods?" Furi asked.

"We don't talk about the North Woods," Mary muttered.

"An ill-advised contract." Smith scratched the back of his head. "It … didn't go well."

"You have to tell us more than that!" Furi said. "I'm sure it's not as bad as you remember."

"Probably worse. Another time, Furi. Another time."

Alice hugged Jacob once more before she started pushing him out of bed. "Out. Time to go."

Jacob grunted in protest, but obliged soon enough. Showers would have to wait. They at least had combs to somewhat tame their hair, but far sooner than he liked, the entire group was moving onto the docks, ready for whatever the day would bring.

✧   ✧   ✧

JACOB PEERED OVER the side of the Bones. It was a good reminder that as much as he'd grown used to heights, there were *some* heights that were still generally terrifying. The narrow and shaky walkways forming the Bones brought that into immediate focus.

"Now I wish Furi wasn't the only one who had a glider pack," he muttered.

Furi grinned at him.

"While we're alone, I want you all to know I spoke with Kat again last night," Mary said.

Alice glanced back at her. "What for?"

"I wanted to understand her thinking better. It's … sometimes she can make rash decisions. She's a great leader, don't misunderstand me, but in times of conflict, she has taken bad counsel before."

"Did you ask her why she called off the fleet?" Alice asked.

Mary nodded. "I did. And I understand her decision better now. She was out in the city during the attack. Kat saw the devastation. The homes destroyed. The people lost. She doesn't want to expose the survivors to more."

"Do you think that's the right decision?" Furi's eyebrows drew together. "Because I don't. It's awful to say, but I know Ballern."

Alice quickened her steps until she was next to Furi. "And will Mordair make that better or worse?"

"Mordair makes everything worse," Mary grumbled. "I see people up ahead. Keep this to yourselves for now."

Jacob didn't think Mary needed to say that. He figured they were all thinking it. If the wrong people on those docks realized who they were, they likely wouldn't have to worry about much at all for very long. And they'd likely be falling from a great height with no gliders.

He shivered at that thought. They followed Furi when they reached the edge of the walkway and turned inward toward the docks and the lifts that waited in the distance.

The Ballern docks were a sight Jacob wasn't sure he'd ever get used to. Each level was large enough to house dozens of destroyers and countless small ships. Their current level, beneath the warehouse district, held a handful of those warships, and it was unnerving to see how many were from Fel.

They stood in a short line for the lift, taking up one entire cage on their own. As unsettling as the lower level might have been, the warehouse district was worse. Fel guards roamed the walkways, the jagged fins of their dark gray warships looming over everything. More of the gray behemoths waited on the level above.

"Act natural." Mary's voice was only a whisper as she leaned toward Jacob. Regardless of that advice, it was hard to ignore the tension in the air. They stayed close to Furi, and the Skyborn likely knew every nook and cranny of that floating city better than the Fel soldiers ever would. Furi led them to an outer walkway, flanked by small single-room homes, bars, and a smattering of vendors.

The farther they went, the fewer of Fel's guards there were. Finally, Furi turned to the left, cutting into the warehouse district where there was no sign of Fel at all, aside from the airships in the distance.

By the time they made it to their destination, Jacob realized Furi had taken them on an indirect course. If anyone had been following, they would have been lost in the alleyways and narrow paths between the metal buildings.

They slipped inside the warehouse, and Furi took a deep breath.

A harsh voice answered their arrival. "State your business."

A man stepped out of the shadows, his brow creased and a sword drawn. But his expression softened when he saw who was there.

"Jakon!" Furi said.

And before Jakon could so much as sheath his sword, Furi crushed him in a hug.

✧   ✧   ✧

A FEW MINUTES later, Jacob and the others took seats in the schoolroom opposite Kura and Jakon. The latter stayed behind Kura's desk as if they were there to teach a lesson that day. To the average onlooker, that would have been plausible if not for Smith's hulking form in the classroom.

"The Stormborn." Kura almost growled the name. She drummed her fingers on the desk, slowly raising her gaze to meet Furi's. "That transmission was you, wasn't it?"

Furi straightened and ran her finger over the patch of the Shadow-wing on her glider pack. "Yes, it was. This is our symbol, Kura. And I meant every word. If we're going to beat Mordair, we have to come together with the Steamborn."

"A Shadowwing?" Kura asked before shifting her focus to Jacob and Alice. "Ancorans, I know your stories. I know the tragedy of your city. But I fear that won't be enough to earn the trust of many Skyborn."

"It will if it comes from Jakon," Furi said.

Jakon held his hands up as he stood. "Look, kid, I'm all for pulling you out of the fire, but signing up for your war is a whole different thing. And becoming a recruiter sounds even worse."

Jacob didn't miss the slight hunch in Furi's shoulders at Jakon's words. But the moment passed, and she steeled herself.

"You think Mordair won't crush the Skyborn like he did the citizens of Fel?" She leaned forward. "Think about all the kids in the market, Jakon."

"Furi, that's not what I—" Jakon sat down on the edge of the desk and crossed his arms.

"Are you going to let them die?" Furi's voice edged toward violence. "Are you going to let them hang from the walls? You know what Mordair did in Fel. We hear all the terrible things the Butcher did in Dauschen and Ancora, but look at what Mordair did in Fel for *decades*. And now he's *here*." She slammed her open hand on the desk, the crack echoing around the warehouse.

Jakon didn't answer. He glanced at Mary and Smith before lowering his gaze. "It's complicated, kid. Maybe it's time to get out of Ballern. For all the Skyborn." He slid off the desk and stood, looking down at Furi. "Sorry. Until next time."

No one said anything as Jakon walked away. Furi wiped at her eye, the muscles in her jaw tensing as her mouth tightened into a flat line.

Mary broke the silence. "Jakon's an old smuggler. He knows sometimes the only way to stay alive is to stay alone, and far away from a battle."

"But he saved us," Furi said. "He saved *me*. He knows how to fight."

Smith put his hand on Furi's shoulder and squeezed. "He isn't Sky-born, Furi. He isn't Steamborn. It's not as personal to him. Sometimes you have to let your friends go, and be happy for the time you've had with them."

"He's better than that," Furi muttered.

"Give him space," Alice said. "He may not want to join us now, but maybe we can hire him later."

Mary laughed under her breath. "That's probably true. He'll do some pretty stupid things for a bit of coin."

"So will we," Smith said.

Mary grinned at him.

"I'd be happy if we could hire him as a chef," Jacob said.

Everyone nodded in agreement with that.

"Enough of Jakon." Kura walked closer to the chalkboard and tapped it with a fingernail, the sound reminding Jacob of how Miss Penny used to get the class's attention. "We have more pressing matters. I doubt you missed the increased patrols on the docks."

"We didn't," Furi said. "A lot of Fel soldiers."

"Yes, exactly my point. I doubt they're here to guard their warships."

Jacob frowned and then blew out a breath. "You mean they're here to keep the Skyborn in check?"

"I suspect so."

Smith rubbed his cheek and looked at Mary before focusing on Kura. "What can we do?"

"The same thing Furi's message asked us to do. Rally the Skyborn and make ready for a battle the likes of which Ballern has not seen since the Deadlands War."

Alice bit her lip. "That might be here sooner than you expect …"

"What do you mean?"

"There's a contingent in Belldorn who want to strike immediately,"

Mary said. "Lady Katherine is holding them back, which I honestly don't agree with myself. I wouldn't be surprised if Archibald makes a move in the meantime."

"Bollwerk? You think they'd send their warships across the sea?"

"They sent them to Fel. They might."

"The stories I've heard of the destruction in Belldorn ..." Kura looked away. "It can't happen here."

"Belldorn?" Jacob said. "What about Dauschen? Midstream? What about *Ancora*? As long as Mordair still has a fleet, no city is safe."

"He didn't need a fleet to level Ancora," Alice said quietly.

Mary groaned and leaned back in her chair. "Look, it is what it is, Kura. Either there will be a battle for Ballern, or your people will surrender to Mordair's tyranny unconditionally. I don't see another way out of it."

"Not unless you run away like Jakon did," Furi said. "I can't believe he ... I can't believe he won't help! He knows pirates, smugglers, and many people who could help."

"So do we," Smith said. "We'll do what we can."

Mary looked at Kura. "You have your warning. Rally your people, or get out of Ballern. I don't want to hear about you being caught up in this if you aren't fighting. That's a death sentence, and you know it. Smith and I are here to appraise the situation and report back to Lady Katherine. I don't have to tell you how chilling it was to see Fel's fleet nestled up to your docks, their soldiers patrolling the walkways."

"No, you don't."

Furi stood up and stepped behind the desk. "I'm staying with Kura. I can help rally the Skyborn. They'll fight when they find out how many survivors live in Belldorn and Canopy. They'll fight when they know the truth about Belldorn. The truth about the assassinations and the Children of the Dark Fire."

Alice shook her head. "You can't stay here without Kura or Jakon."

"Alice is right," Kura said. "Furi, your passion is a light, but you aren't their leader. And neither am I. They lost their queen."

"You did, too," Furi said. "And I'm going to stay because you're going to fight."

"What about Rin and Tatsu?" Jacob asked. "They're going to be worried."

Furi laughed. "If they were worried, I wouldn't have thought they were dead for all these years. No, Jacob, this is my home, like Ancora is yours. The Skyborn have been adrift long enough, and Kura knows it. Don't you?"

She didn't break eye contact with Kura, instead staring the woman down while she waited for an answer.

Kura slowly dragged her fingers across the desktop until her hands clasped together. She sighed and leveled her gaze at the group. "For the Stormborn."

CHAPTER FOUR

MORDAIR STUDIED THE aged mosaic on the wall of the tiny restaurant. The small chair was far more comfortable than the black stone throne he'd been given as Steward. Though, if he was being honest, the darkness of the steward's throne reminded him of the gray pallor that colored Fel.

It had taken all of one day to grow weary of the bickering between the viscounts and archdukes. Petty squabbles and obvious plays for power defined Ballern's leadership. That was something Mordair had fixed in Fel with a handful of bodies on the wall.

But there had been something more interesting in those meetings. Someone always in the corner of the room, silent and observing, until they weren't. And that's who Mordair waited for now. It wasn't long before the cloaked figure appeared at the door, hands grasped in front of them and head bowed as they made their way to the table.

"Please, join me." Mordair gestured to the chair opposite. As much care as he had taken to dress inconspicuously, his guest was not so subtle. The Children of the Dark Fire stood out wherever they went. Mordair had met a handful in Fel who were more discreet, but those in Ballern all wore the same dark robes and displayed the tattoos of metal-plated flames on their forearms.

The priestess slipped into the chair without moving it, betraying the slight form beneath those robes. "Why are we in this place, Steward? And where is the baroness?"

Mordair laced his fingers together and smiled. "She'll be along soon enough. I wanted to speak to you about things I'd overheard in the halls, Marta."

The priestess straightened. "I did not tell you my name."

"People talk."

"Not in the courts of Ballern, Steward. What is your intention here?"

He hesitated, not sure how to respond. It was instinct to lord more information over the priestess to show there was nothing he couldn't find out about her. It was a tactic that had worked in Fel year after year. But she'd already failed to respond as he expected, so he tried another tack.

"As you may know, I welcomed the Children of the Dark Fire into Fel for many years."

"*Welcomed* is a strong word." Marta smiled, and Mordair imagined it was the last thing many had seen in their lives. "You degraded them until they sank so far into their drink they might not be recognized by their own family."

Mordair laced his fingers together. "I did not cast them out. I never made an example of them."

"So you say."

"Many of my closest guards knew a man named Nils quite well."

Marta didn't respond.

"I spoke with him on occasion, and while some of the Children who gathered in Fel had issues, as you say, he was more grounded than the others." Mordair relaxed his hands and casually leaned toward Marta. "As a priestess, you may know the stories he told. Our family line can be traced far into the past to the building of the Great Machines."

The priestess sat up straighter. "Those records were lost. There are only theories and assumptions now, and they carry the weight of so much dust."

"Perhaps."

Mordair waited in silence when the server returned to place an array of cheese and protein boards on the table. He recognized the fried Pilly and slivers of sausage, but other things were not so familiar. Only after the server was gone did he continue.

"I have an interest in the Great Machine to the west and the city that dwells around it."

"You speak again of rumors." Marta's voice was firm, but Mordair could feel a hint of concern behind her words.

"If I believed these rumors, I would have met with you in the throne room. This meeting is as much to protect my interests as it is yours. I want to preserve the legacy of the Great Machines. Doing so will preserve the legacy of the Children of the Dark Fire. I was there in the Deadlands War, Marta. You can bend the history in your books, but you cannot change what my eyes witnessed."

"If what you say is true, your zeal to preserve the Great Machines' legacy could damage our own."

Mordair slowly tilted his head to the side. "Would it? Not if I find your legacy more convenient."

Marta glanced down at the food before picking up a wedge of cheese. She broke an edge off it and chewed for a time before returning her gaze to Mordair. "You play games you do not understand. Our gods are not meant to forward the plans of outsiders."

"Your gods can die."

"You *dare*?" Marta slammed her palm onto the table, rattling the glasses and boards.

Mordair fought back the smile that wanted to creep across his face. "I've stood atop the corpses of your gods in the desert, Marta. Those armies will find their way here in time. Let me help you defend the Great Machines. Give me my legacy so that yours may move on."

Marta's rigid posture relaxed a hair. "In what way?"

"Belldorn is coming. It is only a matter of time. They will attack Ballern, and if all our forces remain in the city, the casualties will be enormous. We need another base."

"And in exchange?"

"Weapons and supplies in quantity. You can work out the details with Patrice. She has my full confidence and authority to make those trades."

Marta drummed her fingers on the table. "Perhaps we can come to an agreement. There are parts of the Great Machines that are holy places, Steward. And your people will not be welcome there."

"I am sure, and my people will abide by your laws. Now, tell me of the magnificent creatures who dwell there. I understand there are several I have never seen here or across the sea."

At this, Marta smiled, an expression that seemed more sincere than anything she'd shown yet. A small crack in the armor, but that was all Mordair needed.

✧　✧　✧

MARTA TOLD HIM of many creatures who thrived around the Great Machines. Two caught his attention. Beasts he'd heard legends of but did not believe truly existed. Giants who could fire superheated liquid into their enemies' ranks, and others so camouflaged one might already be dead before they realized they'd been attacked.

"The baroness is here," Mordair said.

His invitation had asked for an inconspicuous outfit. The baroness donned a leather jerkin and fine pants that could have passed for any of the upper class in town, but her entourage of guards was a dead giveaway.

"Why can't nobles follow the simplest instructions," Mordair muttered under his breath.

Marta grinned. It was the smallest expression, gone well before the baroness could have seen it, but it gave Mordair some small hope that this gambit was going to go well.

"The Baroness of Auxley," one of her guards said.

"Get out," Mordair growled.

The baroness shooed her guards, but they didn't go far, instead lingering around the front of the restaurant. It was far enough they wouldn't overhear the conversation to come, and that was acceptable.

"Why do you have a priestess here?"

"I wished to discuss the history of the city. Who better than those who keep its records?"

The baroness scowled at Marta, then took a seat between her and Mordair. "If you think this place is free of spies, you're a fool."

"I've been accused of worse."

"The baroness has family from one of the nearby villages," Marta said. "She succeeded her uncle after he slew her father."

Mordair blinked. "That is … fascinating, though I did not request such extensive background on our guest."

"And what is it you do request here, Steward?" the baroness asked, wholly unbothered by Marta's statement.

"I wish to assess the potential threat of the Archduke of Willett. Jonas strikes me as a cunning politician. I would prefer he not strike me down."

Whatever the baroness had been expecting, that wasn't it. "And you're asking me?"

"Yes, I'm asking for your help, Yuki."

"How do you know that name?"

Marta didn't so much as blink, even though it had been she who debriefed Mordair just minutes before.

"You're a noble. Many people know your name."

The baroness eyed Marta, but returned her focus to Mordair. "Your silver tongue is some cause for concern, Steward. Regardless, we use titles in Ballern more than names. You will mark yourself as more of an outsider if you do not do the same."

"I appreciate that information."

The baroness inclined her head. "As to … Jonas." She frowned at the use of his name. "He is ambitious and prone to sabotaging the businesses and accounts of his rivals. Tread with caution."

"It is always good to have one's suspicions confirmed, is it not?"

"You didn't bring me here just to ask about the archduke."

"No, I did not. I wanted to get your opinion on strengthening our bond with the Children of the Dark Fire. That is why Marta is here, and why we must be ready for the conflicts to come."

CHAPTER FIVE

OWEN HAD HEARD the stories of Dauschen's destruction. But he'd heard them in the bars and backwaters around Fel, where it was spoken of as a great victory. That was, until the base itself was obliterated, and nearly a third of Fel's forces stationed there died in the collapse.

Mordair had tried to use that as a rallying cry, but most of Fel's citizens were done with war. Their resistance bothered the king enough that the hangings had started again.

Owen's fingernails cut into his palms as he attempted to focus on what good he could find in Dauschen. Homes had been lost, clearly, but new defenses had risen to protect what remained. The towering spike of an airship dock now loomed over the city, eclipsing the tallest of Dauschen's structures by several stories, a crown for the mountains themselves.

They passed the old cemetery, led by only one guard now, and Owen paused at the next street. Looking to the left, it could have been any time in the past—small vendor stalls lined the way, and a handful of shops had opened their doors. But Owen had a good memory, and those stalls now held scant wares compared to those of the past, and the people strolling across the stones carried little in the way of purchases.

The entire place was still stunned by what had occurred there. Of that, he had no doubt. He looked back toward the airship dock when something thudded and screeched.

"Dad, what is that?"

Owen wasn't sure what to tell Vaughn. It looked like a massive hand. A gauntlet of metal and steam and wheels climbed the airship dock, but clutched within its fingers was a load of iron and steel that would have taken twenty men to lift.

One support at a time, the machine rose higher, belching fire and steam into the air like a twisted Fire Lizard.

"Bigger than it looks," the guard said with a smile. "Come, we're nearly to Cage."

Hefina squeezed Owen's arm. "When were we here last? Two years at most? This city was so beautiful."

Owen patted her hand. "It will be again. If Cage is helping them re-build, you know it will be the best it could possibly be."

The guard glanced back at them, raising an eyebrow. "You really do know him, don't you? That man has an infuriating ability to catch every little mistake."

Owen let out a quiet laugh. "He always has. He was an absolute nightmare to play hide and seek with as a child. I swear he'd notice if a single branch on a bush was out of place."

The guard nodded and led them onto the grounds of the airship dock. "Stay away from the ropes marking the construction areas. Those show where the crane has dropped things before."

"Has anyone been hurt?" Vaughn asked.

Hefina scowled at him. "We don't need to know that."

"Not to worry, ma'am. No one's been hurt by anything falling off the crane yet. A couple of close calls, but then we added the ropes."

They continued to a tent at the farthest edge of the construction area, a small trail of smoke rising from a cylindrical chimney in the center. Two men walked out, one holding a large schematic and the other arguing something over his shoulder.

"Cage in?" the guard called after them.

The man with the schematic almost snarled. "Yes, of course Cage is in. It's not like he takes a break to eat or sleep, is it?"

"Everything okay?" Owen asked the guard.

"Oh, sure. That's pretty normal. Come on." He stayed in front of them and pulled the light canvas tent flap open when they reached it.

Inside waited a workspace not so different from where the lure craftsmen worked in the fisherfolk districts of Fel. A small fire warmed the tent, and sparse decorations made the left side of the space feel slightly more welcoming than a prison cell. But the far end held a large table, strewn with plans and inkwells.

Behind it stood a man who couldn't have been much taller than Vaughn, but Owen remembered his hair being less gray. The man's name slipped from Owen's mouth. "Cage."

Cage glanced up, a small crease in his brow growing deeper when he saw who had called his name. "Owen? Owen! Steel and flame, man, what are you doing here?" Cage's slow movements evaporated, and he hurried around the table, rushing over to Owen before the larger man could take two steps.

Owen threw his arms around his cousin and tried to answer. But the memories crashed down like a volley of arrows. Losing his brother so soon after his parents had passed. And they had died so close to Hefina's own parents. It had been a year of loss after loss, and memories of Cage when they were children playing in the rivers were some of the happy memories that kept the darkness at bay.

Cage didn't let go. Owen heard him dismiss the guard who had escorted them, but the younger man never let go of Owen until the tears calmed and the tremor in his jaw stopped.

"It is good to see you, Cage."

Cage patted him on the back and finally stepped away. "And you. But what are you doing here?"

Hefina slid between them and kissed Cage's cheek. "Always a pleasure, Cage. Vaughn has grown a bit in this past year."

"Yes, he has." Cage patted Vaughn's shoulder.

"Uncle Cage, what is that thing building the airship dock?"

"Just Cage, Vaughn," he said. "I'm old enough without the Uncle in front of my name." Cage paused and glanced toward the entrance of the tent. "You can tell it's an airship dock? Well, I suppose not many things are that tall, but I'm still glad to hear it's identifiable. Do you mean the crane?"

"The big hand?"

"Yes, yes, that's the crane, alright. Built by an apprentice of Charles von Atlier, you know? Same boy who killed the Butcher."

"You've met Jacob?" Owen asked, following Cage back to the desk where he offered them one of several uncomfortable-looking wooden chairs.

"Oh, yes, that I have. Fought with him, too. Jacob Anders. Seems a good lad. Though his friend Alice scares me a bit. She killed Rana, did you know?"

Cage's words went from an interesting story to a moment of utter confusion. Owen interrupted. "Are those common names in Ancora?"

Cage shrugged. "Can't say for sure. Why's that?"

Vaughn almost bounced in his seat. "We met a tinker named Jacob! He fixed a clamp on our ship. He's a pretty bad navigator, apparently. And his friend had brilliant red hair. She looked strange."

"Hush, Vaughn," Hefina said. "That is rude."

"I didn't mean it to be cruel!" Vaughn pleaded. "It's just … she doesn't look like the rest of us."

"Are you joking right now?" Cage laughed and slapped the desk. "Did one of the guards put you up to this? Where on earth did you meet them?"

"In Fel," Owen said, "right before they dropped the south wall."

Cage blinked before running a hand through his hair. "Those kids have seen too much, Owen. If you saw what happened in Ancora." He shook his head.

"It can't be worse than here. Half the city is gone."

"No. A couple of blocks were lost, and the base. Ancora was … it was worse in the Lowlands. Like nothing I've ever seen." Cage gestured at the tent flap. "They're rebuilding. They have an arm like ours. One to rebuild the walls that fell in the attack."

"Ancora is a fortress," Hefina said. "How much did they lose?"

"All the Lowlands. Everything outside the city wall besides a lucky building here and there. The rest were buried in an avalanche of Red Death and blood."

Vaughn stepped a little closer to Hefina.

"No need to scare the boy." She pulled him in tight. "It was really the Butcher?"

Cage nodded. "More of my men died in the battles than I care to remember. And as much as I am wary of Archibald, the Speaker of Bollwerk, he's done good things for Ancora. And Dauschen, mind you."

"He's taken Fel now," Owen said. "Granted, it wasn't much of a fight after the wall fell. Mordair sent his own soldiers to attack the fisherfolk. It was … it was the last I want to see of that place, Cage."

Cage reached out and squeezed Owen's shoulder. "Dark days, cousin. But new days are on the horizon. And seeing some of our young allies gives me a measure of hope. Of course, that won't much matter if Ballern and Fel manage to restart the Deadlands War, will it?"

Owen hesitated and studied Cage's eyes. "You think they'd go that far?"

Cage harrumphed. "Come to Ancora with me, Owen. I'll show you exactly how far Mordair is willing to go."

"Please, Dad. I've never been to Ancora! Think about all the stories. With their lights and tinkers. Brad told me they even have chickens."

"Chickens?" Cage asked. "Why is anyone concerned about rare wildlife?"

"Chickens ..." Owen smiled and looked from Vaughn to his cousin. "Is it safe?"

Cage took a deep breath. "Likely safer than here, if I'm being honest. They're crowded in the Highlands now, behind the tallest walls. But I doubt they'd turn travelers away. And I'm sure I could convince Baddawick to put you up for a night." He rubbed at his chin and nodded to himself.

"So be it. Before that, we need rest. In the morning, we can travel, if you have the means."

"Excellent. Let me show you around. You can stay at the old barracks with me and my crew if you like. Or I can see about getting you a place in the library. They had some boarding rooms available last I checked. May smell a bit smokey still."

"Whatever is convenient will do," Hefina said. "Thank you, Cage."

He inclined his head and led them outside once more.

CHAPTER SIX

Samuel eyed the slender bolts in the quiver Drakkar had just handed him. "And you're *sure* these aren't for Emerald Needles? I really don't want to be swarmed by those."

Drakkar pulled his hood down and looked to Lady Katherine.

"Yes, I am sure. They are tuned to the Scythe Beetles. Docile creatures when they are not agitated."

"I could say the same thing about one of Charles's bombs," Samuel muttered.

It had only been a day since the battle for Belldorn, and Samuel was never excited about what came next.

Lady Katherine turned to the gathered soldiers in the Dragonwing stables. Half of the stalls were empty now, as Rin and many others had returned to Canopy. Rin was sure more negotiating needed to be done if he was going to convince Canopy to join the war in full.

Samuel focused on Lady Katherine when she spoke again. "The battle is won for now, but we must see to the city. Several citizens lost their homes, and a number of bodies need burning or burying. This is all secondary to the Carrion Worms that have arrived from the woods. That is what you will utilize our Scythe Beetles for. Fire on the worms, and let the beetles do their work."

"What do you need us for?" one of the infantrymen asked.

"To seal the cracks. Keep your distance, but kill anything that tries to penetrate the city. It's possible the Scythe Beetles will charge, and you have my permission to put them down if the need arises. But remember, they are our allies in this."

"Mindless killers is what they are," someone muttered in the back of the ranks. "As if the Needles weren't bad enough."

Lady Katherine held up her hand for silence. "I empathize with those thoughts, soldier, but Belldorn still stands, and I would not make a different decision now." There was an edge to her words, but it softened as she continued. "Should you encounter one of the Emerald Needles, keep your distance. They will make short work of anyone who attacks them."

A woman's voice rose from the ranks. "Why didn't we chase Ballern back to their walls? We could have ended them, my lady. Look at what they did to our city."

Lady Katherine sighed, and Samuel didn't miss the slight hunch in her shoulders. "You will have your battle in time, soldier. Have patience, and let us rebuild our homes."

It was a measured response, to be sure. But it didn't have the kind of resolve behind it Samuel was used to hearing from Lady Katherine. She was always sure of herself, always confident, and he suspected part of that was because her network of allies was like no other.

Another voice spoke up from a stall beneath a Dragonwing. One Samuel recognized. Tatsu. "If you spoke like that to a commander in Ballern, you'd be executed."

All eyes turned to Tatsu while the dragonrider refilled a trough of Sweet-Flies for his mount. "You did damage to their fleet here, but do not forget that Fel is waiting in their city. This is not the time to throw away your lives."

"Spoken like a Ballern loyalist!" another soldier said, stepping toward Tatsu. "This is why we shouldn't set our prisoners free."

Lady Katherine's voice boomed through the stables. "Speak against me again, soldier, and you will spend the week getting to know our prisons well." She waited until the soldier stepped away from the stable again before continuing.

"Tatsu is correct. We cannot rush into the jaws of Fel. We will coordinate with Archibald, and *only* when the time is right will we consider risking our lives in a further offensive. For the time being, we reinforce and rebuild Belldorn. Have trust in your lady as I have trust in you. Dismissed."

Samuel blew out a breath and hooked the quiver onto his belt before clasping Drakkar's shoulder. "Ready to fly?"

"I do wish they would have left me my own mount," Drakkar said.

"I'll let you drive. Come on."

Samuel followed Drakkar through the crowd of soldiers. Most were stepping forward to speak with Lady Katherine, and Samuel had to admit that was something he'd almost never seen outside of Belldorn. The idea of Parliament in Ancora actually taking time to speak with its citizens was laughable. And to take time to speak with its infantry? Even more so. The citizens gave honor and glory to the soldiers who came home alive, but Parliament didn't care either way, so long as they had the numbers they needed. That had been a cold realization in his time with the Spider Knights.

"Samuel?" Drakkar asked.

Samuel blinked and shook himself out of his thoughts. "Sorry, just thinking about the Fall and some old battles."

"It is easy to remember the worst of times. I find I must force myself to remember the best of times when things are dark."

"Hand me some of those bolts," Tatsu said.

Samuel grinned at the dragonrider as he handed over half the bait boxes. "Coming with us for another bracing adventure?"

"Rust it all. If I can keep *you* from getting run over by Scythe Beetles and keep the rest of these fools from defecting, then yes. Another adventure it is."

Drakkar crossed his arms. "Thankfully, this should be much shorter and less harrowing than our deployment of the Emerald Needles."

"When this is done, you should both come to Canopy with me tomorrow or the day after. Rin will need more than his own mouth to convince them to join this effort."

"I feel like there was an insult hidden in there," Samuel said.

"Not hidden at all. Rin, for all his skill at blending into a crowd, can be overbearing when it comes to protecting his people. Now take your mount."

Samuel smiled at Tatsu as he took the reins from the dragonrider.

✧　✧　✧

THE DRAGONWING LAUNCHED them into the air, and Samuel groaned.

"Are you well?" Drakkar asked.

"I just didn't realize how sore I was until this flying trampoline took off."

Drakkar ran his fingers through the furry patch of hair behind the Dragonwing's eyes. Samuel was fairly certain he heard Drakkar tell their mount to ignore the Spider Knight just because he missed his own mount. It made Samuel laugh under his breath, but it also reminded him how long it had been since he'd seen Bessie.

That moment passed as soon as the Dragonwing shot forward, trailing Tatsu's mount, while Samuel fumbled with the crossbow after pulling his goggles down. The crossbow might have been tied to his wrist, but it weighed enough to be painful when he dropped it at speed. An experience he didn't care to repeat.

Tatsu swung wide, skirting the mountain caves where the Scythe Beetles dwelled before rocketing back toward the ruined outskirts of

Belldorn.

It was hard to reconcile the gleaming towers of glass and stone in the center of the city with the scorched rubble to the south. Ballern had taken its toll. Whether it was a victory for Belldorn or not, the price had been high for both cities.

As devastating as that view was, littered with destroyed crawlers and a handful of smoldering airships among the rubble, the sheer quantity of Carrion Worms chased away every other thought.

"It is like a white sea," Drakkar shouted over the wind.

The thought made Samuel's skin crawl almost as much as the sight below them. Even at that speed, he could pick out clusters of Carrion Worms, and when they slowed, the ground writhed in an enormous fleshy mass near the airships. He didn't want to think too hard about why that was.

Samuel slid the first cartridge of bolts home. "Ready." He turned his seat so he could fire past their mount's wings without risking any damage to the Dragonwing.

Drakkar guided the Dragonwing in a slow circle. Once Samuel glimpsed the Carrion Worms through the gap between the Dragonwing's tail and wings, he fired. When they'd launched bolts into the airships for the Emerald Needle strike, it had been hard to tell if the shots landed. Here they were low enough Samuel could see the dark needle of the bolt sticking out of the pale white flesh.

He turned the crank embedded in the crossbow's stock until the string clicked home again, waited for the next bolt to settle, and fired again. After the fourth cluster was met with a direct hit to a Carrion Worm, Samuel looked toward Tatsu, finding the dragonrider closer to the sea and farther south.

For a moment, Samuel wondered why, and then he saw the Carrion Worms rising from the creek bed, threatening to topple the bridge itself.

Samuel patted Drakkar's shoulder and shouted. "South!"

Drakkar looked to his left and cursed. "Hold tight."

It was all the warning Samuel had before the very air threatened to rip him from the saddle. They were on Tatsu in no time, skimming the length of creek and firing two more bait boxes into the nauseating horde of pulsating Carrion Worms.

The Lowlands in Ancora had given Samuel nightmares for weeks. Most vividly, dreams of those pale fleshy worms tearing through the Spider Knights. They weren't nightmares that would ever fully go away. But what waited below them on the edge of Belldorn would be seared into his mind until his dying day.

"Where are the Scythe Beetles?" Samuel called out when Tatsu came to a hovering stop beside them. He wasn't sure if the dragonrider could hear him over the buzz of wings, but his intent was apparently understood.

Tatsu pointed to the mountains, then drummed out a pattern on his mount's saddle. Drakkar followed, and they were halfway to the stables when Samuel saw it. It could have been a strong breeze or a whirlwind kicking up dust from the ravaged streets. It was anything but.

There were times it was easy to forget how fast the Dragonwings were. They'd flown from one end of Belldorn to the other and back again in the time it would take to walk a single block. Scythe Beetles weren't so quick, but they *were* unstoppable.

Bulky brown carapaces charged through the ruins of Belldorn, crushing brick and Carrion Worm alike in their furor. Every beetle in the world reminded Samuel of a Red Death in some way, but there was something about Scythe Beetles that didn't make his skin crawl. It might have been the way they wielded their horns like a sword crossed with a battering ram. As if they too were soldiers, and this was simply their mission to complete.

Two of the Carrion Worms died before they could so much as turn to view the incoming stampede. The third turned in time to see a Scythe Beetle raise its head and slash with violence without ever slowing. The worm parted like some horrid, congealed mass of grease and greenish blood, spilling its life into the stampede as the Scythe Beetles charged forward to the next bait box.

There, near the fallen arch of a lost building, the stampede separated, half continuing toward the sea while the others made their way south to the creek. There was nowhere for the Carrion Worms to flee. Even the few with enough instincts to try burrowing into the sands found themselves impaled and dragged back into the light.

More and more died beneath the horns and claws of the charging wall of beetles.

"Drakkar!" Samuel shouted. "By the underground!"

Drakkar's gaze flashed toward the arches. He signaled Tatsu with a raised open hand before pointing to the ground. A trio of soldiers were in the path of those Scythe Beetles. It was like the Fall all over again. Samuel could hear the screams. See the buildings topple as an unbearable weight crashed through them.

But Tatsu raised his arm, giving the signal to hold.

"We can't!" Samuel cried. "We have to help them!"

"Hold!" Tatsu might have been yelling, but his voice was more like a whisper next to the buzz of the Dragonwing.

Samuel knotted his fists and watched helplessly as the horde charged toward the soldiers. But in the last moments, the Scythe Beetles dodged around them, instead pulling wide, only to smash together on the other side of those diminutive forms, turning two Carrion Worms into so much pulp as the rest of the Scythe Beetles parted around the soldiers like a river.

"How?" Samuel whispered. "Why?"

Drakkar turned to look at him. "They are like water, always taking the path of least resistance, even to their prey."

"Did you forget they tried to kill us in Dauschen?"

The Cave Guardian smiled. "When we were underground with no other path around us, yes. But here, there are many wide paths. Do you not see that the stone is broken only when there is no way to circumvent it?"

Samuel followed the trail of creatures back through to the edge of the city. Wherever they could go around, they did, unless a bait box was calling them on the opposite side of a wall. Then that wall vanished into an avalanche of rubble.

"Like water, my friend. And like the underground rivers, they will cut through anything that stands in their way."

Samuel watched the stampede of Scythe Beetles as they ravaged the Carrion Worms. He doubted they even needed the bait boxes once the beetles realized what was in front of them. They trampled and sliced through every last invader, regardless of whether it had been tagged or not. Their path left a feast for whatever scavengers would follow that carnage.

The Dragonwings hovered overhead, waiting and watching as the horde made its way down into the creek, turning the very water into a murky green pool of gore. When they were done, and no Carrion Worm still wriggled across the earth, and no bait box called to them, the horde of Scythe Beetles dissipated.

Some filtered back through the ruins, but all made their way toward the foothills of the Dragonwing Mountains.

"Come," Drakkar said. "To the stables. I believe it may be time to return to Canopy to help ensure Rin's success. This city faces threats on too many fronts to be left to its own devices."

"I sure wish we would have known you before the Fall."

"It is perhaps best you did not. I do not think I would have liked you very much."

Samuel just blinked as Drakkar laughed and guided their mount toward the stables. Tatsu followed.

CHAPTER SEVEN

O NCE THEIR MOUNTS were back in the stables, they ventured to a small bar at the edge of town. Or at least what was now the edge of town. Samuel had been surprised to see it open and serving, but Drakkar and Tatsu acted as though it was perfectly normal to be cooking so close to a battle.

They hadn't been at the high table long before Samuel told Tatsu their plan to return to Canopy. He only hoped the dragonrider would agree to go soon, because Samuel knew he'd feel awkward returning to the treetop city without Rin or Tatsu in their party.

Tatsu finished chewing a pastry loaded with strips of fatty meat, spices, and ground potatoes before responding. "It's a good plan. We should go today, before the sun sets. The council gathers every evening in wartime. I suspect everyone will be there. Much like the first time you visited Canopy."

Samuel bit into his own pastry, savoring the rich flavor that reminded him of an Ancoran stew, only with more fat and less salt. "Can the Dragonwings make the flight? I mean, have they had enough time to rest?"

"Once they are full of Sweet-Flies, they can fly for hours. Far longer than we'll need to return to Canopy."

Drakkar finished his pastry and took a long drink of water. "They are as resourceful as the Walkers we prefer in the desert. Remarkable, considering their speed."

"I suppose they are much lighter than your Walkers. Less energy to move less weight."

"But to propel that weight through the air?" Drakkar arched an eyebrow.

"You'd have to ask the tinkers. Frederick enjoys the calculations for that sort of thing."

"I bet he would have gotten along with Charles really well," Samuel said. "You should see his notebooks sometime, Tatsu. More numbers and measurements and nonsense than I'd ever need to know. Jacob makes sense of it, though."

"Tinkers," Drakkar and Tatsu said in unison.

It amused Samuel how quick Tatsu was to speak negatively about some of the tinkers' crafts when he himself was so knowledgeable in the way of machines. Perhaps it was different for him. More instinctive. Regardless, Samuel would have thought that would be a bond when it came to the tinkers.

"Come," Tatsu said. "It is time to go."

"Now?" Samuel asked.

"Yes. This was your idea to leave so soon, Spider Knight, so it hardly seems the time to complain about it."

"I wasn't complaining!" His voice fell to a whisper. "Yet."

Drakkar grinned at Samuel before pulling the Spider Knight off his stool. "I will relay a message to Lady Katherine and tell her of our plans."

Tatsu hesitated and then nodded. Whatever mistrust the dragonrider had in the Lady of Belldorn, some of that suspicion had cracked in the time he'd fought with Belldorn. "To the stables."

✧　✧　✧

BEFORE THEY TOOK to the air, Tatsu warned Samuel and Drakkar they were going to go fast. Samuel had assumed that meant there would be small bursts of speed of varying length, but as he kept his face against the saddle and watched the world below disappear in a green and brown blur, he came to a greater understanding of why Tatsu had warned them.

The Dragonwing Mountains came and went, the chill of the mountain air clawing at them before they dove once more, skimming just above the canopy of the forest. They stayed like that, moving faster than he could comprehend, until the Dragonwing came to a violent stop, forcing Samuel into Drakkar's back and Drakkar into the front of the saddle.

"How was it?" Tatsu called out.

Samuel cracked his eyes open, only then realizing he'd shut them with the impact. "We're … here?"

"More importantly, we are alive," Drakkar said. "You failed to explain how fast our mounts would be traveling."

Tatsu shrugged and hopped down from his Dragonwing, boots thudding against the wooden floor of Canopy's stables. "Not quite full speed. Two riders slow them down a bit."

Samuel groaned and slid off the back of the Dragonwing, only to get affectionately whacked in the face by the beast's tail. "Oww."

"He likes you," Tatsu said with a laugh. "Seen more than one rider in the hospital after a good tail thumping."

"He's growing on me," Samuel said, brushing at the detritus that had gathered on his armor. Small bugs and sap and pine needles had made a mess out of it. "I didn't think I'd ever find a speed I was uncomfortable with. I was wrong."

"It is only a fraction faster than we traveled before," Tatsu said. "You can grow accustomed to it in time, but you feel the pressure from the air with more prevalence at those speeds."

Drakkar rubbed the fur of the Dragonwing's neck as the beast plunged its face into a trough of Sweet-Flies. "I worried my cloak might lash Samuel like a whip."

"It probably would have if I didn't keep my face down on the saddle the entire time. Quite a view, though. I'll give you that."

Tatsu looked to the far end of the stables. "The sun will be setting soon. We must hurry if we wish to attend the beginning of the council's gathering."

✧   ✧   ✧

DRAKKAR STOPPED AT the foot of the ramp after Tatsu led them to it. Metal bands in the trees that formed the stables caught his eye, reminding him of the miniature trees some of the lords and ladies would keep in Belldorn.

"Tatsu, were these trees trained to form your stables for the Dragon-wings?"

Tatsu paused and looked back to Drakkar before following his gaze to the woods. "Observant of you to notice the ties. And yes. For many years, there were anchors all around the stables, securing them to the ground below. It damaged the illusion of the netting, so in time they came up with this as the solution."

Samuel patted a thick branch. "So you trimmed the new growth? Doesn't that hurt the trees?"

"It can, certainly. There are enough fungi to kill even the giants of the Shadowed Woods. Much like we have net walkers to keep that material clear of debris, we have a group of arborists who care for Canopy itself."

"It is impressive, to be sure." Drakkar inclined his head and gestured for Tatsu to continue.

At the top of the ramp, they turned onto one of the main walkways, flanked by countless small homes and storefronts in the treetops of the Shadowed Woods. It wasn't as busy as the streets of Cave, but there were similarities to the stories he'd heard of Ballern.

Tatsu adjusted his cloak when a strong breeze came down from the mountains. They made their way through Canopy and passed the large trunk Drakkar recalled being a hotel.

They turned down another path, crowded with slender trees. Drakkar marveled at that archway, so neatly trimmed, and formed into a nearly symmetrical tunnel for its entire length. The last time he'd been there, he hadn't had as much time to take in their surroundings. He'd been far too preoccupied with watching for an ambush. After fighting together, he felt more of a bond to Canopy. At times it was difficult to extend trust to those outside Cave but doing so had gained him allies from Ancora to Ballern.

The silver tree at the end of that tunnel turned to fire in the setting sun. Tatsu didn't slow as he made his way through the tall doors that came to a rounded peak, but Drakkar didn't miss Samuel's whispered thoughts.

"This place is beautiful."

"Perhaps a new home when the war is done?" Drakkar asked.

Samuel shook his head. "Maybe for a vacation, but I'll still take the stone and brick of Ancora, thank you very much."

Drakkar smiled as he slipped through the doorway, stepping into a chamber of copper and brass and far more faces than he'd expected.

"The council is popular this evening."

He looked toward that voice, finding Allie focused on him. "Madame Councilor." He gave a short bow.

"I believe we are well past such formalities, unless you would prefer I call you Cave Guardian for the rest of your days."

Drakkar's smile widened. "As you will, Allie."

She returned the briefest of smiles to Drakkar before gesturing to the crowded benches. "Find a seat where you can. I assume you are here to give support to Rin's most unsavory requests."

Near the end of the second row, Rin fidgeted in his seat. The tiered ebony thrones at the head of the council chambers were no less imposing than he recalled. Drakkar suspected Rin had already had issues persuading Allie to join in yet another fight.

Samuel led the way to a long bench to the far right. The place was nearly full.

"I've never seen this many people in here," Tatsu whispered. "Let's see how this goes."

The woman beside Allie stood and addressed the room a short time later. "I call to order this evening council. Matters to deliberate include the outcome of the battle in Belldorn …" She glanced at Rin as she trailed off. "And the decision to pursue further measures against Ballern."

Mutterings whispered around the room, sounds Drakkar had heard before. Some of the citizens of Canopy were not subtle about their anger. Any sound at all would be frowned upon in such a formal setting, but to voice protest in that moment was a bold statement in itself.

Allie stood beside the first councilor, who called the assembly to order. She raised her hand. Silence fell, and the speaker took her seat. "You will respect this council in these chambers. Lodge your objections, as is tradition. Speak out of turn, and we will escort you from this place."

She paused to let those words make their impact before continuing. "Many of you protested the engagement at Belldorn. But still, we stand victorious and have walked away with what I consider a tentative alliance with the coastal city. That does *not* mean I am promoting the idea of sending our dragonriders across the sea to engage with both Fel and Ballern. We do not have the strength for such a front."

"Then why are we here?" an older councilman asked from the topmost row of thrones.

Allie turned to face the tiers of her contemporaries, her gaze roaming the thrones until they fell on Rin. "I would ask one of our own to speak to that. One who has spent more time among Belldorn's citizens, and whose experience in Ballern perhaps qualifies him better than any of us. Rin." She gestured to him and then returned to her own seat.

Rin stood and made his way to the end of the risers before taking the narrow stairs down to the floor. "Thank you, Allie." He gave a short bow to the councilor before facing the citizens. "I do not have much more to add than I did the last time we spoke, and the decision was made to engage with Belldorn. But what I do have to add is of utmost importance."

Drakkar liked that Rin spoke to the crowd instead of the council. As if the real decision would be made by the citizens of Canopy and not the whim of their leaders. That was a thin line that was often trampled in cities like Ancora and even Bollwerk. Drakkar was sure Archibald would be offended by the mere thought he didn't always act out of concern for his city. He didn't stop the smile from lifting the corner of his lips.

"I say this to all the people of Canopy. Gregory Mordair cannot be allowed to rule Ballern. He has been given the role of Steward, and with that, I have *no* doubt he will crush the Skyborn. Do you not all remember what happened in Fel? To those who once tended the docks and hatcheries? An entire caste wiped out and hung from the walls like slabs of meat to dry. It will be the same here if Mordair is not brought to heel."

Drakkar stiffened as the chamber exploded into shouts and accusations. Rin stood in silence, waiting for the raucous denials and calls to war to abate. As much as Drakkar had honed his patience over the years, even he was impressed by Rin's composure.

"Is this about to get rough?" Samuel whispered under his breath.

"Peace, Spider Knight," Tatsu said with far less caution.

"Listen to Tatsu," Drakkar said. "Raised voices are not raised swords."

Samuel didn't say more, but the tension in his shoulders didn't leave.

Drakkar knew that posture well and did not think it was entirely unwarranted. The Spider Knight was ready for things to go very bad, very fast.

Rin held up a hand, fingers splayed, when the arguing quieted in the chamber. "While I ask you for peace inside this place, it is not the time for peace in the land itself. Consider what followed in Dauschen and Ancora. You have all heard the stories. We have a Cave Guardian and a Spider Knight in this very chamber. They have seen Mordair's machinations with their own eyes. Imagine the ruin if that were combined with the Children of the Dark Fire's ambitions? This world will be as ash. If not for us, for our children. For future generations. We have to stop this."

The dragonrider let his head fall in a short bow before returning to his seat. Drakkar expected whispers or more shouted objections, but the chamber sat in silence.

Allie stood. "And so now you know what walks behind the walls of Ballern and why I have invited Rin to speak before you once more. The legend, or perhaps more appropriately, the abomination known as the Children of the Dark Fire is no mere tale. Many of us were Skyborn. Many of us heard the old stories before they were erased from our libraries and halls." Allie raised her chin, her eyes glistening, her voice falling to a whisper. "Do you know what they have taken from us? They tried to take everything, but we …" Her voice rose to a thunder. "We are *still here!*"

There were no shouts of protest. There was only a roar, a terrifying reminder that sent a chill down Drakkar's spine. A memory of something his brother once told him. *Rally to glorious war. It is a fool's end. Not even the survivors come home. Not really.*

✧   ✧   ✧

SAMUEL SAT IN silence until the chamber quieted. He'd heard that kind of speech before. He didn't know if it was comforting or terrifying. There were still whispers of objection, but they were drowned out by a new fervor, a demand for schedules and strategies, supply lines and logistics.

Allie started welcoming the observers in the chamber to speak. The first was Tatsu.

"What do you intend to do if the fight moves into the Gray Woods?" he asked. "I agree the alliance between Ballern and Fel needs to be broken, but what allies can we count on? And if we are the aggressors? As you know, the Dragonwings are nearly unbeatable in the open air, but a fight in the forests would not be above the canopy. We could take the Dragonwings underneath it, between the towering trunks of the Gray Woods, but it would be risky with Bombardiers and Tree Killers waiting. Not to mention the rumors of Acidwings nearer the Great Machines themselves. We'd be better off outside the woods."

Samuel perked up at that. He started to raise his hand, frowned, and then crossed his arms.

"It would appear our Spider Knight has a thought in that regard, Tatsu. Might you introduce him to the chamber?"

Before Samuel understood what was happening, Tatsu had his arm hooked at the elbow and was hauling him to his feet. He didn't miss the small chuckle Drakkar let slip.

"Some of you may already know Samuel. He trained here briefly and flew with us at the battle of Belldorn. He is a Spider Knight of Ancora. One who rides a giant Jumper."

That got a few whispers and an awkward smile from Samuel.

"We intended to ask your opinion," Allie said, "but I feared waiting any longer might cause you to explode."

It was the first lighthearted comment of the entire assembly, and it raised more than a few low laughs.

"Please, speak."

"It's … uh …" Samuel started. "Well, you mentioned the woods are hard to navigate with the Dragonwings. What about spider mounts?"

"We have very few, though they are agile on the ground."

"What if … what if you had a lot more? And possibly more soldiers to ride them at your side?"

"Are you referring to the Spider Knights of Ancora? I would not reject their aid if it was offered, but the distance you speak of is nearly insurmountable."

"I know a guy," Samuel said, a smile lifting one corner of his mouth.

Drakkar jabbed him in the ribs.

"Right, apologies. I'm … I'm not good at formal. Actually got reprimanded a few times in … well, that's not important. We know Archibald. Between his warships and transports, we could easily bring a company of Knights to Belldorn. From there, we can take whatever transport is available. We feed most of our spiders the same diet I see you feeding the Dragonwings."

"It is a fascinating proposition," Allie said. "But it is only that. You'll need the pledge of your Spider Knights before we can move forward with this in mind."

"After the Fall …" Samuel trailed off. "After the Butcher and Mordair did so much damage to Ancora, we have far more spiders than we have Knights. I think our leaders would be sympathetic to your plight. And perhaps, even more, they'll want Mordair defeated as much as I do. To let him rule anywhere in the world gives him a path back to Ancora. He could attack my home again, and I've already lost too much."

"Then visit with the Speaker of Bollwerk and those who have taken the reins of Parliament in Ancora."

"I will."

Drakkar stood beside Samuel and waited for Allie to acknowledge him.

"Drakkar. Cave Guardian. Do you dissent?"

"No, Madame Councilor. I agree with Samuel. While I wish war upon no people, there are times when one must fight or lay down their life without protest. I will go to Cave. They have been sheltering refugees from Ancora and Dauschen. The Guardians who are not needed to keep the peace may be willing to fight at our side."

"You intend to join this new war against Mordair?"

"No. The war has always been against Mordair. We just did not know it. I intend to see this war ended."

Allie turned away from the chamber and looked at the other councilors. Each, in turn, placed their thumbs and index fingers together, forming the semblance of a square. It took Samuel a moment to realize they were voting. A few made a different symbol, a circle with an X in the middle. Rin was the last to vote, and he too formed the square.

"So be it," Allie said. "We will join this battle until it has been proven unwinnable, or until a better course of action presents itself. Go, all of you. Spread the word to the citizens of Canopy. We fight."

CHAPTER EIGHT

J ACOB FROWNED AT the transmitter as Mary guided the Skysworn out of the docks of Ballern. He was surprised to hear Archibald's voice, and even more surprised to hear why he was contacting them.

"Are you sure about this, Archibald?" Mary asked.

"No, that's why I need some time to discuss things with Belldorn. If Bollwerk is to send one of the warships that far, our alliance between Ancora and Dauschen will be far less protected than it has been. I wanted you to know Samuel is heading to Ancora, and his logic is sound. The Spider Knights would be formidable in Ballern. I *need* you to get Jacob back to Ancora to speak with the leadership there."

"Why me?" Jacob asked for what felt like the tenth time since Archibald had contacted them.

"Everyone knows you," Alice said, answering the question meant for Archibald. "You're the boy who slew the Butcher."

Jacob understood what Alice and Archibald were saying, but that didn't mean he liked it. He wanted to spend more time in workshops and labs and leave the war behind. He wanted to spend time with his friends and family without worrying they'd be attacked at any moment. With that in mind, perhaps he could talk to Parliament. Was it even Parliament anymore? They'd heard rumors the leadership had changed after so many had died in the Fall, but he didn't know much more than that.

Mary nodded. "Alice is right. And Archibald? There's never been an alliance this broad. Not even in the Deadlands War."

"I know. That's why I am entertaining the idea. Not to mention the future threat Mordair poses. If we are to have peace from Ancora to Midstream to Belldorn, this has to end. With Mordair's seagoing fleet in Ballern, he's within easy striking distance of Belldorn. Should he gain a foothold there, we'd have no way to hold Fel and drive him back. That victory would make both cities vulnerable in one blow. Give me time to speak to Belldorn."

"So be it. We'll be in Ancora in time for dinner, provided the thrusters don't explode."

Smith grumbled something unintelligible over the horn, and despite Jacob's dread for what was to come, a small smile lifted the corners of his mouth. He reached out and took Alice's hand. They were going home.

"Be safe." Archibald disconnected without another word.

Alice crossed her arms and blew out a breath. "I still don't like leaving Furi in Ballern."

"That girl can take care of herself," Mary said.

"Did you *see* all the soldiers? If Fel moves against the Skyborn, they won't have a chance."

"If Fel moves against Ancora, they won't have a chance either," Jacob said. "Maybe Archibald's right. It's like Furi said. We need the Steamborn and the Skyborn together if we're going to win this war."

"The Stormborn against the world."

"Only half the world."

Alice smiled and let out a quiet laugh.

✧   ✧   ✧

IT FELT LIKE an eternity had passed by the time they reached the plains beyond the desert. Jacob half expected to see Midstream or Bollwerk in their travels, but Mary's path had taken them farther to the north, though the view of the Burning Forest had been spectacular. He had a better appreciation for how dangerous those twisted stone trees were now, but it made them no less fascinating.

They passed almost directly through the Bull's Horn, a pair of mountains that acted as a gateway between the desert and the plains in front of Cave. The grasslands slid by underneath them, slowly changing into the foothills of the Ridge Mountains before they entered the range itself and Mary cut the thrusters.

"We're going home," Jacob said.

Alice put her arm around his shoulders. "I know it hasn't been that long, but it feels like ages."

The clouds weaving through the mountains obscured their view for a time, until Mary took the Skysworn lower, and they exited the cloud bank entirely.

A long road took a winding path up the mountain, and at its peak sat the towering walls of Ancora, but something had changed.

"Are you seeing this?" Mary asked. "Smith, get up here."

Smith didn't answer, but it wasn't long before his footfalls sounded on the deck outside. It could have been moments, or it could have been hours, and still, Jacob wouldn't have registered the man's arrival. Instead, he stared at the border of the Lowlands and the pale stone walls that stood nearly as high as those of the city.

"Look, by the old town square," Mary said, pointing off to the east.

"Docks," Smith said. "Lower and wider than I expected, but they look serviceable enough."

"How?" Jacob whispered.

Smith turned to face him with a wide grin. "Pretty sure that crane of yours is how, Jacob."

"That's impossible. Just to get the wall rebuilt. It's not possible …"

Alice undid her harness and hurried to the windscreen beside Smith. "Is that … is that another crane? Two other cranes?"

Jacob blinked and fumbled with the buckle for his harness before joining Alice. "Archibald sent another one?"

"Two," Alice whispered, her voice cracking. "That's why they're moving back into the Lowlands. Gods, Jacob. Look at it."

Huge swaths of the fallen stone and foundations of the Lowlands had been cleared. It took Jacob a moment to remember Ambrose had been using the foundations to rebuild the wall. But his surprise came from far more than that. New foundations for homes had been laid, built of smaller stone that wouldn't have worked for the walls.

One of the cranes still moved on the wall to the far east, and the speed and skill being employed to place larger stones were staggering. Whoever was piloting the crane had mastered it. But there were two other cranes, one building the docks and another helping to rebuild nearby homes.

The outer wall itself was fortified with enormous stones at the base. It made no sense. There was nothing like that in the foundations of the Lowlands. They would have been more suited to holding up the castle or the city walls themselves.

"Swing around to the quarry," Smith said. "I have to see this."

"Quarry?" Jacob asked.

Smith pointed to the west. The far side of the mountain was where invaders often struck from. The base had been sheared off and harvested—rectangular forms dotted the ravine and the flanking mountain. Each slope had been cut away in tiers, like exaggerated versions of the benches where Archibald held his sessions in Bollwerk.

"Charles's place is still there," Mary said.

Jacob forced his gaze away from the quarry and the widened road leading up the mountain. The strange shape of Charles's workshop was indeed still there, and Jacob wanted to go back again. Wanted to step back into that place as if he could wrap the memory of his old life around him.

"Archibald," Mary whispered. "What are you up to now?"

Smith patted Mary's shoulder. "I am quite sure he is solidifying his alliance with Ancora for all time. And perhaps more likely, solidifying his partnership with Jacob."

"With me?"

Smith nodded. "You have a legacy to carry on. We might have Charles's notes and some of his schematics, but you, you actually learned from him. Much like I will carry on Targrove's legacy, assuming the old man does not outlive me."

Mary choked out a laugh as she steered the Skysworn back toward the new airship docks. "That old man will outlive us all." The lower they got, the more people were visible all around the city.

"It's almost strange to see Ancora without one of Bollwerk's ships hovering over it now," Alice said. "Do you think Archibald pulled them all away?"

Smith nodded. "To reinforce Fel, I suspect. Or perhaps to make another supply run. They have clearly been busy."

"Look at those docks." Mary whistled. "Those are going to put Belldorn to shame, and that's saying something."

"Hydraulic locks?" Smith said, leaning forward. "Are those water lines beside the cleats? They must have run the hoses into the reservoirs."

"How?" Jacob asked. "Ancora doesn't have strong enough pumps for water lines that big."

Smith smiled. "Maybe they didn't know that yet. Or maybe Frederick has been up to something behind your back."

"I wouldn't complain if he was." Jacob studied the docks and lines, still in disbelief at how much had been done since they'd been gone. "This is amazing."

Mary drifted into the bay farthest from anyone on the ground.

"Check and see if the dock is ready for us, would you, Smith?"

Smith slapped the control panel and headed to the door. Jacob couldn't hear exactly what he was shouting down to the worker on the docks, but Smith turned and gave a thumbs-up soon enough.

Mary maneuvered the Skysworn until the reinforced bow ran into the hydraulic locks. The long, padded arms opened and rotated forward, hooking over the bow to hold the ship in place without having to tie it off on all corners.

"Eva's going to be jealous," she said with a grin. "Belldorn is too windy to have something this fancy. They'd either snap off the docks or damage the ships."

Smith came back inside as she finished talking. "I think you are correct. And that is likely why the docks are built so low. They will need a higher tier for larger ships, but this will expand Ancora's trading possibilities."

"I want to speak with the dockhands," Mary said. "I'm curious what size ships they plan to have dock here. Why don't you two go ahead and find your families?"

"You know where Bat's old house is?" Jacob asked.

Mary nodded. "We'll come find you when we're done looking things over."

"I need to check the Skysworn," Smith said, reinforcing Mary's statement. "Running the thrusters so long is risky, and I need to be sure we are ready to leave when the time comes."

Alice hurried back to the lockers and grabbed her pack. She threw Jacob's leather satchel to him and started for the door. "We'll see you soon!"

Jacob glanced between Alice and Mary, smiled, and hurried after Alice. The cool mountain air filled his lungs, and he followed Alice across the gangplank and into the reconstruction of Ancora.

✧ ✧ ✧

Jacob didn't recognize the dockhands as he and Alice raced by them. They raised a hand in greeting, and as fast as they said hello, they were hurtling down the stairs that spiraled down two stories to the streets. Jacob's boots hit the stones outside what had once been a restaurant that served some of the best soup in Ancora.

"I bet Smith would have liked The Kitchen."

"The what?" Alice asked, turning to face him. She paused, studying the ground around them before nodding. "It's … easy to forget what was here. The streets are kind of haunting."

"I know." Jacob took a deep breath, and they continued on, passing the docks' supports and several piles of metal plating. That wasn't anything Ancora manufactured. He was sure of it. That meant it probably *was* Archibald shipping supplies in. Jacob wasn't entirely sure how he felt about that, knowing how Archibald liked to manipulate people to his advantage. Regardless of Archibald's intentions, Jacob was grateful.

"That has to be where they're moving people." Alice pointed to the far southern side of the Lowlands. Before the Fall, there hadn't been a direct line of sight to the streets below the lift. In time, perhaps they'd be hidden again, but for now, they were plain to see.

Thick timbers and stone peeked above the edge of the ravine. Homes that looked something like what had once stood in the Lowlands. Homes that looked remarkably like where Alice used to live, only longer and larger and to each other. Jacob realized they were likely apartments or some other kind of boarding house.

"Do you want to go?" Jacob asked.

Alice shook her head. "We go to Samuel's first. We already know my mom is well. Let's find your parents."

Jacob didn't argue. It was farther to the new construction in the west than it was to the gates that led to the Highlands. It was good to see them standing wide open.

They were halfway there when a tremendous thud sounded to the east. Jacob and Alice slowed, looking toward a billowing cloud of dust and debris. Another of the cranes had come to life, maneuvering massive stones into place where the walls would soon meet.

"Wow." Jacob just stood and watched for a time. "We're going to have to find Ambrose, too."

"Yes, we are. It's amazing what he's done here. It wouldn't have been possible without you, Jacob."

He gave Alice a crooked smile and shook his head. "No, any tinker could have done it with Charles's designs."

Alice sighed and placed her hands on her hips. "Keep telling yourself that."

It was nice, what Alice said, but Jacob wasn't so sure. Even if he *had* helped bring the Titan Mech arm into being, it was Archibald who'd had the resources to build them. Smith or Frederick or Targrove could have designed what Jacob did. He knew it. But if they had, would Archibald still have helped Ancora like this? Sending more cranes? Jacob didn't know. He hoped the answer would be yes, but he just didn't know.

Alice slowed.

"What is it?" Jacob didn't see anything out of the ordinary.

"It's the Square. Or it was." She turned in a slow circle, gesturing to the street around them.

Jacob sucked in a breath. They were standing only a few feet away from where the stage they'd once danced on for Festival would have been. There was no rubble left, no sign of what had happened there. As if the entire area had simply ceased to be. The thought sent a shiver down his spine.

Alice shook herself. "I don't know if I'll ever get used to this. Come on. Let's get out of here. It's … unsettling."

"Yes, it is." Jacob nodded and followed. He glanced back, catching sight of the sloping cone of Charles's workshop. He was going to get back there on this trip, even if it was only for a moment.

Closer to the top of the hill leading to the gates, they had a better view of the reconstruction to the south. Jacob gawked at the somewhat chaotic piles of lumber and stone, brick, and tile.

"I guess we know where all the rubble went." Alice looked up at him.

Jacob rubbed his chin. "It looks like they organized it into building materials. That's what they're building the new homes out of? It's a good use of resources, but it's … I don't know."

"It's sad." A small frown crossed Alice's lips. She turned away from the Lowlands and strode toward the gate.

Jacob stayed at her side, greeting two guards with a nod as they entered the Highlands. As different as the Lowlands looked, transformed in an instant by the Fall, the Highlands could have been pulled straight out of Jacob's memory. Almost nothing had changed, except the streets were far more crowded than they had once been.

He squeezed Alice's hand and couldn't help but smile at the small cluster of people waiting to get in to the Wildhorse. Baddawick's haunt looked busier than ever.

Alice started toward the hospital. Next door, the candy shop still displayed Cocoa Crunch in the window. A lure that was impossible to resist for any self-respecting Ancoran kid.

"I wonder if the owners here ever visited that candy shop in Belldorn," Alice said.

"I doubt it. Not many Ancorans journeying to the Crystal Sea."

"Maybe they will now. If they know Belldorn is in the same fight. That has to be a bond, doesn't it?"

"I don't know, Alice. I hope so. There's so much out there to see."

The street curved gently around the corner and opened up when Samuel's home came into view. Bat had left him a tremendous inheritance when he passed. The family home had served generations, and maybe, if they could overcome Ballern, it would serve generations more.

"Do you hear that?" Jacob asked. "It sounds like an engine. A big one." He frowned and looked toward the wall. "I can't tell where it's coming from."

Alice followed his gaze to the wall. "Do you think it's a train?"

"The tracks were destroyed. There's no way." Jacob frowned and cocked his head to the side.

Alice shrugged and walked up to the outer door of the workshop, glancing down the long street that led to the Castle. Parliament stood as gilded and full of excess as ever.

"Do you really think things will change here?" Jacob asked.

Alice turned to look him in the eye. "Did you see the new walls around the Lowlands? We have defenses against Red Death and Walkers and all manner of creatures."

"I know that, but what will that do to the divide between the Highlands and the Lowlands?"

Alice raised an eyebrow. "You really didn't pay attention to Miss Penny's classes at all, did you?"

Jacob raised his hands in surrender. "About what?"

"Most of the merchants moved to the Highlands when the walls were built. It protected their investments and kept them safer from natural disasters."

"Like invaders."

"Yes, Jacob, like invaders. I can't imagine it's an appealing idea to have a Walker stampede through your building and run away with your wealth." Alice lifted the lock on the workshop door. The back panel slid open, revealing a combination. "Do you think they changed it?" But before she finished asking the question, the lock clicked open. "Never mind."

Jacob slid the door open and followed Alice inside. The workbench looked the same as they'd left it, and he almost laughed when he saw the wood and metal still bolted to the floor. "You know, Charles told me that probably wouldn't move again. Guess he was right."

Alice closed the door behind them and threw the bolt into the floor lock. "Let's see if anyone's home."

Of course, they already knew someone was home. They could hear the voices and laughter echoing up from inside the house.

Jacob slipped through the doorway and down the short hall to the kitchen. No one was there, but it smelled like yeast and bread and some sort of roast. It smelled like home when his mom would cook more bread than they could possibly eat for a holiday feast. They continued to the living room, where they found the source of the laughter, and Jacob's heart leaped.

A look of confusion crossed his father's face before the rough stubble of his beard and mustache parted for a wide grin. "Jacob Arthur Anders, what are you doing here?"

Jacob wasn't exactly sure what had happened because he was suddenly crushed in a hug that threatened to steal his breath away.

Alice squeaked when she met the same fate, and they were both ushered into the living room. Jacob's mom stood there with her hands clasped before her, gesturing for them both to come closer. She wrapped them up in the same hug, and Jacob thought he might never escape.

"Hi, Mom."

"It is *so* good to see you two. Come, come, have a seat, will you? We have bread and stew if you would like anything. Alice's mom actually made the stew. She should be back later, dear, if you'd like to wait."

"It's great to see you, Mrs. Anders."

"So formal, dear. I think we can move past that now."

Alice smiled as she stepped away.

"What brings you two back here so soon? After we left you in Cave, I thought it would be weeks before you were back."

Jacob wrung his hands together. "Well, we can't stay all that long. There's trouble in Ballern. How much have you heard about Mordair and what happened in Belldorn and Fel?"

"Snippets here and there."

Jacob's dad stepped closer. "Not much more than that, and you'd have thought we would with as much time as we've spent with the new Parliament."

"The what?" Jacob asked.

His dad offered a small smile. "It looks like we *all* have some catching up to do. Take a seat, take a seat. Will the rest of you excuse us for a time?"

There were various grunts and nods of acceptance as people left for the back of the house or the kitchen. Jacob didn't think they'd be out of earshot, which told him his parents trusted the others in the house.

Alice took a seat at the end of a long, plush couch, and Jacob joined her. His parents sat down opposite them, studying the pair through barely concealed smiles.

"It is good to see you together."

Jacob sat up a little straighter. "Please don't make this weird."

"We would never," Jacob's dad said with absolute insincerity. He continued before Jacob could finish his groan. "In all seriousness, things are changing in Ancora. Those in Parliament who survived the Butcher's reign and were loyal to him have been cast out."

"Alive?" Alice asked.

"Of course! Archibald volunteered to take them into Bollwerk. Reckon he wants to keep a closer eye on them." Jacob's dad leaned forward.

"But why on earth would you ask if they were alive?"

Alice's eyes focused on the carpet. "We've been to … less benevolent places these past weeks."

Jacob imagined that was the nicest way Alice could have possibly made her point. Flashes of Dauschen and Fel roared through his mind. Burned and hanged bodies on the walls, broken children and families caught up in a war that wasn't their own. His fists tightened.

"Jacob?" his dad said.

He shook himself out of that memory. "Sorry, what?"

"Are you okay?"

"I'm fine, yes. Sorry."

Jacob's dad bit his lip, and then continued as if the exchange hadn't happened at all. There was a time his parents wouldn't have let that go without interrogating him for every last thought in his brain, but times had changed. It was easy to forget the days were hard for everyone.

"Yes, well, Parliament. We kept the name, you know? It's easier for everyone to identify who leads this city if as little changes as possible. I think we can all agree there have been enough changes in Ancora."

Jacob's mom smiled. "What did you think of the Lowlands? Remarkable, isn't it?"

"It is!" Alice said. "When Baddawick sent us my mom's message, I was so worried. I had no idea how much had been done here."

"Between the machines and the volunteers, it's been a stunning transformation. Archibald sent laborers from Bollwerk, did you know?"

Jacob's eyebrow rose and he stared at his mom. "He did? He didn't … I mean, he never told us. Just told us about the supply ships."

"They came in on the ships. Helped train the miners on how to run those machines."

Jacob's dad nodded when his mom finished talking. "And that's when I got roped into helping with Parliament."

"What do you mean?" Jacob asked.

"The miners wanted me to speak for them. Baddawick was there, of course. That man has his fingers in everything. The members of Parliament who stood against the Butcher still remain, but everyone else is gone. They elected the rest of us in a Town Hall gathering."

"Samuel will have a seat with Parliament if he wants it. The captain of the Spider Knights volunteered him. I think it's a tribute to everything Bat did for the Knights over the decades."

Alice took a deep breath. "I don't know if Samuel will want that or not. I think he's enjoying seeing the world." She paused. "Despite how much he complains about it."

Jacob grinned and turned back to his dad. "So, you're part of Parliament now?"

His dad sighed. "I hope not."

That got a laugh from Alice. "What do you mean? You could do so much good."

"I know, Alice, I know. It's just … politics. I can't stand them. All the agendas and swindling and lying."

"Maybe it will be better without the Butcher."

"Oh, I'm sure you're right about that. At least for a while. But things always degrade over time, don't they? I approached Parliament on behalf of the miners and got pulled in without thinking about it. After my experience with my lungs, though, I want to fight for them. I do want to do that. And if this is the best way to do it, so be it."

Jacob fought off a shiver that ran down his spine. It had only been months since he thought his dad wasn't going to make it. Everyone thought he'd gotten the black lung. It used to be a shared fate for all the miners until their masks and filters improved.

"I might be able to help too," Jacob said. "With the miners, I mean. We know so many amazing tinkers now. Between all of us, I'm sure we could make better equipment for them. Make the mines safer."

"You'd change a lot of lives, Jacob."

Jacob's mom reached out and squeezed his dad's arm. "When this is all over. Please don't worry about it now. You have enough. You've done enough."

"I haven't done enough until Ancora is safe. And that means Mordair has to be imprisoned or killed." His voice took on a harsh edge. "That's all that matters."

His parents gave each other a look, one he remembered from his younger days. They didn't like what he'd said. He could understand why, but that didn't change his goals. Everyone in Ancora would have peace. Alice would be safe. And Mordair would join his brother in the ground.

✧   ✧   ✧

THE CONVERSATION LIGHTENED after that. Alice gave Jacob a meaningful glare anytime he protested his parents' worries, and he slowly caught on to the fact he was upsetting them. His life might have become swarmed in conflict and terrible things, but that didn't mean he had to worry them with all the details.

Instead, he sat back and let them explain more of what had happened in the Lowlands—the veritable army of Archibald's volunteers, and the unmatched skill of the miners when they took control of the Titan Mech arms.

"I wondered how they dug the quarries without any signs of collapses," Alice said. "That's a really sensitive job."

Jacob's dad nodded. "It is, but the miners know the mountains better than anyone. I'd say it was a natural job for them once they learned their way around the cranes."

"It's amazing, truly."

"If you think the Lowlands are something, you should really visit the train station. The miners finished that first."

Jacob furrowed his eyebrows. "The … train station? You mean underground?"

He nodded.

"That was all buried in the battles after the Fall."

"Well, Jacob, things may have changed a little since you've been gone. Parts of it are still destroyed, but the gates and trestle have been rebuilt. I suspect they'll come back to work on the finer details after the wall is done."

Jacob stared at his dad in plain confusion.

"How?" Alice asked.

"Archibald sent more of those cranes to Dauschen. Some of them mounted to the railroad tracks. Have you seen them? Magnificent machines."

"Of course we've seen them. Jacob designed them."

Jacob's dad blinked.

"No, I didn't. Charles designed them. I just modified them a little bit. And Frederick."

"So modest," Alice said.

Jacob's mom smiled at him. "Between the rails and the airship dock, Ancora can be a hub for travelers and traders alike."

"We're still a bit out of the way in the mountains, Mom."

"You'd be surprised at the things we heard in Cave. There are more than a few residents who want to visit Ancora and Dauschen now that they've met citizens from each. I think the Fall solidified a bond no one realized was missing."

"That makes me sad," Alice said. "It shouldn't take such an overwhelming tragedy for people to want to know their neighbors."

Jacob gave her a small smile. "We all get stuck in our ways, I guess. I used to think there wasn't anything more exciting than sneaking into

Charles's workshop."

Alice reached out and took his hand. "Why don't we take a walk to the underground? I'd like to see what's become of the old shops and station. And your parents can finish talking to their friends."

"Come back for dinner, won't you?" Jacob's mom asked. "Alice, your mother should be here by then, too." She looked up at the clock on the buffet across the room. "Two hours."

Jacob's dad held up a finger. "And you don't have to go sneaking down to the basement of the inn anymore, either. There's a proper staircase just inside the wall beside it. Apparently, it had been there for some time, just bricked over."

Alice mimicked a whine. "But I wanted to climb down the rusted ladder that felt like it was going to fall out of the wall."

Jacob laughed. "We'll be here."

✧ ✧ ✧

WALKING THROUGH ANCORA was more than a little surreal. Jacob remembered how tall everything had seemed in the Highlands before he'd been to places like Bollwerk and Belldorn. Now the inn he'd once felt towered over everything except the city wall itself didn't feel as large.

"I swear this was taller last time we were here."

Alice glanced at him, then looked up. "I know what you mean."

They walked to the end of the street, and Jacob frowned, looking for the nearest entrance to the wall. "Do you think it's in a watchtower?"

Alice paused. "Look, people are going into that one." She pointed to the nearest watchtower built into the pale stone of the city wall. They followed the loose line of Ancorans going in and out, which was an unusual sight in itself. In the past, Jacob had only seen guards making their way in and out. Those guards did their best to keep citizens out, and even Charles needed to use a Steamsworn medallion to get past them.

Jacob slowed in the entryway to the tower, the wide stone steps leading up above them. Instead of ending at a small storage area like other towers they'd been in, this showed the edges of broken stone. A trail of pebbles led to where something had been chipped away to reveal the descending stairs.

They followed the spiral down, voices echoing all around in jarring contrast to the silence they'd sought the first time they'd snuck into the underground. On the third turn, he saw the bricks and large stones that had broken free and crashed down the stairs.

Alice led the way down them, and through a cracked stone archway that took them out onto the platform. They weren't far from the gate with the enormous shell of a dead invader, but it was gone now, buried by a cave-in that might never be moved.

But another curve of the tracks had been cleared entirely, reaching out to the open air of the far wall. Jacob stared at the bright wood of the rebuilt trestle.

"How did they do that? I don't understand how the broken trestle could have supported the weight of an arm while it was being rebuilt."

"I guess you still have a few things to learn."

Jacob blinked at Alice's wide grin.

"Come on, Jacob, look at the *train*."

She grabbed his arm and pulled him forward, snapping him out of his daze at what waited in the underground. The station had mostly survived the collapse, and while one of the inner buildings had been utterly crushed, some of the others were bustling with people.

The bookstore might have been destroyed in the last conflict, but now a small café had taken its place; the same tables and chairs sat around the outside as if the place hadn't seen scores of Ancorans and Fel soldiers alike fall to the invaders.

Charles had said something to him years before when Jacob's

grandmother died. He wasn't sure he'd ever understood those words quite so clearly. *The world doesn't stop, Jacob, and it never will. Take time if you need it, but don't expect the world to wait. It won't.*

He studied the entrance to the catacombs, where the fallen stone doors had been erected once more, and then his eyes settled on the train. A train he'd seen parts of before, beneath Dauschen. But it hadn't been so filled with supplies and people at that point. This looked like something between a passenger train and a freighter full of construction materials.

For a moment, he wondered how the materials would be unloaded before a track switched with a squeal and a Titan Mech arm rolled into the station on wheels.

It settled onto the track next to the train, maneuvering its arm over the car where two crewmen cleared the way for the fingers to close on a bundle of dark gray beams. Steam escaped as the pressure shifted and then cut off as the arm lifted into the air and settled the weight over its center.

Jacob couldn't see the driver, but he didn't miss the lantern hooked on the mining helmet. "It's brilliant. Who knows machines better than the miners?"

"Only the tinkers, I imagine," Alice said, briefly putting her arm around his waist.

Jacob smiled at that and watched the arm move down the tracks, circling to the left as it exited the station. "They must have laid new track to load and unload. They're going to take it to the lift, or maybe have one of the crawler-mounted arms carry it up. Alice, it's more than I could have hoped."

"It's amazing, Jacob. They couldn't have done it without you and Charles. No matter what you say."

Maybe they could have eventually, but it would have taken time for someone else to understand the way Charles worked. Jacob didn't doubt that. They could have asked Targrove or Smith or any of Belldorn's best tinkers. But would Archibald have gotten involved if it wasn't for Jacob? Would they have found the old journals if Samuel hadn't been digging through the rubble? Maybe not.

A scream tore Jacob from his reflections, and his hand instinctively moved for the air cannon on his back. The air cannon that was stowed neatly onboard the Skysworn. His hand balled into a fist.

Alice sprinted toward the train. Jacob followed, vaulting over the railing and onto the bridge, where they raced over the tall arc and came down on the far side. He could already hear the yelling before they reached the scene.

"All will be cleansed! All will be shown the true path to the light. The path of the Dark Fire!" A man in a black cloak stood spewing those words while the limp form of an elderly man lay crumpled at his feet.

"He stabbed that man! I saw it!"

"Guards!"

"You would deny the gods their traitorous enemies? I will smite them in their name, for the time of man has come and gone. This is the age of the Great Machines!"

Alice slid to a stop as the cloaked form raised a long blade above his head. Her wrist launcher unlocked and spun up, but before she could take a single shot, a mountain of a shadow moved.

Jacob winced at the sound of snapped bones, the blade clattering onto the stone platform. The man's feet went out from under him as the mountain lashed out with one violent sweep of his legs, and his voice cracked with violence.

"Threaten my *son*!" He hammered down on the cloaked man's face with a terrible fury before the guards finally reached the confrontation.

Jacob wasn't sure if anyone was going to stop the beating, but the moment the guards arrived, the huge man stepped away and turned, revealing a long, braided beard.

Jacob slowly tilted his head to the side, not sure he could believe his eyes. "Owen?"

"Vaughn is good," Cage said, stepping up behind Owen. "He might end up a little sore from that punch to the ribs, but he'll be okay."

"Cage?" Alice said.

Cage glanced between the shocked look on Alice's face and the shocked look on Owen's face. "So you *do* know them!"

✧   ✧   ✧

A FEW MINUTES later, once the guards had dragged the attacker to jail and the wounded off to the hospital, Jacob and Alice found themselves seated at the café beside Hefina while Owen looked over Vaughn's injuries.

"He punched you?" Jacob asked.

Vaughn winced and nodded when Owen poked a little too hard at his ribs.

"Not broken," Owen said.

Cage stopped just short of rolling his eyes. "I told you they weren't broken."

Alice frowned and studied Cage. "How … how do you two know each other?"

"Me and Owen? He's my cousin. We had a good laugh when we realized we both knew you and Jacob."

"You're from Fel?"

Cage nodded. "I'd appreciate it if you kept that quiet. With zealots like that showing up in Ancora, I doubt being associated with Fel is going to be a positive thing for a while." He turned to Owen and his family. "You three should keep that quiet too. You look like you could be from Dauschen, so stick with that story."

"Why was that disciple here?" Jacob asked. "I thought the Children of the Dark Fire were Ballern's problem."

"They're everyone's problem, Jacob," Owen flexed his fingers against the table. "They've been an annoyance in Fel for years, but I never dreamed they'd … just attack an innocent man."

"He'll live," Cage said. "Let's be thankful for that."

"I never thought he'd punch me when I tried to stop him," Vaughn grumbled. "It does hurt a bit."

Owen ruffled Vaughn's hair. "I know I yelled, but I'm proud of you, son. That was a brave thing. Just … try to be more cautious when it comes to zealots, will you?"

"And perhaps a little less brave when the zealot has a knife?" Hefina asked.

Vaughn grinned.

"Are you staying in Ancora?" Jacob asked. "My mom's cooking a huge meal tonight. I'm sure you'd be welcome."

"We couldn't impose like that," Owen started.

"Then you'll come as my payment for fixing your fishing net after you tried to sink us."

"I didn't try to sink you!" Owen barked out his face twisted in a look of horror.

Vaughn laughed, apparently catching Jacob's teasing tone a bit faster than his father had.

"Yes, well, I could use some dinner."

"You'll come too?" Jacob asked, turning to Cage. "I'd like to hear more about what's been happening in Dauschen."

Cage rubbed his neck and shrugged. "I'd be happy to. It would be good to hear what you've seen in Belldorn. I get most of my news filtered through Archibald, so you know how that goes."

"Do we ever," Alice said under her breath.

Cage laughed and tapped his hand on the table.

CHAPTER NINE

GLADYS STUDIED THE map George had set up across their long dining table. She was certain they wouldn't be eating at that table again for some time once he'd laid down lengths of cork and started pinning down units and estimates and potential strategies. If she hadn't known otherwise, she might have mistaken it for a complicated game.

From everything she knew about him, her father would have loved it. She glanced at the broken mask on the nearby shelf and wished she could see him one last time.

A knock sounded at the front door. "Come in!"

"Gladys," George said, suddenly responding to her voice. "You have no idea who that is."

"So you can't answer my question about *where* we're going to shelter everyone if we get attacked again, but you can snap at me for inviting a guest in?"

George scowled at her.

Someone cleared their throat near the entryway, and they both looked up. Targrove gave them a sheepish smile from behind Theo's wheelchair.

"Is this a bad time?"

"No, no, please come in," Gladys said. "George was just telling me how you were an assassin, and I was about to die. Weren't you George?"

George's lips flattened into a thin line. "You are always welcome in my home, Targrove, Theo. Please, join us."

Targrove offered a nod and pushed Theo's wheelchair closer to the table before sitting on a long bench next to her.

Theo leaned forward and tapped the desert between Midstream and Fel. "You need to secure the north of the city. Why don't you have any defenses on your map here?"

"We have the traps," George said. "And two of the Titan Mechs in addition to four armored crawlers we rescued from the sands."

"Not bad. And the construction on the docks to the south is coming along nicely."

"It will still be months before it's ready for airships."

Theo harrumphed. "Ancora had their new docks functional in a week's time."

Gladys choked back a laugh. Ancora's docks were low to the ground and entirely different from what they were building in Midstream. Of course, she figured Theo was just trying to get under George's skin to take the edge off his obvious irritation.

George sat down on the bench beside Gladys and eyed the older pair of tinkers. "What brings you here?"

"Other than amusement?" Targrove asked, winking at Gladys.

"Yes."

Theo grinned. "What I asked you about already. You need better defenses to the north. In case things go bad. Have you heard the news of Belldorn's defenses? Bait boxes like those used in the Fall, repurposed to defend a city."

"I'm not willing to use Emerald Needles against anyone," Gladys said. "I'll move to Ancora before I unleash something so foul."

Theo gestured to Gladys with an open palm. "What if you could recruit something native to the desert? Something that already lives here in numbers?"

Gladys turned back to the map, following the open space of the desert north of Midstream to the mountains and up to Fel before returning her gaze to the south. "What do you mean?"

Targrove leaned forward and ran his finger over the foothills of the northern Ridge Mountains. "Gareth Cave holds more than the memories of the Deadlands War. We buried more than the Butcher's chaingun and his atrocities there." His voice quieted. "I buried one of my own."

Theo reached out to grab his arm. "It's been so long, Targrove. Tell them. It was a mistake then, but it could be used for good now."

He took a long breath and nodded. "I helped design the original bait boxes, but they were made for defense, not the twisted devices that brought down Ancora. These were made to gather Tail Swords and they would grow defensive of anything encroaching on them in their clusters."

"That doesn't sound bad," Gladys said. "Why is it such a secret?"

"Because I saw what that technology could do in the hands of someone with ill intentions. For Newton to twist it like he did. It is a stain I will never get off my hands. And decades after I thought it buried, it returned to lay Ancora low. That is why it is such a secret, Gladys. It is why I would only trust this information to a handful of people."

"Is this something Jacob could help us with?" George asked.

Targrove looked to Theo.

"We don't know," Theo said. "Jacob's path is one that he must walk. He brought to life one of the most devastating weapons the Deadlands War dreamed of." She held her hand up when Gladys started to protest. "We helped him do it, child. I know. But I have seen so many walk the path he has and come out of it changed beyond all recognition. If he follows in Charles's steps, to use his skills for the good of the many, he may be a boon to all of us. But if he turns to the single-minded task of crushing any threat to his home ..."

"He won't," Targrove said. "Charles taught him."

Theo lowered her gaze. "If he does, there are some things he should not know."

"You act like the mere knowledge means he'll do the stupidest thing he possibly could with it." Targrove crossed his arms. "He's a good lad, Theo. This isn't the Deadlands War, and Jacob isn't Newton."

"I know that, you old fool. Does that mean we shouldn't exercise some level of caution?"

"Whatever answers you hide from that boy, he'll find them on his own. That could be worse. That could be *far* worse, Theo."

George tapped his finger on the table. "So, you aren't unified in this concern."

"A gift for understatement still permeates the Royal Guards, does it not?" Theo said.

George grinned. "For what it is worth, I too trust Jacob. We will do as you ask, but I cannot promise it will always be so."

"A fair offer, and as much as we can ask you for." Theo nodded. "Things change in war. Let us hope the kindness of our friends is not one of those things."

"I'll take you to Gareth Cave," Targrove said. "Meet us at our airship. The trip should not take long, provided the old lock hasn't gotten stuck. Unlikely anyone oiled it in the last thirty years."

Gladys looked at George. "Let's go."

THEO AND TARGROVE'S airship wasn't the smallest Gladys had ever set foot on, but she doubted it was any larger than the Skysworn. She reached up to run her fingers along the curved windscreen where Theo sat to pilot the vessel.

"It's unique, isn't it?" the old tinker said.

"It's beautiful. Is it fragile? Being all one piece like this?

"No more than a standard screen. Granted, that took some work, and

I thought the glassblowers might cast themselves in their forges by the time we finished it." Theo laughed as though that was the funniest thing she'd ever said.

Gladys looked on with an awkward smile, and a sudden sympathy for whatever glassworkers had made that windscreen. The windscreen wasn't all that caught her eye on Theo and Targrove's airship. The control panel itself almost glowed with polished metal and inlaid crystals.

"She's a beautiful ship."

Theo smiled and patted the dashboard. "Frida's gotten a bit fancy in her old age. She wasn't always so gilded. That's the danger when you have a couple of tinkers who grow bored easily."

Targrove harrumphed from the plush seat in the rear of the cabin. It looked like red velvet and gold-threaded rope formed the padded backrest, and Gladys wouldn't have been surprised if that's exactly what it was.

George studied the maps on the wall, leaving Gladys to prod Theo for information about Frida.

"How long have you two worked on Frida?"

"A lifetime, it feels like. And that's not such a bad thing. No one has the same tastes, you know?"

"I could have told you that after running The Fish Head," George grumbled. "You get what's on the menu. No substitutions unless you're one of those terribly unlucky folks allergic to fish."

Theo let out a small laugh. "It is much the same in the workshops. Jobs would come in and our clients would reject the most beautiful work, or work that was too plain even though it met their specifications exactly. We ended up with extra bits and bobbles and slowly upgraded Frida."

"No thrusters, though?" George asked, and Gladys almost laughed at the hopefulness in his question.

"I'll be feeding the Carrion Worms before I ever put thrusters on an airship," Targrove muttered. "That's for the young. Let Smith enjoy those thrusters until he blows himself up and I have to slap even more tubes into his chest."

Gladys grinned. She'd almost never heard Targrove so outspokenly annoyed. Her smile fell a fraction when she realized it was probably because he didn't want to go back to Gareth Cave. What had the old man seen there? What kind of memories dwelled after that kind of horror?

She turned to the windscreen and studied the mountains in the distance. "Not far now, is it?"

"No, dear." Theo adjusted two small levers, and the airship slowed. When it finally drifted to a stop, Theo pressed a button that undid the clamps on her wheelchair so she could spin around. "Are you ready, old man?"

"How are we getting down?" Gladys asked. "Do you use wheels and landing lines like the Skysworn?"

Targrove raised an eyebrow. "My wife calls me 'old man.' Do you think we're in any condition for that kind of excitement, girl? We land and wheel ourselves out on the sand like a properly sane person."

Gladys glanced at Theo's second wheelchair, the one she'd been using in Midstream. Wide, knobby tires replaced the traditional rubber. "We need some of those in Midstream. You know we still pull some of our elders around on sleds to get through the sand?"

Theo's brow furrowed. "You should have told us that a week ago. I could have been working on them while Targrove tinkered with those arms of Jacob's. Never mind that. When we get back, I'll get to work on it. Shouldn't be too difficult to draw up some schematics for your own tinkers."

"We would be honored," George said.

"Make me another bowl of that stew, and we'll call it even." Theo paused before a sly grin crossed her lips. "Just leave out the onions."

Everyone laughed except George as Targrove took the helm and guided them to the sand below.

✧   ✧   ✧

GLADYS HADN'T BEEN back to Gareth Cave since her encounter with Rana. There was a time when it had been one of her favorite places to visit. The inner chambers were always cool, even when the summer sun threatened to burn away her skin.

She didn't think it was going to bother her as she followed Theo and Targrove, leaving the setting sun behind them. But as they turned into the hall that led to the memorial, signs of that conflict were still strewn across the path.

The bodies might have been gone, but the blood still stained the sand and stone where Rana had fallen. Gladys stopped and stared, remembering the feeling of his hands around her neck, the blade held to her stomach before Alice had come. And the warm spatters of blood when Alice had thrown him down.

She willed the tears away as best she could, wiping her cheeks with a shaky hand, trying to block out the roar of Smith's chaingun and the scream of Rana's men as they all met a violent end. Something grabbed her wrist.

Theo held her gaze. "Memories will always burn, Gladys, but they are only part of who we are. Do not despair for the times we'd rather lose. Be better for them."

Gladys bit the side of her cheek and nodded. "Thanks, Theo. It's just …"

"You don't have to tell me anything that brings you sadness. But if you ever want to talk, find someone who will listen. You have friends and family who care. Even Targrove, as grumpy as he is today, would listen to your story."

"Aye," Targrove muttered. "I would, lass. But what do you say we get those bait boxes and get out of this tomb?"

Gladys smiled at him. "I'd like that very much."

George squeezed her shoulder and led the way forward. They continued past a broken table until the memorial overcame the signs of violence. Marble slabs stretched out before them, and then came photos and paintings adorning the walls, leading into the chamber. The glow of countless Fireworms lit the Steamsworn Fist as it stood there in defiance of the dark all around them.

A workshop of biomechanics and old machines Gladys had no name for still stood haphazardly around the edges of the room. It had once been a place of healing and hope. Then the Butcher had turned it into something else. Those machines had never moved again, frozen in a moment of horror.

The entire group stood in that place, lost in thought, until Targrove broke the silence.

"Let's see if that old lock held up." He made his way to the back of the Steamsworn Fist and slid a wide drawer open. "I still remember placing the chaingun in here. It's a wonder Smith was able to fix it." The drawer came to a stop. "George, give me a hand?"

George stepped to the opposite side of the drawer.

"We need to push down, pull forward, lift until it clicks, then push down hard. Got that?"

George nodded. "Ready."

"On three. One. Two. Three."

They moved through the cycle Targrove had described. Gladys wasn't sure what they were doing at first until it dawned on her that the drawer itself was a puzzle lock. Light reflected off the edge of the handles, illuminating the paintings and photographs that hung in memorial even behind the Steamsworn Fist.

A basso thud sounded from inside the monument, and the wide drawer slid free, revealing the complex rails and springs that formed the puzzle lock. George and Targrove gently sat the golden drawer on the stones, the old tinker flicking one of the springs and frowning.

"Held up pretty well. I suppose there was just enough humidity this deep in the cave to keep things from drying out completely." Targrove went down on one knee before leaning his head into the monument. He started to pull himself in, froze, and pushed himself back out. "I'm too old for this. Gladys, would you mind?"

She shuffled around George and crouched down next to Targrove. "What am I looking for?"

"You can't miss it. It's a leather sack sealed in wax. It'll be quite heavy."

Gladys nodded and scooted inside the towering monument. She wasn't surprised it was hollow. Something that large made of solid metal would have been extremely difficult to move, no matter how many people they had to handle it.

She pondered how they would have gotten it through the tunnels and into the chamber itself as she pulled her legs inside and slowly stood, careful not to bang her head on anything. She could just make out the lower shelves, but the light vanished into the area around her head. She couldn't move more than a step in any direction without bumping into a shelf.

"I can't see anything." Her voice echoed, the sound unnerving in the dim light.

"Hold on," Theo said. "I have a lantern here somewhere."

The faint click of an igniter sounded twice before the light danced at the bottom of the monument, only to brighten as Targrove passed the lantern inside from Theo.

"Thanks." Gladys hooked it in the sheaths that ran along her leather vest. It wasn't an ideal fit, but it didn't fall and it kept her hands free.

She had expected to see the wax-sealed satchel and little more waiting inside, but there was much more than that. Small trinkets and broken armor dotted the walls, and rings overflowed an ancient ceremonial tray on the middle shelf.

She froze when she saw it. The rings varied from plain gold bands to intricate silver decorations crafted to look like a Tail Sword. She picked up the last and turned it between her fingers. She'd heard stories of her grandmother's ring when she was younger, and she wondered if that was indeed the same one.

It didn't take long to realize it probably wasn't. Two more of the Tail Sword rings waited in that tray. She ran her finger over the plaque on the front, whispering the inscription out loud. "The dead are never gone."

Gladys hesitated and then pocketed the Tail Sword ring she'd first picked up. It might not have been her grandmother's, but it was something to remember her by. Something to treasure and remember Gareth Cave out in the light, and not buried in a cave.

She took a shaky breath and turned to the next shelf. A wooden plaque carved with a Steamsworn Fist greeted her, three throwing knives sheathed in its edge. Coins and tributes bound in cracked leather and frayed cloth circled the room.

Behind her waited the satchel. The wax was still intact, but fissures ran through it the moment she moved the bag. Gladys bent down to slide the satchel outside and turned back to the wall. Midstream might not have been allied with the Steamsworn until late in the war, but the fist held many artifacts from her people. It drove home the terrible fact so many of them had died in Gareth Cave.

But the last thing she found in that cave almost broke her. A small notebook, written in a childlike scrawl. A simple title greeted her. *Lost to the Deadlands War*. She made it through three pages of names, dates, and causes of death before she reached the blood. She knew what those dark stains were. She could barely make out the last name in the book, and the word Gareth, before the pen trailed off.

Whoever had written those names had been killed there. She was sure of it. Gladys gritted her teeth as she ducked back out of the monument, leaving that grisly piece of history behind.

No one spoke when they saw her. They didn't need to. Gladys realized they probably all knew what was inside that monument. Except George, perhaps, but she didn't need to burden him with old wounds. Instead, she fished the Tail Sword ring out of her pocket and held it up.

"It looks like my grandmother's ring. It was on a memory tray, but I don't think it should stay buried in the dark."

George smiled and gently touched her shoulder. "I am sure its owner would be proud to know their ring came to you, Princess."

Gladys slid the Tail Sword over her finger and studied the tarnished metal. The patter of falling debris drew her attention as Targrove untied the wax-coated satchel.

Targrove peered inside and grimaced. "That'll do. Let's get Midstream a proper defense. One that no army can cross without dire consequences."

Gladys closed her fists. If Midstream could truly be that well protected, then they could focus on helping the war effort in Ballern. She could leave her home again without fear she'd return to nothing but ash and ruin. She wouldn't leave her friends to fight in that war alone.

CHAPTER TEN

A LICE STUDIED THE group standing in the kitchen, still not quite believing who all had joined them. Cage, Owen, Hefina, and their son. Sometimes the world felt overwhelmingly large, like everyone living was a stranger. And other times, you met an ally's cousin halfway across the continent and didn't even know it.

A heavy knock sounded at the front door.

"I'll get it." Jacob almost hopped off the bench as he made his way around the corner.

Owen was telling Jacob's mom how much he appreciated the repair work Jacob had done when a shout echoed from the front room.

Alice's heart leaped, and everyone turned toward the entryway. Jacob reappeared with a tired-looking Spider Knight in tow.

"Samuel!"

"Hey, Alice, it's good to—" But he didn't finish the words before she almost tackled him in a hug.

"You find all sorts of rubbish in Ancora," Mary said, jamming an elbow into Samuel's ribs as she followed him in with Smith.

"We didn't see you after the battle in Belldorn," Alice said to Samuel before pulling away. "Is everything okay? No one hurt?"

Samuel tilted his head to the side for a moment. "I wouldn't say no one is hurt, but me and Drakkar made it through. Thanks to the dragonriders. Rin and Tatsu are as skilled as any Spider Knight I've ever met."

Jacob's mom attacked Samuel with another hug. "Come in, come in. It's so good to see you, Samuel. What brings you back to Ancora?" While Samuel pondered that question, Jacob's mom hugged Smith and a bewildered-looking Mary, in turn.

Samuel eyed Owen and his family, but didn't say anything. "You know how it is, Archibald and Lady Katherine and the mess in Ballern. I've been thinking about ways to get the dragonriders involved across the sea, and I think the spider mounts are the way to do it. And if some of the Knights will come too, all the better."

"Jacob's dad has been working with Parliament since you left. We know something of what's been happening. Please, join us for a meal."

"He's a Spider Knight?" Vaughn whispered to his dad. "I thought they were bigger."

The room burst into laughter.

Samuel shook out his hair and smiled. "We come in all sizes, kid. Do they have Spider Knights where you're from?"

Alice stepped between Samuel and Vaughn, giving the Spider Knight a meaningful look. "These are friends from Fel, Samuel. They helped us on the river, and if you insult them, I will *end* you."

Samuel's eyes widened. "Okay, okay." He held his hands up in surrender. "Sorry, it's just … well, you know. The Butcher and Mordair and things have happened."

"Things have happened to us in Fel too," Vaughn said.

Hefina nodded and smiled at Vaughn. "Do not think Ancora is the only city that suffered at Mordair's hand."

"I don't." Samuel glanced away. "I've seen Dauschen."

Hefina nodded. "As have we."

Smith took a deep breath over the stew pot, paused with his eyes closed, and smiled. "You just don't get Pilly stew anywhere else. Not like this."

"Smith and his soup," Samuel said with a laugh.

Smith narrowed his eyes. "This is stew, you uncultured Jumper."

Samuel grinned and turned back to Owen. "But why come here?"

Owen stepped forward, and for the first time, Alice realized the man might actually be larger than Smith. "The Children of the Dark Fire have come to Ancora. Perhaps that should be our priority."

"That cult from Ballern?" Jacob's dad asked. "Archibald mentioned them briefly, but I thought they were an eccentric organization, not an actual threat. What are the Children of the Dark Fire doing in Ancora?" He leaned against the wall next to the stove. "Did I get that name right?"

Cage nodded. "Perhaps more of a threat than Archibald let on. I think that may be the one drawback to reopening the old railways. Security in Dauschen isn't the best right now, so there will likely be some trouble that slips through."

"Increased trade and shared interests are far more valuable than any risk that poses," Jacob's mom said. "We've lived long enough behind these walls."

"Few people can say that as literally as Ancorans," Cage said. "Even Bollwerk has walls, but the city itself is fairly united. You still have districts there of those better off than others, but not a literal wall to shut them out." Cage eyed Jacob's dad. "I hope you can all bring a modicum of sense to Parliament. Especially now that you have zealots arriving in Ancora."

Alice clenched her jaw, straightened, and spoke over the others. "The Children of the Dark Fire are a threat to everyone on this continent."

"What do you mean?" Cage asked. "They are zealots, to be sure, but we have faced greater threats."

"They orchestrated the assassinations of the Lady of Ballern decades ago. They set off the Deadlands War. And before that, they removed the true line of royals from the throne in Ballern."

"How can you possibly know that?" Owen asked.

"It's in the library in Belldorn," Jacob said. "Old books from Ballern that have been banned and burned so their history would be forgotten."

"History is not so easily forgotten. Look at Fel. We know every ruler, going back to the city's founding after the world was rebuilt."

"Rebuilt from what?" Mary asked.

"We … we don't know."

"Exactly," Alice said. "And Mary's question says it all, doesn't it? It's not like it would take that long to forget. A few decades. A century at most? By then, people only believe what the historians tell them. No one who witnessed it is alive to say different."

"You're talking about lying to an entire city, Alice," Jacob's mom gestured to the room at large. "That's … that seems extreme."

"The Butcher did it." Alice grabbed the edge of the counter with one hand, her knuckles whitening. "And he did it with Mordair's help. How else could people think he was a hero when he was a murderer? A killer of children and grandparents and doctors? He was a monster by any standard, and yet he was *celebrated*."

Jacob's mom crossed her arms. "That's … that's true. But …" She shook her head, keeping whatever else she was thinking to herself.

"There's a meeting at the Wildhorse tonight," Jacob's dad said, holding his hands up to draw everyone's attention. "You should all come."

"Like Parliament or something?" Jacob asked.

"Not so formal as that. More of a … precursor to a session of Parliament. Jacob, tomorrow we'll need you at Parliament. They need to understand firsthand what's happened in Belldorn. And I daresay they don't completely trust Archibald to tell them that story. As for tonight, Owen, I'm sure they'd welcome you. It's not often we hear from someone inside Fel."

"I appreciate the invitation. I'll be there."

Alice wasn't sure if Owen meant he'd bring his entire family or not, but she thought Vaughn might like the Wildhorse. In fact, she wanted to be sure he saw it. "You should bring your family. The Wildhorse is quite a sight."

Owen exchanged a glance with Hefina before nodding.

"I need to talk to the Spider Knights," Samuel said. "But I have to be honest, a clandestine meeting at the Wildhorse sounds intriguing."

"I didn't say anything about this being clandestine," Jacob's dad said.

"Of course not." Samuel gave him an exaggerated wink.

Something clicked in Alice's mind. Jacob's dad wouldn't invite a virtual stranger from Fel to a meeting of Parliament, no matter how unofficial, if he didn't have a strong reason to do it. She wondered why that was. Were other members of Ancora's leadership pushing back at Archibald's help? Or did they not believe a threat still existed from Mordair? The idea of the meeting at the Wildhorse suddenly became far more interesting.

✧   ✧   ✧

JACOB WALKED BESIDE Samuel and Alice late that night, taking in the brightness of the city lights as they made their way down the street toward the courtyard. He glanced at the hospital before turning to Samuel.

"So Drakkar is back in Cave?"

"He probably is by now. Or he will be shortly."

"I hope he comes back."

Alice laughed quietly. "Why would you say that, Jacob?"

"I don't know. Sometimes … sometimes it just seems like going home and never leaving again would be the best thing in the world."

Alice blew out a breath. "Of course. Because how boring is it in Midstream with Theo's assistant, or those dreadfully dull Dragonwings? And don't get me started on the soup in Bollwerk, or the Cocoa Crunch in Belldorn. And why would anyone want to walk through the treetops of Canopy when you could just … stay home?"

Jacob cringed. "Okay, okay! How about going home and staying for a while? Is that better?"

"Yes, but you know Drakkar will come back. He's our friend, and I trust him above almost anyone else. I hope Ancora has learned something from Cave in the time the Lowlanders have spent there as refugees."

"I think that's safe to assume," Samuel said. "Quite a few folks from Dauschen *and* Ancora are planning on moving to Cave."

"That's wonderful. Do you think Cave will come up with another name for the influx of new residents? Like they did with the Melding?"

"Possible, I suppose." Samuel shrugged.

"It's not quite as traumatic as the Melding, though, is it?" Jacob asked.

Alice and Samuel both raised an eyebrow and waited.

Jacob bit his lips as he remembered everything that had happened to drive those refugees into Cave to begin with. The traffic had increased so much that the hidden city wasn't so hidden anymore, with obvious trails and roads leading to the western entrances.

"Never mind." He slouched against the counter.

Alice laughed and slapped him on the arm. "I knew you'd get to it, eventually."

The gate still stood wide open as they walked through the courtyard. Jacob glanced outside, and couldn't suppress the shiver at seeing those pale walls rising around the Lowlands. Things were going to change for Ancora. Things had *already* changed for Ancora. He only hoped they'd continue to change for the better.

✧　　✧　　✧

THEY MADE IT to the Wildhorse before Owen and his family, which was something Jacob wanted to do. He remembered how awestruck he'd been the first time he'd set foot in the Wildhorse, and seeing it now was almost as exciting. The last time they'd been, Baddawick's bartenders hadn't been flinging trays through the air and carrying on with the pianist and the usual entertainment. But the Wildhorse was back, and it was back with a kind of unhinged joy that put a smile on Jacob's face.

He was so enamored with the tables launching trays and the bartenders effortlessly catching them, he almost forgot to turn and watch Owen, Vaughn, and Hefina step through the door. In fact, he did forget until Alice grabbed his hand and spun him around.

Jacob's parents made their way through first, holding the doors for the family from Fel as they stepped inside and froze. The pianist pounded away at a lively jig that wouldn't have been out of place at a far less reputable establishment. Vaughn turned in slow motion, from the long bar with its spotless mirrors and shelves of spirits to the vivid murals that framed the walls, some showing forests that Jacob had never seen the like of.

Owen clasped his son's shoulder and put his arm around Hefina. Jacob's grin widened as he heard them talking about everything they saw, and yet he knew for each thing they noticed, there were a dozen more they wouldn't. At least not this time.

"Welcome, all!" a voice boomed.

Jacob turned to find Baddawick walking out of the kitchen, wiping his hands on a towel before tossing it on the bar top. He didn't miss the look of irritation that flickered across the bartender's face.

"If you've come for the open house, we're gathering in the back. This way." Baddawick gestured for them all to follow.

"Dad," Vaughn whispered. "Why does his hair look like a broom?"

Samuel burst into laughter as they all followed Baddawick. They passed the small area where the picture man often setup, and for a moment, Jacob was at the beginning of the war, sitting with Charles and Ambrose as they struck a deal for bolt gloves.

Jacob's chest tightened, then eased after a few deep breaths as they stepped through a set of wide doors and into a room he didn't recall seeing before. It wasn't quiet, exactly. Another small bar sat against the far wall with a pass-through to the kitchen.

Jacob didn't think they'd walked enough to reach the kitchen, and a moment later, he realized they hadn't. A small train puffed away on a track until it bumped into a blockade. The bartender scooped the plates off and replaced them with a basket of dirty dishes. She flipped a lever, and the train shuffled back in the opposite direction, carrying the load of dishes.

"I love this place."

"Jacob? Alice?"

He turned toward the voice and grinned. "Ambrose!"

The man almost sprinted over to them before gathering them both up in a hug Jacob thought might suffocate them in short order. "What are you two doing here? I thought you were off in Belldorn or Ballern or on some mad adventure!"

"Not since this morning." Jacob grinned at him.

Ambrose blinked. "How is that possible?"

Jacob hooked a thumb at Smith. "If you really want more details than you could possibly need to know, that is the man to ask."

Alice stepped in front of Ambrose when it looked like he might take Jacob up on that suggestion. "Ambrose, how did you get the walls built so fast? Did Archibald really send extra tinkers to help?"

Ambrose stood a little straighter and smiled. "He did! Made a big fuss about it too, seeing as they're in the middle of a war and *need* those tinkers. But they stayed for a few days and trained the miners on the cranes. Magnificent, really. We're still using those bolt cannons you designed too, Jacob. Masons from Cave have been helping us for days, too. Those bolt cannons fastened every brace and bracket you see on the wall."

Jacob couldn't help but look at Alice. Couldn't stop the smile pulling at the corners of his mouth.

"I told you you'd do good here." She squeezed his hand.

"We've done in a week what should have taken months. It's hard to explain what an impact that'll have. Charles would be proud, Jacob. I've no doubt of that."

A loud series of claps quieted the room and Baddawick waved from beside the bar. He looked like he was about to speak, eyed the drink near his hand, and took a quick sip first. "Welcome, all of you, welcome. I think we all know why we're here. The Butcher's pawns may be gone, but they knew how to keep this city running. Perhaps not in a good way, mind you, but we rarely ran out of grain."

"Is the city low on grain?" Alice whispered.

Ambrose shook his head. "Don't know. I suppose we'll find out soon enough."

"Everyone find a seat, and we'll hit the high points. I want to speak to a few of you in private. Some of us have more wealth than we could spend in ten lifetimes, and I have a few ideas about what to do with that."

The crowd slowly filtered around the tables, some faces Jacob had known for years, and others were complete strangers. He still felt a bond with those strangers. Ancorans had lived through a great deal together over the past months, and it nurtured a sort of kinship with the survivors.

Baddawick threw back the rest of his drink and tapped the rim. The bartender nodded, and Jacob had little doubt Baddawick was feeling an inordinate amount of pressure. It wasn't like the man to be drinking that much. He took a deep breath and continued.

"Now, I know we'd planned to discuss the rebuilding of the Low-lands—"

"What do you mean, *planned*?" Jacob's mom asked.

"Well, Ms. Anders, I thought you might be the most knowledgeable, given your relationship with your son."

She frowned and glanced at Jacob. "What do you mean? Speak plainly, Baddawick. We're all tired."

"Right. Right you are!" He shook his finger in the air as if scolding himself. "We'll touch on that a bit still. Progress on the wall is well ahead of schedule. Ambrose tells me we should be sealing off the last of the wooden barriers tomorrow. That's cause for celebration, if you ask me. According to Frederick, there's still the matter of mounting the defenses along the top of the wall, and we should see them in the next shipment."

A small round of applause sounded through the room.

"A handful of families are already moving back to the Lowlands. We don't have much as far as accommodations for them yet, but I urge you to visit and take a woodworker with you. We have funds to help furnish those homes, but those of you who can help, please do.

"Which brings me to what I wanted to speak to you all about." Baddawick started to reach for another drink, paused, and walked away from the bar. "The Fall was a nightmare for us all. But it was one battle in a war we didn't realize was upon us. And I say to you now that war is not over so long as Gregory Mordair holds power." Baddawick stood straighter, projecting his voice. "We must join the war in the west."

Surprised protests started in the back of the room until Baddawick held up his hands.

"We're here to discuss it, but in some fashion, Ancora *must* be seen supporting the efforts of Bollwerk and Belldorn. They've supported us in ways I never imagined, and this is not the time to walk away. This is the time to solidify an alliance with our trading partners that will endure longer than anyone in this room will live."

"And Fel," Owen said, raising his voice. "Or some of us, anyway."

The briefest smile crossed Baddawick's face. Jacob thought if the man had been fully sober, he might never have slipped like that. Jacob looked back at his mom and dad and found them both hiding devious smiles from the rest of the room.

Sometimes his parents were rather unbelievable.

"Yes!" Baddawick said. "We have one of the kind fisherfolk from Fel in our midst."

"Are you mad, Baddawick? Fel is the enemy!"

It took Jacob a moment to find the speaker. He was surprised to see one of Ambrose's men.

"Mad? Quite so. Have you seen my bar?"

That got several muffled laughs and caught the speaker off guard.

"Let Owen tell you his story. Let Hefina speak to you, and their son Vaughn. Listen to the story of their family hung from the walls by the Butcher and his brother, and tell me you don't believe them to be an ally."

Ambrose's man immediately fell silent. Those weren't the kind of words a decent person would shout back at, and Jacob doubted Ambrose liked to work with indecent folks. That was more like something Mary would have done in her less honest days of piracy.

He looked around for the captain of the Skysworn, finding her at a table with Samuel and Smith. Jacob smiled at her, which caused her brow to raise.

"Owen," Baddawick said. "Please, come here and tell your story."

And so he did, but with details Jacob didn't know.

"Hi, everyone." Owen wrung his hands together and flashed a brief smile. The braids of his beard caught the warm yellow glow of the lanterns in the Wildhorse, and Jacob could see patterns he'd never noticed before. "I know when you hear that I'm from Fel, that my family is from Fel, you probably think the worst. And in regard to some folk in my city, you'd be right to do so."

The few whispers Jacob had heard cut off abruptly with that statement.

"I've heard stories of Ancora. The kindness of people here." Owen's voice took on a harsher edge. "But I've also heard stories of the broken city, and the unkindness pushed onto those deemed unworthy by your own leaders."

There wasn't a single protest in that room, and that was something Jacob wasn't sure he'd ever expected. So often, the Highlanders would stand up for the worst sort of treatment, but maybe the breaking of the Butcher's stranglehold really had set other things in motion.

"Unworthy." Owen nodded to himself. "It's something I know. A label I'm familiar with as most of the fisherfolk of Fel wear that same label. The more I learned of Dauschen and Ancora, the more I realized Fel was the testing ground for the Butcher's madness. I can't say if it was Gregory or Newton who wrote the laws that broke our city. All I know is that it was broken, and later abandoned when Mordair took his loyalists to Ballern.

"It was small things at first. Patrols guarding the streets would get too physical, too violent. And instead of men being locked up until they were sober, they were beaten to death in the gutter. Some of the bartenders tried to help. I remember not so long ago, maybe a year past, a man outside The Crooked Blade bumped into an airship pilot. He tripped on a cobblestone, nothing more, but it wasn't an hour before he was hanging from the wall, guts ripped out like a damn fish.

"His family followed. Everything in their house was piled in the town square and set on fire. Made them watch. Threw a … a …" Owen held a hand over his face. "You don't need to know what Mordair did to that family. You only need to know how much good that family did in Fel. They took care of the fisherfolk. Brought us medicine and food when the rivers grew stingy. Good people."

Owen looked at his wife and took a shaky breath.

"That's what it took for some of us to realize something was wrong. And I have so much sympathy for Ancora. Years spent under the manipulation of any Mordair, a ruthless family with grand ambitions to spread their empire. We learned to live with horror in increments. Tiny transgressions that built over months or years until the public torturing of our citizens became a regular spectacle. It's still … it's still a shock when it touches your own family.

"It was my brother they took. Hung him from the walls they did, after an assassin ran him through. I tried to get him down and got lashed for it. It was a silly thing. I knew he wasn't in that body anymore. And if they'd hung me next to him, where would that have left Vaughn and Hefina?"

Silence reigned in the room. The only sound was the pianist and muted banter from the front of the bar.

"It wasn't long after my brother died on the blades of the Red Hand that we noticed the changes in the bookstores. The Children of the Dark Fire had arrived in Fel. Many believed them to be harmless. Some thought quite the opposite. And we were right.

"If Ancora is joining the fight, the fisherfolk need to know. Many of our people have family in Dauschen. Many of us lost … so much. I'm going to return to Fel. I'm going to bring Mordair a fight on the sea he'll never be prepared for. He may have defenses against a grand fleet, but he won't see the fisherfolk coming. I owe him blood."

"Thank you, Owen," Baddawick said, clasping the man on the shoulder like an old friend. "I think there are many in Ancora who understand better than we'd like."

Owen nodded and took a seat next to Hefina. She reached out and held his arm while Vaughn stared at his dad like he'd just seen the man for the first time.

Someone sniffed loudly, and Jacob turned to find Smith's teary face. Mary stayed close to him, and Jacob realized there were several more people in that room who had been torn up by Owen's story. It almost made him feel bad that he wasn't affected in that way; he was inspired. It was a story that could have come from anyone in Dauschen, or anyone who'd witnessed the Fall in Ancora. How did you find a bond stronger than that?

Baddawick swirled his drink and studied the room. "That brings us to why we're all here, doesn't it? I know we need to reinforce Ancora. We need to keep our people safe." His voice rose. "Part of keeping them safe is throwing down Mordair. I don't care if he rots in a prison cell or on the end of a pike. He must be stopped. I've spoken to Samuel, and have an understanding of what the city of Canopy intends to do."

"A bunch of pirates!" someone grumbled in the back.

Mary stood and slammed her hand on the table. "So are we, you daft Pilly! Now shut up and let the man speak."

Baddawick cast Mary an awkward grin before clapping his hands together. "Right then. I know there is much to discuss in the coming weeks. We need to keep an eye on our supplies and be mindful about feeding the city. I'll have you all know I've already made a sizable purchase of grain from Cave, and our current shortage will be resolved in days."

"We don't have the budget for that," Ambrose said, interrupting Baddawick. "We scarcely covered the supplies for the wall, even with Archibald's gifts."

"This isn't coming from the city's budget," Baddawick said, sitting his drink down. He studied his hands for a moment before meeting

Ambrose's eyes. "I've spent my own reserves on it, and I plan to spend much more than that. It's why I have meetings with the heads of the wealthiest families over the next few days. Ancora's reconstruction will not stall on our watch."

Ambrose sank into his chair, his jaw somewhat slack as he listened to Baddawick.

The more the eccentric tinker and businessman spoke, the more Jacob liked Baddawick. And he'd already liked the man quite a lot.

"It still leaves the conflict in Ballern. And what we are to do about it. Canopy is throwing the power of their dragonriders into an alliance with Belldorn. If you understand the history of Canopy, and the fact it essentially became a refuge for Belldorn's prisoners over the decades, then it should be jarring to hear they have formed a partnership. Canopy has given blood and resources to defend Belldorn, and they are joining the efforts in Ballern. So shall we. Not one single drop of blood from the line of Mordairs will ever set foot in Ancora again."

Baddawick gestured for Samuel, and the Spider Knight joined him, the silver accents of his armor glinting in the warm yellow light.

Samuel eyed all of those in attendance. Jacob didn't envy the Spider Knight, standing in front of what represented this new Parliament. How much pressure did that put on Samuel not to say the wrong thing?

Alice reached out and squeezed Jacob's hand, her brow wrinkled with creases. Jacob knew she was worried without even asking.

Samuel closed his eyes for a moment and then spoke. "I grew up in Ancora. Some of you may know I came from the Lowlands, lived there until my uncle took us in. A lot of you knew Bartholomew. A lot more of you probably knew him as Bat. I watched him die, just like I watched men and women die in Belldorn. You can wish this conflict to be over all you want, but the truth is, it's not.

"I'm going back to Belldorn. I'm going to take as many of the Spider Knights with me as I can. And those who won't come, or can't come, I'll ask for their mounts for the dragonriders. Because, you see, the woods aren't safe for the Dragonwings, and the dragonriders need more mounts. The Grey Woods harbor invaders like you can only imagine."

Samuel turned and focused on Jacob, his voice lowering as he stepped forward. "A Tree Killer might have stolen Jacob's leg, but imagine what a cluster of Acidwings or Bombardiers could do? Firing boiling liquid and detritus at a distance? It would be like taking a cannon shot to the chest. And without room to maneuver as they've been trained, the Dragonwings would be far more vulnerable. We need them in the city, not hobbled by the woods."

"What about Ancora?" Jacob's dad asked.

Jacob looked at his dad, surprised at the question before he realized the calm tone and easy inflection gave Samuel the opening he needed to put any fears to rest. Maybe Parliament was the right place for him after all.

"Ancora will stand, as it has always stood. It is stronger today than it has ever been, and our alliance with Bollwerk and Belldorn and the rebellion in Fel will forge a new world. A world where the Steamborn do not suffer, and the Skyborn do not starve on their docks." Samuel looked at Owen, his voice rising. "A world where fisherfolk are not murdered in their homes as a statement of politics. A world where the Steamsworn are not whispered of as some lost legacy of a terrible war and are instead *all* united under one banner. This is a time for an alliance between the Steamborn and the Skyborn. This is the time of the Stormborn, and we will *not* fall again."

Owen's shout startled Jacob so badly that he almost fell out of his chair. The huge man came to his feet and pounded on the table. Ambrose joined him, as did Smith, and Mary, and so many more faces Jacob knew.

The thunder in that room drowned out the music and chaos in the background. Jacob and Alice joined in the cacophony. A crash of defiance he would not soon forget.

CHAPTER ELEVEN

PATRICE SLUNK THROUGH the narrow alleys of Ballern. No one turned away from her or cringed at her presence, which was a quaint benefit of being in a new city. Fel knew only her reputation as an enforcer. Only feared her skills as one of Mordair's assassins.

Her king would likely complain about her unscheduled absence, but if she had to listen to one more of those pompous archdukes waxing about his own superiority, she was going to stab every last one. Repeatedly.

The Baroness of Auxley was somewhat more tolerable. At least she seemed to have some sense about her, a ruthlessness that would have served her well behind the gray walls of Fel. Time would tell if the Children of the Dark Fire were all as foolish as their pawns strewn about the city. Someone needed to educate them on the basics of trailing their mark.

Patrice hadn't gone more than a few blocks before she identified her tail, and she lost the man completely in the span of a single alley. It was a simple thing, slipping into a shop where a similarly built woman lingered. The red scarf she'd wrapped around her head and shoulders to hide her clothes did the rest.

The task of losing the cloaked and tattooed spy done, she headed for the market. It wasn't the most inconspicuous place for a meeting, but her contact with the Children of the Dark Fire had insisted on it. That was fine with Patrice. One must get to know a people before one can learn how to break them. She doubted the same tactics Mordair had used in Fel would work in Ballern. The Skyborn were far more resilient than the fisherfolk.

But departing the courts in irritation made her far too early for that rendezvous. It gave her time to stroll up and down the aisles, studying what Ballern considered items worthy of sale or trade. It was quite different from the fisherfolk's markets, and she found herself stopping at more than one booth.

Closer to Fel's warships, several weavers displayed brilliant throws and shawls fit for a king of Fel. She ran her fingers down a shimmering garment, enjoying the smooth feel and the way the light reflected on the threads.

"You have a good eye, dear."

Patrice looked up and met the vendor's gaze. "How much? Do I want to know?"

"Oh, it's not so bad." She gave a dismissive wave. "They aren't in demand this season."

That felt like a remarkably bad negotiation tactic for a vendor. "Do tell."

"Oh, you must be from Fel, aren't you? These are more popular when it gets colder, but there are only a few months in Ballern when folks wear them regularly."

"How much?"

"Two silvers. I know it might seem a little steep, but they are crafted of the finest spider silks. Widow Makers, in fact."

Patrice pulled a gold piece out and handed it to the woman. "We don't have much made from Widow Maker silk in Fel. I'll take five."

"Very well! I thank you. Now, these Fel coins are a bit heavier than our pieces."

Patrice held up her hand. "Keep the extra. For your skills."

"Pick out whatever colors you like."

Patrice grabbed four of varying colors. Rich blues and pale greens slid across her fingers, but the last was never a choice. She plucked a large red throw with a hood sewn in to one corner. Perhaps a bit on the nose, but there were times one needed to make an impression.

The vendor held out a canvas sack for Patrice. She dropped her purchases inside and thanked the vendor, moving on to a cluster of food stalls. One of the men sitting on a barstool saw her and almost jumped out of his seat, running down the aisle with a sandwich in tow.

"Hey!" the chef shouted. "Hey, this isn't a charity, you thief!"

"I'll pay for his," Patrice said. "And another."

"Bah, it's not the coin so much as the principle." The cook ran his fingers through his hair and then immediately started making another sandwich.

Patrice pursed her lips but didn't comment on it. She'd traveled enough to know people had *very* different opinions of what constituted clean hands. Although very few would have considered hers clean, no matter how well she scrubbed the blood away.

"What are you selling?" Patrice asked. "It smells delightful."

"An old family secret. But seeing as you're willing to cover for some of the riffraff, I suppose I can let you in on it. It's a plain cheese sandwich, grilled until it's almost burned, which is not so special in itself. It's what we add that's the real trick to it." He leaned in conspiratorially. "It's a cheese from a village far to the southwest."

"And how does cheese from a village make this special?"

"Well, it's not the cheese; it's the seeds we grind to make it."

"There's no milk in it?" Patrice eyed the sandwich with a newfound suspicion. She'd had cheese without milk in it before. That was not a pleasant memory.

"Trust me. I know you don't know me, but you ask anyone on the docks whose sandwich is best, and they'll tell you it's Hal's. So long as Jakon isn't making sandwiches that day, at least." He said the last with a hearty chuckle as he flipped the sandwich and wrapped half in three quick motions.

"You're quite good with your hands."

"A byproduct of my old profession." He smiled and handed her the sandwich.

Patrice raised an eyebrow. "Please, do tell."

"I was a magician! The best illusionist in all the docks, I tell you."

Patrice smiled and bit into her sandwich. It was warm and gooey, with a sharp bite like the best cheeses she could get in Fel. The man was either a liar or had found the best use of seeds she'd ever encountered. Other than brewing poisons, of course.

"They don't like magicians much up top, though." He pursed his lips and nodded toward the airship docks. "You know how it is. Even the Bones frown on us."

Hal's story started to come together, and Patrice didn't think the next words she spoke would be a wild guess. "Card games or shell games?"

Hal froze for a moment before offering a wide grin. "Shell games. Best at it I was."

"Until you got caught?"

"Aye, until I got caught. Let me off easy if you ask me. I can't run my games anymore, but they still let me set my grill up at the market. It's better money than running a table, anyway. Some of those Skyborn have sharper eyes than you'd think."

"You can't trust anyone if there's a reward for turning you in. Keep that in mind when you make the terrible decision to open a new table." She checked the small handwritten menu for the price of the sandwich, put two extra silvers down and excused herself.

Patrice wandered the market, keeping her canvas tote close as if someone might try to steal her new garments at any moment. It was a silly, and refreshing, concern. What a scene she could make, eviscerating a thief in such a densely packed market. It would do nothing to help her blend in, though, and she let the idea fade from her mind.

She stopped below one of Fel's ocean liners, the red and gray flag snapping in the mountain winds far above her head. The market was shielded from the worst of the northern winds, but open to anything rolling in from the sea when the winds shifted.

Patrice turned and wandered past the great stone docks and smaller marinas that dotted the entire landing around the market. She found more than one vendor touting the sharpest blades in Ballern. If that were true, she'd need to find a Fel blacksmith to educate those fools. Each blade she tested had far too little give. They might have had impeccable craftsmanship in the hilt, but it would have been an easy task to snap them in half.

Her path took her to the first row of vendors in the shadow of Ballern's mighty wall. She followed it to the archways leading into the heart of the city. Instead of trailing the thickest crowds, she veered off to a dark alley on her left.

Odd as it might be, she felt more at home there than among the bright stone buildings of Ballern. The shadow made it feel more like Fel, and Fel was the city she'd come to think of as home. She didn't like the idea of spending so much time in Ballern, but what Mordair needed, he would have.

She stayed there in the shadow and watched. No one would notice her; their eyes, adjusted to the brilliant sun, made it too hard to see inside the darkness. It wasn't long until she noticed the arrival of the Children of the Dark Fire.

Patrice hadn't expected her contact to show up alone. After all, if he were that large a fool, she wouldn't have been doing business with him.

This was something Mordair needed done without any ties back to him personally. With the archdukes and royals watching him constantly, seeing him strike a deal with the Children of the Dark Fire would probably cause a great deal of suspicion.

As the last cloak entered the market, Patrice left her shadow. She'd long ago learned how to follow a man without him noticing. Some people thought they could feel eyes on their back, but in her experience, that was a lack of skill on the part of the predator.

She passed close enough to slit the man's throat, close enough to see the metal-plated flame tattooed on his forearm, and thought about how she could do it—follow him to the ground and stuff him under a table where no one might notice for a few critical seconds.

Instead, she passed the disciple, brushing against his arm as she swiped the pendant from around his neck. Anyone foolish enough to wear jewelry on top of their cloak was begging for it to go missing.

That amusing sidebar done, she made her way to the southwest corner of the market. It wasn't a particularly busy section, but there were still people who would be within earshot if they weren't careful. One cloaked figure sat at a small table with two chairs, his back to the sea. This man knew what he was doing. She could see how he listened to everything around him, watched every movement that was within striking distance. A paranoia she could admire.

"Lane."

The hooded face rose to see who had spoken his name. His complexion looked not so different from anyone else's from Ballern, but he had pale blue eyes the likes of which she'd only seen in the far west.

"Welcome, Patrice." He gestured to the chair beside him. "Won't you join me? With our backs to the sea?"

She slid into the chair and smiled as if she was meeting an old friend. If it wasn't for Lane's hood, they might be inconspicuous, in truth.

"Your fellow disciples are clumsy. I could have killed them several times over."

"I saw you follow Victor through the market. The fact he did not notice you, I admit, was impressive."

Patrice smiled and handed Victor's necklace to Lane. "Tell him to be more careful, would you?"

Lane ran his thumb over the studded metal flame. "I will do as you ask. As to the matter at hand? You speak on behalf of Mordair?"

Patrice studied the citizens milling about the market. Some might have been in earshot, but none were paying attention. They were all caught up in shopping or food, and she began to appreciate Lane's choice of meeting place.

"I speak on behalf of Fel, and I have resources to spare."

"Very well. First, I've heard stories of your past. If you would humor me, I wish to confirm the veracity of my spy's information."

Patrice laughed and offered a nod. "Considering we will also be relying on your spies, I would like to hear this history myself. Hopefully, their information is better than their ability to follow me on the street."

Lane took a sip of his drink, breaking eye contact for only a moment. "Even in this city, we are outcasts. It is unusual for anyone to take notice of their lesser, or at least who they believe to be their lesser. We could learn much from you."

"Tell me what you've heard."

"There were only two things of any note. One, you were orphaned when one of the villages between the Black Mountains and the North Woods was crushed by the Steamsworn. I have my doubts about this, as you do not appear old enough to have been alive in the Deadlands War. And second, your first assassination attempt was against the Butcher himself. And when that failed, Gregory took you in to raise you as his own personal assassin. How does one twist oneself into that logic, Patrice? Two of the most violent Steamsworn who double-crossed their allies to usurp a throne? You are a contradiction. Loyal to the betrayers of your own people."

Patrice's smile slowly fell into a flat line the longer Lane spoke. The facts weren't exact, and some were far from the truth, but it hit home. And it hit closer than it should have. They had spies inside Fel, of that she had no doubt.

The difficulty was either she denied those facts and lost a potential trail to a spy in their midst, or she confirmed what was right in an effort to keep those threads of a trail alive. There would be a hunt after this meeting.

Patrice spread her fingers on the table and gave Lane a slow nod. "It wasn't me who was orphaned in the Deadlands War. It was my parents. Their village, their families, were crushed by a mechanical god, or so they called it. We know what it was now. It was a Tower Mech created by Charles von Atlier himself. The Mordairs were the only Steamsworn with the backbone to go against Atlier." She paused as two guards walked by on patrol. Satisfied when they left, she continued in an even tone. "So yes, I joined them, and I carved a path to the throne for them, and I will continue to carve a path for Gregory until I lie dead in the sands, or he does. Is that what you want to hear, Lane? Do you understand where my loyalties lie, and why, should I find you a threat to our king, you won't leave this table alive?"

Instead of shock or fear or anger, three completely reasonable reactions to her words, Lane *smiled*. He steepled his fingers together and laughed under his breath.

"Our alliance will be the stuff of legends, Patrice. I am honored you have shared your story. For that, you will have my weapons and the aid of the Children of the Dark Fire. Are you certain you do not wish your goods delivered to Ballern? Conflict is coming. There are whispers all along the docks, and it would not be like the Speaker of Bollwerk to leave an opportunity unexploited."

Patrice shook her head. "No. Your people know the terrain of the Great Machine better than anyone. If we fail to hold Ballern, that is where we're going."

Lane nodded. "You wish to ambush your enemies with the unknown. It is an admirable plan, but we do not have the airships to withstand a direct assault from the likes of Belldorn."

"Leave that to Fel and Ballern, but make your forces ready for battle, Lane. Dark times are coming, and none of us are getting out of this without the other."

"Very well. As for the other supplies? The harvest and spice shipments?"

"Those you can bring to Ballern. Keep the people fat and happy and celebrating as long as we can. Morale has as much to do with perceived stability as it does actual stability."

Lane's smile grew. "Should you ever wish to switch careers, I would be thrilled to welcome you into our fold. At times it is difficult to manage such a widespread network of loyalists."

Patrice lifted her hand, revealing the trio of throwing knives she'd concealed underneath.

Lane raised an eyebrow. "Have we not come to a mutually beneficial agreement?"

"We have, which is why you're still alive. And old habits, well … they're why *I'm* still alive." She pointed to a trio of people in the market, who suddenly had their eyes locked on the pair. "Your people need better training. They're obvious even when uncloaked."

Lane chuckled and relaxed into his chair. "Train with them sometime, Patrice. It would be our honor to host you."

Patrice stood and gathered her bag. "Until next time, Lane. Try not to get yourself killed."

"And you."

CHAPTER TWELVE

"YOU REALLY DON'T have to come with me," Jakon said.

Furi could tell he was trying to talk her out of joining him, but she wasn't falling for it. She wanted Jakon on their side, and the more time she spent with him, the more likely she was to convince him to fight. And she didn't want him to go to the base outside the Red Woods alone.

Instead of answering, Furi walked up the loading ramp and undid the latch.

Jakon blew out a breath and nodded to himself. "Alright then. I haven't taken The Ray out since her last tune-up, so if we get stranded, don't go yelling at me."

"When have I ever yelled at you?"

Jakon crossed his arms and furrowed his brow. "I may be thinking about my regular crew." He flashed a grin and gestured for Furi to follow. "Just you and me today."

"Did you bring food?" Furi asked.

Jakon gaped at her. "I'm sorry, are you asking if *I*, the greatest chef in Ballern, brought *food*?"

"Yes."

Jakon placed his hand over his heart and let out a long sigh. "I am wounded. But yes, we won't starve."

The loading ramp clicked closed behind them, cutting off the natural light from outside and leaving them in a dim yellow glow. Jakon led the way past the engine room and down the hall that would take them to the cabin.

Furi didn't think she'd ever get used to the sudden switch from practical wood and bare steel to plush fabrics and upholstered chairs. Jakon's cabin wouldn't have been out of place in a palace, and yet somehow it worked perfectly aboard The Ray. It didn't hurt that those plush seating arrangements were bolted to the floor, of course; otherwise, Jakon would have had quite the mess every time he took The Ray out.

Furi settled into the copilot's chair beside him, looking over the levers and dials while they waited for the dockhands to clear them. The signal came soon enough, and Jakon let The Ray drift backward before spinning the ship out toward the Crystal Sea.

The Ray might have looked like any other airship with its massive gas chamber floating overhead, but Furi knew from experience it was anything but. She doubted there were many faster ships in the air outside of the Skysworn itself or perhaps the small short-range strikers. She supposed that came in handy when you spent half your time smuggling.

Which begged another question. "Smuggle anything good lately?"

Jakon spluttered and his head twitched as he eyed Furi. "You can't just say things like that."

"Why? We're the only ones on this old bucket of bolts!"

"She didn't mean that," Jakon said, patting the dashboard. "Still, it never hurts to make good habits. And no, for your information. When would I have time to smuggle anything when I'm chasing you and your friends across the sea while trying not to get blown up?"

"There were at least one or two days in there where you didn't get shot at."

Jakon laughed and eased the throttle forward. It wasn't a violent leap like the Skysworn, but the engines roared near the stern of The Ray. Jakon guided them higher as the clouds sped by ever faster.

"Don't think I don't know why you're actually here," Jakon said. "You can try talking me into this fight all you want, but I'm done with risking The Ray."

Furi thought about all the times he'd put The Ray at risk to protect his friends. She didn't think Jakon was a lost cause yet. And his network was valuable. Even if Mary knew the same people as Jakon, she'd made enemies out of several of them.

If worst came to worst, at least she'd get some of Jakon's cooking out of the trip.

✧   ✧   ✧

LEAVING EARLY IN the morning meant they reached the other side of the sea well before midday, and the Red Woods reached up to greet them in short order. To the south, she could just make out the Bay of Sorrow, the coastline trailing north until it nearly intersected their path.

"We'll set down at the old base," Jakon said. "See if anyone's returned yet, or if any messages were left behind for a new rendezvous spot."

"And lunch?"

"Yes, definitely lunch. I'm starving."

Furi smiled and watched the windscreen as Jakon started their descent. She admired Mary's piloting skills, but Jakon's flights always felt smooth. At least they felt smooth when he wasn't trying to escape certain death. Maybe that was more of a difference in the airships, but either way, Furi enjoyed riding with him.

"It sounds like Kura will support your efforts in Ballern," Jakon said, keeping his eyes focused on the windscreen.

"I know. It's such a relief. I don't think Mordair is going to have anything good planned for the Skyborn."

Jakon harumphed. "I imagine not. Are you sure it wouldn't be best to leave the city? They'd welcome you in Belldorn or Ancora. I'm sure of it."

Furi rubbed her hands together. "I can't do that, Jakon. It's not just about me."

"You might not survive it." Jakon sank into his seat and glanced away. "I've seen good people die in uprisings, Furi."

She studied Jakon for a moment before focusing on the windscreen, now filled with distant mountains and trees rising on either side of them. "There's more to this than just living another day, Jakon. Beck died in Belldorn. I watched him die. I can't … that can't be for nothing. And everyone on the Nightingale? Everyone in Ancora?"

"I know what you're saying, Furi, but you have to stay alive if you want to help people in the future. If you don't … if …" Jakon leaned forward as they descended to where the docks for the base should have been. But there weren't docks there anymore. There was only ash and rubble and the scorched remains of everyone who called the place home.

Jakon's fingers tightened on his wheel so hard Furi heard the leather protest beneath his grip. "This wasn't supposed to happen."

Furi didn't say more as Jakon guided The Ray forward, giving them a terrible picture of what had occurred. She could still hear the explosions from the time she'd run from the attack with Alice, but she'd had no idea just how bad it was.

The landing gear on The Ray whined as Jakon settled them onto a patch of flat grassland. Or what had been grassland. "There was a shelter here. If we're lucky, some of my clientele might have made it inside before the bombs hit."

Furi didn't tell him how quickly the attack had come. How no one would have survived if they weren't already in the shelter, but she followed him to the loading ramp anyway, watching the swirl of ash when the metal hit the ground.

Jakon pulled a sword and a crossbow off the rack before heading down the ramp. Furi followed, keeping one hand on the daggers sheathed at her waist.

It was the smell that came first. Burnt meat and rot so thick it could have choked a Carrion Worm, which made her wonder about something else. "Where are the Carrion Worms, Jakon?"

"It's solid stone beneath our feet, Furi. It's one reason the base was built here. Some think it was a collapsed mountain. I honestly don't know what it was, but it keeps the worms away. Come on."

They hadn't gone far before Furi realized they were walking through the ashes of the market. It was easy to forget what had been there until she saw the skulls, burned to the bone and left to scream in silence.

Jakon didn't look down. He strode forward like it was the most important mission he'd ever taken. Furi wasn't sure if he was putting on a brave face, or if the carnage simply didn't get to him like it did her. She didn't think that was true, though. If it were, he wouldn't be running from the fight with Mordair.

Jakon swept his gaze from the woods to the collapsed building next to them. They were inside the makeshift village now, not far from the docks and the base. He circled to the back of the detritus and scraped at it with his boot, grimacing when a handle revealed itself.

He pulled it open, and light flooded the basement below. Furi almost retched when the smell hit her. Bodies littered the floor with enough bolts stuck in their chests to look like a Stone Dog had lodged every quill on its back into them. But she knew the bloated face of one of the men by the scar under his eye. He'd been on the last smuggling run out of Ballern.

Jakon cursed and turned away. "No bombs did this."

"Who?" Furi whispered.

"Look at the bolts, Furi." Jakon tensed and bit off the words. "Fel did this. Mordair. They bombed the docks and the village, and then killed anyone who survived. This is just a graveyard now."

Furi reached out and squeezed Jakon's shoulder.

He turned and smiled, but she didn't miss the tears in the corner of his eyes. Furi thought it might have been a stretch for Jakon to call some of those pirates and outlaws friends, but they didn't deserve what they got. The village didn't deserve what it got.

"How many times?" Jakon whispered as he led the way to The Ray. His pace quickened and grew heavier as they moved. "How many bloody times?"

"You've seen something like this before?" Furi asked.

Jakon clenched his fists and nodded as he started up the ramp to The Ray. "A village in the North Woods along the Black Sea. They objected to the hangings of several fisherfolk. Mordair slaughtered them. Redlins was the town. It was something like the Pirate's Cove of the North Woods, though … shorter, as one of my contacts liked to say."

"What? I had no idea. Mordair doesn't even rule over the North Woods, does he?"

"No. He never has. It was an act of war, but few cities have the power to break Fel's walls."

"You never told me about Redlins."

Jakon didn't say anything as they walked back to the cabin, not waiting to make sure the ramp had closed completely. Furi was relieved to get away from the smell of that place.

He stepped closer to a locker at the rear of the cabin and pulled out a small grill. It snapped into place on the floor before a flame flickered and burst into a round inferno. He sat a skillet on top and took a deep breath, opening a cooler and pulling out two long portions of fish.

"I don't tell a lot of people about Redlins, Furi." He uncapped a glass canister filled with a spice mixture, one Furi was certain she'd see at the market. "Those of us in the guild remember, and that's good enough."

Jakon sat in his chair and was about to turn around, but he stopped, staring out at the remnants of the Red Woods' docks. "Let's change our view a little. Watch that skillet, would you?"

Furi nodded as Jakon let The Ray drift into the air. It wasn't long before they were caught in a gentle breeze, slowly turning, seeing the Bay of Sorrow and the Red Woods before the mountains appeared far in the distance.

Jakon turned his chair around and leaned over the grill before grimacing. "It's going to smell like fish in here for a week."

"Good fish, at least."

He smiled at that, seasoning the fillets before dropping them on the oiled skillet, where they hissed and seared.

"Will you tell people about me, Jakon?"

He raised an eyebrow. "What do you mean?"

"When I'm gone." She almost whispered it as she looked away. "I mean, if things don't go well in Ballern."

Jakon froze. He sat staring at Furi before shaking himself out of a daze. He opened his mouth to speak and then ran his hands through his hair.

"Damn, kid. You don't have to lay the guilt on so thick. You already told me what happened here. I just … I didn't think it was this bad. I can't … I *won't* leave you and the Skyborn hoping people from Bollwerk and Belldorn will come to save the docks. That's not something I'm leaving behind, Furi. A fight is coming. And I owe Mordair. I owe him a great deal of pain."

It was the answer she wanted, but it didn't make her feel any better about seeing the village. That had been worse than she'd expected, and it had brought memories of the Belldorn's underground screaming back to the surface.

One thing Furi agreed with Jakon on was that she just wanted the war to be over. She wanted her friends to be safe, but she understood with painful clarity that it wasn't going to happen without a fight.

CHAPTER THIRTEEN

A S MUCH AS Drakkar wanted to leave immediately for Cave, he was
glad they had chosen to rest. Rin explained that the Dragonwings
could make the flight with fewer stops after an overnight feeding. The
other option was to take a different mount, but Drakkar found himself
more attached to his own than many of the dragonriders.

The second advantage was climbing aboard a supply ship bound for
Bollwerk before dawn broke. It would take most of the day to reach the
desert city, but when they did, they and the mounts would be ready to
move. The supply ships were not so slow and lumbering as the warships,
but Drakkar missed the speed of the Skysworn. A speed he found readily
enough once he took to the air with Rin and the Dragonwings.

Daylight still lit the skies when the Ridge Mountains came into view.
Rin fell back, letting Drakkar take the lead when they crossed into the
foothills. It wasn't long from there before the fields and pastures between
the mountains opened onto trails that would take them to Cave.

Drakkar had tried to explain where to land, but after his third try to
tell the dragonrider how to choose between the valleys and arches to
locate the stables, Rin had wisely told the Cave Guardian to take the lead.

A smile worked its way across Drakkar's face when he saw two of the
Nameless perched among the stones. It was a rare thing to surprise one
of the many guards who stood watch over Cave's gates, but Drakkar
enjoyed a challenge.

He tapped out a quick pattern on the Dragonwing's plated harness, and they dove, the wind snapping his hood behind him as it threatened to lift the goggles from his eyes. Drakkar flew beneath the first of the Nameless, only to rise before the second, hovering before the astonished faces.

"What in all the seas are you doing, brother?" called out the first guard.

"Showing my friend the path to Cave!" Drakkar gestured to Rin, who hovered behind the Nameless. The dragonrider gave a small, somewhat awkward smile and wave.

The Nameless held out their fists. Drakkar opened his hand in response. Together, their gesture formed the Fist of the Steamsworn. Apart, it was the greeting of the Nameless, a tradition borne of the horrors of the Deadlands War and the unlikely soldiers who had fought beside Cave.

Drakkar pulled the reins back on his Dragonwing before tapping out another pattern. His mount swooped down between two thin walls that towered over the field and funneled them directly to the stables.

He feared the stable hand might die of surprise when the child could do no more than splutter at the sudden arrival of two Dragonwings.

Rin slid off his mount and eyed Drakkar. "You're getting far too much enjoyment scaring the life out of your countrymen."

Drakkar gave him a sly smile. "You could not possibly understand the depths of my enjoyment."

Rin laughed and shook his head, focusing on the stable hand. "They eat Sweet-Flies. You can care for them as you would a Walker. Keep clear of their tails and their mandibles. They aren't poisonous, but they'll take your arm off." He paused. "Assuming you have the room?"

"Sir, absolutely, sir." He bounced on his heels, unable to contain his excitement. "I just … I'd heard of Dragonwings, but I'd never seen one. It's … they're … and you *rode* them!"

"Which stalls would you prefer the Dragonwings in?" Drakkar asked.

Rin looked around and pointed to the far wall. He walked over and glanced at the stable hand. "Are these acceptable to you?"

"Yes, sir!"

Rin tapped on the bar running across the stable, and his Dragonwing darted over to it, dancing on the metal before settling down.

Drakkar slid off his own Dragonwing and did the same. He unfastened his pack from the saddle and threw it over his shoulder before offering the stable hand a few coins. "Sweet-Flies. Just like a Walker, and we'll have more coin when we return. We're on our way to the temple, and I'd like a quick meal at The Rock Inn. Take care of our mounts. If anyone asks after them, give them my name. Do you know it?"

"No, sir, I'm new this week. I grew up in Ancora, sir."

Drakkar offered him a smile. "My name is Drakkar. Take care of yourself. I have many friends from Ancora."

They took their leave, Drakkar leading the way down the corridor to the city proper. It was still odd to see so many people in that corridor. The sounds of the city grew louder as they reached the threshold, and Drakkar's steps slowed as the city of Cave sprawled out before them.

He turned to take in Rin's expression, and it reminded him somewhat of the shock on the faces of the Nameless. Drakkar smiled at the dragonrider. "Welcome to Cave."

"I'd heard stories, but … but this is grand, Drakkar." Rin gestured to the mixture of stone buildings and wooden walls that formed the chaos of Cave's streets. Some areas held more concentrations of stone than wood, like the rings of a tree, telling the story of the city.

"Come. We will see Alana first. I would prefer to be done with that, as it has my nerves on edge."

Rin nodded and followed, but Drakkar didn't think the dragonrider was hearing everything he'd said. He led Rin over one street to their right, passing the flickering lamps of the district before taking him down a crowded street.

Drakkar smiled when he saw some of the larger musical groups had returned to the cobblestones. When last he'd visited, Cave had been too choked with people to allow room for the usual buskers. It felt like a glimmer of normalcy in a long darkness.

A music shop had its windows open, the delicate notes of a flute echoing out before they were swallowed by a trio of wandering guitar players. Music brought the city to life, and there was no place in the world as homey as Cave.

"This place is amazing, Drakkar. Oh, street vendors. I do need a snack. What coin do they take here? I didn't think to ask."

Drakkar patted his satchel. "Do not worry, my friend. I have plenty for this trip." He led them past the first cart, as he wasn't fond of the sweet fish balls that particular chef specialized in, and instead brought Rin to a small stand serving steamed buns.

If he was being honest, the buns in Midstream might have had a slight edge over those of Cave, but the thought of that thick stuffing of beans and Sea Claw made his mouth water.

"Four, please."

The vendor nodded and pulled the glass door open on her cart. She flipped them into the air one at a time, catching them without looking at a tray in her other hand. Drakkar offered up two silvers, and they went on their way.

Rin didn't wait for an explanation about what the buns were. He dove face-first into the gummy dough and said something unintelligible through a mouthful of bun. A short time later, he clarified, "This is so good. The salt and that chewy texture? Why don't we have these in Canopy?" There might have been more words, but Drakkar couldn't make them out.

Drakkar finished his own buns before pointing off to one of the taller buildings with what looked like a small house built on top of it. "That is the Temple of the Cave Guardians. We will find Alana there."

"Does she have steamed buns?"

Drakkar smiled.

They soon found themselves standing in front of the ten-foot-tall doors to the temple. Drakkar pushed his way inside, surprised at the unusual quiet that waited for them. Drakkar assumed there was a meeting or some other gathering that had drawn some of the residents and refugees away. Or more had returned to Ancora already than he'd expected. That was not to say the temple was not busy.

"Rust it all, Drakkar. How did they build *that*?"

Drakkar followed Rin's gaze up to the wide holes in the second floor that allowed four massive columns to reach beyond. "Do you mean the mosaics, or the bronze gargoyles set around them?"

"Mosaics?" Rin squinted at the decorative work that adorned the ceiling. "Those aren't paintings?"

"No."

A cloaked figure stepped into their path. "All are welcome in this place who do not mean harm."

Drakkar inclined his head. "Thank you, brother. I seek an audience with Alana."

The guardian stepped to the side and gestured to the rear lift. Drakkar continued past, motioning for Rin to follow. It wasn't a particularly large lift, but it served its purpose even with the burden of so many staying within.

They stepped out onto the roof a short time later, and Rin's steps slowed while he studied the brilliant yellow glow in the distance. "It's like a sunset, but underground."

"A sunset that never changes," Drakkar said. "It does not compare to the sun itself."

"Maybe not, but it's quite a sight. Not something you expect to see underground."

Drakkar turned and made for the narrow stairs that led to the open doorway of the home atop the temple. Alana stood inside, perfectly centered, as though she had been waiting for their arrival.

"Alana."

The stern look on the woman's face cracked a hair. "You remembered my request."

"Of course."

She touched the shaved side of her head where intricate tattoos arched around her ear. "I do hope the times have not been cruel. It is rare to see you so often in so short a span."

Alana studied Rin, her amber eyes locked on the dragonrider. Drakkar waited, and it didn't take long before Rin started to fidget. So even the dragonrider had his limits for uncomfortable eye contact.

"Alana. It is good to find you well."

She shifted her focus back to the Cave Guardian. "And you, Drakkar. What brings you to the temple?"

"I have brought a friend. This is Rin of the Skyborn, Dragonrider of Canopy and acquaintance of Allie."

"I have no more masons to send, Drakkar. If that is what you seek."

Drakkar held up a hand. "No, no. Not at all. I have another request. One that is perhaps more important even than the rebuilding of Ancora."

"Oh?"

He took a breath to center himself and met her gaze. "Canopy rides to war with Belldorn and Bollwerk. Ancora intends to send Spider Knights. I fear these things together will leave Midstream and Ancora vulnerable."

Alana looked away, glanced at Rin, and then returned her focus to

Drakkar. "And you wish the Cave Guardians to join in this conflict? What of protecting our own homes? And those refugees who still remain here for shelter and protection from that same conflict?"

"The Skyborn are joining the battle against Mordair. I do not believe they have the resources to stand up to them, but I do believe we have the resources to help."

"There are whispers in the walls, Drakkar. Stories of a new alliance between the Skyborn of Ballern and the Steamborn of Ancora."

"They're true," Rin said. "All of it. We're fighting back."

Alana slowly turned her gaze to the dragonrider. "And what has fighting back gotten you? What has fighting back *cost* you?"

"Everything," Rin said without hesitation. He ran his fingers through his hair. "Is that what you want to hear? I could be killed just for going home. And I'd do it again to protect my friends and keep my family safe. Allie has given me a new home in Canopy, but I'll still fight to save the Skyborn."

"Brave of you." Alana turned back to Drakkar. "But why involve Cave? We are safe here."

"We will not be if the battle is lost in Ballern. Allie sends the dragonriders to join them. If Belldorn falls, Canopy will no longer stand between whatever comes from the west and Bollwerk. If Bollwerk falls, we cannot resist."

"That is a long chain of events with no certain outcome, Drakkar. I understand your concern. Give me this night to think on it. I will have an answer for you in the morning."

Drakkar nodded. "We leave for Ancora after dawn. I travel with a dragonrider and a Spider Knight for the offensive in Ballern. Remember that alliance, Alana. Knights and pirates, dragonriders and Steamsworn, facing Mordair as a unified front. It is our best chance."

"Be well, Drakkar. Visit me when the sun breaks."

Drakkar bowed and gestured for Rin to follow. He continued to the edge of the roof and stopped, looking over the bustling streets of Cave.

"What was that?" Rin asked. "I thought we were going to have answers."

"We will have answers in the morning, Rin. For tonight, I will show you the docks and take you to The Rock Inn. They seem to be some of the Ancorans' favorite places, so you may find them interesting at least."

Rin sighed. "Could be worse ways to spend an evening."

"Far worse." Drakkar smiled and led the way back to the lift.

✧   ✧   ✧

RIN BLINKED AND started to sit up before groaning and flopping back down on his cot. The rough wooden walls looked vaguely familiar. "What … what happened?"

Drakkar beamed at him, dressed and suspiciously awake. "It is nearly dawn. Come. Breakfast awaits, and then we can hear Alana's decision.

"But my head." Rin sat up, one eye closed, marveling at the thunder inside his brain.

"I told you to stop after two Sweetwing smashes."

That name. Rin remembered that name. The barkeep's specialty. They'd ordered them with dinner, and then …

Rin groaned and took a deep breath. "Remind me to listen to you next time. It didn't taste *that* strong."

"They never do."

It was a bad way to learn the Cave Guardian's advice was impeccable, but he supposed his head still wasn't as bad as some of the concussions he'd had over the years. A memory of falling off the ladder on the Bones and cracking his head on the railing came to mind. His stomach roiled at the thought.

Rin pulled his boots on before picking up the leather jerkin and dark fabric from Canopy. He took a sharp breath and stood up, wincing at the movement.

"Are you able to walk?"

Rin started to protest before he found the wide grin on Drakkar's face. "Humor now, is it? Tell me you have a better cure for hangovers than we do in Canopy."

"Apparently you will be able to put that to the test this morning."

Rin grumbled and picked up his backpack, following Drakkar out of the room and down a narrow hall flanked by several more doors. Snores rattled the walls, and Rin found himself somewhat jealous.

Drakkar almost hopped down the stairs, light on his feet, but Rin dragged his boots forward, letting them thud down each stair like a dropped boulder. They made it down to the bar proper, and he stared at the cluster of people in that place.

They weren't loud or raucous like the night before, but they were clearly awake and enjoying their breakfast.

"What can I get you, boys?" the barkeep asked.

"Whatever the greasiest thing you have is," Rin muttered.

"Not ready for another smash yet, eh?"

Rin tried to scowl at the barkeep but winced at a lance of pain instead.

"Something for the hangover," Drakkar said. "He has had a rough morning." The Cave Guardian pulled up a barstool and sat down.

Rin did the same, guzzling a glass of water when the barkeep sat it down. The next thing to show up was red and thick, with a brown streak running through the glass. It looked as appetizing as a trough of Sweet-Flies, but smelled like horseradish.

"What is this?"

The barkeep's nose scrunched up. "Probably best you don't ask. Just drink it. You'll feel better by the time your Walker eggs are done."

Eggs didn't sound too bad. Especially when compared to the somewhat terrifying glass sitting in front of him. Rin wasn't one to worry until after he'd made a mistake. So, he picked up the short glass, braced himself, and took the entire thing down in one go.

His eyes flashed wide a few seconds later when the heat hit him. Fiery like the best chopped Pilly dishes of Ballern. The texture bothered him, a little too grainy for something he was drinking, with a heavy aftertaste of salt. Rin smacked his lips and looked at Drakkar.

"Not too terrible, is it?"

"No, the texture is a little weird, but not bad. My face is on fire, though."

"Helps with the recovery!" the barkeep said with a little too much enthusiasm.

By the time their eggs arrived, Rin found himself covered in sweat and drinking more chilled water.

"Better?"

Rin nodded to the barkeep. "I'm sweating like it's the dead middle of a rainstorm in the southern desert, but other than that, yes."

The barkeep sat a bowl in front of Drakkar and then Rin. "This should take care of the rest."

Rin salivated at the rich smell coming up from the bowl of eggs. They'd been mixed in with oatmeal to form something that reminded him of a chunky stew.

Drakkar handed him a wide piece of flatbread that looked like a crepe. Rin watched the Cave Guardian tear off a piece of another bread and dip it into his egg stew.

Rin followed by example. The bread had a sour edge to it that wasn't unpleasant and complimented the savory eggs and chewy chunks of meat better than he imagined. He didn't think the sheer volume of oil waiting in the bottom of that dish could possibly be healthy, but he had to admit he was feeling better.

"Good?"

Rin looked up at the barkeep and nodded before swallowing. "Amazing. I've never had anything quite like it."

"We only serve it for breakfast here, so you had good timing."

Drakkar slid a gold coin to the barkeep.

"It's included with your room, Drakkar."

He shook his head. "Take it. You have put great effort into taking care of my friend this morning."

The barkeep shrugged and slid the coin into his apron.

Rin finished another glass of water when Drakkar said it was time to go. Soon enough, they were walking back through the streets of Cave, and Rin was quite happy it didn't feel like his head was about to explode.

✧   ✧   ✧

DRAKKAR STOOD IN the center of the house atop the temple. Alana waited for them, standing a little off to the side in what indicated a more casual welcome than she often gave. Rin appeared to be far less nervous in this new encounter, and Drakkar was glad to see the dragonrider settling into the slower pace of Cave.

"We have discussed your request, Drakkar."

"I give you thanks for taking the time, Alana. It is good that you hear the people of Cave and give thought to their words."

"There's no need for such formality."

"Oh good," Rin said, letting out a long sigh. "So, are you going to fight with us? I'd understand either way. It's … if you told me I'd be fighting beside Belldorn soldiers one day, I would have laughed at you."

Drakkar and Alana stared at Rin.

"So, maybe a little formality still?"

Alana smiled at the dragonrider. "It is our tradition, yes. A fine balance either way, though we give our guests much more freedom to speak their mind."

Drakkar inclined his head. "Is there a message I may carry forward? One I can deliver to our allies in Ancora and our brothers and sisters in Midstream?"

"There is a third message I wish you to carry, Cave Guardian. To Allie in Canopy. I look forward to greeting her again in the dark of Cave, but I will see her in Canopy before that happens."

Drakkar could see Rin frantically glancing between him and Alana from the corner of his eye. "It would be my honor."

"We cannot leave Cave unguarded, Drakkar. Not entirely so. I will not send the full force of our Guardians into battle, but I will send enough to support our allies. Tell this to the people of Ancora who do not still dwell in Cave. Tell it to those of Midstream, and our lost family in Canopy. Tell them the doors are open once more, and Cave is the beacon in the shadows it was always meant to be."

Drakkar extended his fist, and Alana closed her hand around it. "A symbol of what came before, and what is yet to come."

Alana smiled. "Atlier changed you, Drakkar. And it was not for the worse."

Pressure welled behind Drakkar's eyes as memories of Charles came flooding back. Memories of a bloody legacy, a redeemed tinker, and a man he was proud to have called a friend.

"Go now," Alana said, drawing Drakkar out of his thoughts. "The Guardians make for Bollwerk. From there, they will spread between Midstream, Fel, and Belldorn. A web to catch anything Mordair deploys back across the Crystal Sea."

"Fel is broken, Alana. The fisherfolk may be willing to fight, but the will of the city has been long extinguished."

"They will be protected, regardless. And if they cannot be protected, they will be evacuated as fast as the Guardians can take them." Alana hesitated, and then hugged Drakkar. "I'll be in Canopy if you need me. Allie won't face this battle alone. I don't care if she left Cave behind. We won't leave *her* behind."

Drakkar tightened his arms around Alana. And for a moment, it felt like times long past, when all their friends had still lived in Cave, and the world had not been quite so mad.

"Thank you," Rin said when Drakkar and Alana broke contact. "I can't explain to you what this will mean to the Skyborn. They've heard so many stories about Cave. Lots of them are pirate stories, if I'm being honest, but the city is everything those stories promised and more."

Alana inclined her head. "When you speak to them, tell them they are welcome in Cave. But perhaps to be cautious around the Sweetwing smashes."

Rin blinked as Alana and Drakkar broke down into very informal laughter.

CHAPTER FOURTEEN

Gladys reached up and tapped on the sand skiff's sail. They'd scarcely made it home from Gareth Cave when Archibald contacted her. And now he wanted to talk to them in Bollwerk.

"I just want to stand up," Gladys muttered into the microphone. "It feels like we've been sitting down for an entire day."

"Archibald wants to speak to us in person, and if he is unable to join us in Midstream, then Bollwerk is the nearest point." George said it like it was a simple fact, and not an hours-long trek across the desert. "It is better than a journey to Belldorn, is it not?"

George didn't quite make it around a sharp sand dune, and grit sprayed up over the edge of the skiff, pinging off Gladys's goggles.

"We wouldn't have to have any *journey* if you hadn't mentioned the bait boxes over the transmitter."

"It is good for Archibald to know what defenses we are capable of."

"I know, I know, but Targrove said it could take him a while to get them working. What if he doesn't? It might not even be an issue."

"We will dine at The Fish Head. Does that not take some of the frustration out of this travel?"

"Maybe a little." Gladys thought George was a little too good at changing the subject some days.

Grumbling done, Gladys settled in to read for the rest of the trip. She hadn't spent much time doing that lately, and she wanted to dig further into the history of Midstream. Sometimes their city felt so isolated, it was hard to remember how many places the settlers of Midstream had come from after it was established.

She looked up from time to time, watching the dunes race by as George guided them around stones that could shatter the skiff and cacti that would make for a terribly unpleasant day. Her focus wavered when Bollwerk's silhouette came into view, and she put her book down to watch the city grow on the horizon.

✧   ✧   ✧

THE RUSTED WALLS and giant armor plating of the desert city dwarfed the skiff as they made their way closer. George slowed to gain more precise control over the skiff. As the sand thinned, he deployed the wheels and guided them into the hangars just inside the city walls. The bays were usually reserved for airships being built or under extensive repairs, which meant there were rarely prying eyes there.

A black column of smoke caught Gladys's attention. "Is that a fire at the old factory?"

George glanced over his shoulder and grunted. "I am not sure, Princess. It is not dense enough to be a large building on fire."

The sand skiff's tires squeaked to a stop on the metal floor. They wouldn't have inertia when they needed to leave, but they could get back to the sand with a little help from the dockhands. Except Gladys didn't see any dockhands in the repair bays. In fact, she didn't see anyone at all. That gave her some cause for concern.

George was out of the skiff and on the ground, already surveying the area before Gladys climbed out.

"Keep your blades ready. I do not like the quiet."

But the quiet had a sound. A distant chant Gladys couldn't quite make out. She strained to hear the words, but it was no good.

Bootsteps sounded nearby, and a throwing knife slid silently out of its sheath and into her hand.

A frazzled-looking man dressed in pants and a leather jerkin slid to a stop. "George? Gladys? Archibald sent me. I'm to take you to the Temple of the Steamsworn. The council is sheltering there."

"We were headed there anyway," Gladys said. "Why is the council sheltering?"

"Protests at the factories. Did Archibald not tell you? Been going on for two days now. They want no part in the conflict with Ballern."

George cursed under his breath.

"I have a crawler nearby. Closer to the stables. Come."

"We will not."

The man froze and lifted the brim of his leather hat, turning back to George. "Why?"

"Your city is wrapped in unrest, and I do not know you or who you are loyal to."

"Archibald sent me. I am loyal to Lady Grey and Archibald alike. So much as the council annoys me at times with their petty laws and mild punishments, I am still loyal."

George narrowed his eyes. "Should you be lying, you will not live to see your betrayal."

"Rust and steel! My name is Walter Jones. You're friends with the Ancorans, yes? Jacob and Charles and the others? I'm Archibald's cousin. You might know me as Dr. Jones."

"The tinker?" George's posture grew less rigid.

Gladys relaxed her hand around the blade between her fingers.

"Yes, yes. I was sad to hear what happened to Charles. He knew my father, but we have to get you off the streets."

George hesitated before nodding. "Lead the way."

Jones pulled his hat down and scampered forward. Gladys thought the man could use a lesson in being inconspicuous because crouching down like no one could see you in broad daylight was not the way to do it. Although his obvious concern and paranoia did give her some confidence that he wasn't leading them into a trap.

The stables were one block north, and not so vacant as the hangars. Stable hands milled about, one briefly glancing toward Jones but saying nothing. Jones pulled a canvas cover off one of Bollwerk's crawlers and hopped inside.

"We're warmed up and ready to go. Get in."

George held a hand out to Gladys. Instead of waiting to open the door, she put one foot on the tread and vaulted over the side. George followed.

"You can lie down in the back, or we have goggles in the console."

Gladys had been in crawlers numerous times on the streets of Bollwerk, and she never recalled needing goggles. The moment Jones pushed the throttle forward and didn't stop accelerating, she began to understand the offer, and was happy she'd put them on.

The goggles were large and unwieldy compared to those on the sand skiff, but they hid a large portion of the wearer's face. Gladys thought that might be a good thing if they were truly in danger from the protests.

Jones raced them over three blocks before turning with a speed that felt like he was trying to throw everyone out of the crawler. The treads screamed on the paved streets of Bollwerk, and Gladys didn't doubt there would have been sparks if it were night.

Brick and aged bronze rose all around them, accented by tarnished copper and glass as the trails of smoke in the distance grew lighter in color.

"New fires," George said when Gladys pointed them out.

There were no other crawlers on the road, and few pedestrians to even see them drive by. Nonetheless, Gladys was happy when the crawler slowed and whipped into an alley next to the council building. Jones hurried them out, leading the way to the street and pounding on the front door.

Two guards opened the single door that wasn't hidden behind armored plates. That was new, and it bothered Gladys more than she cared to admit.

"The Princess of Midstream and the Royal Guard here to see the council."

One guard stepped to the side, allowing the trio to pass.

"Go to the hall," Jones said. "Trust no one until you've spoken to Archibald. There are those on the council who would go far to undermine him."

"Thank you," Gladys said.

Jones nodded. "I'll be in the workshop should you need anything. Please don't venture out into the city alone."

With that, he walked away, leaving George and Gladys to compose themselves as they made for the lift.

"Things may be worse than we know," George said.

"I think it's just a question of how much worse, George." She rubbed her hands together. "I'm worried."

The lift rattled when it came to a stop in front of them.

George glanced at her. "We will have our answers soon enough."

✦   ✦   ✦

THE LIFT OPERATOR opened the gate for them when they reached the council Hall. It was a grand place, flanked by bleachers that led to the council's heavy benches at the far end. But instead of the immaculately dressed council that normally awaited visitors, all looking down on whoever entered with something just short of disdain, it looked more like the cramped shelters they'd thrown together in Midstream after Fel bombed the city.

Gladys eyed the room, recognizing few people in that place, though there weren't nearly so many as she'd expected. It might have been because they were usually only there when the council convened, or it might have been because of the riot outside. Her gaze eventually fell upon the wispy hair and thin face of Archibald.

She started toward him, George close behind.

Archibald ran his fingers through his hair and shook his head, speaking with a slightly younger woman with a wide-brimmed leather hat studded with vent holes.

"Archibald." Gladys waited for him to meet her eyes.

"Gladys! You're here. And safe, I'm glad to see."

"You could have warned us about the riots outside."

Archibald frowned, and his brow crinkled. "It's not so much a riot as an energetic protest."

"It is why you did not wish to use the transmitters, is it not?" George asked pointedly.

Gladys blinked.

"Yes … yes, it is. I'm sorry to drag you both here, but there are some things that must be done as securely as possible. And what you told me about … well, that is the sort of thing we need privacy for. That and other sensitive matters.

"Lady Grey, would you join us? Should something happen to me, I think it best someone from the council remains aware of what is happening. Someone I can trust."

"Even regarding Theo's assistant?" Gladys asked, not sure she wanted *anyone* else to know about Targrove's survival.

"Yes, Princess. Even him."

Archibald swept the maps up with a flourish and started back to the lift. The other three followed, Gladys stealing looks at Lady Grey. She'd heard things about the councilwoman over the years. She'd even seen her in The Fish Head once, but she'd never gotten a chance to speak with her.

"I'm Gladys."

Lady Grey looked down and studied her for a moment before smiling. "You may call me Liz."

Archibald cast a look back at Lady Grey that Gladys couldn't quite decipher, although she did take note of Archibald's very high eyebrow.

"You're kind of a legend in Midstream."

"Really?"

Gladys nodded. "The way you took down your assassins?"

Liz smiled. "That was a very long time ago, dear."

Gladys pulled her cloak open to reveal the dozen throwing knives along her vest. "I very much liked that story."

"My, but I do appreciate your choice in blades. May I?" She held a hand out.

Gladys handed one over as Archibald closed the lift.

Liz flicked the edge of the knife with her fingernail before studying it with one closed eye. "The weight is impeccable. Did one of our bladesmiths make this for you?" Liz answered her own question when she turned it over. "Ah, no, I see the mark of an old Midstream forge. Royal, isn't it? I doubt they thought these would see real use, but the quality is superb." She flipped it into the air and caught it effortlessly with two fingers before handing it back to Gladys.

"We still have traditional bladesmiths in Midstream. If you ever want to visit, I could show you. They can make custom knives! They'd be happy to make some for you, I'm sure."

"If we live through the war, my princess, I would be thrilled to visit Midstream."

As dark as Liz's response was, Gladys couldn't help but beam at George when he caught her gaze. The stories of Lady Grey were almost as believable as the legends George used to tell Gladys when she was younger. More than once, she had pretended to be Lady Grey when George was training her late into the night. It was a strange thing to meet someone like that in person.

They took the hall that would lead to the workshop, but passed it, heading for the Steamsworn monument that now stood open. It felt strange to see the monument open and welcoming all to study the room within. Gladys had little doubt there used to be a great deal more in that space. Archibald had likely hidden it away when they decided to keep the room open.

He slid the door closed behind the group, and her ears felt the change in pressure. She looked up at the monument of the Steamsworn Fist. It might have been the same size as what sat in Gareth Cave, but it loomed so much larger in the small room. Gladys rubbed her thumb over the Steamsworn Fist on her bracelet, one mirrored in a tattoo on the base of her neck.

"One of my transmitters is hidden here," Archibald said. "Liz knows about it and a few other transmitters in case there is an emergency and we lose access to those in my quarters. It is also why this room remains proofed against spies and curious ears."

George rubbed his chin. "So you were not concerned the transmitter would have been intercepted, were you? Your concern lies in those who might overhear you in this place."

Archibald nodded. "Many know my bias toward Gladys. With the unrest inside our walls, I would not risk her being taken."

George glanced between the Speaker and the Princess. "Was she not safer in Midstream?"

"I'm right here," Gladys said. "It's not like I would have come if I didn't want to."

She didn't miss the smile that came and went from Lady Grey's expression.

"There is more to the situation than that," Archibald said. "The warships are deployed. One in Belldorn, one in Fel, and while I was absent, the council fractured."

"In fairness, the council has long been fractured," Liz said. "It simply worked up the spine to act on those old wounds."

"Fair enough." Archibald nodded. "And now you tell me Targrove has more bait boxes? That can summon Tail Swords? We're rushing back into a war that should have been buried decades ago."

"Targrove?" Lady Grey said. "You're telling me Targrove is *alive*?"

Archibald almost scowled. "Yes, Theo's assistant is actually Targrove. At times, that pair is too clever for their own good."

Lady Grey shook her head. "You could have told me with some ceremony."

George clasped his hands together. "The Mordairs would not have left Targrove's weapons buried. That has become painfully obvious at the cost of our friends' lives."

"Yes, but even in battle, those technologies have remained hidden. When Charles showed up with that blasted rotting chunk of Sky Needle, I knew something had gone wrong. Now Lady Katherine deploys Emerald Needles while Targrove establishes a perimeter of Tail Swords? Where does it end?"

"Have Ancora or Cave contacted you today?" Archibald asked.

A small frown crossed George's face. "No. Should they have?"

"They will both be joining the efforts against Mordair."

"Ancora?" Gladys said. "How? I mean, they don't have people to spare after the Fall."

"They have Spider Knights, Princess," Archibald said. "And it is my understanding that the dragonriders of Canopy will be training with some of their mounts."

"Is that wise? With our defenses in Dauschen and Ancora so depleted? We'll have no allies to help us defend Midstream."

"You will have Cave Guardians. I spoke with a contact from Cave. It is my understanding Midstream was one of Drakkar's biggest concerns."

"I always liked him."

Lady Grey crossed her arms. "You leave out details, Archibald."

Everyone focused on her.

"The Cave Guardians will be in Belldorn as well. Cave has a long history with Canopy, and that is a bond we cannot underestimate the value of."

A knock sounded at the door. It was faint through the soundproofing, but obvious in the heavy quiet of the small room.

George reached out and undid the latch, revealing a disheveled Frederick standing in the doorway.

"Apologies for my tardiness." He stepped inside and pulled the door closed.

"Is that … blood?" Gladys asked, looking at Frederick's forearm. A red stain soaked the cuff of his sleeve and smeared across his leather apron.

He blinked at it, rolled the cuff back, and sighed. "Not mine."

"Is it getting worse?" Archibald asked. "Are the workers still safe?"

"The factories are okay. They haven't assaulted anyone who hasn't approached them first, but I don't know how long that will be the case."

Archibald took a long breath.

"You already know the answer," Liz said. "When the next transport returns from Fel, you deploy our forces inside the walls. There are times peacekeepers must keep the peace."

"How long until they arrive?" George asked.

"Five hours. They are supposed to be put on leave and rotated out. We will have to keep some here, which will diminish the forces going to Ballern."

"What other choice do you have?" Gladys asked. "You can't just give up Bollwerk to fight Mordair. Bollwerk is the trade hub for this entire continent."

"And it will remain so," Lady Grey said. "Archibald, let me give the orders. It will shift some of the attention from you, and perhaps I can convince the mob to at least let the firefighters through."

"The fires are still contained to one bonfire and one supply depot," Frederick said. "I suppose that is *some* measure of good news. But we cannot reach them without breaking the lines of protesters."

Gladys looked to Archibald. "That settles it. We're deploying the Tail Swords around Midstream, and you are focusing your attention on Bollwerk. We can keep ourselves safe for a time. So long as no airships come our way again."

"Even then, the docks are well defended," George said. "It will be easier when the new docks are built, but for now, we are safe."

"What is this about Targrove and bait boxes?" Frederick asked.

"He took us to Gareth Cave," Gladys said. "There were several hidden there, and Targrove wants us to deploy them to protect Midstream."

"Is that wise?"

Gladys clenched her fists briefly. "He said they don't work like the new ones. This will cause the Tail Swords to cluster, but they won't attack unless something approaches."

"That's an interesting change from what we've seen with the Fall and the bait boxes in Belldorn." Frederick rubbed his chin. "I suppose the Butcher had some hand in making Targrove's creation more deadly than it was intended."

"You'd have to ask Targrove."

Frederick harrumphed. "Maybe I will."

"What of the production?" Archibald asked.

"Everything is on schedule," Frederick said. "We'll have a dozen

Titan Mechs completed and ready to deploy against Ballern.”

Gladys stood a little straighter. “What? How? When?”

“I believe he answered all three of those questions, Princess,” George said. He turned to Archibald. “Is that something that is known outside of this city?”

“No,” Archibald said. “I’ve told no one. Not a single transmission has gone out, and the workers in the factory are being paid extremely well for their silence.”

Lady Grey nodded. “There are few things that will garner loyalty better than coin.”

George crossed his arms. “Some days, I wish that weren’t true.” He glanced between Liz and Archibald. “You should know Targrove is already moving forward with the bait boxes. By the time we return to Midstream, the perimeter will be well guarded.”

“So be it,” Archibald said. “And you know what aid is coming to Midstream. I will send a small airship if I am able, but as you can see …”

“You have your own problems,” Gladys finished.

“Yes, indeed we do.” Archibald hesitated. “There is something more you may consider, though risk is inherent.”

“Tell me,” Gladys said. “If I can help, I will.”

“With Midstream’s defenses in place, you could travel to Fel once more. There is news from the city that word has spread of your presence there. Your short time made an impression, and it could instill some goodwill for you to speak to those who remain.”

“We will consider it,” George said. “Let us see if our defenses are truly set, and then we will see.”

“Of course.”

When an awkward silence filled the room, Frederick spoke up. “How are the Titan Mechs doing in Midstream? Are they running smoothly?”

“Yes!” Gladys said. “They’ve been invaluable in the repairs. Of course, Targrove is helping maintain them, so I may have a somewhat skewed opinion on how reliable they are."

Frederick grinned. "You couldn't ask for a better tinker."

"No, no, we couldn't."

"If you all would like," George said before pausing. "And if it's safe. We were thinking about visiting The Fish Head."

"I cannot," Archibald said. "I do appreciate the invitation, but matters here need our attention."

George nodded.

"Another time," Lady Grey said. "It was good to meet you both formally."

"You too," Gladys said.

Frederick crossed his arms and tilted his head toward the door. "Well, those two may be too scared to go with you, but I'd be happy to escort you to The Fish Head. A rice bowl sounds great right about now. And maybe a sake?"

George smiled. "Lead the way."

CHAPTER FIFTEEN

J ACOB STOOD ON the cobblestones in front of Charles's old workshop. The grass to either side had grown tall and started to drop seeds across the stone. The building itself could have been straight out of his memories, so unchanged but for minor damage to some of the roofing and gouges where invaders had stalked over it.

He took a deep breath, ducked to the left, leaving the locked door behind, and pushed through the high grass. His fingers still fit in the edges of the gap, and he slid the panel out of the way. A barrel sat just inside, but it moved easily enough with proper leverage.

Light leaked through a few gaps in the walls, but most of the workshop looked the same as the last time he'd seen it. Jacob spun the igniter on a small lantern, and it burst to life, the reflector casting a bright yellow glow all around the room. Two Jumpers weren't thrilled with the sudden change, and Jacob could hear them scampering in the shadows.

He stood at Charles's old bench for a while, basking in memories from a time he had far fewer worries. The surface showed gouges with freshly exposed wood, which Jacob had little doubt had happened when the workshop was raided.

But even those raids had missed what he'd come for. He ran his finger over the smooth surface of the workbench and turned around, walking to a barrel filled with various damaged springs and nails. Jacob pushed it to the side and bent down to the puzzle lock. The catch was easy enough to undo, but moving the stone proved a bit more problematic on his own. It didn't require as much force as before, but it still wasn't light. The stone thumped down, sending up a cloud of dust.

Once he knew the pattern of the dial underneath, it wasn't nearly so challenging. Of course, that was partially because they hadn't fully locked it, so it could be operated by one person far more easily. With the phrases lined up, it was little effort to lift the hatch, since the seal had been broken before.

Jacob clipped the lantern to a pocket on the shoulder of his vest and peered into the dark. His boots scraped the edge as he slid down to the ladder and made his way inside. The old armor still stood there, as if it had been waiting. Jacob had certainly been waiting since he found the entry in one of Charles's journals. A suit of armor like an exoskeleton. A mad creation like a Titan Mech not much larger than a person.

He reached out and undid the buttons on the uniform, cursing himself that he'd missed it when they were all there before. He made it to the bottom button and pulled the jacket open. There were some things, no matter how ready a person thought they were, that could still shake them.

Underneath the jacket was a webwork of metal brackets and braces. The assembly could have been mistaken for a prototype of a Titan Mech. But this was something far different. Jacob slid the sleeves off the exoskeleton and laughed at the structure of the arm. It looked almost exactly like the arm brace he'd used to kill the Butcher. A model for the braces he built for those who'd lost limbs in the Fall.

Charles had never stopped tinkering with that suit of armor. That was something Jacob had come to understand, piecing together what he'd read in the journal and what he'd seen Charles building on occasion. Charles's scribbled words and schematics all linked back to his projects. As much as the old man had given up on war, part of his curiosity couldn't leave his creations behind.

Jacob slid his pack off and sat it on the table below the wall of weapons, glancing at the array of tools on the workbench. He pulled out one of Charles's last notebooks from the Deadlands War and flipped to the rough schematics in the back. Comparing those sketches to what the old tinker had built was a masterclass in craft. The math was simple enough, if you had something to measure with, or measure at all, but Charles had written those notes in the field. And yet, when Charles finally moved on to prototyping that wearable Mech armor, he'd used the exact same measurements.

The rust felt like a violation beneath Jacob's fingers as he checked the length of the brackets and the ratios of the gears. Almost every single one fit into the numbers in that notebook perfectly. The armor, as it was, would never move again. Rust had long done its work. The only way Charles's Mech suit would function would be to rebuild it all. Jacob might be able to reuse some of the braces, but little else.

And once it was assembled, getting it back out of the crawlspace would be a nightmare. That meant he needed to drag the tools up the ladder after breaking down the armor. It was the only way to get everything he needed out of the underground lab. Jacob blew out a breath and scratched his head. He didn't think they'd be in Ancora long enough to try rebuilding Charles's creation entirely, but he certainly wasn't going to leave without trying.

✧　✧　✧

ALICE HAD TOLD him he should have taken a clock, and by the time he hefted the last leg of the Mech suit up and over to the workbench, sweat pouring down his face, he figured she was probably right. He unlocked the front to step outside and check the sun's position, and yelped when he found Alice standing there, fist raised to pound on the door, or possibly his face.

"Do you have any idea how late it is, Jacob?"

He glanced up at the sun, pursed his lips, and nodded. "Yes."

Alice almost growled. "We're going to be late for lunch."

"Okay, okay, but hold on." His words quickened with his excitement. "You have to see this. Do you remember me telling you about the Mech suit?"

"You mean the one you mentioned fifteen times this morning? No, not at all."

Jacob held his fingers up. "Right, well …" he gestured to the interior of the workshop.

Alice sighed and stepped inside, freezing when she saw the layers of braces and springs and brackets laid out across the workbench.

"What are you building?" She stepped closer, her frown deepening. "And why is it rusted so …" She looked up to meet his gaze. "Was this all in the storage room underground?"

Jacob nodded and walked over to the bench, picking up the aged fabric and leather of the armored jacket. "It was underneath it."

"No way. How did we miss that?"

"I just assumed it was a display. You know, like a museum? Where they prop things up on frames or mannequins or place it in a shadow box."

Alice rubbed the back of her neck. "We should have known. Charles wasn't really the type to keep old things around like that, was he?"

Jacob thought about the array of items Charles *had* kept. From the workbench to the weapons to the notebooks, all of them could serve a useful purpose. But armor that had aged far past the point of being useful? He smiled and gave a slow shake of his head.

"You're right, Alice. We should have looked closer. But even if we had, I hadn't read the journal yet. I wouldn't have known what it was."

"I think you could have figured it out."

"Maybe. It's one thing to build a machine from a schematic. It's another thing entirely to figure it out backward."

"Remember how much you loved taking things apart when we were kids? Come on, Jacob."

Memories of his mom flashed through his brain, slack-jawed when she found him with the laundry barrel disassembled, the crank broken down into its component parts. He wasn't sure if she was angrier at that moment, or more surprised when he reassembled it and it still worked. Granted, it didn't work as well, but it still worked.

"That's … that's a fair point." He grinned and stepped closer to the workbench.

"What is it? Like a miniature Mech?"

Jacob nodded enthusiastically. "Yes! That's exactly it. Except you wear it like a bug wears an exoskeleton." He picked up a leg and stood it upright. "Here, grab that other leg."

Alice did, and her hands jerked up when she started to lift. "It's lighter than I would have thought."

"I don't think the entire suit weighs more than a hundred and fifty pounds or so."

"Still not something you'd want to be dragging across a battlefield."

"You would if you were inside it. Now it'll be heavier once we get armor installed, and I think that might be why Charles never finished it." Jacob forced the leg over the hip joint, pulling a curved bracket down to lock them together.

Alice undid a latch on the back of the leg and swung it open. "You can step right into it."

Jacob nodded. "The only drawback is you need operators of specific dimensions, or they won't fit. Not ideal, considering how different everyone is. It wouldn't be practical to build everyone their own Mech."

"No, but you could have two or three standard sizes." Alice frowned at the assembly before her eyes lit up. "Or build them larger and anchor the pilot with inserts!"

Jacob started to dismiss the idea before he really thought about it, and then he focused on the spacious braces where he could anchor almost anything he wanted. It wouldn't be that hard to have a range of inserts. "A brace inside a brace held down by the mass of the pilot. It's … Alice, that could work."

"Good. Now, think about that while we go meet my mom for lunch."

He leaned just a little closer and kissed her. "Thanks, Alice."

She rolled her eyes, but he didn't miss the small smile on her face. "Come on then."

✧　✧　✧

AFTER MAKING SURE the front door was locked again, Jacob followed Alice out into the Lowlands. It still hurt his heart to see so much of the city wiped away, but what was rising in its place kindled a new hope for a future Ancora was never guaranteed.

They took the long hill down from the workshop, passing one of the few surviving structures that had once been a seamstress shop. Jacob didn't know if she'd survived the Fall, but it was obvious no one had been back. The front window was still broken and the mannequins within weathered and worn.

The road north descended into the deepest parts of the Lowlands. Jacob and Alice had both lived there in the past, but there was no trace of his old street now. Even the oversized paving stones had been ripped up and repurposed for some other project, perhaps the wall itself.

Alice put her arm around his waist as they walked farther into the Lowlands, circling the cliff where the bent poles of the old lift had been replaced with polished steel. They could see the new homes in the distance now, only a few blocks from where Alice's house had once stood.

"I miss the Pillies."

"They were fun to roll down the hill."

"That is *not* what I meant, and you know it."

Jacob grinned at Alice. "It's different now. You know … everything's different now."

"It's a clean slate, Jacob. I'm looking forward to seeing what gets built here. With proper airship docks and the train reopening, there's a great deal of potential for Ancora."

"And not just for the Highlands, for a change."

Alice squeezed him a little tighter, causing him to trip and stumble over her shoes, but he didn't complain. Sometimes having her close made everything in the world feel right, even when he knew so much was wrong.

The closer they walked to the new block of construction, the more impressed Jacob was. The long building towered three stories into the air and ran the length of the flattest section of the Lowlands cliff. Heavy timber stood out along the front and sides, forming a pleasant design in the wooden beams that made up the frame. Farther down, he could just make out more foundations for additional buildings.

"It looks like it belongs, doesn't it?" Alice said.

Jacob nodded. "It reminds me of our old house, just a lot bigger."

"I think it's brilliant building apartments here. It's like something you'd see in Bollwerk or Belldorn, but now we have it in Ancora. And before you even ask, I don't count the few giant apartments in the Highlands."

Jacob laughed because that *was* what he'd been thinking. He looked up as they approached the stairwell. "They could build more of these in the Lowlands to make up for the airship docks. In case the city expands, you know?"

"Yes. I was worried when I saw how much land those docks took up.

But … do you really think people will move back to the Lowlands?"

"Your mom did. I don't see why not." He gestured to the new wall around the perimeter. "It's going to be as safe as the Highlands when they're done."

Alice sighed. "I think you're right." She turned and started up the stairs. Jacob followed, admiring the simple railing that had clearly been hammered out by a skilled blacksmith. He was surprised to see it hadn't been cast, but he supposed there was likely a reason for it.

They made their way to the front of the landing and turned right, heading down four doors before Alice lifted a heavy black knocker and let it fall. Footsteps sounded inside before a deadbolt clacked. The door opened in silence, revealing a thin woman with fiery red hair muted only by a handful of gray streaks.

"Alice, Jacob!" She welcomed them both with hugs. "I'm so glad you could come by. I know you're busy with your friends, but sometimes I need to see my family."

"So do we," Alice said. "You about gave me a heart attack with your message."

"I did worry about that, dear. Baddawick assured me he would make things clear, so you didn't worry. I assume that was not the case?"

"No. It wasn't. But look at this place." Alice turned in a half circle, gesturing to the low couch and rough wood of the kitchen table.

Jacob immediately wanted to sand it down and smooth it out, but he also figured that might come off as a bit rude.

Alice's mom led them through the living room. It wasn't a huge space, but Jacob thought it would be plenty for a family of four, and it was downright spacious for one or two people. The kitchen pass-through bore a shelf with far more polish and stain than the table.

Jacob ran his hand over it, impressed with the glass-smooth feel, before he glanced at the table.

"You noticed the table, I see."

Jacob stiffened and gave Alice's mom an awkward smile.

"So subtle," Alice said, jabbing him with her elbow.

"It's not done yet, so it might be a little splintery. Some of the craftsmen will be here tomorrow to work on it."

"It has good bones," Jacob said.

Alice's mom blinked. "Right then. This is the kitchen. The stoves are all connected, which is quite a marvel, one I think Jacob would like. There's a large reservoir built into the cliff side for the gas." She led the way deeper into the apartment, revealing three doors.

"Two bedrooms, if you two would ever like to stay over. Of course, the second isn't furnished yet, but it may be after you come home … from your travels?"

"We'd like that," Alice said.

"And the third room, well, it's small, but it might be my favorite."

Alice slipped inside, and Jacob followed. There was a faint scent of smoke, and when Jacob looked to the left, he knew why. Dozens of books lined the wall, some showing faint burn marks.

"We rescued what we could from the wreckage. Ambrose and the Spider Knights collected quite a few from the rubble. Almost all the apartments here have more books than most of us will read in a lifetime. It was … it's a nice reminder of what we lost."

Jacob thought that was a rather odd way to put it, but he was fairly sure he understood. Just because the Lowlands wouldn't be the same again didn't mean the district's past wasn't worth remembering. And what few things had survived were worth treasuring.

Alice reached out and hugged her mom again. "You have to come to Belldorn sometime. The Crown Library is like nothing you've ever seen."

"I'd like that. Maybe when this is all over, we can take a trip together."

"Yes, let's plan on it. That would be lovely."

Alice's mom clapped her hands together. "Well, then, are you ready for lunch? The new restaurant is just downstairs."

Jacob blinked. "You have a restaurant? In your building?"

"Yes, we do."

"I could get used to an apartment like this."

Alice rolled her eyes and led the way back to the door.

✧   ✧   ✧

THEY PUSHED THROUGH the two-way doors and found a crowded restaurant beyond. Jacob was still trying to take it all in—the open flames on the grill and stools set up before it—when the cook shouted at them to find a seat wherever they'd like.

"What's that smell?" Jacob asked.

Alice closed her eyes and inhaled. "Oh, I think it's Sea Claw!"

The entire scene fell into place in Jacob's mind when she said that. The fishing nets tacked to the wall for décor, the reeds lashed together that formed the low tables, and the rough iron stools with peculiarly comfortable seats.

"You're from Cave," he blurted out when the chef approached.

The man gave Jacob a slow blink. "I was told Ancorans were observant. What gave me away? The cloak? Or perhaps the seal of the Cave Guardians on the wall behind you?"

Jacob gave the chef an awkward grin and glanced at the wall, finding the crossed spears and bonded hands that echoed the Steamsworn Fist.

"You'll have to forgive him," Alice said. "I think he was just excited about the prospect of getting some properly prepared Sea Claw."

"Oh!" the chef said, his face brightening. "Have you been to Cave, then? One of the refugees?"

"She's my daughter," Alice's mom said.

The chef tilted his head to the side. "My friend. Just because I say Ancorans are observant does not mean I am *not* observant. Even without your hair, she is your duplicate." He didn't so much as give them a chance to stop laughing before turning back to Jacob. "Now, tell me where you found this Sea Claw."

"Lakkan made it. Down by the docks."

The chef straightened and pursed his lips. "Well, I will not prepare you anything in a skillet then. Lakkan has no rival for that. But I *will* give you the best grilled Sea Claw you'll find anywhere between here and Cave."

"Do you know Drakkar?" Alice asked.

"I know several Drakkars, young one. It is a common name in the depths of Cave."

"His brother is one of the Nameless," Alice said. "He's a Cave Guardian."

The chef laughed under his breath. "Yes, I know *that* Drakkar." His movements slowed, and he studied Jacob and Alice. "You are the Ancorans. Friends of Atlier?"

"Is that a good thing or a bad thing?" Jacob asked.

The chef grinned and gestured to the full restaurant. "I have come to know many Ancorans these past weeks. And if you all enjoy Sea Claw as much as our treasured refugees, it is a good thing indeed."

They were light words, but Jacob still remembered what Drakkar had thought of Charles when he'd first joined their group. He hadn't been there to make friends. He had been there to keep an eye on a man they thought to be a monster after the Deadlands War.

The chef plunged his hands into a cooler filled with ice and water, pulling up Sea Claws and impaling them in two quick motions before dredging them through spices and dropping them on the fire. "If you see that Cave Guardian, tell him you met Branddur. I would like to see his face when you tell him that. We spent much time together as youths."

"He's a good friend," Alice said.

"Loyal to a fault, I used to say, until he abandoned the Nameless and became Drakkar once more. I don't think it was until that point I realized how many layers there were to my old friend."

A customer down the bar asked for another drink, and Branddur spun away from the fire, a graceful move that betrayed the training he must have had with the Cave Guardians. Drakkar was the only other person Jacob had seen move with that kind of grace and precision. Outside of the dancers in plays at Festival, at least.

"What brought him here?" Alice asked once Branddur was well out of earshot.

"His food stall burned down in Cave not long after the refugees started arriving," Alice's mom said. "It … things got out of hand when he accused a group of Ancorans of doing it."

"How did he go from accusing Ancorans of burning his booth down to opening a restaurant in *Ancora*?"

Alice's mom laughed. "Some of us helped him pay to rebuild. Or at least we donated coin to help him. Whatever he chose to do with the coin was up to him. The Temple of the Cave Guardians got wind of what we were doing. I think … I think it was a turning point in our relationship with Cave. I'd never heard that kind of honesty from them."

Jacob thought about how blunt Drakkar could be at times. "I've heard plenty of honesty from Drakkar. I could use less honesty, if I'm being honest."

"Or repetition," Alice whispered.

Jacob scowled at her before breaking into a grin.

Alice's mom shook her head at both of them. "So, Branddur came with us."

"I did at that," he said as he returned to the fire. "I was coming here as an escort. Alana asked a few of us to join the caravan, and I didn't have much else to do. I didn't expect to find a new home so quickly, but the pale stone and brightness are so different from Cave. I rather like the natural light." Branddur raised his voice. "And it doesn't hurt that Ancorans are terrible at cooking Sea Claw."

Half the room held up their glasses and shouted, "Fire!"

Branddur grinned at the tables and went back to his flames. "You can tell a few of them have been in before." He pulled the skewers off the fire and started dropping them onto plates, sending a few out to the tables, and throwing the last on the bar in front of the trio. "Soft shells. No need to peel them or crack them." He hurried back out to the restaurant floor as fast as he'd delivered their plates.

Each plate had a small ramekin of dark sauce, which Jacob eyed with some suspicion. "The last time I had a sauce that dark, I thought my face was going to melt."

"No spice!" Branddur called from the tables behind them. "Well, lots of spice, but little heat."

"Oh, just eat it, Jacob," Alice said, casting him a smile that gave him no confidence at all.

He braced himself and took a small bite with the sauce. It wasn't hot. Instead, it was salty, almost briny, with a rich depth like the soup at The Fish Head. And then the buttery flavor of the Sea Claw followed it, all brought together by the smoke and char of the open flame.

"Wow." Alice stopped and stared at the charred piece of Sea Claw. "The spices are amazing."

"I thought you might enjoy Branddur's cooking better than some old jerky before you meet with Parliament tonight," Alice's mom said.

"You're right, but it doesn't matter what we're eating as long as you're here, too."

Right behind Jacob, Branddur clapped his hands together with two quick smacks, almost sending Jacob's skewer into the air. "You are adorable. All adorable. You told me of your daughter, but you did not *tell* me of your daughter."

Alice's mom smiled at the chef. "I did tell you I thought you'd like her."

Branddur walked away with a flourish. "Fair, fair. That you did."

They finished their meal, talking about the days they'd lost and the promise of the days to come. But nothing quite settled Jacob's nerves. It was time to visit Parliament, and he hadn't been inside the Castle since he slew the Butcher. As much hope as he had for the Lowlands, darkness still lived in the back of his thoughts.

CHAPTER SIXTEEN

Afternoon came as Jacob and Alice walked through the gates to the Highlands. They stopped to watch one of the Mech arms working on the wall. The last gap was nearly closed now, and Jacob didn't think it would take the rest of the day to finish.

"It's getting late," Alice said. "We better get to the Castle."

Jacob took a deep breath. "I'd rather be back in the workshop."

"Why doesn't that surprise me at all?"

He smiled and led the way into the Highlands. Instead of taking the usual path by the hospital and candy shop, they turned to the right, cutting up the street that ran right past the Wildhorse. Even with the time they'd spent there, the district felt unfamiliar to him.

They had gone nearly three blocks before he recognized the inn Alice had stayed at after the Fall, and another small bar Charles had once taken him to. He paused and studied the street, laughing to himself.

"What is it?"

He glanced at Alice. "I was just remembering an old lady who called me a Steamborn. Like it was the worst insult she could possibly spit at me short of, well, spitting at me."

"I'm sure even people like that have changed now," Alice said. "Most of them, at least. I suppose some are so stuck in their ways they'll always be nasty."

Jacob gave her a tight smile and eyed a clockmaker's shop as they passed. An older woman sat behind a glass counter, enough lenses strapped to her goggles that she could have been mistaken for a tinker. The store beside her had once catered to the elite of Ancora, carrying rare foods and spices from all across the world.

"I'm surprised that store closed."

Alice glanced at it and shrugged. "Maybe they should have catered to a customer base that wouldn't get exiled for betraying the city?"

"Ouch."

They turned down the next street, a more modest stretch of the Highlands filled with more essential stores, like the local grocer and what had become the main butcher shop to all of Ancora. Across the street, a bell chimed as someone walked out of a candlemaker's shop.

Jacob froze in his tracks as the young man looked in his bag and nodded before starting off down the street. "Reggie!"

His steps slowed, and he looked around. Alice called out his name too, and he locked onto the pair behind him. "Jacob? Alice? What are … how did …" Reggie's confused half-question broke down into a wide smile as he sprinted at the pair and slammed into them both, pulling them in tight enough Jacob thought his ribs might bruise.

"What are you doing here?" he asked as he stepped back and studied the pair, finally getting a complete sentence out.

"It's so good to see you, Reggie!" Alice glanced at the candlemaker's shop. "Is Bobby with you?"

Reggie shook his head. "No, no. He's been helping with the wall; you know how it is. We both volunteered to train with the Spider Knights, and well, that got us volunteered for other things." He scratched his head and laughed.

"Have you been here the whole time?" Alice asked.

Reggie nodded. "We thought about going to Cave. Still might when everything's done. We've met several people from Cave now, and I have to say they're a lot more respectful than some of the Highlanders."

"They really are."

"But what are you two doing here? Last I heard, you were off in Belldorn."

"Who let that slip?" Jacob asked. "Baddawick been talking again?"

Reggie let out a low laugh. "Maybe a little. Nothing that seemed all that sensitive, though. The man knows how to keep a secret." He looked down at his watch and cursed. "I have to get these candles over to the Castle. They're having some special session, and apparently no one thought to check the candle supply for the toilets."

Jacob couldn't stop the curling of his nose at that thought.

"Exactly," Reggie's face scrunched up.

"We'll walk with you," Alice said before leaning in conspiratorially. "We have to speak at that session."

"Wow. I don't envy you. That's a big group to be talking in front of."

"Umm …" Jacob started. "How big?"

JACOB WASN'T ENTIRELY sure where he'd expected the session of Parliament to be held, but he certainly hadn't expected it to be in the throne room where he'd killed the Butcher. Gone were the golden throne and the dais it had stood upon. In their place was an enormous circular table.

That would have been intimidating enough as it was, but around the table sat a ring of slightly raised chairs. Nothing so pompous as an actual throne, and Jacob thought it was just to give those seated behind the table a clear view of what was happening around it.

Conversation stopped when Jacob, Alice, and Reggie stepped into the room.

Reggie gave them all an awkward smile and raised his bag of candles. "Right, if you need candles, they're by the door. Right here." He sat them down and patted the bag.

"Don't go," Jacob said, and Reggie paused.

"Why in all Ancora would I *not* go?"

"Because if they talk about the Fall, they need to hear from more people than just us," Alice said, gesturing for Reggie to stay.

Alice's reasoning made far more sense than the answer Jacob almost blurted out, which would have essentially been *because numbers.*

Jacob's dad stood from his seat beside Jacob's mom and gestured to a line of empty chairs along the back of the room. Everyone would be able to see them there except for the representative immediately in front of them, but Jacob assumed that seat would simply turn around.

He recognized a few faces from the night before. Baddawick, despite his protests that he'd never wanted to dabble in politics, sat beside a captain of the Castle guards. Opposite them was a Spider Knight, identified by his armor, but someone Jacob didn't recognize immediately.

He and Alice took their seats. Reggie glanced between their audience and the chairs and sat down with a thump. Jacob wasn't surprised to see a good number of Highlands residents at the table. The old Parliament might have come and gone, but the Highlanders would be working toward whatever benefits they needed to maintain their standard of living. Considering how many Lowlanders were there, Jacob imagined that wouldn't be nearly as simple as it used to be.

Heavy bootsteps crashed down the hall, and Jacob almost choked out a laugh when Samuel skidded to a stop just inside the door. He glanced at the table, nodded to the other Spider Knight, and then casually walked back to the row of seats to sit beside Alice.

Baddawick stood, commanding the attention of everyone in the room. "I call this special session of Parliament commenced. We are here to bear witness to the testimony of one Jacob Arthur Anders, Alice Morrow, Samuel Payne, and ... Reggie. What is your last name, son?"

"I ... I brought the candlesticks," Reggie said with a smile caught somewhere between a hysterical laugh and a scream of terror.

"Yes, well. Welcome, Reggie Candlestick."

A few muffled laughs went up around the table.

Baddawick turned back to the round table. "The Fall was not the end of the conflict with Fel. I believe most of us at this table would agree with that."

A few nods and short agreements were the only response.

"The taking of Fel was also not the end of Mordair and his threat. Jacob, Alice, and Samuel have all spent time in Bollwerk and Belldorn. They've witnessed these events with their own eyes. I know there is great skepticism in the reports from Archibald, but here we have the young man sentenced to have his hands removed by the Butcher."

"The Butcher's dead," someone said, interrupting Baddawick.

Baddawick shifted his gaze slowly to the man who'd spoken out of turn. "His legacy is not. If you wish to project an air of incompetence, one fit for the previous Parliament, by all means, continue. Otherwise, keep silent, and we will discuss the testimony of our allies while they are not *in the room*."

By the time Baddawick finished talking, the light-haired man was no longer meeting his gaze, instead focusing intently on the wood grain of the table.

Baddawick stared at the man a moment more before turning to Jacob and the others. "Apologies, friends. There are some members of this Parliament who have not risked their lives or gambled their security in the name of protecting their city. What I would like to hear from you, as we all witnessed parts of the Fall, is what has happened outside these walls."

When Baddawick paused, Alice interjected. "Loads. Loads has happened. We can't possibly tell you everything we've seen."

"As interesting as that would be, that is not what we need to hear,

Alice. We need to understand if the things Archibald has told us contain enough truth that we should act. For instance, he tells us Bollwerk's warships have left their patrol around the desert city."

"They have," Alice said. "We saw one in Fel and another in Belldorn. They fought alongside Lady Katherine's Brigs. A two-section fighter armed with flak cannons."

Jacob was fairly sure everyone had stopped listening the moment Alice confirmed the warships had indeed left Bollwerk. It was uncharacteristic of Archibald to send the strongest defenses of his city away, and judging by the shock on everyone's faces, they already knew that. It had likely triggered their doubt in the first place, and Alice had changed that in two words.

"I saw it, too," Samuel said. "Saw one of those warships tear through Ballern's line above Belldorn." He gestured to the room at large. "If this is all to debate Archibald's benevolence, understand this. If he wished, he could level the Highlands in a day. Rubble and ash like the Fall a dozen times over. Archibald may be an ambitious bastard, but he isn't your enemy in this fight."

"What of his spies?" Baddawick asked. "The one called Skysworn Mary and her pirate guild?"

Jacob tried to choke back his laugh, but it escaped. He put his hand over his mouth and tried to hide it with a cough.

Baddawick raised an eyebrow.

"Sorry. It's just ... Mary would quite literally knock your teeth in if you called her Archibald's spy. Their partnership is ... well, tenuous on the best days. And Smith? The only problem people have with Smith is the fact he's a Biomech." Jacob didn't give anyone a chance to respond to that before he lifted his pant leg and looked Baddawick in the eye. "And he's not the only one."

"You listen to the words of a Biomech!" A woman snarled. "Unbelievable."

Jacob didn't look at the woman who spoke. His eyes were all for Baddawick, and the knowing smirk that flashed across the old man's lips.

"Why don't you tell us the story of that leg?" Baddawick asked. "Some of the people in this room have known you since you were a child. They would surely know better than anyone if you'd slipped into the madness."

Baddawick's plan clicked into place before Jacob's eyes. There was still hatred for Biomechs in Ancora. He planned to sway Parliament's opinions on more than Archibald's alliance. He was going to use Jacob as leverage to gain acceptance for Biomechs inside the city walls. Whatever his intention for *that* was, it would be far easier than trying to hide his leg all the time. Of course, he probably didn't need to worry about that since he'd shown it to the entire room.

Jacob bit his lip and leaned back in his chair. "It started in the skeleton, where I met a Tree Killer who wasn't too fond of trespassers." It wasn't a story he'd told very often, and it had hurt his chest when he saw how upset his mom had got when Alice had interjected far more details about the capping of his leg than he'd remembered. Part of him was quite happy he didn't remember that.

"And you're still of sound mind?" Baddawick said. "And even Smith is? How is that?"

"It's the metals," Jacob said. "Some metals will poison your blood. Lead to madness. But others are harmless. It's what caused the berserkers."

Some of the members of Parliament had blank faces as Jacob explained that to them, but he continued.

"Other metals can be in your body for decades and never hurt you. It's just unfortunate so many had to suffer before we learned that."

Alice leaned forward when Jacob finished. "Did you know Targrove studied Biomechanics in Belldorn? Does it not at least make you curious how two of the largest known cities could be so accepting of Biomechs while Ancora sits back in its mountains in fear?" Her words grew harsh. "There are things I learned in this city, like kindness and love and how to defend my friends, but I learned awful things too. How to judge, how to fear, how to hate anyone who was different from me. My hair marked me as other, and growing up, I heard every insult you could imagine. I learned to ignore most of it without fighting, but it takes a toll. Some days I had to either remember to be kind … or accept that I may not be who I thought I was."

"I knew Jacob before the Fall," Reggie said, raising his voice. "Seemed like a nice kid. Damn good at Cork, I can tell you that."

"Language," Baddawick whispered. "This is a session of Parliament, after all."

"Sorry, sir. But I knew Jacob. And I met him again after the Fall, after he got his leg. Did he change? Yeah, sure. But did he act like a berserker? No. He acted like a kid who'd seen too much. And you've all heard what they've been through out there. That'd change any of us. The Fall changed *all* of us. I was just happy to find out some of my friends were still alive."

Alice gave Reggie a sad smile. "Us too, Reggie."

Someone started to speak, but Baddawick cut them off with a glare. He turned back to Alice. "Can you tell us of Belldorn and what you found in their library? Many at this table believe Archibald's proclamations on the topic to be dubious, at best."

She grimaced and nodded. "There was a lot. You have to remember they have manuscripts and books dating back centuries. I've never seen anything like it. You could fit twenty of the Castle's libraries inside the Crown Library." Alice paused. "Probably more. I can't overstate how big it is.

"They have books from Ballern there, from before the arrival of the Children of the Dark Fire. They detail the assassination that spurred the Deadlands War. Things didn't happen the way we thought they did."

"You can't trust something just because it was in a *book*," a middle-aged woman said. "You don't know what their agenda was when they wrote that ... *history*."

Baddawick clearly favored the woman, because she wasn't met with any glare or interruption at all. Jacob tried not to laugh at that, as he figured the woman would be rather offended.

Alice sat up straighter. "It was published by the monarchy's press. Our friend, Furi, tells me everything that went through that house was vetted. And yes, that means some things may have been glossed over, but the *year* of her death didn't match up with our own records. History was changed in Ballern after that to spur another assassination. One that would start the Deadlands War."

"What does any of this have to do with Fel and Mordair?"

"Don't you see? An alliance between the Children of the Dark Fire and Mordair is a perfect storm. If they rule Ballern together, their strength increases by untold factors. The power of Fel's fleets and the cunning of a religion that has rewritten centuries of history. No one will be safe."

"Ballern's government is capable enough," Jacob's mom said. "They can prevent that kind of takeover."

Alice blinked at her.

Jacob worried at first, but then he realized his mom already knew the Queen of Ballern had been slain.

Alice looked down, covering a smile behind her hand as she composed herself. Jacob thought she must have had the same realization. Alice leaned forward, taking on a slow cadence to her words.

"The Queen of Ballern was in league with the Skyborn resistance. She could have stood up to him. She would have. But Mordair had already assassinated the Queen of Ballern. We were in the palace when it happened. The city is his now."

The table erupted in protests and accusations. Those who had believed Archibald shouted as much. At first, the objectors accused the others of being in league with Archibald, and then Mordair, and the raised voices showed no sign of calming.

"If this is the kinder, gentler version of Parliament, I'm glad I didn't see the old one much," Jacob muttered.

"The old one tried to *kill* you," Samuel hissed.

Jacob froze before a quiet laugh escaped his lips. He reached out and took Alice's hand, watching the chaos unfold. He grinned at Reggie, who now pressed himself against the back of his chair. Samuel rubbed his forehead and cursed.

Baddawick stepped closer, whispering so only they could hear him above the shouts of disbelief echoing in that room. "Well done, Alice."

CHAPTER SEVENTEEN

THE STABLES WERE empty when Samuel walked in. Well, empty of Spider Knights, at least, as the stalls still held dozens of mounts, all happily chewing away at their Sweet-Flies or resting. Samuel made his way to the far end where Bessie would normally be staying, and when he found those wide black eyes and furry head staring at him, he couldn't help but smile. Reuniting with the Jumper was a far more appealing scenario than listening to members of Parliament shouting at each other.

Samuel slid the bolt open and stepped inside, not making it three steps before the spider head-butted him into the wall. She smacked him a few times with her pedipalps before he managed to get his hands up and start scratching her above the eyes.

"It's good to see you, girl. Sorry I've been away so long. But I have good news. We're going on a trip! Of course, we're going to go fight people, so that's maybe less-good news. But a trip!"

He stayed there for a while with the spider until she went back to her trough of Sweet-Flies. Samuel took that time to check her wounds. She wasn't bandaged anymore, and the only signs she'd ever been injured were a few pale streaks near some of her joints.

Relief flowed over him before he remembered what else he was there to do. Then the nerves came back in force.

Samuel paced back and forth outside the stables. He wasn't looking forward to convincing the Spider Knights to lend him their mounts, along with as many volunteers as they could spare, and he gestured wildly to himself in silence, trying to find the right words.

"Should we tell him we're here?"

Samuel froze when he heard that deep voice. He turned to the stable closest to the entrance, where two cloaked forms waited. "Drakkar! Rin! What are you doing here?" He stepped closer and exchanged grips with both of them in turn.

"We came to deliver news," Drakkar said. "Cave will be joining Canopy in the war effort, as well as sending a contingent of Guardians to Midstream and Ancora. Our allies will not be forgotten in this conflict."

"That's good," Samuel said, nodding quickly. "I can use that to help convince the captain to let more of the Spider Knights come to Ballern."

"Umm, Samuel?" Rin said.

"No, no, I think it will work. Think about it. If the Cave Guardians are here—some of the best fighters around, not to mention lots of Ancorans have gotten to know Cave better than ever—then some Spider Knights could join us in Ballern."

Someone cleared their throat behind Samuel, and he nearly jumped through the roof, instinct sending his hand looking for a halberd that he didn't have. He was met by the cool, clear gaze of someone he hadn't expected to see in Ancora. "Nora?"

"At ease, Samuel. What is this talk about Ballern and the Knights?"

As she spoke, Spider Knights started filtering in from the other end of the stables, their mounts effortlessly strolling across the stone, appearing unburdened by the armor they wore.

"You're a captain now? When? How?" He cringed as he realized some of those questions might be offensive.

"Is that how you address your officers, Samuel?" Nora asked.

He shook his head and stood up straighter. "We're going to Ballern, Captain."

"My father told you a long time ago to call him Lewis when you weren't serving in the Spider Knights."

"I'll always serve the Knights, Captain. Are you not embedded in Dauschen anymore?"

"Obviously. Call me Nora. I don't like formalities, Samuel." She gave him a small wink when he didn't respond, utterly confused at *what*, exactly, he should call her. "Tell us about Ballern, then, Spider Knight."

Samuel was so distracted by the fact one of Archibald's spies from Dauschen was back in Ancora, and now the captain of the Spider Knights, that he forgot all about how nervous he was. Instead, everything he needed to say came pouring out effortlessly as the other Knights got their mounts settled in the stables.

"The fight against Mordair has moved to Ballern. Word is he's been installed as Steward there, and I don't think we need to imagine what will happen next. Belldorn might have turned away Ballern's attack, but they won't withstand the combined force of two fleets. No one will. And they'll come for Ancora in the end. Maybe it will be months, or maybe we'll be their first target, but Mordair has to be stopped."

Nora listened, tilting her head slightly at various points in Samuel's story. "And what is it you want from us, exactly?"

Samuel gestured to Rin, who stepped forward. "This is Rin, dragonrider of Canopy, and a friend I trust. He rides with us to Ballern, to face Mordair and the Children of the Dark Fire."

Nora frowned. "That strange cult everyone has been talking about? The same that attacked our train station?"

"They attacked Ancora?" Samuel asked, his heart hammering in his chest.

"Tried. Fisherfolk from Fel subdued one of them."

"So you know they're real, and a threat." Samuel paused. "Parliament gave me the impression they didn't believe that."

"Oh yes. He's locked in the Castle prison. Only a fool would believe the Children of the Dark Fire to be a fable at this point." Nora turned to Drakkar. "And you, Cave Guardian. Has Cave grown so soft on Ancora they send their own Guardians to our gates?"

Drakkar let a slow smile etch across his lips. "Cave sends protection to its allies, so that those allies may send reinforcements to the front. Our Cave Guardians will be here, and Midstream, and even Bollwerk will have our spears. Cave marches to Ancora as we speak, and it will not be long before they will help guard your walls."

Nora inclined her head and then turned her focus to Rin. "And what of the dragonriders? Do you fly to face Ballern on your goodwill alone?"

"No, Captain. I am of the Skyborn of Ballern, as many of those from Canopy are. We fight for our families who remain and our friends who cannot escape."

Nora glanced at the Spider Knights all around them in those stables. Samuel followed her gaze, catching nods and shakes of heads as though she were taking a poll at that very moment. She looked again at Rin.

"Mordair cost me my father and my brother." She didn't sound angry or distraught, and the simple delivery chilled Samuel. "I'll see him torn down and hung from his own walls for that. You have my blades, Dragonrider, and those of my Knights who wish to join you."

The nearest Spider Knight slammed the butt of his halberd against the stone. "Aye!"

Half a dozen more did the same, the sudden crash of metal on stone riling up their mounts in the stables. More than one climbed up their gates to peer at the commotion of their riders.

But that wasn't all Samuel needed. He waited for things to quiet before he asked Nora one more thing. "The fight won't just be in the city. We need spiders and training for Canopy. They've offered to train you to ride Dragonwings in exchange."

One of the men who had shaken his head no had a sudden change of heart. "Take me. I'll fight with you."

Nora smiled at him before turning back to Samuel. "There are still many mounts without regular riders. We have the spiders for your request, but no way to transport them to Canopy, much less Ballern."

Samuel rubbed his hands together. "Leave that part to us."

CHAPTER EIGHTEEN

JACOB AND ALICE hunched over the workbench in Charles's old lab. Another gear split when he tried to pry it off the elbow joint. Jacob sighed and flopped onto his stool.

"This won't work. Half the gears that aren't broken are stripped, and the ones that are in good shape are seized."

Alice sat her ratchet down and rubbed her palms into her eyes. "I thought Samuel was going to be here by now. I'm not dragging this thing over to the Skysworn on our own."

"Maybe Smith can carry it," Jacob said with a laugh.

"Oh, I'm sure he'd love that. Could you carry this pile of rust to the other side of the city?"

He chuckled and turned the page on another of Charles's workbooks. It wasn't a journal, not really. This one didn't have any of the personal thoughts Charles had included in his journals. This was all about materials and ratios, and what could hold up to the pressure applied by various boilers.

Jacob made it through three pages detailing the tolerances of copper before he finally put his head down and groaned. "I need to rebuild this entire thing, Alice. Maybe we can save a handful of braces. Don't worry about stripping the gears. We need to break it down further if we're going to drag it over to the Skysworn." He gestured to a section she had been working on. "You got the rust off. It looks practically new."

"Except for the pitting, sure," Alice said, skepticism plain in her voice.

"It should still be good enough for a prototype. Let's just—"

A horn turned the air to thunder, startling Jacob and bringing him to silence. The moment it faded, it came again, a claxon that could rival a ruptured boiler.

"What is that?" Jacob asked.

"I'm pretty sure that's the new warning system Baddawick was talking about."

Jacob scratched his temple. "When was Baddawick talking about a new warning system?"

Alice leveled her gaze at him. "Honestly. How do you pretend to be listening so well when you're clearly not? Come on."

The moment they stepped outside, Jacob knew something was wrong. Spider Knights raced through the gates of the Highlands, turning north as they rushed toward the wall.

But as the claxon quieted, another sound took its place, a rhythmic hammering like that of an army marching. One of the Spider Knights didn't turn with the rest of his comrades. Instead, he charged across the open field that had once been a congested area of the Lowlands.

Samuel's armor glinted in the afternoon sun, radiant and impossible to miss, the perfect complement to Bessie's new armor plating. How that spider still managed to move in silence boggled Jacob's mind.

"What is it?" Alice shouted as Samuel grew near.

"Invaders. Red Death on the northern slopes."

"What about the station?" Jacob asked, not understanding why the Spider Knights were rushing to the wall instead of the train station.

Samuel's words came out in a rapid tumble. "You won't believe it. You just won't believe it, Jacob. Come on. You have to see this."

"I don't have my air cannon!"

"Neither do I," Alice said, but it didn't stop her from taking Samuel's hand and swinging up onto Bessie's back.

Jacob glanced between Alice and Samuel, getting the distinct impression this was a terrible idea he wasn't going to escape. He sighed and took Alice's hand, bumping Bessie's leg in the process. The spider helpfully pushed him up, almost flinging him off the other side.

"Hold tight!" Samuel's shout was all the warning they had before Bessie took off, tearing down the slope to the intersection below. Jacob yelped and latched on to Alice's waist as Bessie made a violent turn.

"What if she jumps?" Jacob asked, the idea somewhat terrifying in their unsecured state.

"She won't. Probably." Samuel shrugged, which was about the least reassuring thing he could have done.

They surged past the new apartments and restaurant on their way to the north wall, flying over construction supplies and rubble alike before the wall loomed over them.

Bessie started bouncing up and down mid-stride, and Jacob cursed under his breath, reaching around Alice to lock his hands on Samuel's saddle. Alice did the same, apparently noticing the same movement a second before Bessie left the ground.

Alice's scream was something to behold, and Jacob took more than a little satisfaction as Samuel winced away from it.

"Sorry!" Samuel yelled back as they slammed into the wall.

Jacob waited for the tug on his fingers as they fell backward, but he should have known Bessie wouldn't do that to them. Instead, the spider stuck her butt out, propping her riders up as she scampered higher and crested the wall next to a trio of Spider Knights.

"Red Death to the north," a Knight shouted. "Nora ordered us to stand down."

Jacob's worst fears had run away with his thoughts, imagining a tide of Red Death like the Fall. The swarm in the mountains was nothing so dire, but without the permanent defenses mounted along the top of the wall, that many Red Death could pose a serious danger to anyone in their path.

Spider Knights clustered along the walls, but they didn't move forward. They held at Nora's command where she stood on the road below. And standing beside the captain of the Spider Knights were two cloaked figures, one who gave signals to something farther down the mountainside.

A resonating chant echoed back along the mountains, and a line of Cave Guardians stepped out of the train station as if they meant to leap down the valley. Instead, they raised spears, shouted in one voice, and lowered their weapons.

"Are the Spider Knights just going to watch this happen?" Alice asked. "There's a Red Death for every one of them."

Dust and dirt swirled around the charging Red Death as they scampered up the mountainside. The Cave Guardians's chant rose and traveled down the walls as more of them stepped forward, just outside the pale stone of the Lowlands wall.

"They were on the path to the station?" Jacob asked.

Samuel nodded. "Drakkar insisted the Knights stand down so they could see how the Cave Guardians operate. I understand why. Their formations aren't like ours, and we need to understand them better to work side by side."

The ground shook with the stampede of Red Death. There wasn't any going back now. There were only the Spider Knights to clean up the mess if Drakkar had miscalculated. The thought sent a chill down Jacob's spine, and he wanted to look away. Wanted to stop the memories from flashing behind his eyes.

Instead, he slid off Bessie's back and stepped to the edge of the wall. Alice joined him, wrapping her fingers in his as the pulsating line of Red

Death crashed into the waiting Cave Guardians.

Their cadence changed. A low chant shifted into something calmer, like a series of directions laid out for every person to follow, and each word brought another strike from the Cave Guardians. They met the forwardmost Red Death with a diagonal sweep of their spears, the flat tips cutting into carapaces like so much paper.

When the beetles reeled back, losing limbs and wings and eyes in that first strike, the Cave Guardians lunged as one, bringing their spears down and forward in a single graceful movement.

Chitinous legs thrust into the air before curling around the dying bodies of the beetles. Red Death scrambled over their fallen, but the chant of the Cave Guardians continued, each of them coiling and striking like the traps Jacob had built for Midstream.

Twice more, the call repeated; even those Guardians not engaged with the beetles mimicked the movement of the others. A deadly dance that brought the stampede to an end in short order. What Red Death remained scampered away, vanishing into the valleys until they were mere dots on the distant mountainsides.

Nora held her fist out to Drakkar. The Cave Guardian wrapped his hand around it.

"Show off," Samuel muttered.

Jacob squeezed Alice's fingers and laughed. Ancora was in good hands.

CHAPTER NINETEEN

F URI'S ANNOYANCE WITH Jakon turned to awe when she realized what was actually happening. He'd been insisting she help him set up his booth for the day in the market, which sounded like a fantastic waste of time. Jakon fixed a signature broth that was in high demand by the locals, but something else happened when the first customer came by.

They didn't just hand over coin. Furi would have missed it if she wasn't glaring at Jakon for making money in the market instead of plotting with Kura. A tiny slip of parchment folded no bigger than a coin. Jakon slipped it into his apron and thanked the patron.

Furi watched him go, and before she could so much as ask what that was all about, the same thing happened again. Except this time, it was a child who delivered the paper. It was in the bottom of the soup bowl she'd brought. Jakon thanked her, and she danced away with a precariously sloshing soup, as happy as could be.

"What is happening?" Furi whispered.

"How do you think I always know what's going on in this city, Furi? It's not magic."

"And it's clearly not your charming demeanor."

Jakon scowled at her before laughing. He spoke low, low enough it was unlikely he'd be overheard. "This is the best way to find out about jobs and other goings on that may be best to avoid. When I'm not here for a while, I get more visitors than usual. I promise, once the lunch crowd has thinned, we can pack up and get back to the Bones."

Furi sighed. There were certainly less entertaining places to be stuck while she was waiting on Jakon. She settled in soon enough, helping serve some customers and taking coin from others. A few even came with coded notes after Jakon gave his customers a subtle nod as if to approve her as a contact.

In two hours' time, Furi had noticed at least seven different people passing paper to Jakon. The coding was brilliant, she thought. If someone found a note and didn't know how to read it, they might think a child had sketched out a random series of pictures.

"You're going to tell me how this works," Furi said, frowning at a sun with a little hat and several squiggly lines that made no sense to her eyes. There was exactly one word in Mokuskrit, and the rest looked like nonsense.

"I am, am I?" Jakon said with a smile as he packed up his pot and burner. The entire assembly broke down into three crates. The heaviest was the gas tank, but that crate had wheels. He locked the other two on top and patted the handle. "Ready?"

"As if you need to ask." Furi led the way through the crowd, both making sure people cleared a path and that those same people didn't get hit by Jakon's trundler.

The crowds thinned at the outskirts of the market. She turned down an empty alley that would take them closer to the dock lifts without walking down any of the main streets of Ballern.

"Some days, I think you may be more paranoid than I am," Jakon said.

"Is that such a bad thing?"

Jakon harrumphed. "In this day and age? Not in the least. It's quite a good trait in a pirate and smuggler. If you are ever in need of some extra coin, I may know some captains looking for help."

"Are you trying to hire me, Jakon?"

"Only if we survive this war." He flashed her a quick smile.

Furi grinned and kept up her pace. It wasn't too fast or too slow, but nice and casual to anyone who might catch sight of them.

When they started toward the nearest lift, Jakon called out. "Wait. The Ray is docked by the second bank. It'll be easier if we go there."

"It's a lot smaller, though," Furi said. "We could end up waiting forever."

"And because so many of the Skyborn will think that, I bet we won't wait any time at all."

"And what are you going to bet?"

"Nothing, because I don't want to take your money."

Furi scowled at Jakon, but continued farther down the block anyway. The crowds closer to the city gates and the market thinned considerably by the time they reached the fountain that marked the center of the district. Furi always thought it was a bit dramatic, showing the death of an unknown lady, cradled by another royal with a blade in her back.

Now that she knew the history of Ballern, she wondered if there was more to it. In fact, Furi wondered if it depicted the assassination that started the Deadlands War, or if it showed something older.

"Jakon, how old do you think that fountain is?"

He slowed and glanced at the worn stone and tarnished bronze accents. Furi followed his gaze up to the hilt in the second royal's back. "Some say it's the first fountain built in Ballern, before the original palace burned down."

"So older than the Deadlands War."

"Oh, yes, much older than that."

Furi continued on, taking one of the narrowest alleys in all the city. It wasn't a problem for her and the light load she carried, but she heard Jakon curse more than once when his trundler scraped the stone walls. His frustration aside, they reached the other end without incident, and

Furi groaned when she saw the line for the lift.

"Aren't you glad you didn't take that bet now?" Jakon asked.

"No one. Not a single person. Are you joking? I thought this place would be crowded."

Jakon grinned. "The far bays might be a long walk from the restaurants and warehouses, but sometimes it's good to keep a low profile."

"Smugglers," Furi muttered.

He laughed and reached out with one hand, pulling the gate open for Furi. She stepped onto the lift, and while it was obviously smaller than the main lifts, Jakon followed her in with little issue.

"Make room, pirate trash," someone barked behind them.

Furi stiffened at the woman's deep voice, and she didn't miss one of Jakon's hands slipping inside his vest. Furi leaned to her right and froze. "Kura?"

"What?" Jakon said, twisting around to see who had joined them.

Kura almost doubled over with laughter. "Come on, make room. That part wasn't a joke."

Jakon pulled the trundler farther into the lift and Kura closed the gate. The metal cage rattled, and the switch squeaked when Furi moved it to the position for level three.

"How was the market today?" Kura asked.

Jakon glanced down at his stack of crates. "Good. Not as busy as I would have expected, but times are strange. Although there were a large number of regulars."

"Hmm," Kura said with a nod. "Anything interesting?"

"I haven't checked the messages yet. Furi looked at a few, but I was ready to get away. Fel's warships and soldiers have too large a presence there for my liking."

Kura crossed her arms. "Mordair does know how to intimidate, does he not? Rumor is the Baroness of Auxley has turned in a minor duke for treason against the crown."

Jakon's lips tightened into a thin line. "Imprisonment?"

"No." She laughed without humor. "Execution."

Furi stared at Kura. "Already? They just made him Steward!"

"And he likely wants to make a point." Jakon almost spat the words before he focused on Kura. "I went to the Red Woods. I saw what he did to the villages there."

Kura looked around, as if anyone could be listening in through the clattering cage of chains and gears. "And?"

"It wasn't just the bombers." Jakon grimaced and his hand tightened on the trundler. "The underground shelters had been raided, too. Fel bolts were still stuck in their corpses."

Kura didn't show anger, didn't show the kind of rage or fear Furi had felt walking through that destruction. She just looked sad, as if the inevitable had finally come home to make itself known.

"Check your messages, Jakon."

"Why do I have a feeling you already know what these messages say?"

Kura gave a small smile. "I may have sent a handful your way. The rest come of their own volition. Remember that."

The lift clanged to a stop, and Kura slid the gate open. She paused and turned to face the pair. "Tonight. Be at the warehouse. I am afraid this city is about to eat itself alive, Jakon, and Mordair knows how to bait the trap."

She said no more, only walked away in silence, her loose jacket catching the wind before she tied it tighter around herself.

Jakon grimaced, looking after Kura before turning and pointing to the north. "Come on, Furi. The Ray is close by."

When Jakon said close by, he wasn't kidding. Furi blinked when she stepped out of the lift, finding the flowing scrawl of The Ray's name not two bays down.

"How'd you get so close?"

Jakon gestured to an empty bay on the other side of the walkway.

"Like I said before, some folks don't like to walk." He led the way past a sleek modern airship. Furi didn't think it was fancy enough to belong to a noble, but it was certainly nicer than anything the Skyborn would be running.

Across from it was an ancient beast, the shoddy patchwork clear to see on the gas chamber. It was exactly the kind of death trap she had loved riding in when she was a kid. Something about not knowing if you'd have a safe landing or a crash landing was a thrill all in itself. Of course, the Skyborn lived on the docks, so even their shoddy-looking repairs could hold up to a great deal of stress.

The trundler thudded as it cleared the walkway, and Jakon started up the loading ramp. He paused at the top, fumbling with his keys to find the right one.

Furi waited near the end of the ramp, the gap between the side and the walkways a dizzying drop to the diminutive-looking city far below. Clouds moved in from the mountains, and soon enough, she knew she wouldn't be able to see from one end of the docks to the other.

"Pull the ramp," Jakon said.

Furi shifted the box she was carrying to cradle it in her left arm before reaching out and forcing the lever up. A catch clicked in the wall, releasing whatever held the ramp in place, and it quickly rose, dimming the light all around them.

Jakon opened a porthole, letting in more light before he wheeled the trundler into a locker. He took a deep breath and gestured for Furi to set her box inside, too. That done, they took a seat in the cargo hold on a pair of collapsible chairs.

"Well then, let's see what we have." Jakon unrolled the first parchment and frowned. "I don't know this symbol. Rust it all. Who wrote this?"

He opened another, and his furrowed brow softened. Then another.

"What is it?" Furi asked.

"Do you know this symbol?"

Jakon held up a shred of parchment. At first glance, she didn't recognize any of it except the Mokuskrit symbol that meant "For." But the last symbol she knew. Furi stood up and ran down the corridor to the cabin, leaving Jakon behind with a somewhat perplexed expression.

"Furi?" he called after her.

But she couldn't stop. Adrenaline hammered through her veins as she reached the locker and pulled her glider pack out. Jakon was standing up by the time she got back, worry creasing his brow.

"This. *This* is the last symbol." She ran her fingers over the embroidered patch. "Stormborn."

Jakon's head jerked back like he'd been slapped, and he stared at the small bits of parchment and cloth with a far different expression. He sat down again and spread them out, reading them aloud.

```
For the Stormborn.
United as one. Steamborn. Skyborn. Stormborn.
The Stormborn are ready.
Eyes to the sky. Stormborn.
On the Bones live the Stormborn.
```

One after another repeated similar phrases. One after another pledged themselves to the Stormborn. But it was still so few who had given Jakon that parchment.

"It's not enough," Furi said, and she hated the disappointment in those words.

Jakon spluttered. "Not enough? Furi, this is every guild and gang across the entirety of the damn docks. Every last one. I don't ... I've never seen anything like it."

A chill raced down Furi's spine, lingering in her fingertips as she took in Jakon's words. "Those ... those weren't just individuals passing you information?"

"No, Furi. They're couriers. Messengers for whatever organization they represent." He turned the last note toward her, perfectly rectangular with a gold accent running the length of it. "This is the Order of the Last Guard."

"But they aren't Skyborn."

"No, Furi, they aren't. They live in the palace under Mordair's nose. *They* are how I communicated with the queen before her assassination." Jakon lifted a small lantern off the wall behind him, struggling with the hook for a second before it came free. "Now, every royal ambition is going to run rampant."

"We already live with nothing on the docks. What more do they want?"

He sighed and studied Furi's face. "I don't know, Furi, but I don't want anyone I care about to find out. The queen was their blockade. Furi, the maps, the schedule, everything came from her. She was so bent on helping the Skyborn … but the Children of the Dark Fire have a stranglehold on every royal, from the barons to the archdukes, and half of them don't even realize it."

Furi's heart ached for what could have been. To have an alliance with the queen. What could they have accomplished? "And now Mordair sits on the throne."

"Not yet, he doesn't."

"He might as well. If the archdukes think for a moment they can bend him to their will, they'll give him too much rope."

"It's possible. If they see him as a way to break off the influence of the Children of the Dark Fire, it's possible." Jakon bit his lips as he lit the lantern, dropping every last message into it until nothing but ash remained.

Furi wondered how much information had been burned in that flame. How much had been forgotten to the fires? And a terrible thought echoed in the back of her mind. *Would the Skyborn burn with them?*

CHAPTER TWENTY

I T MIGHT HAVE taken some doing, and if Jacob was being honest, a bit of whining, but Smith finally agreed to call the maintenance on the Skysworn done and help drag the Mech parts back to the ship. No single piece in particular was all that heavy, but the idea of carrying it all the way across the Lowlands to the Skysworn was nothing to be excited about.

Jacob picked up extra bolts and cogs from one of the remaining barrels in the workshop, adding them to another crate he wanted to take with them.

"Are you sure you need *all* of that?" Smith eyed the rapidly filling crate with a great lack of enthusiasm. "You can use whatever you can find on the Skysworn. Better yet, we'll be in Midstream soon. You know how well Targrove will have that workshop stocked by now?"

Jacob paused with another sack of springs over the third crate, and then dropped it in anyway. "Okay, last one. You convinced me."

Smith turned to Alice. "Sorry, but I think you'll have to stay here. No room left on the ship."

"I understand," Alice said solemnly.

Jacob looked the crates over and the trunk Smith had piled the larger Mech pieces into. "Come on. It's not *that* bad."

Smith slapped him on the back and laughed. "I might think otherwise if I didn't have my biomechanics to rely on."

A loud knock came at the front door.

"It's open," Jacob shouted.

Light flooded the workshop as two cloaked figures stepped inside. Jacob smiled at Drakkar and Rin.

"Come to help us carry things to the Skysworn?" Alice asked.

Rin's nose wrinkled. "Definitely not. I thought it was supposed to be cold in the Ridge Mountains. It is like an oven."

"Some days it is, some days it isn't," Jacob said. "Keeps you guessing."

Smith reached out a hand and traded grips with the pair. "Are you coming with us to Belldorn? We need to stop in Midstream, but it shouldn't add much time to the journey."

Drakkar shook his head. "We do need to visit Midstream, but the Dragonwings would not enjoy riding on the deck that long."

"You *have* been paying attention," Rin said with a smile.

"You're not staying in Ancora, then?" Alice asked.

Drakkar looked at Alice. "Not now, no."

"Oh, good. I don't want to go to Ballern without everyone together. Furi is there by herself, and I don't want to leave her alone. I mean, I guess she has Jakon and Kura?"

"Don't worry about that," Rin said. "Furi can take care of herself. Plus, someone needs to add a little stress to Jakon's life. Furi'll be fine."

Smith pulled the collar of his shirt down and adjusted a dial on his biomechanics. He grabbed the crates and balanced them on the trunk before picking them up as if they were no heavier than a box of strawberries.

Rin gawked at him. "Is that … is that all your biomechanics?"

"Mostly. That and picking up heavy things regularly."

Rin blinked. "Very funny." Jacob caught the smile that flashed across the dragonrider's face.

"I will hold the door for you," Drakkar said.

"Thanks." Smith walked outside, and Jacob scrambled to make sure he had everything before following the tinker.

Alice pulled the front door closed behind Rin and threw the lock.

"What's taking you to Midstream?" Smith asked as they started down the hill.

"I would like to introduce the Cave Guardians to those they will be working with. Gladys also tends to make a good impression, so I wish them to meet her."

Alice chuckled. "You think they'll feel protective of her, don't you?"

"I do," Drakkar said. "Do we not all feel something for the desert princess?"

"Allie has a lot of respect for her," Rin said. "I think a lot of the council does in Canopy. It's hard not to wish the best for someone who has been through so much. Her people have endured hardships I cannot imagine."

"We all have our struggles," Drakkar said. "The best we can do is help where we are able."

"Good thing Mary isn't here," Smith said as he adjusted the crates in his arms. "She'd be accusing all of you of getting soft. Don't tell her, but I know she'd secretly agree with you. If we weren't shuffling off to Belldorn to fight Ballern, we'd probably be staying in Midstream, too."

Jacob looked past the airship docks to where the last section of a temporary wooden wall had been erected. It was gone, and the stone was nearly done.

"What is it, Jacob?" Alice asked quietly. "Are you okay?"

"It's just ... the wall. Once they get the top installed, it'll be just as good as the Highlands. Look at it. It's twice as high as the old wooden walls, and once the defenses are mounted on top nothing will be able to climb over it."

"Samuel tells me they're going to smooth the walls out more as well," Drakkar said. "Something Nora told him about."

Jacob nodded. "That makes sense. If it's sheer enough, nothing can even make it to the defenses. Or at least not climb it well."

Rin looked at the wall before focusing on Jacob. "If they're going to take the time to smooth out the stone, why not just use armor plating like Bollwerk?"

"It's possible, but it wouldn't last as long in the mountains. Our weather would corrode it pretty fast."

"I didn't think about that," Rin said. "A fair point."

They slowed when they reached the remains of an old foundation. The road split, one branch returning to the Highlands and the other leading to the airship docks.

"We'll see you in Midstream, then?" Alice asked.

"Unless you are in and out as fast as Smith claims," Drakkar said. "Which I highly doubt."

Smith raised an eyebrow. "Insult the Biomech while his hands are full. I see how this is going to go."

"Until Midstream, my friend." Drakkar clapped him on the shoulder.

Jacob exchanged grips with Drakkar and Rin after Alice finished crushing them both with a hug.

"Fly safe," Rin said, and the pair took their leave.

"Almost there." Smith took a deep breath and looked to the Skysworn. "Let's get on board and get in the air."

Alice stepped forward, followed by Smith and Jacob.

✧ ✧ ✧

JACOB CLOSED HIS book when Alice grabbed his arm and pointed out the window. They were still over the desert, but Midstream was on the horizon.

"Not long now," Alice said.

"You hear that, Smith?" Mary tapped on the horn. "We're almost there and nothing blew up. All that fretting over your thrusters for nothing."

Smith let out an exasperated sigh. "Any time I find a leak in a pressure gasket, I am going to fret, as you say. Do you understand what happens if that seal ruptures? It could—"

Mary closed the lid on the horn and rolled her eyes. "He'll be talking for another five minutes, then he'll be fine."

"Isn't he going to notice you muted him?" Alice asked.

Mary shrugged, but the movement cut short. She threw open the cover on the horn again.

"—and that is why I cannot simply—"

"Smith!" Mary shouted. "Cut the thrusters and look out the window. What is that around Midstream?"

Smith didn't protest getting cut off. Instead, his boots thundered across the deck beneath them.

"Harness," Mary said.

Jacob fumbled with his latch while Alice smoothly fastened hers. His clicked home, and not a moment too soon. The inertia slammed him forward and sent his backpack skidding up to Mary.

Once things settled, Jacob and Alice both hopped out of their seats and hurried to the windscreen. Mary expanded a collapsible telescope and peered through it before cursing.

"Are you seeing this, Smith?"

"I am, but I don't quite believe it. There must be fifty Tail Swords around the city. They do not appear to be attacking anyone."

"Deploy the landing skids," Mary snapped. "We aren't going all the way to the docks until we know what's happening."

"Agreed. They aren't in natural clusters. Something is drawing them in." Smith's heavy footfalls echoed up from the belowdecks. It wasn't long before Jacob heard the whine of the hull as it split open and the landing skids deployed.

"I'm setting down by Targrove's workshop," Mary said, her words less harsh. "I have a sneaking suspicion that old man may know exactly what's going on."

"Didn't Targrove help design the original bait boxes in the Deadlands War?" Alice asked.

Jacob nodded.

Alice turned back to the windscreen, giving a slow shake of her head. "Oh, I have little doubt this has something to do with him."

"Look," Jacob said, pointing out the windscreen. "That's the sand skiff George and Gladys used to get me to Bollwerk. It's clean. They've had it running."

Mary circled to the east, crossing the path the bomber had torn through Midstream, only now the scorched sands were buried underneath the grains blown in from the desert. The buildings that took the most damage had been demolished and removed, but a few that could be saved still showed damage. If Jacob hadn't known what had happened there, he would have thought the scaffolding was for new construction or even restoration.

Alice leaned into the port side window. "There are far more people here than the last time we came. I'm surprised they aren't still sheltering in Bollwerk."

Mary glanced back at Alice and grimaced. "So am I. Let's find out what's going on here."

The Skysworn took a sharp turn and drifted north before Mary leveled them out. The descent wasn't subtle, and Jacob had a moment to wonder if he should be back in his harness before Mary pulled up at the last second and sat the airship down on the sand as gently as a glassblower with a new creation.

"Shut it down and lock it up, Smith. We're not taking any chances."

"Understood."

Valves hissed and groaned as Smith started shutting down the Skysworn's engine, steam billowing from the vents to either side, ruffling a cluster of Tail Swords. The bugs didn't move far, though, instead watching the Skysworn.

Mary blew out a breath and spun out of her chair. "Let's find Targrove. And if he won't talk, let's see if Gladys will."

✧ ✧ ✧

JACOB SQUINTED AGAINST the sudden assault of windblown sand and found himself quite glad they were close to Targrove's workshop. He only hoped it was closed, and the walls weren't folded down to let the sand and desert winds in.

They passed several Midstreamers, most of whom appeared to be in a hurry. That wasn't how Jacob tended to think of the desert city. They were often laid back, going about tasks with a deliberate methodology. He didn't recognize anyone, but they each offered a nod of greeting.

The shorter adobe buildings on the outskirts of town were soon dwarfed by taller structures with decorative arches. The workshop stood beyond a building with a three-story tower. Jacob was happy to see three of the walls closed to the elements.

Alice hurried forward and looked inside before gesturing to the others. "He's here."

Jacob jogged the last few steps and peered inside, finding Targrove sipping a steaming mug with Theo, a clay teapot between them on a low table.

"Alice, Smith!" Targrove said. "Jacob, Mary. It is good to see you all. What brings you to Midstream?"

"Fuel and supplies." Smith brushed sand off the top of his boots. "But our agenda shifted when we found Tail Swords surrounding the city."

"Remarkable, aren't they?" Theo smiled and looked out toward the desert. "I never would have thought they could be so calm."

"Was this your doing?" Smith asked, turning his gaze to Targrove.

"With help from Gladys and George, yes. These old bones have a hard time getting into the old hiding places."

Smith frowned, his brow furrowing. "What old hiding places?"

"Let us say there was more than the chaingun you took."

"The cave?"

Targrove inclined his head. "Sealed away a long time ago." He gestured to the Tail Swords near the dry riverbed. "Remarkable how many boxes still functioned. I always said the power of the sun was the future of the desert, did I not? Admittedly, I didn't expect to be quite so literal about it." He sipped his tea and smiled.

"What are they for?" Jacob asked. "The bait boxes I've seen just caused bugs to go berserk."

"Not berserk, Jacob. The boxes trigger their defensive natures. Some bugs, when called to defend, are far more aggressive than others. It was also a different frequency. The Tail Swords are unique. More like Widow Makers than Red Death or Emerald Needles."

"Tell me you aren't calling Widow Makers," Mary said.

Targrove grumbled. "What kind of madman do you take me for?"

Theo sipped her tea, failing completely to hide a wide grin.

Alice turned to the others. "Look, at least we know the Tail Swords aren't an immediate threat. We can relax, right?"

"Right," Mary muttered. "Like a bloody vacation it is."

"If you have some rum, it certainly could be." Targrove raised an eyebrow and waited a moment before continuing. "Do you?"

Mary narrowed her eyes before she slid a flask out of her vest and tossed it to Targrove.

"That's my girl."

"I'm not your girl."

"My valued and loyal colleague."

Mary grimaced. "Never mind. I'm your girl."

Theo leaned forward and gestured for Targrove to come closer. As soon as he did, she smacked him in the back of the head.

"Thanks, Theo."

"My pleasure, Mary. Now, what is it you all intend to do?"

"Refuel, resupply, and get back to Belldorn." Mary glanced at Smith. "I want to be there for whatever Eva gets roped into by Kat."

Targrove screwed the lid back on the flask and handed it to Mary. "Lady Katherine is not one to act rashly. I'm sure there will be some measure of reason to her response."

"You obviously didn't grow up with her," Mary muttered.

Targrove smiled and sipped at his cocktail. "No, no I didn't."

Theo wheeled her chair back from the table and spun to face Mary and the others directly. "We spoke with Kura. There are rumblings on the docks about the Stormborn. I hope you understand what Furi has ignited among those people."

"It's not just the Skyborn," Alice said. "The Spider Knights are coming to Belldorn's aid, too."

"Truly? That I had not heard." Theo tapped her teacup and eyed Alice. "Tell me, do you know of Ballern's superstitions when it comes to those of the old blood?"

Jacob had heard that term before. It referred to a bloodline often marked by red hair and pale skin. A bloodline like Alice's.

"I've gotten enough strange looks growing up in Ancora not to be surprised by much of anything," Alice said. "You try to ignore the people who stare, but ..." She shrugged.

"It is more complicated than simply being different in Ballern, dear. In Ballern, people like you are seen as a living blessing. One that brings good fortune to all who associate with them. I do not know how many alive today in Ballern even remember *why* that is."

When Theo didn't say more, Jacob's curiosity got the better of him. "Why do they like the old blood so much?"

Theo took another sip of tea and leaned over to set the cup down. "That is a rather long story, Jacob. I'll try to be brief, so you understand what else I have to say. Belldorn and Ballern both have long superstitions with folks who look like you, Alice. I'm afraid Ballern has forgotten most of that past, wiped away with the coming of the Children of the Dark Fire. But some traditions go on, even if we forget their origin.

"It started well before the Deadlands War. Ballern was a city of chaos, of blood and rivals who would gladly kill each other for the slightest wealth. Legend says those times lasted five hundred years. It remained an abyss of death for centuries. While the rest of the world began to flourish. Ballern remained frozen where it was."

"How is that possible?" Alice asked. "The city is beautiful, and it's clearly stood for decades. Centuries, even."

Theo inclined her head. "Yes, but not because of the warlords who ruled Ballern for so long. Because of a woman who would become queen. A soldier from the other side of the Silver Gulf."

Jacob tried to wrap his brain around what Theo had just said. "That's … that's east of Ancora. No one crosses the Silver Gulf."

"Few do anymore," Theo said. "Fel's great ocean liners still make the journey on occasion for trade. There were times when explorers were bolder, and the glory of discovery drove them better than greed ever could."

"My family is across the Silver Gulf?" Alice asked.

"Somewhere in your history, it is quite likely. But that is not our concern today, Alice. Our concern today is those who are not against the Stormborn, but who are not willing to throw themselves into the fold with the likes of Kura and Furi. Skyborn who could be allies and not bystanders."

Alice glanced at Jacob, and he didn't like the sad smile that crossed her face.

"What is it?" he asked.

"Theo wants me to go to Ballern."

"What?" Jacob shook his head. "Theo didn't say that at all."

"I want Alice to go to Ballern," Theo said flatly.

Jacob's protests died on his lips, and he stared at Theo. "Fine, then I'll go with her."

Theo opened her palms and gestured to Targrove.

He scowled at her and sipped his drink. "Giving me the hard part, eh?"

"You can still sit on your butt and drink, so I wouldn't refer to it as the hard part."

Targrove grinned and turned his focus to Jacob. "You can't go to Ballern yet. And I emphasize *yet*. Help Frederick in Belldorn. He should be arriving with a fleet of supply ships any time now. They're going to need you to help with the carrier."

"Carrier?"

"We can't very well swim to Ballern, can we? We have no way of getting to the fuel reserves in the city without a battle, and a battle without fuel is a death sentence. Where would our ships land? Even those that are suited for the sea would be torn apart by Fel's armada. We need what Ballern already has. A carrier."

Jacob's mind spun at the idea. He didn't know enough to design something as monstrous as a carrier. He didn't know enough to design a small airship! What was he going to do, build a glider pack and bolt it to an airship? The entire idea was mad. "Sir, I have no idea how to do that."

Targrove raised an eyebrow. "You'll have some of the best airship designers on the continent. You'll have Frederick. And *you* have seen a carrier with your own eyes. You, with the mind of a tinker. They will need you. You can use my workbench at Theo's shop as well. The best equipment you could find."

"Are you coming too?" Jacob squeezed his hands at his side.

Targrove gave him a small smile. "No. Airships were never much interest to me, Jacob. Unless you want to make a Biomech float, I'm not who you want."

"Have you done that?" Jacob said, trying to picture what that might involve.

"Simon," Targrove and Theo said in unison, turning to each other with a laugh.

"That poor boy." Theo sighed. "It's a good bit of luck you were indoors. Had him stuck in the rafters of the factory for three hours. I miss him."

"What happened?" Jacob asked.

Targrove looked away for a moment. "The Deadlands War happened. Took him away, as it did to so many. War will do that." He turned and met Jacob's gaze. "It will take more than that. Smith knows, and Mary has seen the worst of humanity and come out better for it.

"But you, Jacob and Alice. You've seen what power can wreak. How the war machine can swallow a city whole, and the innocents vanish with it. I've seen it more times than I can tell you." Targrove leaned forward. "We may never end war, but we can end *this* war. And it must be done. But it will cost you. It will cost us. Everyone pays a price. Even those who never see blood spilled on the sands and stone. War turns life into one tragedy after another, until *you* become the tragedy. Don't lose the light between the dark places. Sometimes it's all you have."

Alice stepped closer to Targrove, putting a hand on his shoulder. The old tinker smiled, but it cracked, and he turned away. She put her arms around him for a time before turning back to Theo.

"I'll go to Ballern. For Furi, and the Stormborn. For Ancora, and my friends."

Theo gave her a sad smile. "It is a luxury to know what you're fighting for, Alice. May we meet again when times are not so dark."

✧   ✧   ✧

ALICE DIDN'T LIKE the idea of splitting up again, but she understood why Theo thought it best. Once the old tinkers had explained it, even *she* thought it best. Alice tightened her grip on Jacob's hand.

"You're still coming to Belldorn with us, right?" Jacob asked.

Alice nodded. "No one here is heading to Ballern right now. It'll be faster in the end."

Jacob blew out a long breath and squinted against the blowing sand.

Alice dragged him toward the next block. "Let's find Gladys. We need to get a message to Furi, and other than the Skysworn, Gladys's transmitter is our best option."

She let go of Jacob's hand when they reached George's home. The door stood open, so she knocked on the wooden frame, peeking inside. "Hello? Gladys?"

For a second, no one answered, and then there was a calamity on the stairs as Gladys sprinted down them faster than one of Cave's Walkers. She didn't slow when she hit the wooden floor, instead shouting Alice's name and running into her at full speed.

"It's good to see you too." Alice laughed, pulling Gladys closer in a hug. "What's happened? Is something wrong?"

Gladys pulled away and hugged Jacob before responding. "Everything? I don't know. Targrove set up new defenses around the city."

"We saw."

"Of course you did. They're hard to miss. I want to go to Ballern with you all, but I can't leave Midstream again. It's too big a target. What if Mordair attacks us again and we aren't here to defend it? But I want to go with you."

"You have to help your city," Jacob said. "That's … don't feel bad about that. We'd both do the same for Ancora."

Alice nodded. "If Ancora weren't so well protected right now by Cave Guardians and a new wall, we'd be right back home, too."

Gladys paced from one end of the area rug to the other, following the angular pattern woven into the reds and browns.

"Has Drakkar arrived yet?" Alice asked.

Gladys shook her head. "No, is he coming with the Cave Guardians? They're scheduled to arrive today."

"He's flying from Ancora."

Gladys's steps slowed. "But not on the Skysworn?"

"On a Dragonwing, actually. They're planning to take some of the Spider Knights on the next supply ship, but Drakkar won't be waiting for that."

"To Belldorn?" Gladys asked, finally growing still and taking a deep breath. "The Spider Knights are going to the front?"

Jacob nodded. "Can you believe that? The dragonriders are going to train with them. Use the spiders in the forests around Ballern where the Dragonwings don't have as much space."

"That's smart. That's very smart."

Alice rubbed her hands together. "Gladys, could we use your transmitter? I need to tell Furi I'm coming to join her."

"Of course! Is the Skysworn's transmitter not working?"

"It is, but Smith and Mary have to take care of getting supplies, and we wanted to see you more than listen to Smith count off crates and barrels."

Gladys chuckled at that. She walked over to the shelves and pulled a copper box from underneath the second bookshelf. "Here."

"Thank you." Alice took the device and turned it over in her hands. The dials appeared to be labeled the same as the Skysworn's, and that would make things easier. She tuned them to Kura's frequency and clicked the button.

"Skyborn, do you have a moment?" Alice tapped her foot and waited. "I hope she's around."

They stood for another minute before taking seats at the table. Alice studied the wide range of maps and pins.

"George," Gladys said. "He's a little obsessed with maps right now."

Alice smiled and pressed the transmitter again, relaying the same message. "Skyborn, do you have a moment?"

This time there wasn't a large delay. Instead, static greeted them, followed by a somewhat flummoxed voice. "Who is this, and how do you have this frequency?"

"Friends from … from across the sea. Is Furi there?"

"Alice?" Kura asked, her voice sounding a little less strained. "Is that you?"

"It is, but I wasn't sure we should use our names. Mordair has intercepted more than one transmission."

"Technology," Kura muttered. "It always has drawbacks, doesn't it? Furi! Come, speak to your friends."

A few clicks and thumps sounded over the transmitter before Furi's voice answered. "Alice?"

"Hi, Furi. I wanted to tell you I'll be in Ballern soon. Theo thought it could be good to be seen with you? It was a long story that made it sound like I'd be your good luck claw."

Furi laughed at that. "That's your legacy. Who needs a Mantis claw when they can have an Ancoran?" She paused for a time. "It's not a bad idea, though. I know why Theo said that. It's a superstitious lot who live on the docks. How soon will you be here?"

"Not for a day or two. Unless Mary is bringing me, I'll probably catch a ship in Belldorn."

"Belldorn!" Furi's words came out rushed, her excitement palpable. "Alice, you have to do me a favor. Bring one of the books from the Crown Library."

"That doesn't narrow it down, Furi."

"No, no, *listen*. Get a book from the old Ballern press. Any that details the assassinations and the history of the Children of the Dark Fire. We found several there, Alice. They'll let you take at least one."

"I don't know if they will, Furi."

"Then have Jacob steal it for you!"

"What?" Jacob said, sitting up ramrod straight. "I mean, I could? But I'd feel bad?"

Alice grinned at him. "Let me try more respectful avenues first. If that doesn't work, we can let our pickpocket loose."

Jacob groaned.

The others laughed.

✧ ✧ ✧

BY THE TIME Mary and Smith had acquired the supplies they wanted and traveled back from the docks to the city, Drakkar and Rin had made their appearance. Jacob sat beside Alice on the deck of the Skysworn, looking out over the north edge of the city where the Cave Guardians gathered close to the Tail Swords.

Jacob wasn't sure if the Tail Swords or the people were more uncomfortable with their newfound proximity. He pulled the lid off the bucket of steamed buns Gladys had given them and peered inside.

"Gladys said there was enough for dinner for us, but this is like a week of food."

"She probably expected us to share them." Alice snatched up another bun and grinned.

One of Midstream's Titan Mechs strode by, vibrating the ground and sending tremors through the Skysworn's landing gears.

Alice pointed at the towering Mech. "Between those, the Tail Swords, and the Cave Guardians, I don't think Gladys has much to worry about."

"I hope you're right. The best weapon is the one you don't need." Jacob squished a steamed bun between his fingers and took another bite. The rubbery texture on the outside was fantastic and a bit sweet; the perfect complement to the salty chunk of meat and sauce in the center.

"I know we just saw Drakkar and Rin, but I feel like we should go talk to them," Alice said.

Jacob looked down at the bucket of steamed buns. "Maybe we should share."

"Full already?"

Jacob grinned at Alice before hopping to his feet and holding a hand out. He pulled Alice up. "Let's go say hi. George looks like he's being awfully formal down there. Gladys may need us to rescue her."

Alice laughed at that and led the way to the hatch that would take them belowdecks and down to the loading ramp.

✧　　✧　　✧

"I DO NOT know." Drakkar's words were the first sentence Jacob could make out as they approached the gathering. "Alana makes for Canopy with a good number of Guardians. The Nameless are among them, as there are some among you now."

George stood beside Gladys and Helena, a rather stern expression on the older woman's face. She kept her arms crossed, appearing unimpressed with anything Drakkar had to say. Drakkar, of course, looked wholly unbothered.

Jacob waved to Helena, and her grim expression cracked. But it was only a moment. A quick nod, and she was back to judging every word being exchanged there.

Gladys squeezed her hands together and focused on Drakkar. "Are you sure you want to station so many of your people here? I don't want you to feel like Cave isn't guarded well enough."

"It is not an immediate concern. Cave is not a target that would give Mordair an advantage. It is also located behind Belldorn, Bollwerk, and Midstream. The distance he would need to cover is great, and I do not believe he would abandon his gambit for that."

George rubbed his chin and spoke with a formal cadence. "We welcome you all."

Gladys gave George a somewhat annoyed look. "Of course we do. You can stay in the south barracks near our new docks if you would like. Almost all of our dock workers still live in the barracks in the mountains. Two hostels have been rebuilt closer to the city center. Few have moved into them yet. Furnishings are sparse, but you're welcome to them."

"Thank you, Princess." Drakkar bowed.

Rin crossed his arms and looked toward the Tail Swords. "Which one is farthest off the ground? I don't like being at eye level with those."

Gladys grinned at the dragonrider. "Try the hostels. One of them has a tower that is four stories tall."

"Like a short tree in Canopy," Rin said. "I can live with that. It's only one night, right?"

"And a short night at that," Drakkar said. "Once our mounts have had their fill of food and rest, we leave early in the morning."

"Helena coordinates most of our defenses here," George said. "She can show your people around. And if you have any suggestions on a perimeter or other defenses, we would be glad to hear of them."

Drakkar looked to the Tail Swords, a light amusement in his words.

"I do not think your perimeter is a concern."

"We have several of the javelin traps Jacob designed." Helena uncrossed her arms. "They are deployed beyond the river and in the base of it. A few were destroyed by the Tail Swords. The Mechs can place additional traps easily enough if the need arises."

"Gladys and George have told me of your knowledge of this city and land on which it resides. I would be honored to review this further with you."

Helena inclined her head. "Let me show you to the barracks, and then we can tour the grounds." With that, she turned and started down the street.

"Better follow her," George said. "She is not the most patient of us."

Drakkar raised his hand and held up two fingers. The semicircle of Cave Guardians turned toward Helena and followed.

Hours passed before they saw Rin and Drakkar again. Jacob and Alice managed to finish off their bucket of steamed buns with the help of Gladys, George, and the old tinkers. It was night before Drakkar found them, another Cave Guardian at his side.

"Welcome," Targrove said, gesturing for the pair to join them in the shop. "There is more food if you would like."

"We have had our fill, thank you. I wanted to introduce you all to someone. Or perhaps it is better to say I wanted to introduce someone to you."

"Did you lose Rin?" Alice asked.

Drakkar laughed. "Lost him to sleep."

The second Cave Guardian pulled the hood of his cloak down, and Jacob frowned. If he didn't know better, he would have thought he was looking at a younger version of Drakkar. The same sharp cheekbones and hairline paired with a piercing gaze.

"This is my son, Rikken." Drakkar beamed at the group.

The entire workshop fell silent. It wasn't necessarily hard to believe. After all, Jacob knew Drakkar had a son, but he rarely spoke about his family. However, the sudden introduction caught everyone off guard. And it was clear some of them had no idea.

"I'm sorry, what?" Gladys asked.

George slowly blinked. "You … have a son?"

Rikken fidgeted and scratched the back of his neck before offering a small half-smile.

"Any family of Drakkar is family to us. I'm Alice." She stepped forward and held her fist out. Rikken didn't hide his surprise, but quickly wrapped his hand over Alice's.

"It's good to meet you. Drakkar's told me of the Ancorans who were friends with Atlier. I guess I never thought I'd actually meet you." His voice wasn't as deep as Drakkar's, and he might have been a Cave Guardian, but he didn't speak with such pointed enunciation as Drakkar either. He sounded more like he could be from Ancora himself.

"Why didn't you introduce us when we were in Cave?" Mary asked, scowling at Drakkar.

"Probably because Mom's a nightmare," Rikken muttered.

It was Drakkar's turn to scowl, but he broke down into a laugh soon enough. "She does not appreciate guests in the house without several days' warning. That is the truth."

Rikken rolled his eyes.

Jacob held his own fist out to Rikken in the greeting of the Steamsworn.

"You're a Biomech, right?"

"Jacob. Yes. Though you really need to talk to Smith if you want to see the more advanced biomechanics." He gestured to the larger Biomech.

Smith raised his fist. "Welcome, Rikken. It is good to meet you."

Targrove stood and stepped closer to Drakkar's son. He eyed the Cave Guardian and then extended his own fist. "Do you know who I am, son?"

Drakkar started to shake his head, but then he winced in slow motion when Rikken spoke.

"You're Targrove. Dad's told me all about you. I'd love to hear some of your stories about the Deadlands War. Dad just gets bored with things like that. I mean, after all, what's that have to do with defending Cave? But I love old stories! And it doesn't get much older than you, does it?"

Drakkar almost shrank as Jacob watched, the Cave Guardian covering his eyes as if he could unsee everything that had just happened.

Targrove, on the other hand, shook like he was choking to death on a chunk of jerky instead of a laugh.

Theo extended her hand and exchanged grips with Rikken. "Son, it is an honest pleasure to meet you. I did not know a Cave Guardian, one who has walked with the Nameless, could be so thoroughly embarrassed. Absolutely brilliant."

Drakkar groaned.

Mary crossed her arms and grinned. "I think I know why we haven't met the kid before."

Targrove shook his finger at Drakkar, raising one eyebrow. "I always knew you Cave Guardians weren't more machine than man when it came to secrets. You would have had me believe you never told *anyone* about me."

"Oh, he told me and Mom the first day he was home. Barely even closed the door." Rikken lowered his voice in a terrible imitation of his father. "You will not believe who I encountered this week. The mad tinker Targrove!"

"Mad, am I?" Targrove said with a chuckle.

Drakkar raised his hands, palms open. "It is the name the Cave

Guardians gave you long ago. Please, take no offense."

"Quite accurate, really," Theo said.

Targrove tried to scowl at Theo, but he broke down into laughter again. "It has been some time since I heard a tale as grand as that. What brings you to Midstream? I wouldn't have thought you old enough to be serving with the Cave Guardians."

"He is as of this year." Drakkar stood a little straighter. "It is not his first mission, as there was an issue with him lying about his age last year."

"Cunning, ambitious, and far too honest," George said. "I rather like him."

"Will you be staying with us in Midstream?" Gladys asked.

"I will be, yes. Alana asked me to keep Midstream safe while she travels to Canopy."

"You are getting orders directly from Alana now?" Drakkar asked. "Your training goes better than you led me to believe."

Rikken shrugged. "It's okay, I guess."

George looked to Drakkar and nodded. "We will be sure Rikken and the other Cave Guardians remain as safe as possible."

Drakkar placed a hand on Rikken's shoulder. "Thank you."

"Does Rikken know about the transmitters?" Gladys asked.

"The what?" Rikken glanced at Drakkar.

"You told him about me, but kept your transmitter secret?" Targrove asked.

"Don't worry," Gladys said. "I'll show you how it works. You can talk to your dad even when he's as far away as Belldorn."

"Oh, I've heard of those! I thought they were just rumors, though. And really, how practical is it to have an antenna the size of a building?"

Gladys grinned. "We might have one or two smaller than a building."

CHAPTER TWENTY-ONE

WITH THEIR DEPARTURE set so early in the morning, the whole crew of the Skysworn slept onboard. Jacob stared at the bottom of the bunk above them, listening to Alice's quiet breathing and the occasional restlessness of Smith nearby.

He wasn't sure how long it took for the gentle chittering of the Tail Swords outside to lull him to sleep, but sleep did come, and it was mercifully peaceful. No dreams disturbed the darkness. No terrors to bring him screaming into alertness, searching for a weapon.

Some days, it felt like those nights were far too few.

It wasn't until he heard a voice over the horn that Jacob stirred. That was an odd thing. Normally, Mary or Smith's first footsteps would wake him, although that wasn't always the case.

"Jacob, Alice, come to the cabin."

"Mary? On our way," Jacob muttered in the general vicinity of the horn.

Alice groaned beside him. "It can't be morning already."

The ship tilted and the roar of the boilers grew louder. Jacob frowned at the light coming through the far door. It should have been dark. It should have been pitch black outside.

"Alice, I think we overslept."

She mumbled something unintelligible. After another minute she yawned and sat up, throwing her legs over the edge of the bunk and smacking her lips. "Yuck. I need a toothbrush."

"Maybe we should worry about why it's light outside first?"

Alice shook her hair out and flopped onto Jacob's shoulder. "Fine. The toothbrush. Then food."

He squeezed her and then stood up, grabbing a shirt from where he'd tossed it onto the bunk above them. Fully dressed, they both started lacing up their boots before clomping over to the stairs and heading down the corridor to the engine room.

Smith glanced over his shoulder, keeping both hands on a pressure valve. "You two finally awake? Good, good. If Mary keeps talking to me, I will *never* finish this swap. Do *not* forget to clip into the safety line when you head for the cabin."

"Why would we need to clip into the safety line?" Jacob asked around a yawn. The ship shook and rattled, and the telltale whine of a turbine accelerating caught his attention.

"Are we in the air?"

Smith grinned. "Mary said to let you sleep. I didn't think you'd sleep until the Bay of Sorrow."

Alice squinted at Smith. "You're telling me we're at the bay already?"

"At the bay?" Smith offered a bemused smile. "No. I'm telling you, we're halfway over the bay. It's nearly midday. Mary has Lady Katherine waiting to speak to you. Go."

Jacob's grogginess evaporated. Alice grabbed his arm and dragged him, both stumbling over to the ladder. At the top, she spun the lock and pushed it open, the wind howling across the opening.

"Stay low," Smith said. "Or you better be wearing a glider pack."

"Well, that's terrifying," Jacob muttered, following her up the ladder and grabbing the safety line she offered. With that looped around his belt, he clipped it to the nearest cable abovedeck.

The hatch slammed closed behind him, and he winced at the boom. But then the fresh air hit him, both figuratively and literally. The scent of the sea and brine filled his nose while the wind tried to push him off his feet. Alice crouched and moved forward, making it to the cabin door in short order.

Jacob followed, opting to lean into the wind. By the time he caught up to her a minute later, he figured that hadn't been the best idea, wondering just how much of his face had been sheared away by the nonstop gale.

He stepped inside the cabin, unclipping from the safety line before closing the door behind him.

"Nice hair," Mary said.

Jacob and Alice stared at each other and laughed. Alice looked like someone had glued clumps of her hair into semi-vertical spikes that slowly fell without the wind in their face. Jacob figured his didn't look any better, given Alice's grin.

"They're here, Kat."

Lady Katherine's voice sounded across the transmitter. "I understand you have need of a book from our library. That is not something we would authorize under normal circumstances. And now that we understand the sensitive nature of them, I need to understand what your intention is."

"And then we can borrow it?" Alice asked.

"Possibly."

"I don't know if you understand how important this is to Ballern."

Mary glanced back at Alice and shook her head, discouraging Alice's approach.

Alice frowned and tried again. "I'm sorry, I mean, I don't know if you fully understand how valuable this could be to your allies in Ballern."

"I don't," Kat said simply. "You're right about that. The information I received from the Skysworn was incomplete, at best. Meet me for an audience after your arrival. The halls of the Crown Library. I will take our audience there. Inform your tinker that our own will be waiting for him on the second floor of the library."

Alice's lips flattened into a tight line. "We'll be there."

"Excellent. Kat out."

The transmitter silenced, its quiet buzz receding to nothing in the quiet roar of the wind outside.

"What did you tell her?" Jacob asked.

Mary sighed. "Exactly what Gladys said last night. The Skyborn need it to gather more recruits."

"That's the heart of it," Alice said. "I'll … I'll explain it to her in more detail. She must let us take one of those books. It could be the only way Furi will be able to persuade several of the Skyborn to rebel."

"Pull out your jump seats and get in your harnesses. We'll know soon enough."

Jacob looked out the windscreen. A dark shadow loomed on the horizon, growing wider and taller as they closed on the towering city of Belldorn.

✦　✦　✦

"I DON'T LIKE splitting up," Jacob said, combing his hair and squinting at the small mirror in the berth.

Alice squeezed his arm. "You know we don't have a choice. You have to help with the carrier. Think about it like this. The faster you get them working in the right direction, the sooner you can come find me in Ballern."

Jacob closed his eyes and nodded. "I know. And you'll have Furi and Jakon. As far as friends go, you could do worse."

"I won't tell them about that ringing endorsement. I wouldn't want them to feel uncomfortable being showered in such mighty praise."

Jacob let out a quiet laugh. "Stop it. You know what I meant."

"I did. Now stop fussing with your hair and let's get this done."

Alice led the way out of the Skysworn. Smith and Mary were already waiting on the docks when they stepped outside, and Mary tapped her watch.

"Close the hatch, would you?"

Jacob pushed the heavy metal hatch over and let it slam closed, the sound echoing out across the docks. After that, he followed Alice over the gangplank, looking down toward the base of the docks. They weren't low, exactly, but they felt far less intimidating than the high-flying airship docks of Ballern.

The Hall sat close by, home to the most critical parts of Belldorn's government, encased in a monolith of glass and steel and brick. It was the first place they had ever met Lady Katherine. When the lift opened, they turned away from that building and headed to the right, toward the plaza with the Crown Library.

A buzz ran through the city, the streets alive with activity that ranged from guards marching in patrol to vendors selling a variety of foods from carts. It was hard to believe how normal Belldorn appeared so soon after a battle there.

"So many people are out," Jacob said. "I thought ... I don't know. Maybe they wouldn't be with the fighting?"

Smith glanced back and smiled. "You still have to live your life in between, Jacob. If the battles return to Belldorn, the crowds will thin again."

"It was different in Ancora," Alice said. "There wasn't a city to go back to. We all just crowded into the Highlands and ... waited."

"Until we found the underground," Jacob said. "Then we almost got eaten by Widow Makers."

Alice let out a short laugh and slapped Jacob's arm.

"I understand what you mean," Mary said. "It takes some getting used to. Smith and I have been on the run before. It's … it's similar. You catch little pieces of normalcy where you can. But it's never easy."

Smith stopped at one of the food carts and traded a few coins for a small pile of wrapped squares. "Now, here is a treat. Caramel Crunch. It can be hard to find when it gets too warm. Tends to melt."

Jacob pulled the wrapper off, which tried to prove Smith's point by sticking to the candy like glue.

"You don't have any false teeth, do you?" Smith asked. "Well, anyway, you won't have them after this." He grinned and popped the entire square into his mouth.

Jacob exchanged a look with Alice, and they both did the same.

Alice's nose curled up as she tried to chew, and Jacob would have laughed if he didn't feel like his mouth was glued shut.

"How," Alice managed to blurt out, "how do you eat this?" But she kept chewing, and so did Jacob.

It tasted salty until something crunched on the inside, releasing a sweet liquid that washed some of the salt down. Then he could taste the caramel. It almost felt like a taffy only sweeter. Just on the edge of being burnt, but in the best possible way.

"It's so good," Jacob said. "Thank you!"

He was pretty sure Alice was trying to say thanks too, but it came out as more of a hiss.

By the time they managed to finish eating their treats, the rotunda of the Crown Library stood high above them. Smith led the way to the door, holding it open as the group stepped inside and formed a circle on the first floor.

It wasn't quiet, like the times they'd been there before. Jacob could hear dozens of voices speaking, and some of them were heated. Movement surged along the balcony of the second floor.

"We will find the tinkers there," Smith said. "I will stay with Jacob."

"I'll stick with Alice as long as I can," Mary said. "Depending what Kat has up her sleeve, this may be the last time you two see each other for a while."

Jacob turned to Alice. "We've done it before, right?"

"We have."

He stepped closer and leaned in to kiss her, trying to cement that memory of her lips on his and her cheek in his palm. She wrapped her arms around him and squeezed before stepping away.

"Soon," Alice said. "And keep a transmitter with you. I'll be with Furi at some point, and I can use hers or Kura's."

"You will need to," Smith said. "I do not believe the transmitters in our collars will have that range. Though they may in the evening."

Alice clasped her hands together and smiled at Jacob.

"Love you."

"Love you too."

With that, he sighed and turned to follow Smith up the stairs. Jacob glanced back once to watch Alice following Mary away.

✧　✧　✧

THE VOICES GREW louder as Jacob climbed the stairs.

"I already told you that won't work! You'll flip the whole carrier as soon as you load the first hangar."

"You're wrong."

Jacob could see the first speaker, whose long gray hair was pulled back in a braid. It was an unusual style among tinkers, and a dead giveaway it was Frederick. "And do you have time to rebuild it if I'm not?"

Jacob cleared his throat before the other man could answer.

Frederick looked over his shoulder and then spun to face the newcomers. "Jacob! Smith! Thank the bloody sands you're here. Help me talk some sense into these men. I believe you know Tobias, my assistant."

The second man crossed his arms and scowled at Frederick, only offering a curt nod of his balding head in greeting.

"Hi." Jacob only spared Tobias a glance, taking in the sheer width of the man's shoulders. The rest of the room paid their group no mind. Jacob recognized one or two tinkers from Theo's workshop, but most of them were strangers.

It only took a moment to find the patterns. Most of the tinkers in that room wore an apron, some leather, others woven from a lighter material. All of Theo's tinkers wore thick leather. Jacob suspected the others were all from different workshops, or even cities.

Frederick caught him staring at a cluster of tinkers in the corner. Two of the women had lighter aprons on. A brown-haired woman with biceps to rival Smith's sketched on a large parchment while the others watched.

"Tinkers from Bollwerk," Frederick said. "Natalia!"

The brown-haired tinker looked up.

"This is Jacob. I believe you already know Smith."

"We've met," Natalia said, a small smirk lifting the corner of her lips.

"Oh, I don't need this," Smith muttered under his breath.

Jacob raised an eyebrow, glancing between the pair. "Are you two—"

"Not now, Jacob."

"He means not in a while," Natalia said with a laugh.

"Still have excellent hearing, I see." Smith cast her a small smile.

Natalia winked at Smith and then turned back to her rough schematics.

Frederick clapped his hands together. "Yes, well, Natalia helped me incorporate your designs into the Titan Mech, Jacob. She's one of the best when it comes to taking a design and making it simpler for the factories."

"That's incredible," Jacob said. "She's here for the carrier too?"

"We all are. And you know it's important if Archibald let us out of Bollwerk for the time being. Doesn't hurt the city's on the verge of a riot. Makes it hard to work the factories when you have protesters kicking down the doors."

"Getting bad?" Smith asked. "Gladys and George told us something of it, but I was not sure how severe it was."

"We've seen worse. We'll likely need the factories to accomplish this carrier build, so that might get interesting."

Smith harrumphed and crossed his arms. He leaned over the table piled with blueprints and notes and sketches.

Jacob leaned in beside him, realizing it was a rendition of Ballern's carriers. He traced the hull with his finger and shook his head. "This isn't right. I remember these gas chambers being on the far corners, plus one in the middle on all sides. And it isn't just the large chambers. There were smaller pods along the entire bow. I think it was to act like some kind of ballast."

Tobias cursed and threw his pencil on the schematic. "Are you joking? We've been working on this for three bloody days, and the kid just tells us where the whole thing is set to fail in ten seconds?"

"Sorry?" Jacob said, raising an eyebrow.

Frederick tried to answer, but he was laughing too hard. "No, no." He finally choked the words out. "This is why we wanted him here in the first place. Intel from the pilots and crew is good, but they don't have the eye of a tinker."

"It's not like he was standing on it."

Jacob and Smith exchanged a glance before Smith shook his head. Jacob grinned at him.

"Go see what Natalia is working on," Frederick said. "They've been debating over a method to connect these platforms into one giant carrier."

"Does it have to be one?" Jacob asked, looking over the schematics. "You could divide it up into two or four pieces." He paused and frowned. "No, never mind. I think four pieces would destabilize it. You'd almost have to have the gas chambers hanging overhead if you did that."

"That's Natalia's specialty," Frederick said. "Talk to her."

Jacob nodded and headed across the room, glancing toward another heated debate at a table of tinkers with a rough paper model of an isolated gas chamber. He almost walked right into Natalia's table before he switched his attention back to where he was walking.

"Hi," Natalia said. "Join us. Did I hear you have an idea for the platform?" She glanced over Jacob's shoulder. "Come over here, Smith."

Smith made his way across the room, hands in his pockets.

"How's my favorite biomechanical masterpiece?"

"Good, Natalia. Other than the war, of course."

Natalia let out a harsh, staccato laugh. "You and me both, Smith. You and me both."

Smith grabbed a small wooden chair and spun it around to sit with the group. Jacob took the last of the upholstered chairs. "Tell us what you have."

Natalia gestured to the blueprint of one of Archibald's warships. "This is how those monstrosities were put together in Bollwerk. We thought about building two platforms and joining them, but I'm afraid the stress would be too much on the welds. What say you, Jacob?"

He glanced between the blueprints and Natalia. "Ballern's carrier isn't supported in the center. This wouldn't work without the gas chamber floating above the deck. And the whole concept of a carrier doesn't work if the gas chambers block the deck."

"Hence our problem," Natalia said.

"Why not break it into two carriers? You don't need them together. Distribute the weight. Two large gas chambers on the shorter sides. Then place pontoons in the middle arcing away from the carrier to stabilize it."

"We considered that, but pontoons are susceptible to attack."

"So are the gas chambers themselves. And unless you're going to make them larger than the carrier itself, you can't armor them."

"How did Ballern protect theirs?"

"Only from above," Smith said, pulling a rough sketch across the table. He pointed to the base of the gas chamber. "The anchor is inverted, so the gas chambers are protected by the deck itself. Very little rises above the plane of the deck."

Natalia ran her fingers through her hair. "Gods, I wish you two were here yesterday. Would have saved us some arguing."

Jacob realized something else at that moment. "Nothing's been built yet, has it?"

Natalia blew out a breath. "Some of the deck has been. But as to what it's going to be attached to? That's why we're here. And Archibald wants these done in a week." She laughed. "I have no idea how that's going to happen."

"We don't have a week," Jacob said, perhaps a little too quickly.

"Kid, I respect your sense of urgency, but we can only do so much. Even in Bollwerk's factories. Especially now with the protests."

"Archibald will quell the protests if he needs to," Smith said. "He's done it before."

"Eh, maybe," Natalia said. "He has a clean image now, Smith. I doubt he'll want to revisit the old days. Iron fists aren't too popular with Bollerk's residents in these times. That's the stuff of warlords and kings, not benevolent speakers."

"Belldorn does not have the space to build one of these." Smith hesitated. "Not even if it is broken in half."

Jacob rubbed his neck. "They could."

"How?" Natalia asked. "Have you seen the factories here? There's barely space to assemble a Porcupine, much less a vessel that can *carry* a Porcupine."

"The docks Ballern built. You can probably salvage some of the armor they laid for the dock, too. Some of those buildings that were bombed were iron. Melt it down. Are you going to tell me Belldorn doesn't have enough space to smelt it?"

Jacob noticed Frederick and a couple others had gathered behind Smith and were listening intently. Normally that would have intimidated him, but the longer it took to build these carriers, the longer that gave Mordair to get settled in Ballern. Time could cost them everything.

"I've seen the Porcupines," Jacob said. "The amount of bronze and brass and steel it would take to build a single cannon could form an entire plate of the carrier if you use this design. May I?" He held out his hand for a pencil.

Natalia sat back and eyed him before handing it over.

He sketched a beveled tooth like one he'd seen Charles use on a much smaller scale. "If you use this design, they'll lock together but still have room to flex. If you lose a gas chamber, the entire plate could buckle, but if you lose a gas chamber, the carrier is going to sink anyway.

"Cut it into quarters, and then cut it again to fit your factories. Bollwerk can probably make a plate twice the size as one in Belldorn, but that doesn't matter because they're going to be two separate carriers."

Tobias asked what Jacob was talking about, and it was Frederick who answered.

"He's saying to build one carrier in Belldorn and another in Bollwerk. Utilize the temporary docks Ballern built on the beachhead."

Natalia rubbed her face. "If we use your idea, Jacob, then we can build a hollow support structure to bear the weight. Struts and triangles, and that would allow the deck to be far thinner than it would be otherwise."

Jacob nodded. "Yes, and the hangars don't need to be heavy. They can be as simple as tarps. Just make sure you have something to anchor each airship, or you could lose some."

"Weight distribution will be important," Frederick said.

"Maybe not as important as we are thinking." Smith tapped the edges of the plate. "What if we anchor the Porcupines to the carrier? Turn them into a defensive point *and* a kind of secondary gas chamber."

Jacob nodded quickly. "Yes, yes! And for the pontoons, we can put the arms on a ratchet. The same as we use for the waist of the Titan Mech. You'll be able to pivot it in and out as needed. While the Porcupines are anchored, the pontoons can be hidden. Because once the Porcupines deploy, no one in their right mind will be focused on an empty carrier."

Tobias cursed under his breath. "If we incorporate those changes, it removes half of what we were planning to build. We really could have this done in a week."

Natalia looked up at Frederick, her words rushed. "You already have the designs for the steering. What about the gas chambers?"

"Solved."

"Draw them up so we have plans in Belldorn and Bollwerk. And get a transmitter anchored in every factory. Contact Bollwerk and tell them to start smelting anything the city doesn't need. Someone get Lady Katherine's permission to tear down the rubble around Belldorn and smelt that too. I want these plans done by morning."

"You heard the lady," Frederick said, clapping his hands. "Prep the docks for a factory. Get the Titan Mechs over there, and you can have it roughed out tonight. Move!"

"Segment the gas chambers," Jacob said before everyone left, remembering one of Charles's lessons. *If you can die if something breaks once, make sure three other things have to break first.* "More than you would on a Porcupine or a warship. Redundancy is key."

Tobias eyed Jacob before giving him a sharp nod. "Belldorn tinkers with me. We prep the factory while Bollwerk finishes the schematics."

The arguing in that place had stopped entirely. Now there was only movement and quiet concentration as the tinkers who specialized in actually making giant machines work started stepping through the math.

Jacob looked up when someone squeezed his shoulder.

Smith smiled down at him. "Charles would have been proud of you."

It was a nice thought, and he smiled at Smith's words. But he wasn't so sure proud was the right sentiment. It felt more like Charles would have understood *why* he was doing what he was, even though it was going to end in war. War was coming for them, no matter what they did, and if they weren't ready for it, Jacob knew what that might cost them.

✦　✦　✦

ALICE STAYED CLOSE to Mary. She didn't like leaving Jacob behind in that mass of tinkers. They needed to build the carrier if they had any hope of stopping Mordair in Ballern, but it still made her worry for Jacob. After knowing Charles and Targrove and even Smith, she knew what war could do to the people who created the greatest weapons.

Mary's boots remained silent on the stairs. Alice didn't understand how the Skysworn captain did that. Every step *she* took echoed out around them like a small Pilly bouncing down the stairs. The long curve of the staircase came to an end on the lowest floor. Mary glanced at the shadow behind the stairs, her hand never leaving the hilt of her dagger.

"How many guards does she have down here?" Mary muttered.

Alice frowned and looked back at the staircase again, stiffening when she saw two pairs of eyes staring back at her.

"Come on," Mary said. "The sooner we talk to Kat, the sooner we can get out of here. Too many people for my liking. At least, too many people if you aren't trying to pick their pockets."

"Now you sound like Jacob."

Mary led the way down a corridor of bookcases and stone arches until she finally exited into the room where Alice had first met Jakon. Glass cases and sealed shelves, each with its own hygrometer to measure the humidity within, covered every wall in the center of the archives.

The Lady of Belldorn sat on one of four red velvet chairs in a corner. Alice was certain those hadn't been there the last time she saw the archives, but it was possible she'd been too distracted by all the books in the library's collection.

But that didn't much matter now to Mary, who was far more focused on the other woman in the room. "Eva?" She almost leaped at her, wrapping Eva in a strong hug.

"Kat asked me to come."

"Please, join me." Kat gestured to the empty seats. "I'll tell you all why."

Alice slid into the chair beside her while Mary and Eva took the other seats beside the lady.

Kat looked tired. She wore her hair pinned back beneath her crown, letting the red and gray strands flow down her back. It was the exact opposite of Jacob's, which had apparently decided no comb could hold it down that day.

"Now, Alice, tell me what you intend to do with these books if I choose to loan one to you." Kat leaned forward, resting her forearms on her thighs. "No one will hear us in this place. The acoustics are made for it."

Alice glanced at Mary and Eva. She had her suspicions about why Lady Katherine had asked Eva to join them, but she didn't speak them aloud. Instead, she focused on Kat. "Furi is working with the Skyborn in Ballern. You already know that. Kura is key to the resistance there. She's well respected in the community."

"She is," Mary said. "Has her hands in a bit of everything, I think. Smith and I had both heard of her well before we met her."

Alice nodded. "Well, some of those Skyborn who respect her aren't willing to help the Stormborn. They're already blinded by the Children of the Dark Fire. Even Furi didn't completely escape their rhetoric. She still catches herself repeating their propaganda. But that part doesn't matter. What matters is Mordair could leverage that influence to his own uses. And I think he will as long as his ambitions and the agenda of that cult line up."

"But why the books?" Kat asked.

"The books prove what the Children of the Dark Fire did." Alice clenched her fists before making an effort to relax them. "How they replaced the heir to the throne. All they had to do was wait once that was done. The queen was supposed to be their pawn, but she was delivering information to the resistance. She *knew*, Lady Katherine. She knew, and then Mordair killed her."

Kat looked away, exchanging a look with Eva and Mary. "And so long as their agendas are united, we face a unified enemy."

"Yes, and we need as many Skyborn as we can get. The Stormborn need more soldiers inside Ballern."

Lady Katherine took a deep breath and placed her hands on the arms of her chair. She studied Alice for a moment before nodding. "So be it. I do not know if this will be enough to sway those who have shown loyalty to the Children of the Dark Fire, but it is perhaps better than what you hoped to take."

Alice watched as Kat stood, walking over to a floating case on the wall. It was one of the few that were locked in the entire archive. Kat's fingers danced over the yellowed parchment inside, most of the books unbound and only a few showing signs of any organization.

Kat slid a thin volume out. There was nothing on the binding. No legendary Ballern publishing house or other identifiable markings. It wasn't anything that Furi had asked for, and worry started to gnaw at Alice's gut. And apparently, she didn't hide it well.

"Don't concern yourself," Kat said, patting the volume in her hand. "I'm still letting you take the book."

Alice frowned. "Then what is that?"

"This is the original manuscript for the book. Handwritten notes, research that never made it into print. I had our librarians scour the archive for anything within three years of the date of your books. Anything that mentioned the Children of the Dark Fire. I admit, I didn't expect them to find this."

"Do you think that will help?" Eva asked.

Kat held it out to Alice. The parchment still felt supple beneath her fingers, though its color and the scent of musty vanilla betrayed its age. The first page revealed far more than she'd expected.

The Failed Treatise and the Third War
Essay by Yan Wu

"How?" Alice whispered. "How can you possibly have this?"

"Yan Wu was a dissident, Alice," Lady Katherine said. "One of the first Skyborn, from a time when the docks weren't meant to house people day and night. She defected when the Children of the Dark Fire rose to power. Yan was also the source of some of our rarest Ballern publications. Loyal to the Skyborn until the day she died, and one reason our prisons here are so welcoming to all from Ballern."

Kat said more, but Alice was fixated on Yan's tight scrawl. Some passages were in Mokuskrit and others were in the standard tongue, and the few characters she recognized told her each was a translation of the other. She flipped to the center of the notebook and froze, her voice a whisper.

"It's almost word for word."

"What is?" Mary asked.

Alice read aloud.

All they needed was a gifted calligrapher to forge the documents. A simple theft of the royal seal put everything in order. With the placement of their forgery in the royal vaults, the Children of the Dark Fire only needed to wait.

When the last daughter of the second king passed, a cult inherited Ballern. With support inside the monarchy, the Children of the Dark Fire's goals were realized. It took time to replace the rulers of Ballern, but they have succeeded far more than I care to detail here. Many fear a new war comes on the horizon. The dangers surrounding the Great Machines, divine guardians according to the Children of the Dark Fire, have grown too large for even the most devout cultists. And make no mistake, a cult they are.

Their homes are now overrun by their own foolishness. The Children of the Dark Fire will seek to expand east. This expansion will come at the cost of the Skyborn, the largest threat to their power. The Children of the Dark fire will leave them in ruin.

Kat walked over to another case and pulled out a bound book, a gilded griffin on its spine. "Take care of these." She handed Alice the printed version of *The Failed Treatise and the Third War*.

"How long have these been here?" Mary asked.

"Since Yan Wu moved here. Decades, Mary."

"And no one knew?" Eva asked. "No one ever found this?"

Kat gave a slow shrug. "If they did, they didn't understand the significance of it. Or were unconcerned because it cost Ballern more than it cost us? Or assumed it was a lie printed by Ballern? More propaganda to catch us off guard? A million possibilities, Mary.

"Now, Eva, Alice, you need to get those documents to Furi. I have a ship waiting for you. An old pirate vessel we seized a long time ago."

"I can take them," Mary said.

Kat shook her head. "No, Mary. I need you here. There are still strangers in my guard, and I want to review my protocols with you."

"Is there a threat?" Mary sat up a little straighter.

Kat gave her a sad smile. "There is always a threat."

Mary sighed and nodded. "I'll stay. I can help keep Smith in line if he starts yelling at your tinkers."

Alice laughed at that.

"What?" Mary asked.

"Nothing, I was just thinking if anyone was going to yell at the tinkers, it would probably be you."

Kat and Eva both burst into laughter, only to immediately cover it with a cough.

Mary narrowed her eyes. "I'd be mad at all of you if you weren't right."

Alice grinned at the captain of the Skysworn. Smith might be the most patient person she knew. Mary, on the other hand, didn't hesitate to let her feelings be known.

Eva leaned forward. "Well, Alice, are you ready to take a trip? Let's go see what kind of junker Kat got us." She winked, but if Alice was being honest, she was a bit concerned about the ship too.

"Let's swing by the Skysworn," Mary said. "I'm sure Alice needs to grab a bag or two. Kat, I'll find you in the Hall as soon as I get the Skysworn locked up."

With that, they parted ways.

CHAPTER TWENTY-TWO

ALICE WRUNG HER hands together. She felt the weight of the glider on her back and the leather satchel in her hand. "Did they find him?"

Eva smiled at Alice. "You fancy that boy, don't you?"

"Yes …" Alice said, dragging out the word. "I thought that would be obvious by now." She looked out to the docks. Several lifts ran to and from their level, but there were no crowds there like those in Ballern.

"Why don't we put your gear on the ship? We can wait a bit longer for Jacob, but we need to go if we plan to be in Ballern before tomorrow."

Alice nodded and followed Eva across the gangplank. Usually, the ramps onto the airships were so wide that she didn't think about the lack of railings. But the decommissioned freighter had chains serving as railing on the narrow path, and she was glad of it.

She glanced at the patchwork hull and gas chamber. Rust showed through in some spots, but the gas chamber was polished and pristine above the deck. It was a jarring contrast, and one Alice suspected helped the pirates who used to run the airship keep a low profile.

Colors from every city's flag she could think of lurked somewhere on the vessel, from blue to gray to red to green. It wasn't attractive, to say the least, but it would fit in if they docked on the Bones. Over the opposite side of the airship, she could see a Titan Mech far below, tearing into the burned wreckage at the edge of the city.

"And the boiler looks better than the paint?" Alice asked, pointing up to the gas chamber.

Eva laughed and glanced back at her. "*Much.* It may even be in good enough shape for Smith's tastes."

"I can have him look it over if you'd like," Mary called from the end of the gangplank.

"Please, no," Eva said under her breath. "We need to *leave*, not wait for him to check every last gasket."

Mary grinned.

Alice followed Eva onto the deck and into the cabin. It wasn't as large as the Skysworn, but with only two of them onboard, it felt plenty spacious.

"Lockers are all yours. I already have my gear stowed by the captain's chair. Kat stocked us with enough dry food for a week, so that shouldn't be an issue."

Alice's gaze roamed along the ceiling, where more than a few water spots stained the wood. "As long as we don't end up in the sea." She took a deep breath and stashed her backpack and glider in the locker, double-checking for what must have been the fifth time that both books were safely stowed away.

"This old freighter holds more fuel than most destroyers. We could be deployed for a week and still have reserves." Eva leaned into the windscreen. "I think that's him."

Alice didn't bother to check the window. She hurried back to the deck and sprinted across the gangplank, her hands strategically touching the chains of the handrails as she went. She skidded to a stop beside Mary.

"Good eye," the captain of the Skysworn said, raising an eyebrow.

Alice grinned. "It was Eva."

Mary raised a hand to Eva as Jacob made his way down the dock. "I'm going to say goodbye to Eva. Just scream if you need anything."

"Thanks, Mary."

She watched Jacob's movement, amazed at how far he'd come in so short a time. There was barely a hitch in his stride to hint at the Biomech leg hiding beneath his clothes. And what would the future bring? She didn't know, but she was happy to be at his side, except for now she wouldn't be.

"I still don't want to split up," Alice said as he reached her. "This is exactly what I wanted to avoid."

Jacob blew out a breath. "I know. I don't either, but it's the only way we can bring a large group over at once, Alice. We have to do this."

"I just don't like it, even if it *is* our only real option."

"Me either." Jacob scratched the back of his neck. "I don't like the idea of you being over there alone. You'll have Furi and Kura, but still. Everyone else we know is so far away. It doesn't seem fair I'll still be here with Smith and Frederick."

"Mary too, she's staying."

"Really? I thought I saw her boarding that … ship?" His lip curled up as he actually looked at their airship.

"It's not as bad as it looks. We'll blend in, and it has a huge fuel supply."

Jacob blinked. "Hopefully that's not what we're carving on your tombstone. 'Drowned, but had fuel.'"

Alice snorted a laugh and swatted his arm. "How were the tinkers?"

Jacob gave a half smile. "Grumpy? We have a strategy, though. It's going to take some time, but the work will be split between Belldorn and Bollwerk."

"Kat gave me *The Failed Treatise and the Third War*. And some of the original notes by the woman who wrote it."

"That's incredible!" Jacob paused and nodded. "Smart. Harder to call a book a forgery with that in hand. I'm just glad she agreed to it. We need Furi to pull as many Skyborn in as she can."

"This will help."

Mary and Eva's voices rose as they returned to the deck.

Alice sighed. "I guess this time, it really is goodbye for now."

Jacob slid his arm around her waist and pulled her close. She reached up to his face, the stubble getting long enough to be a bit annoying when they kissed. But at that moment, she didn't care. He waited for her to kiss him, and she grabbed the sides of his face, holding him tight, remembering his warmth.

She stepped away after a time and smiled at him. "Soon. I'll see you soon."

"Yes, you will."

With that, Jacob said goodbye to Eva before leaving the docks with Mary in tow. Alice climbed aboard the freighter and settled into the cabin as Eva prepared to launch. Alice closed her eyes and listened to the rattle of the boiler. She'd see Jacob soon, but for now, it was time to focus on Ballern.

CHAPTER TWENTY-THREE

FURI SCOWLED AT nothing as they left their latest meeting in disappointment. "As many pledges as you got in those notes, there are still a quarter of the coalitions with no interest in the Stormborn, Jakon."

"Mostly, I am unconcerned," Jakon said, leaning forward over the table in his smuggler's hold. "The Abernathys are admittedly a potential problem. If anyone is going to inform on our doings, it would be them."

Furi grimaced. "Do you know how long I thought the Abernathys worked for the queen? They always touted that, you know? Queen's orders, queen's taxes, queen's seizure."

Jakon thumbed through a pile of maps that wouldn't have looked out of place in the Crown Library. "She worked against them for years, but the Abernathys are deep in the pockets of Viscount Allerton. They aren't any better than enforcers for a crime ring, Furi."

"You think they'll be a problem?"

Jakon tilted his head to the side. "Sometimes they're good customers. Sometimes the viscount pays them to kill people. It kind of depends on the day you meet them, Furi. But those who ignored the call to the Stormborn, or spoke out against it … none of them have as much influence as Kura."

"They think we're lying."

"It's human nature, Furi. The Children of the Dark Fire got their hands on them decades ago. Do you know how hard it is to change someone's mind if it's been poisoned for that long? You're talking about children, parents, and their grandparents. Multiple generations taught the same lie."

Furi crossed her arms. "That's why I need Alice to bring the book."

Jakon ran his finger across the edge of a map and pulled it from the stack. "Until she does, we should assume she won't make it. Every plan needs a backup, and every backup needs more backups. Here." He jabbed his finger down in the center of a faded cluster of trees.

It took Furi a while to figure out what was depicted on the map. "The Gray Woods?"

Jakon inclined his head.

Furi ran her finger over the names printed in the forests. "What are these?"

"Villages," Jakon said. "Well, they were the names of villages some thirty years ago. Some have merged, and others have died off. I give you backup plan number one."

Furi frowned at Jakon. "How are the villages of the Gray Woods a backup plan?"

Jakon sat back in one of the chairs he'd used to smuggle people to the Red Woods. People who'd died in Fel's raid. The sudden memory overwhelmed her, and her heart pounded in her chest. She wanted to move, *needed* to move.

"Are you okay?" Jakon asked.

Furi nodded, a little too quickly to be nonchalant about it. "Just … just remembering the Red Woods."

Jakon lowered his gaze to the table. "Yes, that was a tragedy. It is also why the Gray Woods will be a backup plan, Furi. What if Mordair turns his fleet against the docks? Decides to kill off the Skyborn while they're still in the air?"

Furi stared at him in horror. "He'd kill his own allies."

"Do you not think him capable of it?"

She stifled a shiver.

"Exactly. If something happens, we need a place to flee. Of course, we'll have to get the word out, both to the villages and to the Skyborn. Mordair will hear of it, I am sure. But it will at least split his focus."

"Who do we reach out to?"

"Leave that to me. I've made more than a few runs for those villages." Jakon grinned, and it was equal parts reassuring and unnerving. He held a finger up to ask for silence.

Furi held her tongue, about to ask him why when she heard it. The faintest footsteps. They could have been someone walking by on the docks—until the clicking started. Jakon pointed to the ceiling and then to the lockers behind the seats.

As soon as Furi stood, Jakon stepped closer to her, whispering so quietly she could barely hear him.

"You do not hesitate. Whoever has come onto this ship is no friend of mine."

"How do you know?"

"They aren't on the deck, Furi. They're on the roof."

The roof. It all fell together in an instant. Jakon had a window in the roof of the cabin. If he'd been in there, he would have been an easy target for an attack. Or worse.

Jakon slipped out of his boots. Furi did the same, and they moved to the lockers. He handed her a short sword, a standard issue for everyone who trained with the fleet. Beside that came a crossbow and a bandolier of throwing knives.

Furi hooked the sword sheath to her belt and put her arms into the leather armor Jakon offered. Less than a minute and they flanked the door. The porthole was so dirty no one could see into it. Great for hiding things for smuggling, but the drawback was no one could see out of it.

Jakon pulled a bolt out of the frame, putting his eye up to the hole and watching. A moment later, he opened the door and gestured for her to follow. Furi stayed close behind him, sticking to the outer wall where they wouldn't cast a visible shadow if someone looked in the portholes.

They paused at the corridor leading to the cabin, waiting and listening. Jakon raised a finger over his lips and pointed to a gap between the supports where Furi could hide. She unsheathed her sword and slid inside the shadows, making herself as small as possible and keeping the blade out of the light.

Furi leaned forward and watched Jakon walk down the corridor and up the stairs to the cabin, making a racket as he went. He banged on the walls until he reached the top. "I don't see anything up here. I think you're just hearing things."

He pointed at Furi and then disappeared as if he'd stepped into a locker. And Furi realized that was exactly what he'd done. She slipped into the shadows and stared at the plain gray metal of the supports she hid between.

It came fast. The crash reminded her of the sudden explosions across the Nightingale before it sank, and it caused a tremor to run down her legs. Furi's grip tightened on the sword as loud footsteps sounded through the corridor.

"Nothing! You said you saw him."

"He can't have gone far. Down the stairs. Find him!"

Furi gritted her teeth as boots slammed into the steel of the hallway just outside her hiding spot.

"He's here—" the man's words choked off in a gristly crack.

"Assassin!" Jakon called out.

Furi took a steadying breath as steps of the man's closest to her moved back into the hall. She ducked out of the shadows, her eyes checking the corridor from one end to the other and finding nothing.

"Big man, Jakon. You had this coming. You going to throw that dagger at me?"

Furi slipped in behind the man.

"Time for you to catch a bolt," the assassin growled. "You've got nowhere to go."

Jakon held his hands in the air. "I suppose I am yours. And you won't have to split the reward with your fellow here."

The man slowed and started to level his bolt thrower.

Furi took three rapid steps, only the third loud enough for the man to hear, but his reflexes were quick. He caught the thrust of her sword on his bracer, slamming it into the wall. But Furi had trained for tight quarters. Combat lessons that had been drilled into her head day in and day out until muscle memory was all that was needed.

She moved with the ricochet of the blade, spinning underneath his arm, twisting the sword back and up until the only thing stopping it was the top of their would-be assassin's skull. She stared at his wide eyes, and her heart hammered as she stepped away, ripping the blade free.

Furi cringed while the man kept clawing at his neck as if he could put the blood back where it had come from. The struggle didn't last long before he fell forward and stilled.

"I appreciate that you didn't kill him like that on the carpet," Jakon said. "This one was a bit cleaner." He pushed the other man down to crash to a stop a few feet from Furi. "That window isn't going to be cheap, though."

Jakon stomped down the stairs and bent down, pulling the rear collars of the men's shirts down. He frowned at the skin underneath. "No tattoo? I would have pegged these fools as Abernathys."

"Look at his arm," Furi said.

Jakon cursed and moved the other body, cursing again when he revealed a matching tattoo. "It's abstract, but that's a metal flame, I have no doubt."

"Why doesn't it look like those of the Children of the Dark Fire? It's all squares and sharp edges."

He grimaced. "So they can show allegiance to Children of the Dark Fire without having their actions traced back to them directly. It's a message. And one they meant us to relay, no doubt."

"You mean they sent these two here to die?"

"Maybe." Jakon rubbed his chin. "They certainly weren't up to the task." He studied her face. "Are you okay, Furi? I know this kind of thing is … unpleasant."

Furi nodded. "I'll be alright. I've seen worse."

"That's a good attitude. We'll probably see worse before this is done, too. We'd better contact Kura and tell her what happened. And it wouldn't hurt to warn our friends across the sea. Come on. We need to get something to drag these fools off the ship." He glanced down at the blood. "And a bucket."

✧   ✧   ✧

FURI WAS THANKFUL Jakon hadn't asked her to mop up the blood after they'd retrieved their boots. Instead, he got to work on it while she tried to remember the frequencies for the Skysworn. She was still shaken from the fight, and the wind whistling through the top of the airship wasn't helping anything.

The dial felt hard under her finger. She turned it back and forth until her mind finally reassembled the pieces of what she needed.

"Skysworn, over. Is anyone listening?" Silence answered, and worry gnawed at her. "Skysworn, come in." Furi closed her eyes and waited, the terrible wet sounds of the mop bucket in the corridor churning her stomach. Seeing Jakon toss the bodies into a wheelbarrow hadn't been too bad, but the sounds were getting to her. She didn't want to know more than that.

"No answer?" Jakon asked when the mop mercifully fell quiet.

"No."

"Hmm. Give me a minute." Jakon's bootsteps echoed down the corridor until they hit carpet. Furi glanced back at him, watching him open a locker and dig through a chaotic pile of paper. Or at least she'd thought it was chaotic.

He held up a piece of that paper about ten seconds later. "This is only for emergencies, which I think this qualifies. We're not supposed to have this, so maybe don't tell her where you got it."

Furi studied the frequency scrawled across the page. "Who is it?"

Jakon rubbed the back of his neck and gave something between a wince and a smile. "It's Lady Katherine's private frequency."

Furi felt her jaw going slack. "*How* did you get this?" Her mind raced through a dozen scenarios, bought it from a spy, found it on a job, traded for a top-secret list of transmitter frequencies, but only one made any real sense. "You stole this from Mary."

"And won't she be glad I did?"

"No!" Furi shook her head. "No, she won't, Jakon."

"Go on. It'll be fine. This is more important than any argument I'll have to have with Mary. Besides, she's stolen plenty from me over the years."

Furi huffed and turned back to the transmitter, moving the dials while she was still irritated, which kept the idea of contacting Lady Katherine directly from overwhelming her.

"And call her Kat! No formal names."

Furi closed her eyes and muttered a curse, then crushed the button for the transmitter. "Kat, are you there? Please, it's important. I need to get a message to Mary."

Silence.

Furi clicked the button again. "Kat, please." She hated the tone of her voice. It sounded like she was pleading, and that was far too close to begging. She'd been raised not to ask for help, and it was a hard habit to break.

"Who is this?" a voice hissed over the transmitter. "How do you know this frequency?"

Furi's heart leaped. "Kat? I'm … I'm a friend of Alice. We met at Mary's. I can't use my name because assassins just tried to kill me and my … my chef friend."

Another voice sounded in the background, and relief flooded through Furi when she recognized Mary. Although her words were far less reassuring. "I'll kill him."

"Please, please listen. Tell Gladys, tell Canopy, tell anyone you can. The Children of the Dark Fire sent assassins after us."

"How do you know?" Kat asked, the anger bleeding away from her words.

"Tattoos. They look like the metal-plated flame, but they're wrong. Too square and not shaped right. The chef thinks it's to show allegiance, but not be able to tie them back to the Children of the Dark Fire."

"Damn. He's probably right. How did you get this frequency?"

It was Mary who answered. "I let him on my ship. How do you think he got it?"

Jakon cringed and then raised an eyebrow. "Consider us even for that basket of truffles you took."

"That was *ten years ago*," Mary hissed. A string of curses followed while Kat tried to quiet her down. "Fine, *fine.* We're going to talk about this, though. What you did is dangerous."

"Not as dangerous as assassins," Jakon said. "These two were admittedly not very good, but that doesn't mean the next won't be."

"You were right to contact us," Kat said. "Keep the frequency. If you have another emergency, contact me directly."

"I tried the ship first," Furi said. "We were worried when no one answered."

"It's okay," Mary said. "The others are helping with the docks. I don't know if the transmitters can reach through that much metal anyway."

"What about Alice?"

"She'll be there soon," Kat said. "I'll warn her about the assassins. I'll contact Gladys and Jones, too. Get to a safe place and keep a low profile. Emergencies only, okay?"

"Okay."

"Be well."

The transmitter went dead.

"See?" Jakon said. "Everything's fine. Now Gladys and Archibald will know there are assassins in play, and whatever egocentric fool sent marked assassins in the first place has shown their hand."

Furi grimaced. The leaders of the Children of the Dark Fire weren't fools. And if they knew there was a high probability of those assassins failing, then what else did they have planned for the Stormborn and their allies?

CHAPTER TWENTY-FOUR

"ASSASSINS, KAT?" MARY said, pacing back and forth across the throne room. "We need to take precautions. Keep your armor on at all times. I don't care if you're in the bath. Wear your armor."

"Mary, that's …" Kat sighed. "We can worry about me once we have contacted the others."

"Gladys is better defended in Midstream than she has been in years, and Archibald still has his walls, doesn't he?"

"Walls, yes, but what is inside those walls, Mary? The unrest near the factories poses a threat on more than one front."

Mary stopped and pinched the bridge of her nose. "How is he going to deal with that? They can't wait any longer. If those carriers are going to be built before Ballern regroups and attacks us again, they can't wait."

"I suspect he'll deploy his Biomechs, Mary. It's … it's what I would do."

"You can't just attack your own citizens."

"No, but you can put them in a position where they are out of the way. Let them have their protests, but keep them far enough from the workers that it's not a safety issue."

Mary cursed under her breath. "This is a mess, Kat. Every time it feels like we have a handle on one situation, four more crop up."

"Welcome to leadership. Did you not deal with the same organized chaos in the guild?"

"Uh, yeah, I did." Mary put her hands on her hips. "And do you know what I did, Kat? I cut a deal with the *Speaker* of Bollwerk to get out of it."

Kat grabbed either side of the transmitter table and bowed her head. "Come and sit with me, Mary. Let's talk to Archibald."

Mary nodded and walked back to the table, sliding into one of two velvet chairs Kat had placed by the transmitter. The brass device with its long antenna normally hid behind a false panel in a marble column, but now it stood exposed.

Kat turned the dials and pressed the button. "Fire Lizard, this is Sea Claw, over."

"Codenames?" Mary asked. "Do you think Archibald's new frequency could be compromised already?"

"It's hard to know if you've plugged all your leaks. He's been monitoring the line, and there hasn't been any activity, but it's best to be safe."

"Fire Lizard." Archibald's monotone response was unmistakably him.

"News from across the sea. An assassin came for the chef, tattooed with an abstract of the metal-plated flame."

"Assassins are nothing new. I will increase my patrols, but I have other concerns, Sea Claw."

"As do I. The threat has come full circle. Do you not think it wise to delay our own strike? Reinforce our cities against all external threats."

Archibald let out a sigh that degraded into static. "There was a time I would have agreed. But the time for that has passed. How long until you see the same unrest that plagues the desert city of Bollwerk? Without action, the same fate will come for Ancora, Belldorn, even Dauschen, where the scars may never fully heal. Think on that. If you still believe inaction is the best course, I implore you to reconsider."

Kat looked like she was about to say more and then fell silent. Mary reached out and squeezed her hand.

The Lady of Belldorn pressed the transmitter again. "Bolster your guard. We will speak again."

"You do the same." Archibald's voice grew quieter. "And make sure it is people you can trust. Keep your circle small. If the coalitions of Ballern are involved, there is more at play than we know. Fire Lizard out."

Kat blew out a breath.

"Are you still considering holding off on deploying to Ballern?" Mary asked. "You can't give them that kind of time."

"I know," Kat said with a grimace. "Part of me knows that, Mary, but I don't want to send my people to their deaths."

"I'd rather march into the fight than end up under the rule of the Children of the Dark Fire."

"Maybe. Maybe, Mary. But time is all any of us really has, and having it cut short is the worst tragedy of all." Kat spun the dials on the transmitter and pressed the button again.

"George, are you there?" Kat waited for a time before static came back and cleared.

"Sea Claw, yes, I am here."

A loud thunder sounded in the background, followed by an old but stern voice cursing at great length.

"Everything okay?" Kat asked.

"Yes, yes," George said with mild annoyance. "Targrove just dropped the arm of a Titan Mech on a crawler. It's fine. Well, it is not fine. It is quite broken, but the people are fine, and that is good."

Mary couldn't help but laugh and shake her head.

"George, I need you to listen closely. Assassins have been identified in Ballern. They came for The Ray."

"Survivors?"

"All, thankfully. The assassins bore tattoos made to resemble metal-plated flames, but not done in the traditional style of the Children of the

Dark Fire."

"Understood. If memory serves, those are the assassins working for the Auxley district. Tread carefully."

"Auxley? The baroness?"

"Yes, Sea Claw. Cunning and ruthless are the nicest things I have heard about that woman."

"Didn't you say the same thing about me?" Kat asked the question so innocently, Mary could only blink.

George laughed. "Perhaps. But you like my soup, so there is far more to compliment about your person."

Kat exchanged a small grin with Mary. "Be careful, will you? Keep her safe."

"Always, Sea Claw. You must change your codename. I find myself hungry now."

"Goodbye, George." Kat shook her head and disconnected. She twisted the dials again and clicked the transmitter. "Freighter, this is Sea Claw."

There wasn't a delay on this broadcast. The answer came quick and sharp.

"Codenames?" Eva's voice crackled with static. "Rust it all. What's happened?"

Mary leaned closer and answered before Kat could. "Assassins in Ballern. They boarded The Ray."

"Is everyone alive?" Alice asked, her voice rising in the background.

"Everyone besides the assassins. Find the others as soon as you dock. Take no chances."

"What are you doing about the Sea Claw?" Eva asked. "Hopefully not making drawn butter."

Kat snorted a laugh and pushed Mary away. "No, Freighter. She will be well protected, but thank you for your concern."

"Good. What about the construction efforts? Is the factory ready?"

"Not yet. They're still working on it."

"Well, don't keep us waiting forever," Eva muttered. "I've no desire to be fending off assassins waiting for you to make up your mind on some small nuance."

Kat didn't answer, instead biting her lips.

Eva didn't miss the delay. "Sea Claw ..." She dragged out the code-name. "Are you already dragging your feet on something?"

"The safety of the city," Kat answered, a little too fast.

"Let us know when you decide if we're worth saving," Eva snapped, and the transmitter went dead.

Mary wanted to shout with joy at Eva's unmitigated guilt trip, but she reined herself in. Kat, on the other hand, groaned and let her head thump down on the table.

"Why did I take this job?"

Mary grinned. "Why don't we start with organizing your guards?"

CHAPTER TWENTY-FIVE

OWEN STUDIED THE broken wall of Fel as the small airship crested the last of the foothills. Home. Part of it still felt like coming home. There was no arguing with the fact things had changed. Only one fishing vessel made its way down the river, and the city had never looked so open.

Fel's walls had been impenetrable the entire time he'd lived there. There were stories of invasions during the Deadlands War, but even those had been brought to a standstill or had the tide turned by Fel's formidable army. But now the city stood open, with little more than a paddock fence to keep out unwanted wildlife.

"You didn't have to do this," Owen said to Cage, who sat in the pilot seat.

"Are you joking? Nora offered to lend me her jump ship, and I sure wasn't going to say no."

Owen smiled and looked back at the city. It might have been their home in many ways, but it felt even emptier knowing Vaughn and Hefina were back in Ancora. They'd be safer there, Owen was sure of that, but it didn't make him any more comfortable with the distance.

Cage pulled up and took them high above the city walls. There was a time any ship crossing into Fel's airspace would have been shot down, but the remaining ballistae were silent along the wall and ridges.

"It's so empty," Owen said, leaning closer to the window in the small cabin. "And gray."

Cage nodded. "Easy to forget, isn't it? Dauschen and Ancora are vibrant by comparison. Fel wasn't always so dark, though. Or so my grandfather used to say."

Owen's focus shifted from the streets to the fast-approaching dock. Cage swung wide, taking them west of the tower where Mordair once ruled. The archway connecting the docks to the city looked small from their vantage point, dwarfed by the sea that opened in the distance.

The airship docks were dead. There wasn't another word for it in Owen's mind. The dockhands were few and far between. So much so that no one even gestured at Cage or acknowledged the ship's arrival as they floated into one of the smallest bays.

"If you decide to do something stupid," Cage said, "I'd appreciate a little warning. *And* an invitation." With that, he powered down the small turbines on the jump ship. "Tie us off, would you?"

Owen grunted as he unwedged himself from the small space in the cabin and pushed the door open. It swung up instead of to the side, which was both interesting and undeniably odd. He grabbed an aged leather pack from the rear locker and threw it over his shoulders.

Outside, Owen picked up one of the anchored ropes with a spring-loaded clamp on the end. It snapped onto the railing of the bow, and he repeated the process on either side of the ship as Cage climbed out. Owen took another moment to crank the winch on the deck, tightening all three ropes and stabilizing the jump ship.

"Thanks, Owen. I doubt I'd ever hear the end of it if she blew away. I have a few bars to visit, so if you need me before our rendezvous, check there. Are you going to go looking for those transmitters?"

Owen nodded. "Some things you have to see with your own eyes."

"There were enough of them hidden in Dauschen. I wouldn't be surprised at all if Archibald managed to keep a few spies active in Fel."

"I'll check the docks. And I want to run by my house. See if everything's still there."

"Three hours, Owen. We're in, out, and back to Ancora."

Owen wasn't sure about that as he looked down at the bay below Fel. There were more fishing vessels left behind than he'd expected. That wasn't all. One of the smaller armored destroyers sat unfinished in dry dock. He nodded regardless and strode toward the walkway that would take him into the city, while Cage went farther down the docks. Likely to visit one of many unlicensed bars hidden in the sea caves.

Owen laughed under his breath and headed back into his city.

✦ ✦ ✦

OWEN UNFOLDED THE small piece of paper and studied the frequency scrawled across it. If he found the transmitter, those numbers would get him in touch with Nora. But the other numbers, added as an after-thought, would get him in touch with some of the fisherfolk who had been spies.

The question in Owen's mind was, would they fight for Fel? Or would they fight against the tyrant? Spies he didn't like. They made him question their loyalty at every turn. All of them except Cage. But Cage was blood, and that got more trust from Owen than anything else.

The lift slowed to a stop, and Owen stepped out into the wide streets of Fel. Mordair's red and gray banners still fluttered sporadically around the city, but many of them had been torn down. No bodies remained on the far walls, and he was glad of it.

Owen pulled his vest tighter and struck out toward the caves of the fisherfolk. The walk played tricks on his mind, one step feeling as if nothing had changed and no time had passed, with locals dining on an outdoor patio. The next moment, he remembered his wife and son were far from home, and he likely wouldn't see them for some time. His thoughts darkened at the end of the block, the cold gray of the jagged mountains rising far above.

He remembered his brother. Remembered the iron fist of Mordair strangling the life from his city. Remembered the raid that came for the fisherfolk. But fisherfolk didn't lay down for tyrants. Fisherfolk defended their own.

Owen's hands curled into fists, and his steps fell heavier as he reached the path to the caverns.

No guards waited at the checkpoints. Each shack stood empty, one with a broken window and dark stain Owen didn't linger on. His fingers brushed the hilt of his broad knives sheathed at his waist. One of the fisherfolk would rarely be seen without a blade of some kind. Be it for cutting line, cutting net, or cutting throats.

The tunnel dimmed the light all around him, but enough of the lanterns were lit to show the way. Only a few people walked in that place, but he could hear voices ahead. If he didn't know what had happened there, he could have imagined it was a day of rest on the river.

Owen crossed through onto the docks, his boots echoing with each step on the wood. One of the larger bars was gone. Ash and rubble stood in its place, burned through to the stone beneath. It was hard for a fire to do that kind of damage so close to the water. Fisherfolk had pumps and hoses that could cover the entire cavern in minutes.

The dark stains and cut hose nearby told him the rest of the story. He didn't need to see that to know the story, though. It was one of his last visions as he'd fled with his family.

Laughter echoed around him, and a few boats thumped against the docks on a gentle wake.

He followed the docks toward those voices. Light gave away the inlet where a favorite restaurant had operated for a decade. The laughter led him there, to a small gathering of fisherfolk who sat around a bar, the scent of fried fish and spiced beets lingering like an old friend.

A thin reed of a man worked the grill and fryer behind the counter, the kitchen open to the air. He hadn't slowed over the years, and Owen supposed that made sense. The man had opened the place when he was barely twenty.

"Trevor," Owen called as he walked past the tables and occupied barstools.

The entire place fell silent.

"Owen?" Trever squinted at him, a turner in one hand and a basket for the fryer in the other. "Owen!" Trevor dropped both of the utensils and hurried to the older man. "Rust and steel. We all thought you died."

Owen threw his arms around Trevor and gave him two hard thumps on the back before responding. "Came close enough. I fled with Vaughn and Hefina as … well, you know."

Trevor nodded and made his way back to the grill. "Grab yourself a beer, Owen. I have more than I'll ever be able to sell with the city empty."

Owen inclined his head to the other fisherfolk. A few he recognized, but their names escaped him. A larger woman with piercing brown eyes inclined her head and took a long pull from her stein. The conversation started up again, and Owen closed his eyes, basking in the familiarity of it all.

"What are you doing here?" Trevor asked as he walked by with a plate of fish for another patron.

"I'm going to Ballern," Owen said in no uncertain terms. "Mordair killed my brother. It's time to be a thorn in his side."

"Cheers to that!" someone shouted from down the bar.

Owen picked up a stein and leaned over to the tap. It was a sloppy pour, but he just needed a drink.

The larger woman called out to Owen. "Are you serious about that? You're going to go after him?"

"I doubt I can get to him," Owen muttered, clenching a fist. "But I know a thing or two about his fleet. We all do. Get onboard those ocean liners, and we could do some real damage."

She said something to the men at her table, but Owen couldn't make it out. She raised her voice again. "Name's Fiona. I've seen you around the docks from time to time. Where's your boy?"

"Ancora," Owen said. "They're taking refugees if anyone needs shelter."

"Shelter?" Fiona said with a laugh. "I have fish and beer. What more shelter is there?"

Owen smiled at that, but some other people didn't find it so outlandish.

"How safe is it?" a younger man asked.

Owen tilted his head to the side. "They have their walls rebuilt, so I reckon it's a bit safer than Fel."

He studied his beer for a time. "If I can get my girl there safely, I'll come to Fel with you. I can't leave her alone here. She's only twelve."

Fiona crossed her arms. "How are you going to get to Fel, Owen?"

"Flew in this morning. Been up to the airship docks?"

None of them said yes.

"There's an ocean liner in the dry docks, and at least a dozen small fishing vessels docked at the base of the mountains."

"You mean to take a netter across the confluence?" Fiona's eyebrow arched higher as she spoke. "Where the Black Sea meets the Gray? Are you mad?"

"No, I'm practical. Do you think anyone on Ballern's boat docks would notice a fishing vessel coming in or out? I don't believe they would."

"It could work," Trevor said, pointing at Fiona with his spatula. "Stow the nets to keep the balance, and you could clear the confluence. It's been done with smaller boats than that."

"The confluence has swallowed *larger* boats than that too. But ... I admit, I'm intrigued. Very intrigued. Who else have you recruited?"

"You're the first group I've spoken to."

That got a booming round of laughs.

Trevor wiped his eyes on his sleeve. "Oh, aye, Owen. You've got some work to do then. This raggedy bunch isn't going to do much against a fleet."

"No stronger backs in the world than fisherfolk, Trevor. I believe that with all my heart."

"Then step up and say it." Trevor gestured out to the river and beyond. "Folks these days who have a piece to say use Mordair's stage in the square. If you're serious, tell your story there. It'll spread."

"I'll spread the word here," Fiona said. She hooked her thumb over her shoulder. "This lot will help."

There were a few muttered words of agreement.

"Give us two hours," Trevor said. "Two hours, and we'll have as many fisherfolk as we can find out in the square. And that's saying something. We don't much like the square, you know."

"I know." Owen glanced down at his foamy beer and drank the rest in a few gulps. "Two hours. I'll be there." He dropped a few coins onto the bar. "Thank you. All of you."

✧   ✧   ✧

Owen made his way farther down the dock, but it wasn't long before he realized the far ends of the docks were empty. So many had left, or had they been lost in the raid? Either was a weight on his heart.

Plans had changed. He wasn't going to go hunting for old transmitters now. He had to prepare himself for talking to whatever fisherfolk showed up. Owen walked back to the tunnel and took the path into the city, heading toward the second street from the outer wall. It wasn't the nicest part of Fel by any stretch, but it had been home for a long time. Memories of past generations lingered there, some fading to fuzzy dreams, while others were locked away forever in a photograph.

Owen stopped in front of the narrow residence his family lived in. He'd always thought the tiny living spaces in Fel were similar to the rest of the world. That all changed when he traveled to Cave and Belldorn to study fishing styles from across the lands.

Then he realized how close together the walls of Fel were. Both the city walls and those he called home. Owen slid the house key in and cracked the door open. The warm scent of cinnamon mixed with musty air. Hefina's incense, still cloying and welcome.

Owen closed the door behind him and stood in the entryway for a moment, letting the memory of that place flow around him. He glanced at the long couch, almost too big for the area where it faced the stairs. He checked the cooler in the kitchen to make sure nothing would rot while the family was gone. Assuming they ever came home again.

That done, he headed upstairs, passing Vaughn's bedroom on the second-floor landing before turning and heading to the third floor. The stairs were only wide enough for one person. Every wall hung with paintings and photographs in frames narrow enough they wouldn't be bumped off the wall.

Owen stepped into the long bedroom. A room he could nearly touch wall to wall with his fingertips outstretched. Their bed at the end took up the entire width of the room. Owen sighed and turned away from it, pulling open the closet. Inside waited his spearfishing gear. He grabbed both launchers with their quivers.

Behind that was a small cabinet. Old photos rested within, leaning against a stud in the wall. Owen took a deep breath and lifted them out, flipping through images he couldn't bear to burn, but couldn't bear to look at either. He pulled out two of his brother and left the rest behind.

Owen walked to the dresser and took one more photo. One of the celebrations on the docks from two years before. Vaughn looked so young, but so happy. His hands were a little blurry due to his inability to sit still for any amount of time, but it was still one of Owen's favorite photos.

He opened the bottom drawer in the dresser and grabbed a rolled-up sleeve of knives. He stuffed those and the spearguns into a large carpet bag from under the bed. Bolt throwers had long been outlawed in Fel, which was another reason he exceled at hiding things. It took some work to remove the false bottom in the dresser drawer.

Two cylinders waited there. He'd purchased them in Cave some ten years prior, along with two dozen bolts. All of it went into the carpet bag. Owen slid the clasp closed and ran his fingers over the intricate vine pattern made of faded greens and reds.

He placed a hand on their comforter, still unmade from the last time they'd slept there. Owen studied it before heading back downstairs. His time would be up soon enough, and he had no intention of being late.

✧　✧　✧

OWEN STOPPED ON the street corner and stared at the gathering crowd. There might have been fisherfolk there, but whatever Fiona and Trevor had done, there were far more people waiting at the stage than he'd expected.

He started down the street, hand closing tighter and tighter on the carpet bag. Speaking to large groups had never been a comfortable thing for Owen. The closest he normally came was teaching some of the young fisherfolk how to care for their rods and nets. This was different.

Owen reached the back of the crowd and started weaving between them until he heard a familiar voice.

"I really hoped this wasn't going to turn out to be you."

He turned to find Cage with his arms crossed. "It wasn't a choice."

"It never is, I suppose. Go on, then. I'll keep an eye on the crowd for you. You're paying my bail if I have to cut anyone."

Owen laughed and moved toward the stage, the smile not leaving his face when he saw Trevor and Fiona sitting on the side of the stage. Trevor waved to Owen to call him over. Seeing them gave him comfort he hadn't expected, calming the nerves he tried to ignore.

"You made it!" Trevor said.

"I do prefer to be on time. Most fisherfolk do."

Trevor scoffed at that. "You clearly don't run a bar." He reached out and put a hand on Owen's shoulder. "You said some good things at the bar, Owen. These people need to hear the same."

"They'll hear more than that." Owen started up the stairs and sat his carpet bag on the edge of the stage. It was a show of trust, and if he'd learned one thing in his lifetime, trust was earned.

Fiona cast him a smile before she turned to the crowd and shouted. "Listen up!" Her voice carried over the general conversation and chaos of the gathering, and silence flowed out from her words like a ripple in a lake.

Owen didn't wait. The longer he waited on things, the more nervous they made him, and that had long ago taught him not to delay.

"Fisherfolk! Some of you know me. I am Owen of house Kriss. A house that rose and fell long before the Mordairs claimed their rule over our city. And ever since, my family has been one of you, the strongest community in all the cities of the north.

"To those of you who don't know me, I wish we had met under better circumstances, on the water or behind a stein. I bid you welcome." He paused. "I won't waste your time this day. Mordair killed a great many of us in his last raid. Tried to lay the blame of the siege on the fisherfolk. That was all a ruse. My message, my *offer*, is simple. Come with me to

Ballern to strike a blow against our fallen king.”

"Why?" Cage shouted, and Owen had to try not to smile at his cousin's rather obvious prompt.

"I'll answer that question." He'd moved Ancorans with that story. He could move his own brethren with it.

"Unworthy. We've all heard the word. We've all lived it and struggled against that label. Some of you may have even used it against us, and I harbor no ill will toward you. It's what you were taught behind these walls. But I've been to Dauschen and Ancora. I saw what that kind of hostility in Fel was truly a harbinger of. And I tell you, as many as we lost in that final raid, we were lucky."

Owen reached into the pocket of his vest and pulled out a dark photograph. "This is my brother. *Was* my brother. Until they strung him from the wall."

The gathered crowd mumbled and shouted similar stories, and Owen waited for them to quiet again. And it took some time before the overlapping tales of horror subsided.

"You all remember the changing of the guard. That's what they called it. They'd get more violent for less and less serious crimes. Do you remember what happened at The Crooked Blade? A man with too much drink bumped into an airship pilot. Innocent enough, but it wasn't an hour before they gutted him like a fish and hung him from the wall. It was the start of a war inside our own walls, and it cost us all far too much.

"His name was Carl Lawrence. I remember his name. I remember what they did to his family." Owen's mouth twitched as fury bled into his voice. "I remember the screams of his daughter when they threw her into that fire! I remember the good that family did for the fisherfolk. I remember Carl Lawrence. I remember his daughter Bethany, and I will see the Red Hand dead before I close my eyes for the last time!"

The crowd stared at Owen.

He raised his chin and stared back, biting his tongue to hold back the tears that wanted to escape.

Fiona drew a slender blade from her belt and hammered it into the stage. "The king is dead." She slammed the hilt down until the blade shattered.

Trevor followed her lead.

They came in pairs and threes after that, men and women, children who Owen would never let see the dawn of a battle. Knives thrust into the wood and broken off until the stage's entire edge was a gray waste-land of broken blades. It was a fisherfolk tradition reserved for the death of a leader. But there was a darker side to it. One Fiona had called upon with her words and her gesture. A call to battle, and a cry for blood.

CHAPTER TWENTY-SIX

A LICE STARED OUT at the docks above Ballern while Eva hunted for an empty spot on the docks.

"This was a lot easier when Fel wasn't taking up every last bay," Eva muttered.

The turbines of the freighter whined and quieted as Eva adjusted their flight path.

Alice kept an eye on the docks. It looked busier than the last time she'd been there, even out on the Bones. Seeing men and women standing on the far edges, clustered in small groups, was strange. It didn't dawn on her why until she saw a woman pass a satchel to someone else.

"They're on the Bones to keep their conversations private, aren't they?" Alice asked.

"Probably. Doesn't look too private today, though, does it?" Eva blew out a breath. "We aren't finding anything on this level, Alice. We'll go down one more. It's a bit rougher. Known for its thieves as much as its empty bays."

"Do you think that's still a problem with Fel patrols everywhere?"

Eva pursed her lips. "Good point. Maybe not. And … it's not like this old freighter is going to be a big target for anyone." She pushed the steering levers forward, and the ship slowly drifted down. Eva cursed when the lower level opened before them. "Are you joking?"

Even there, every small bay looked to be filled from one end of the dock to the other. Eva steered them to the end and swung around the corner.

"There!" Alice said. "That's The Ray. That's Jakon's ship. And look at all the open bays."

"I hope he doesn't mind a neighbor."

Eva guided the freighter into the bay beside The Ray. The ship might have been small for what it was, but Alice tried to sink into her seat as Eva drifted in with a mere foot of clearance on either side.

"And done." She powered the turbines down and sighed. "I'm ready to stretch my legs. How about you?"

Alice was already out of her seat by the time Eva stopped talking.

"I'll take that as a yes."

"Sorry, definitely a yes." Alice rubbed her hands together. "I want to get these books to Furi and Kura, and the crowds on the docks are making me nervous."

Eva studied the traffic in front of them before nodding. "Good news is we're right next to a lift. Let me get the ship tied off. We can take that lift up to the warehouse district's level and be there in no time."

Alice picked up her backpack and left the glider in the locker. She hesitated and then tossed a cloak over her shoulders too, the gray hood helping to obscure the fact she had anything on her back at all.

Eva followed, grumbling when she had to kick the gangplank five times to get it unstuck. She tied the ship off like she'd done it a thousand times before, which, Alice thought, she probably had, and they were on their way.

As crowded as much of the docks were, Alice was glad to see the path to the narrow lift on the other side of The Ray was anything but crowded. They only had to wait behind one group, and in less than five minutes, the lift took them up.

"This place sure is lively," Eva said.

"Have you been here before?"

She nodded. "Not often, mind you, but when you spend enough time around Mary …"

Alice grinned. "Say no more. Did she get you into any trouble? Anything that would have you stripped of rank and berated by Kat?"

Eva turned to Alice and narrowed her eyes. "That sounds awfully specific, Alice."

"I promise Mary didn't say a word." Alice flashed her a grin. "You just have to remember *I've* spent time with her, too."

The lift rattled to a stop, and Eva pulled the lever that opened the gate. She offered Alice a small smile, and they pushed out into the crowds, walking across the narrow platforms like it was Festival in Ancora.

Only in Ancora, you couldn't feel the ground shift beneath your feet with all the boots walking around you. The sensation unnerved Alice, but she kept her cloak pulled tight, leading the way for Eva.

It was jarring to be in that space, hearing a great deal of happy banter and joking along that section of the docks. A few buskers were set up, performing small plays with marionettes while others entertained with rudimentary magic tricks.

The crowds thinned somewhat when they reached the residential areas outside the warehouse district, and Alice almost tripped when she saw a blue banner with an abstract Shadowwing emblazoned across it in glittering black sequins.

"Go," Eva hissed.

Alice nodded and continued on, not sparing a glance back for the flag that bore the insignia of the Stormborn. She kept her eyes forward but focused on her peripheral vision. It was a trick Jacob had taught her, and one that had helped her avoid pickpockets on several occasions.

The small homes gave way to the warehouse district and the bays for several of Fel's warships. Gray shadows loomed over the area, cannons polished to a dark sheen, some of their barrels pointed directly into the docks as if they meant to attack.

Alice shuddered at the idea. The docks in Ballern weren't like the docks anywhere else. They weren't merely a military target. They were home to thousands.

The warehouse district teemed with Skyborn and Fel soldiers alike, though in the distance, the gray uniforms overwhelmed all others. It was as if the Skyborn all avoided the warships as best they could, and Alice had the same instinct.

She turned the corner and headed to the last walkway to the south, taking it east until she reached the school. The handle felt cold to the touch when she pushed inside, half expecting to find a crowd of people, but instead only finding three.

The conversation between Furi, Kura, and Jakon fell silent.

"Alice?" Furi said, standing up straighter. "How did you get here so fast? I didn't think we'd see you for a while."

"This is Eva," Alice said, glancing between her and the group.

"Jakon," the chef said, stepping forward to greet Eva. "Mary has told me a great deal about you."

Eva narrowed her eyes. "She's told me a great deal about you, too."

Jakon's grin lit up like a torch. "This is Kura and Furi, if you didn't already know." He gestured to each as he said their name.

Alice pulled off her cloak and backpack and walked over to Kura's desk. "Did I see a Stormborn flag out on the docks? How is that already there?"

"We have a few craftspeople who have pledged to the cause," Kura said. "Some of them have little else to do."

"You have the books?" Furi asked.

Alice nodded, sliding the pair out of her bag, and placing them on the table side by side.

"Yan Wu's original manuscript," Kura said, tapping on the notebook. "To think it was in Belldorn all these years."

Alice opened the book and the notebook to the pages she'd committed to memory. She wasn't sure how many times she'd read them at that point, but the text was easy to recall, even when the books weren't in front of her.

"These passages. These show how little was edited from Yan's original writing. It's proof the book tells the true history of Ballern."

"Or at least as true as Yan believed it to be," Jakon said.

Kura nodded and read, speaking only the last line out loud. "The Children of the Dark fire will leave them in ruin." She glanced at Alice before focusing on Furi. "Not all the Skyborn can read Mokuskrit. Having Yan's translations on the same page is a boon."

"Enough of them can," Furi said. "Enough that even if they can't read it themselves, they'll know some who can. Someone they'll trust."

"Take these to William at the bookstore by the market," Kura said.

"William?" Furi asked before her eyes lit up. "The clerk?"

"He's not merely a clerk, Furi. William has long been the owner of that store. Ever since the previous owner fell out of sorts with the Baroness of Auxley. And that owner has been in prison since then. Either that or they buried him at sea."

"Are you sure?" Jakon asked.

Kura nodded. "He's long been a Skyborn sympathizer. I've gotten crucial information from him in the past year. Information that has kept more than a few of us out of prison." She closed the books and handed them back to Alice.

"Furi, stay with Alice. Eva, Jakon, we need to plan for what happens when things go wrong on the docks. And with some already placing Stormborn flags around the walkways, things *will* go wrong."

Furi squeezed her hands together and gestured to Alice. "Ready?"

Alice nodded. "Eva, we'll be back soon. If you need to get back to Belldorn, don't wait for me. We're with friends here."

"Oh no, I'm not leaving you here, Alice. Anything happens to you, and I'd never hear the end of it from Mary. You lose one shipment of Pilly eggs …" Eva rolled her eyes.

Kura called out as Furi and Alice reached the door. "And if William tells you that's interesting and says no more, you ply him for more detail. He's on his own side in this. Remember that."

Furi inclined her head and pushed through the door. Alice followed.

✧   ✧   ✧

"ON THE BRIGHT side, it's bad luck to steal from old blood."

Alice raised an eyebrow. "Are you saying I'm carrying everything because it's *bad luck* to steal from me?"

"Yes. Definitely." Furi grinned.

Alice shook her head and trailed the Skyborn across the docks. They kept to the outside near the Bones until they needed to cut back for the lift. The crowds thickened there, and Alice grimaced when she realized it would be no short wait.

"Listen," Furi whispered.

So she did, catching snippets of conversations with no real weight. One couple argued about where to eat for dinner, while another bantered about a new game they'd played down at the bar. Another woman mentioned her favorite bard from the Gray Woods was in the city, and she didn't want to miss them.

But it was the words the woman said next that caught her attention. "More than one person says he's one of the Stormborn! Can you believe it? Grimhelm the bard? A Stormborn?"

"Nonsense," her friend said. "That's utter rubbish. No bard announces their allegiance to a bunch of traitors before walking into the city they're betraying. Think about it."

"I … I suppose. But wouldn't it be wonderful?"

"Yes, yes." The friend lowered her voice. "Did you bring the flags?"

The first woman opened her bag and tilted it just enough that Alice caught sight of the symbol of the Stormborn.

Furi bumped her with her elbow and gave a small shake of her head. "Don't stare."

"Right." Alice turned her attention back to the lift. She tried to pick out the voices of the two women again, but it was hard as more Skyborn walked between them.

Soon enough, they were in the lift with far more people than seemed safe, riding down to the city proper. Alice took a deep breath of free air once they unloaded and their feet hit the cobblestones. Furi wove through the crowds on the street, leading them to the other side, where the sidewalk was empty by comparison.

Alice was struck again by how clean Belldorn looked, the light stone and polished windows catching and casting light all around the people who milled about its streets. She stuck close to Furi when the Skyborn almost leaped into an alley to avoid an oncoming cluster of people.

"There now," Furi said. "Not so bad."

"So many people."

Furi grinned. "And now you see how pirates manage to keep their trade alive in Ballern. It's a bit busier than normal with Fel here, but you'd be surprised how much traffic the docks get in a month." She pushed her way through the front door of the bookshop, setting off a small bell.

But the bell didn't sound before Alice caught the words of the woman at the counter. "That cult disgusts me."

She and the clerk both turned to see who had entered the store.

A smile worked its way across William's face when he recognized

Furi and Alice. "Welcome back! Two of my favorite patrons. Looking for more quality history books?"

The woman pulled the hood of her cloak back and eyed the newcomers.

Alice didn't miss the flash of gray armor beneath the brilliant greens and blues of the cloak. "You're from Fel."

The woman raised an eyebrow. "I am, girl. Aren't you the bold one?"

"I heard what you said. You don't like the Children of the Dark Fire."

"Oh, and do you intend to do something about that?" she asked with some amusement. "Run off and tell one of those cult Carrion Worms what a Fel soldier said?"

"Of course not. I don't like them either."

The woman paused and turned to William. "You know these two?"

William nodded. "I do. They don't seem to fall in line quite as easily as most of the locals."

"I've heard they aren't falling in line much at all up on the docks." The woman lifted a coin purse and doled several out to William before picking up her bag. "You all take care. I don't want to hear about any of you getting tied up in this mess with those fools calling themselves Stormborn."

Alice felt Furi stiffen at her side. She stepped in front of the Skyborn to hide any temporary awkwardness from view.

The woman adjusted the canvas bag and inclined her head to William. "A pleasure, sir. I will return." Her graceful movements didn't hide the edge of a golden vambrace, or the ropey muscles of her forearms. She moved like she could have been a dancer. Given the Fel uniform, Alice suspected she was anything but.

She paused in front of Alice and Furi. "If you hear anything about the Children of the Dark Fire plotting against the steward, I would be most appreciative of the information."

"Of course. How can we reach you?"

"Come to the palace and ask for Patrice. The guards will show you to me, or let you know when to return."

"You work in the palace?" Furi asked.

Patrice nodded.

"But you don't like the Children of the Dark Fire?"

Patrice gave Furi a flat smile. "I thought we had established the fact no one in this room likes that cult."

"Yes, ma'am."

"Good, that's very good. William, be well. As to you two, I'm sure William can sell you some wonderful propaganda."

William scowled and waved as Patrice left.

"She seems nice," Furi said.

William shrugged. "She pays, and she prefers the less curated books. That is someone I can respect. Now, what are you two doing back so soon? I gave you enough entertainment to last a month."

"Is the shop empty?" Furi asked.

William nodded.

"Alice, show him."

Alice pulled out the two copies of *The Failed Treatise and the Third War.*

William smiled at the first. "Ah, yes. One of the Children of the Dark Fire's more butchered accounts, or so they say. You know …"

Furi turned the book sideways to show the gilded griffin on the spine, and William's sentence died.

"That … that's …"

"You've read it before, though, haven't you?"

"Copies and reproductions, yes. But I've never seen a first edition." William gently took it from Furi's hands, turning it over and gently cracking it open.

Alice cleared her throat and tapped on the notebook.

William glanced at it. "One moment."

Alice opened it to the title page and waited.

William eventually looked again and froze. "That … that can't be … how did you … how did *it*?" He looked up at the door and stepped out from behind the counter, rushing over to throw the deadbolt and post the closed sign.

"Both of you with me. In the back. Now."

William scooped up the book and manuscript and led the way to a blank wall. He pushed on a length of wainscoting and a door beneath the stairs swung open to reveal a small office. Books lined every wall and shelf, and where there wasn't any space left, the books rose in towering piles. Four stools were all the seating in the cramped room.

"Sit, please, sit."

Alice studied that space, reading title after title, and catching sight of more than a few marked with the gilded griffin. "I thought everything from that publishing house was destroyed."

Furi glanced at Alice and then looked at where she was pointing. Her brow furrowed, and she stood, taking a closer look at the back wall. Her voice didn't hide the awe. "You have banned books."

"I have a great deal more than that, Furi. But nothing like these. These are priceless. I've never seen such an early edition of *The Failed Treatise and the Third War*. And you have the manuscript! Yan Wu touched this paper with her own hands. This is *history*, Furi. This is what the Children of the Dark Fire want buried forever."

"They may want it buried more than you know," Alice said. She leaned forward and gently opened the pages to the same passages she'd shared with Kura. Alice didn't say anything else. She didn't need to.

William was glued to the text, his fingers tracing the handwritten Mokuskrit and comparing it to the published passage. He looped back, starting at the beginning again, his brow furrowed as if something didn't make sense.

"How well do you know that book?" Furi asked.

"I wrote papers on it for the University. Lectured on it. I know it as well as anyone … but the oldest I ever found was a later edition. We don't know how late. I always assumed it was fourth or fifth, but the differences here are monumental."

William pulled the glasses from his face and rubbed at his eyes. "If you didn't have the manuscript sitting right in front of me, I would have thought this to be some kind of propaganda. A fake meant to undermine our own monarchy." William cursed and stared at Furi. "What do you know of the Stormborn?"

"I've heard of them," Furi said, and Alice could have applauded how level and collected she sounded. "They're defying the Children of the Dark Fire, yes?"

William smirked as if he saw right through her. "You know more than you say. They're defying the steward, Furi. Only those of us who know the history of the Children of the Dark Fire would say the Stormborn are denying that cult. No one else knows who rules Ballern from the shadows.

"Kura teaches some of the Skyborn what came before, but even she doesn't know all of the Children of the Dark Fire's transgressions." William's gaze trailed up to the books on the wall. "But those transgressions are far in the past. So far, I thought there was no way to untie their lies from our history."

"There are more books like this in Ballern," Alice said. "Yan lived there for years, and she took books and writings with her. That's how we got the manuscript."

"So it's not all lost," William said, running his hand across the edge of the manuscript. His hand tightened into a fist. "The Children of the Dark

Fire and Mordair are conspiring, which, somehow, I suspect, comes as no surprise to you two. They've bribed Skyborn and royalty alike, feeding rumors and outrageous claims about Belldorn and even the archdukes themselves."

"Kura thinks you know something," Furi said. "She didn't say that outright, so don't get mad at her, but she wouldn't have sent us to you otherwise."

William bowed his head. "It is hard for me *not* to know things, Furi. Scholars from the Skyborn and royalty both visit this shop, and I endure inspections from the Children of the Dark Fire. I hear things. At times, things I am not supposed to hear. At other times, things I am paid not to hear."

William leaned back in his chair, and his gaze flickered between Furi and Alice. "And here you are, Skyborn, with a friend of the old blood. Heirs to a world that never came to be."

"You have influence over the Skyborn who might join the Stormborn," Furi said. "That's what Kura told us. You wanted to know what we know of the Stormborn, and I'll tell you."

Alice reached out and touched Furi's forearm. "I will tell him. It should come from me. The … old blood, as you say."

William stared at her with an intensity that made her skin crawl. Alice took a deep breath and dove into the most abbreviated story she could.

"The Stormborn are moving, William. Their banners already fly on the docks, and more will come from across the sea. The royals of other cities support their cause, but I dare not say who. The threat is here, in Ballern. Spies and pliable ears who will share anything for a bit of coin. We need those who would bend their ear to the side of the Stormborn."

William lowered his gaze. "I have supported the Skyborn as best I can, short of violence. I cannot condone it. I despise it regardless of how unavoidable it is." His hand moved over the Mokuskrit passage again before balling up into a fist. "But this. If this exists in Belldorn, so much of what we know of them was a lie. There is one thing I will tell you. It is hearsay—understand that, both of you. There is a rumor that an assassin has been sent to Belldorn to strike down the support of the Stormborn."

"Sent to Belldorn for what?" Furi asked, narrowing her eyes.

"To serve as one of Lady Katherine's guard, so when the time is right, she can be removed."

Alice wanted to scream at the man and tell him what a fool he'd been, but she could see the moisture gathering at the edge of his eyes, the redness running through them. And Alice had a strike of her own to make.

"This is your moment, William. This will be for you what the Fall was to us Ancorans."

"Ancorans?" William sat up straighter, as if she'd slapped him.

"Mordair brought ruin to my city, and I will bring ruin to him. You can't always sit back and be the observer. Sometimes you have to make the hard choices, like Yan Wu did when she defied the Children of the Dark Fire." Alice slammed her palm down next to the manuscript. "Tell her story."

"No one will believe me without these," William pleaded, gesturing to the book and notebook.

Alice stood and motioned for Furi to join her.

"Keep them. Consider them a gift from the Stormborn."

William stared. Alice held his gaze until she turned and walked out of the room. If that didn't convince him to offer aid to the Stormborn, or at least not stand in their way, nothing would. William was like Jacob before the Fall. Like *Alice* before the Fall. Books and theories were a wonderful thing until the real world came to burn them down.

Then it was time to fight.

CHAPTER TWENTY-SEVEN

ALICE WAS TREMBLING by the time they made it back to the lift. She'd taken a risk. A massive risk. And if it didn't pay off, it could cost her *everything.* "Lady Katherine's going to be so mad about those books, Furi."

Furi hissed at Alice. "Are *you* mad? You just found out there's an assassin in her ranks, and you think she's going to be worried about those books? Did you *see* how many books are in that archive?"

A larger group stepped into the lift behind them, and Alice stopped talking, waiting in a nerve-racking silence while the door closed, and they rose into the air. Furi squeezed her arm, and they both listened to what was happening around them.

"I'm telling you, those Stormborn are the only choice we have. You heard what that steward did to his own city."

Another man scoffed. "Please. Do you know anyone who was actually in Fel? I talked to those sailors at the market, and they were there. They saw what happened. That was Belldorn attacking that city, not Mordair."

And back and forth they went. Talking as if debating their favorite place to eat lunch and not the fate of thousands. Alice stared at her feet and waited until the lift stopped. The instant the gate opened, she grabbed Furi's hand and slipped out ahead of the group, anxious to get away before she said something she'd regret.

"Can you *believe* those people?" Alice whispered, her nerves giving way to anger as she leaned against Furi. They hurried out toward the

Bones.

"They don't know better, Alice. They've spent their whole lives being taught to trust their teachers and leaders and books."

"But you heard them. They act like the lives of everyone on these docks aren't at stake, and they are. You think the steward won't do here what he did in Fel? You think these people won't see their families hanging from these docks?" Alice spat a curse and sped up.

Furi matched her pace. "Alice, look." She pointed down the next walkway, and even in her fury, Alice slowed. Hanging from the level above them was a tapestry large enough to match the blood-red banners of Fel opposite them. Only these were a deep royal blue, emblazoned with a brilliant silver Shadowwing that caught the light like a prism.

Shouts echoed from the walkways above them, and Alice could just make out a shoving match between a trio of Fel guards and a group of Skyborn. Or were they Stormborn now?

"Alice, let's go."

Alice nodded, and they continued on, dipping into the warehouse districts where the shouts grew muffled, and the tension she'd felt in the air subsided, but only just.

✧   ✧   ✧

Furi hit the door to the warehouse without slowing. "Kura!"

"Furi? Furi, is everything okay?" Kura shouted back, apparently catching the frantic tone in that one name.

Jakon stood with his arms crossed and one eyebrow raised.

Eva leaped out of her seat as soon as she saw the look on Furi's face. "What's happened?"

"They're sending assassins after Lady Katherine. We need to reach them *now*."

"What?" Eva stiffened.

Kura looked at Jakon. "Get the transmitter up."

He nodded and walked to the back corner, where he started prying open a section of the wall.

"What else happened?" Kura asked.

"We spoke with William," Furi said, talking faster as she went. "He's … he's not a staunch ally, Kura. He doesn't want to be involved, but we may have convinced him. I hope we convinced him."

"Sit." Kura gestured to the chairs in front of her desk. "Sit and tell me what he said. But if he told you about an assassination plot, I doubt he's an enemy."

Furi rushed through the story almost without taking a breath. Alice filled in a few details until Kura started asking more questions.

"And you left the manuscript with him?" Kura leaned forward.

Alice nodded. "It was the only way to persuade him, Kura. If we'd left with that, there was no chance he would have risked helping the Stormborn. He wouldn't have believed us without it, and how could he convince anyone else without it?" She turned her gaze to Eva. "Do you think Kat will forgive me?"

But Eva was just staring at Alice. "I don't think it will matter if she's dead, Alice."

Jakon pulled a long line from the wall, placing the transmitter on Kura's desk. Kura reached out and turned the dials before pressing the button. "Kat, this is Ballern." They waited, the only sound the gentle rise and fall of crackling static.

Every second tightened a band across Alice's chest. Were they already too late? Had Belldorn already suffered the loss of their leader? Had anything happened to her friends?

"This is Kat."

A collective sigh escaped the group.

Kura leaned forward. "We've learned of an assassin in your ranks,

Kat. Do not trust your guards."

"That isn't terribly unusual, Ballern." Kat's voice almost sounded like she was laughing. "How reliable is your source?"

"The Steamborn had to turn over the manuscript to convince them to reveal this. It's reliable, and you should take precautions."

Kat's voice sobered, her entire demeanor switching in an instant. "Understood. Mary, lock us down."

Alice heard Mary's string of curses grow fainter as footsteps sounded over the transmitter.

"I can't stay in this tower forever, Ballern." Kat's voice was calm. Almost too calm. "This will need to be addressed."

"You could detain your guard, I suppose."

"No. That would tell the assassin we know of their plot. I need to bait them."

"Bait them!" Eva snapped. "Have you lost your mind, Kat? You need to stay hidden and keep Mary out of this."

"I'm not staying out of this," Mary answered.

"Then I'm coming back there right now."

"No. Stay in Ballern. You can do the most good there. Let me worry about Kat. It's not the first time we've dealt with a threat against her."

Eva grimaced.

"The manuscript is a loss," Kat said. "It may be the most compelling piece of Yan Wu's writing we have in our archive. But it is not the only one."

"I'm sorry," Alice said. "I didn't see another way."

"Peace," Kat said. "Do not worry about what is done. You may have saved my life and gained allies in a single encounter. Perhaps, when this is done, your contact will be willing to share some of the things they have collected over the years. If they were swayed by the writings of Yan Wu, I suspect they are in possession of a great many items of interest."

Alice sat back and stared at the copper transmitter. She hadn't thought of that. She'd only thought about losing that one piece of history, not the fact William might have another, or dozens more. If they survived, she had to know. What if he had more of the history, like what was hidden in the Crown Library of Belldorn?

"Will you send our allies?" Kura asked. "It is my understanding there is hesitation across the sea."

It was the politest way Alice could imagine Kura asking about whether Lady Katherine was committed to helping the Skyborn, but she still cringed.

Kat hesitated. "The situation is complicated, but this threat will not go unanswered. Give us time to complete the ships. Keep your ear to the ground, or to the sky, as the case may be. When the fleet is ready, the Stormborn will not fight alone."

The transmitter went dead.

"That went well," Alice said with an awkward smile. It was, in reality, the best answer they could have hoped for. But in this case, the best answer meant war, and in war, Alice knew, nothing ever went to plan.

CHAPTER TWENTY-EIGHT

Targrove might have given Jacob permission to use his personal workbench in Theo's shop, but Jacob still felt like an impostor leaning over a master's space. It had taken him almost ten minutes to find a tensioner because Targrove's didn't look like any he'd ever seen before.

Instead of a lever, it was a wheel mounted on a crank. The face of the wheel was marked with measurements. Several of those were Mokuskrit, as if the device wasn't confusing enough. Once he got it secured to the edge of the workbench, though, Jacob started to appreciate it a great deal.

Hardened rods with flares slid into openings in the plate. The gear ratio on the crank took most of the work out of it, even on the heaviest of springs in the joint of the brace he worked on. With so many lengths to choose from, the tensioner could pierce the smallest of places.

Jacob turned the crank, the wheel pulling against it with the slightest resistance as one of his heaviest springs stretched forward just enough to reach its anchor. Instead of awkwardly lifting the spring off the tensioner, he slid the flared rod out of the bottom, and the spring smacked against its anchor, perfectly aligned.

As he looked over the wearable arm, he realized it was enough for a test. The skeleton of it was there, but he'd have to add armor. That would add enough weight that he'd need to anchor it to the torso, or it would be too heavy for anyone but Smith to use at length.

Jacob slid the arm out of its clamps, and it naturally flexed slightly with the springs. It was just the balance he wanted, not fully extended and not fully bent. The legs wouldn't be that easy, he knew. There was enough room in the arms that they didn't need to fit someone's exact measurements to be functional. The legs were a different beast. They needed to be adjustable, but how to accomplish that without compromising their integrity was a question he didn't have an answer for yet.

The door to the workshop opened, and someone's bootsteps stomped on the throw rug just inside the shop.

"Break's over."

Jacob turned to find Smith casting him a smile. "Already? It feels like I just got out of that cockpit."

"You and me both. Come on, now. We are still the best Mech pilots here, and if that carrier is ever going to be finished, we need to work."

Jacob sighed and sat the arm back on the workbench. There would be more time later. For now, Smith was right. The carrier was their priority.

✧   ✧   ✧

JACOB JUMPED WHEN Smith let out a thunderous yawn from the copilot's seat of the Titan Mech.

"How do you *do* that?"

"What?"

"Sound like an avalanche when you yawn."

Smith grinned. "I don't know, but I am sure Mary would love to know, too."

Jacob turned back to the windscreen. Ballern's base to the south of Belldorn had been leveled and cleared. With the help of the Titan Mechs, they'd already driven supports into the ground and built up the entire assembly area. What armor plating could be salvaged had been, and they'd taken the rest to the factories to be resmelted.

"Mech Two, this is Mech One, over," a scratchy voice sounded over the transmitter on the control panel.

"Mech Two," Jacob answered, fighting off a yawn of his own.

"We have the first of the new plates coming down the beach on a load of crawlers. Ready to put your plan to the test?"

"Yes, Commander," Jacob said.

"Stop calling me that."

Frederick's voice broke in across the transmitter. "You never should have told him you were one of the lady's bridge commanders, Wilkes."

"I am aware of that now, Frederick," Commander Wilkes muttered.

A green blur dove through the sky and landed in the center of the work area. Jacob watched the Emerald Needle for a time, beautiful in its own way, before the bug took to the air again, flashing its metallic wings in the fading sun.

"They aren't attacking the city," Jacob said. "I'd always heard they were some of the most aggressive bugs you'd find."

"Some fool probably disturbed a hive and wrote that," Smith said. "I prefer to make my own opinion about these things. Look." He pointed to the northwest.

Jacob turned and watched as a massive platform caught the sunlight, turning to a blinding fire as dozens of crawlers churned through the sands below it. The sheer volume of machines being used to move the enormous plate cast doubt in his mind.

He bit his lips and turned to Smith. "Do you think we're going to blow a hydraulic line trying to lift that?"

Smith shrugged. "That would be an easy enough fix. I am more con-cerned we could break the teeth off every load-bearing gear in the Titan Mechs' shoulders."

Jacob groaned at the thought. It wouldn't bring them to a complete standstill, as they had more Titan Mechs on hand, but it would set Frederick's schedule back by days.

"I am impressed by the crawler pilots, though. I did not believe they could transport that weight across the sands without being stuck in earnest."

"It's still a limited window. High tide will cover too much of the beach."

"If that becomes an issue, we can revisit the idea of carrying the platforms with the Titan Mechs or using Archibald's warship to lift them."

Jacob nodded. The problem with using the warship was that it provided the entire northern wall of Belldorn's defenses at that moment. Two of the Porcupines were under repairs, which left precious few resources to split between defense and reconstruction.

Watching Frederick coordinate everything made Jacob's head spin. He might have had ideas when it came to machines and schematics, but organizing hundreds of pilots and crew was intimidating. Smith said it was because Frederick had learned to manage as many tinkers in his time in Bollwerk, but that still didn't feel as overwhelming as what was happening in Belldorn.

They watched as the crawlers left the beach and hit the empty stretch that had once been the outskirts of Belldorn. Much of the debris had been cleared or repurposed, even slated for resmelting or used as supports for their construction site, but it did not leave the area without obstacles.

The crawlers crashed over small hills and mounds. They sank into pits of loosely filled foundations, sending tremors through the plate like a thunderclap. Jacob's jaw didn't relax until they reached the scorched earth and dirt of the construction site, and Frederick's voice came over the transmitter.

"Smith, Jacob, take the far side."

Jacob maneuvered the Titan Mech closer to the beach, crouching so the long arms could slide underneath the plate. As soon as they were locked in, every man and woman in those crawlers walked away. Jacob kept his eye on the lead pilot of the crawlers, who finally raised his hand to signal everyone was clear.

"On three," Frederick said.

"One."

Jacob tightened his grip on the levers to straighten the legs.

"Two."

Smith placed his hands on the wheel that controlled the tilt of the waist.

"Three."

Jacob eased the levers forward, and the gears of the Titan Mechs whined in protest, the enormous plate trembling before enough torque reached the cogs that weight gave way to force. The Titan Mechs rose into the air, and he almost shouted, but they weren't done yet.

"One step for every count," Frederick said.

Smith pivoted the waist, and Jacob shifted the legs, taking one step forward with Frederick's voice. Every impact sent vibrations through the metal, through the Titan Mechs, and into his hands.

But they moved. One step after another, they moved, until they stood at the far edge of the construction area. They positioned the plate above the only segment where struts had already been placed, the triangular supports waiting to show them if their plan would work, or they were going to have to start anew.

The plate clanged when it hit the supports, a split second between the impacts, and the Titan Mechs stepped away.

Silence reigned before Frederick's voice exploded over the speakers mounted on his Titan Mech.

"I told you he was right! You didn't want to listen to a kid and look at us now. Half the build time. Tell the others. Get the next plate before high tide. It's time to build this carrier!"

Chills ran down Jacob's arms.

Smith clasped his shoulder and grinned. "I believe Frederick approves of your plan, Jacob."

Jacob gave a small nod and smiled, the relief almost taking him to his knees. "Yeah, I think … I think you're right."

✧   ✧   ✧

"Who do you trust?" Mary asked.

Kat slumped into her chair and squeezed her forehead. "You. Eva. There is resistance in Belldorn, Mary. I'm sure you've seen it and heard it on the docks. Outrage that I let the city be attacked. Outrage that we destroyed empty buildings."

"As if you could have stopped it. Who else do you trust?"

"I trust who you trust, and few others."

"Samuel and Drakkar are in Canopy, or on their way to it to train with the Spider Knights and dragonriders. Targrove and Theo are in Midstream, and I wouldn't pull Gladys away from there either. If assassins have targeted you, it's reasonable to assume they will target her and Archibald as well. The others are in Ballern, which leaves us two trusty Biomechs." Mary ground her teeth together and pulled out the base of her portable transmitter. She turned the dial and clicked the button in her collar.

Smith answered fast. "Mary? I did mention we would be working until we collapsed, did I not?"

"Of course you did, Smith."

Smith hesitated. "Is everything okay?"

"When was the last time everything was okay?" He started to respond, but she cut him off. "We just got word assassins are targeting Kat. We need you."

Mary heard Jacob's voice in the background. "Assassins?"

"Where are you?" Smith asked. "We have Frederick and Wilkes with us, but the others need to continue working."

"*We* need to keep working," Jacob said.

Smith relayed exactly what Mary had said, explaining the fact there was an assassin after Kat. After that, Jacob's insistence on staying in the shipyard fled.

"Where are you?" Smith repeated.

"In the tower. Come as fast as you can."

"How did you find out about this?" Smith asked.

"Alice and Furi met an informant in Ballern." Mary almost growled. "Let's call them that. I can give you more detail in person."

Smith cursed and disconnected.

✧   ✧   ✧

SMITH SWITCHED BACK to the transmitter on the Titan Mech. "Frederick, we have been summoned by Lady Katherine. Could you manage the shipyard while we are absent?"

"Done and done, Smith. Don't keep the lady waiting."

Smith popped the canopy for the Titan Mech. "Come, Jacob. I do not like this. We need weapons if we are to defend Belldorn's throne."

"Isn't that going to make it a little obvious Kat knows?" Jacob asked.

"Yes. And it could deter whoever means to kill her. Now hurry."

Jacob opened his backpack and tossed a bolt thrower to Smith before opening the locker in the back of the Titan Mech. He offered Smith a sword and retrieved the handheld air cannon from a high shelf inside.

Smith nodded. "I am glad one of us was prepared."

They scampered down the side of the Tower Mech, racing over to the crawler drivers celebrating their victory. Jacob recognized a man from Bollwerk, noting his leather hat, and called out his name.

"Walter! Walter Jones!"

The driver turned toward the voice and squinted at the two figures racing at him. "Smith? Jacob? What brings you down to see us lowly drivers? Strange seeing you outside Bollwerk."

"We need to get to the tower, and fast. Can you take us?"

"It'll keep our formation from bringing the next plate if I do."

"Drop us off and go. That's all we ask."

Walter rubbed his chin and nodded. "Hop on and strap in. We'll make this quick."

It wasn't until they were already moving that Smith told Walter exactly what was happening. "A threat against Lady Katherine was identified. That is why we are in a hurry."

"What?" Walter cursed. "You should have said that in the first place. Hold on."

The whine of the treads on the cobblestones escalated, and so did the roughness of the ride. Walter shouted over his shoulder. "I haven't been here a day, you know. Caught the last supply ship after Archibald told me what's been happening here."

Jacob sank back in his seat, realization striking him. "You're one of Archibald's spies."

Walter grinned in the rearview mirror. "I'd appreciate it if you kept that to yourself."

Smith leaned forward and held on to the back of Walter's seat. "Contact him after you drop us off. Let him know about the threat. He needs to be vigilant too, as does Gladys in Midstream."

"I'll be sure they all know," Walter said. He took the next turn like it was the level streets of Bollwerk instead of the rough cobblestones of Belldorn, and Jacob thought his back might never recover by the time they stopped skidding into the turn.

The Tower loomed above them, framed by the airship docks as they raced forward. Another dip in the cobblestones rattled their teeth before the crawler skidded to a stop.

"Go!" Smith said as he vaulted out of the crawler behind Jacob. Smith clicked the transmitter in his collar and whispered as if he was speaking to Jacob. His voice sounded breathy with the exertion of running from the crawler. "Mary, we are coming to the rear lift. Are there any guards we should be aware of?"

"Kat?" Mary asked. "Any guards?"

"No. Hardly anyone knows about the rear lift. They should be clear."

"Come on," Smith said to Jacob.

He followed the larger tinker across the wide rotunda that greeted all visitors to the Tower. A pair of guards waited at each hall, silent and watching. Smith said nothing more as he led the way past the central lift and into the far hall.

Jacob nodded to a guard, but still hurried past without a word. They followed the outside curve of the Tower before Smith stopped, glancing both ways down the corridor before opening what Jacob thought was a closet.

Inside, a narrow dark path waited, so narrow and musty Jacob would have believed they were in the underground caves beneath Ancora. Smith angled his shoulders so he could move faster, jogging through that darkness until they reached the end.

"Where is it?" Smith grumbled.

Something clicked and shifted, and a light bloomed in the wall, revealing a lift not much wider than the gunpod on the Skysworn. They stepped inside, and Smith pulled the lever before the cables whisked them into the air.

"Mary?" Smith said. He clicked the transmitter again. "Mary, are you there?"

Jacob's heart pounded in his ears. He didn't hear the crackle of a response. Not a whisper back from Mary.

"The walls are too thick," Smith said. "The cages can block transmission when the metalwork is in such a fine web."

Jacob racked the small slide on the handheld air cannon. He would have preferred the full-sized weapon currently sitting in the locker on the Skysworn, but this would have to do.

Smith watched him for a moment before strapping the bolt thrower to his arm and testing the mechanism. The barrels spun up and retracted as smooth as could be. He locked a cartridge of bolts into the feeder and took a deep breath.

The lift slowed, and the doors opened. Four guards faced the towering doors to the throne room, a spreader held between two of them while a third hammered it home with a sledgehammer.

Mary's voice crackled across the transmitter. "Where the hell are you? They're at the doors!"

The guards turned toward the sound, dropping the spreader to the floor with a crash and clang. But Jacob already had the air cannon in his hands. He'd already heard Mary's cry. He didn't have to wait to see the throwing knives rising into one assassin's hands while a woman raised an arm with three barrels mounted on top of it.

Jacob fired, the boom of the air cannon, small though it might have been, utterly deafening in the enclosed space. The sound rebounded off the ceiling and walls and raced through the corridor. Smith emptied the entire cartridge of his bolt thrower into the man in front of him, raising his sword when it clicked empty, but not before the barrels on the man's wrist fired, and Jacob grunted when three bolts knocked his leg out from under him, sending him to the floor.

He fired again, catching the woman's helmet. It caved in with a spray of gore, and he rolled away as her body twitched on the polished marble.

In one movement, Smith raised his arm across his chest, engaging the overdrive on his biomechnics before he brought his blade down on the last guard. It split the man in two, and Jacob almost retched at the spilling of blood and viscera.

Smith grabbed the spreader and slammed it into the door. The lock gave with a squeal, and he forced his way inside the throne room.

Jacob scrambled to his feet, following after Smith as he primed his air cannon again.

Inside were more assassins, and another broken door. Jacob tried to understand what he was looking at, two dead in front of the throne, and his brain screamed at him to make sure it wasn't Kat or Mary.

Smith didn't hesitate. He hurled his sword at one of the last guards stalking toward the throne. The man's armor folded in on itself, the blade of the sword snapping in two as the body crashed into the marble floor.

Someone moved behind the throne, the last guard distracted by the ruthless destruction of his comrade. He didn't see Mary's blade. Didn't hear her silent steps. Didn't react until the knife split the flesh of his neck, but even then, she didn't release him. She followed down, raising the dagger only to plunge it into the armpit of that guard, the seam at his waist, and the exposed joint at his groin. Only when his hissing cries slowed did she let go of his body.

"Where's Kat?" Smith said.

"Here," a shaky but somewhat reserved voice answered.

Jacob hurried over to Mary while Smith headed for Kat. "Are you okay? Are you hurt?"

Mary shook her head and took Jacob's hand when he reached for her, letting him pull her to her feet. "We're both fine. As fine as we can be, anyway." She flexed her arm and winced. "Though I wouldn't argue a trip to the hospital. Are they all dead?"

Blood ran down one side of Lady Katherine's face. She wiped at it as she walked around the throne, leaving a mess behind. She winced and prodded at a cut that ran from just above her eyebrow up into her hairline. She touched the blood and frowned at her hand, holding one eye closed.

"*That* was a bit closer than I would have preferred."

Mary laughed and grabbed her ribs. "Let's get you stitched up. Then we can get me stitched up."

"Eight of them?" Smith said, looking around the room.

"Just four," Mary said.

Smith shook his head. "We killed four in the hall. That is far more than one."

Lady Katherine cursed and tied a handkerchief around her head. "Eight of them. I thought *one* might have slipped through. But eight?"

"How long have they been in your guard?" Mary asked, studying the blank faces on the floor.

"I don't know. They alternate, Mary. We thought that would be best. Rotate the guards out of the fleet to keep them from recognizing too many patterns."

Jacob glanced back at the door. "You don't need to know patterns if you're going to come through the door with spreaders like those."

Lady Katherine gestured to him. "Jacob, your leg."

He looked down and raised an eyebrow. It was somewhat odd to see a bolt stuck in his leg but to not feel any pain. One of the things he thought he might never grow accustomed to with his biomechanics.

"Careful," Smith said. "Make sure it didn't damage any hoses."

Jacob prodded around the bolt, finally figuring out where it was lodged. "It's between the lower plates. I think it's safe."

Smith nodded before Jacob pulled the bolt out and lifted the hem of his denim pants. The older tinker whistled.

"Yeah, that got a little close." Jacob ran his finger over the bent plates. He could see the impact marks from the two that hadn't stuck, and the bent rod from the one that had. "I'll need to hammer that out. Next time we get a break from the assembly floor."

"I will help when we are done."

"You're going back to work?" Mary asked, her voice rising. "After all of … this." She gestured to the blood and bodies all around them.

"I'm going back to work, *especially* because of this. We have to finish the carriers. How many more assassins can Mordair send before one of them gets to Kat or Gladys or Archibald? Will he send them to Canopy? Ancora? We have to remove him."

"Jacob's correct," Lady Katherine said. "If anything, this has shown me Archibald was right to hurry." She winced as she pulled the handkerchief away from her wound, pausing to make sure the bleeding had stopped. "We're going to Ballern. And Mordair won't be able to run like he did in Fel."

"I hate to agree." Mary eyed the corpses on the floor and turned her gaze back to Kat. "But you can't afford to wait."

"I want a timeline on the carriers." Lady Katherine's voice hardened. "Consult with Frederick and contact the factories in Bollwerk. Summon every Stormborn who can answer our call to arms. Those who are not already in Ballern, tell them to be in Bollwerk or Belldorn by the time the carriers will be completed. We will transport them all. Send word to Canopy. When their training is complete, have them come to Belldorn. It is time to remove the king of Fel once and for all." Lady Katherine crumpled the blood-soaked handkerchief in her fist before letting it fall to the stone floor.

EPILOGUE

J ACOB STOOD ON the carrier's flight deck with Frederick and Smith, studying the schematics of what was to come. Completing the expanse of metal was only one step in the massive project. They still needed hangars and gas chambers and pontoons and a thousand other details if the ship was going to get off the ground, much less carry a fleet.

Even though he knew how large that carrier was. Even though he'd walked the perimeter two times that same day, it was hard to comprehend standing in the corner of it. The only real point of reference was a Titan Mech on the opposite side. It could have been no taller than a person if he didn't know how far away it was.

"That's why I think we need to install the pontoons first." Frederick tapped on the schematic. "Easier to fit the gas chamber around a structure than try to guess how much space we need to leave."

Smith crossed his arms and nodded. "I will not argue that. Tobias had a good idea, running channels for the pontoons, and I think we should still do that. But splitting the chambers *before* we install them will prevent any impingements."

Jacob turned back to Smith and Frederick. "And I'm pretty sure we don't want the carrier leaking air over the middle of the sea. It's not going to float."

Smith's lips twitched. "Not for very long, it's not."

Frederick rolled the schematic up and tapped it against his hand a few times. "Why don't you two kick off for the night? You've been going nonstop."

"One more hour," Jacob said, raising an eyebrow as he looked at Smith.

Smith's shoulders slumped just a hair. "One more hour."

✧   ✧   ✧

BY THE END of that hour, Jacob rather regretted his decision. There wasn't much to do with the Titan Mechs, which meant Jacob and Smith got to climb the supports underneath the flight deck and help run cables through a seemingly endless gauntlet of brackets and hinges. The welders would follow in the morning and bond the cables to key points across the carrier, and Jacob didn't envy them that job.

They made it to the far end before Smith declared the job done. Jacob followed him back to the Skysworn. They'd considered staying at Mary's, but with things as they were, they also thought it better to keep Kat moving with a smaller group. If they were all at Mary's, it might draw more attention while the few officers she trusted combed through the ranks of the fleet for any more potential assassins, an unsettling idea at best.

Jacob checked the time as they reached the docks. Ten minutes before Alice was supposed to contact him. He'd cut it close at the docks, and he would hate to miss her transmission.

"Almost there," Smith said as the gate to the lift opened.

"That obvious?"

Smith smiled and led the way to the Skysworn. "If you need me, find me in the morning. I fully intend to sleep like the dead in the next five minutes." He slowed beside the sleek form of the Skysworn, opening the chain that blocked the gangplank. It wouldn't really stop anyone from boarding the deck, but most of the ships on Belldorn's dock still chained their gangplanks.

Jacob followed Smith to the cabin, where they parted ways after Smith's reminder to lock up before he came below deck. Jacob settled into Mary's chair, checking to be sure the transmitter was on, and waited. It wasn't long before a small burst of static resolved into Alice's voice.

"Skysworn, this the Freighter, over."

"The Freighter?" Jacob asked. "Are you staying on that tiny ship you told me about?"

Alice chuckled at that. "No, no. I just wanted some privacy, and there isn't much of that at the warehouse. Pilots and Skyborn and potential allies. I think our friend has made a lot of new friends here, Skysworn."

Jacob smiled. He knew Alice was talking about Kura and the warehouse, and new friends likely meant more Stormborn had joined the fold. That was excellent news.

"How's the new boat coming along?"

"Big," Jacob said. "Sometimes I forget how big. You won't believe it. I've heard the other half is coming together faster, though. That's probably good since they'll be transporting a lot of our friends from back home. It's good to hear your voice again."

Alice laughed a little. "It hasn't been *that* long, Jacob."

"I know, I know. But it's going to be at least a few more days before we can test. Maybe even a couple of weeks. That's … that's a long time."

"I'm sure you can find *something* to keep yourself occupied. We have so much to do here, it's making my head spin. Our teacher is something to behold, though. You should see her work."

"I will. As soon as I can. I still wish I could be there with you."

"I'll be looking forward to it." She paused. "But how big is the new boat? As big as the one we visited on the Crystal Sea?"

"I still don't know how they built that one. Ours won't be quite that big. Although, combined, I think it might be close."

"That's hard to imagine. I can't wait to see what you all came up with."

"Me too."

They stayed silent for a time. Jacob looked up at the stars, catching a glimpse of an airship crossing the moon. It was a beautiful sight.

"Can you see the moon?" Jacob asked.

"Barely." Alice's voice sounded strained, like she was bending far to one side to look out the windscreen. "Why?"

"Nothing, nothing. I was just watching an airship cross it here."

"That sounds nicer than what I can see, which is basically the grate of the dock above me and a tiny sliver of the moon past the lift."

"That … okay, my view sounds a little bit nicer."

Alice laughed. "You'll have to show me the view from the docks when we make it back there."

"I'd like that. We'll find a good view."

"It's a plan."

There wasn't much else to say, but they stayed on the transmitters for almost another hour, talking about nothing and everything and things that might yet come to pass. It was hard not to be too specific over the transmitters, just to be safe, but hearing Alice's voice brought some peace to Jacob's heart. And that would be enough to get through another day.

Note from Eric R. Asher

Thank you for spending time with Jacob and Alice! I've been blown away by the reader response to this series, and am so grateful to you all. As you may have guessed, we aren't done with the story quite yet! The next book of Jacob and Alice's adventures is called Stormforged.

If you'd like an email when I release a new book, sign up for my mailing list (www.ericrasher.com). Emails only go out about once per month and your information is closely guarded by a ravenous Pilly.

Also, follow me on BookBub (bookbub.com/authors/eric-r-asher), and you'll always get an email for special sales.

If you enjoyed Stormborn, please consider leaving a review on a platform of your choice. Reviews can make a huge difference and help make sure we get more Steamborn books.

Thanks for reading!
Eric

Coming in 2023. Preorder today!

Stormforged

The Steamborn Series, Book #8

By Eric R. Asher

Books by Eric R. Asher

Shop ebooks, audiobooks, and paperbacks at ericrasherstore.com

The Theme Park at the End of the World

The Steamborn Series

Steamborn

Steamforged

Steamsworn

Skyborn

Skyforged

Skysworn

Stormborn

Stormforged

Stormsworn

The Vesik Series
(Recommended for Ages 17+)

Days Gone Bad

Wolves and the River of Stone

Winter's Demon

This Broken World

Destroyer Rising

Rattle the Bones

Witch Queen's War

Forgotten Ghosts

The Book of the Ghost

The Book of the Claw

The Book of the Sea

The Book of the Staff

The Book of the Rune

The Book of the Sails

The Book of the Wing

The Book of the Blade

The Book of the Fang

The Book of the Reaper

Dreams of the Forgotten Dead

Garden Gnome Graves

The Vesik Series Box Sets

Box Set One (Books 1-3)

Box Set Two (Books 4-6)

Box Set Three (Books 7-8)

Box Set Four: The Books of the Dead Part 1

Box Set Five: The Books of the Dead Part 2

Mason Dixon: Monster Hunter

Episode One

Episode Two

Episode Three

Episode Four

Want to receive an email when one of Eric's books releases?

Visit ericrasher.com to get started.

About the Author

Eric is a former bookseller, cellist, and comic seller currently living in Saint Louis, Missouri. A lifelong enthusiast of books, music, toys, and games, he discovered a love for the written word after being dragged to the library by his parents at a young age. When he is not writing, you can usually find him reading, gaming, or buried beneath a small avalanche of Transformers. For more about Eric, see: www.ericrasher.com

Enjoy this book? You can make a big difference.

If you've enjoyed this book, I would be very grateful if you could take a minute to leave a review on the platform of your choice. It can be as short as you like. Thank you for spending time with Jacob and Alice.

www.ingramcontent.com/pod-product-compliance
Lightning Source LLC
Chambersburg PA
CBHW061118310726
48974CB00002B/581